AMPLITUDE

DIMENSION SPACE BOOK THREE

DEAN M. COLE

CANDTOR PRESS

Amplitude: A Post-Apocalyptic Thriller (Dimension Space Book Three)

Published by CANDTOR Press, LLC

Amplitude: Dimension Space Book Three is a work of fiction. Names, characters, places, and incidents are either the products of the author's imagination or are used fictitiously. Any resemblance to actual persons, living or dead, events, or locales is entirely coincidental.

Cover Art © 2019 Raphael Francavilla

ISBN-13: 978-1-952158-03-2

For R.C. Bray and Julia Whelan.
Thanks for breathing life into these tales o' mine. You've made Vaughn and Angela real for a multitude of audiobook listeners (see what I did there?).

Another Great Series by Dean

The Complete *Sector 64* Series
1947 - *First Contact a Sector 64 Prequel Novella*
Today - *Ambush - Book One of the Sector 64 Duology*
Tomorrow - *Retribution - Book Two of the Sector 64 Duology*

(Read the sneak peak of *Ambush* at the end of this book.)

PART I

"You can't do the end of the world in a ... boy meets girl way."

—Terry Southern

"Hold my beer."

—Dean M. Cole

CHAPTER 1

"Today, vee shall plumb the deepest reaches of the quantum realm. The collider's High-Luminosity upgrade vill shine the light of discovery upon hidden dimensions und singularities."

Unfortunately for the world, the German scientist had no idea how right he was.

Doctor Hans Garfield smiled inwardly. The director of CERN's High-Luminosity upgrade had said those words for the benefit of both the reporter and her cameraman just a few short minutes ago. In the intervening moments, he'd stood the world of theoretical physics on its head.

The first successful collisions at the collider's new and significantly increased power levels had resulted in a resounding success.

This was going to be his Nobel Prize.

Hans placed a hand over his heart as he imagined the medal hanging there.

A slap on his back snapped Doctor Hans Garfield from his reverie.

"We did it—!" Shouting to be heard above the cheers of the control room's multiple occupants, the exuberant man paused and then shook his head curtly. "Sorry. You! You did it, Doctor Garfield!"

Hans gave the postdoctoral candidate his best, most disarming smile and then tilted his head toward the man. "You vere correct the first time, Sampson. *Vee* did it," he said, his German accent rendering we as vee.

Turning from the man, Hans stared through the control room window. The large, cylindrical body of the ATLAS detector filled the majority of the view. He smiled and then nodded again. "Yes, vee did do it."

He gave Sampson a sideward glance. "Now please tell me that *vee* captured all the data."

The man's head bobbed up and down rapidly. "Y-Yes." He bent over his keyboard, his fingers pecking out a series of commands. "Here's the energy graph." Sampson stopped typing and pointed triumphantly, indicating a spike in the readings. "There it is, sir."

Hans gave the man a beatific smile. "There it is, indeed."

That spike of Hawking radiation would be the key to his Nobel Prize. The event that it represented was the penultimate moment that Hans had been working toward his entire career.

A feminine voice at his right shoulder rose above the excited cheers of the room's numerous occupants. "Is that it?" The reporter pointed at the computer screen. "Is that the black hole?"

Nodding, Hans turned toward the woman. "Yes and no. It is not the black hole itself, but the decaying remnant of the short-lived singularity." He gestured toward the peak in the data. "That spike represents the burst of Hawking radiation that emitted an instant after I ... uh, vee created the black hole."

The woman from The New York Times tilted her head inquisitively. "Hawking radiation?"

Hans nodded. "Yes, it's a type of energy that Doctor Stephen Hawking theorized vould be released by an evaporating black hole."

The woman nodded dutifully, although Hans doubted she had comprehended a word of what he'd said.

After a furtive glance through the control room window, she looked at Hans again. "Aren't you worried that you'll create a black hole that will end up swallowing the entire planet?"

It was all Hans could do not to roll his eyes. "No, no. This is simply not possible. As I vas telling you before, an MBH–"

"MBH?"

Failing to stop the eye-roll this time, Hans sighed. "Yes, a micro black hole."

The reporter, Miss Preston, he believed, nodded and scribbled something in her notes. She looked at her cameraman. "Are you getting all this?"

The man nodded.

Hans wasn't sure why a newspaper would need a video. He supposed it had to do with providing content to their online readers.

The reporter looked at Hans with raised eyebrows. "Please, continue."

After checking on the status of his ongoing experiment, Hans turned back to the woman. "Anyway, the MBH is of no threat to us." With a sweeping motion of his arm, he gestured toward the ATLAS detector. "Vee are not doing anything that nature hasn't done millions of times right here on Earth." He pointed upward, jabbing his finger toward the ceiling. "In our very atmosphere."

The reporter tilted her head. "What do you mean?"

Hans lowered his arm. "Cosmic rays vith energy levels a million times greater than anything vee vill ever achieve on Earth bombard our upper atmosphere constantly. You see? Nature must create MBHs all the time. If they vere dangerous to us, the Earth und all celestial bodies vould have ceased to exist billions of years ago as micro black holes turned each one of them into a singularity. It vould be a cold, dark, lonely universe."

The woman chewed on his words for a moment and then tilted her head. "So you've detected these bursts of Hawking radiation in our atmosphere?"

Hans blinked, surprised by the insightfulness of the reporter's question. He nodded for a moment but then shook his head. "No." He waved dismissively. "But that is likely because vee have never been close enough to an actual collision."

Miss Preston tilted her head toward the ATLAS detector. "Until today?"

Hans smiled and then nodded. "Precisely."

The reporter looked through the control room's wide observation window. "And all of this is possible because of the luminosity upgrade?"

"Sehr gut, Miss Preston. Yes, vee recently completed the High-Luminosity Large Hadron Collider upgrade. Vee now have ten times more power than previous experimental runs."

He turned from the lady and looked at the computer console again. "Now if you don't mind, vee have another iteration in the vorks."

Not waiting for the woman's response, Hans turned back to Sampson. "How are vee coming?"

The American postdoctoral candidate nodded excitedly. "We're up to ninety percent!"

Hans returned the nod. "Sehr gut."

He smiled inwardly. The selection committee would have no choice but to choose him for the next Nobel Prize in Physics.

Sampson pointed excitedly. "Here it comes!"

After glancing at the large cylinder of the ATLAS detector, Hans bent over his console and stared at its display with rapt attention. Twenty-three tera electronvolts! The energy level had reached the threshold. "Start proton-proton collisions."

Nodding again, Sampson toggled the command on his console.

It took several moments for the streams to cross. Finally, data began to flow from the detector. However, it was only the normal shower of gluons and muons that resulted from the multitudinous collisions of the highly energetic particles.

Then Hans saw one data point rise above the noise.

Sampson sat back and pointed again. "There it is! It's happening!"

A grin began to spread across Hans's lips, but then the smile faltered as the undulating spikes of energy and data suddenly flatlined.

"Vhat happened?!"

The postdoctoral candidate shook his head. "I don't know." He stared at the display. "This doesn't make any sense."

Miss Preston stepped forward. "What is it? What's going on?"

Hans shot her an annoyed glance. "Vee seem to have lost the data stream."

"You mean the experiment shut down?"

Hans threw his hand toward the screen. "Does that look like live data to you?"

The reporter pointed through the control room window. "Well, if the experiment has shut down, then why is that thing glowing now?"

"Vhat?" Hans blinked and looked up from his console. Staring through the window, he tilted his head. The woman was right.

A nervous murmur rose as every occupant of the large room stared through the observation window.

At the center of ATLAS's radiating assembly of pipes and conduits, the detector's massive cylinder glowed faintly.

Tilting his head, Hans stared at the soft light. "Th-That is not possible ..."

Suddenly, the cylinder's glow brightened.

Sampson looked up from his console. Then he stood, pushing his chair back. "What the hell is going on?!"

Hans stepped back and then looked at Sampson. "Don't just stand there, idiot! Shut it down!"

"Y-Yes, sir." The man dragged his gaze from the glowing assembly and focused on his console's display. He punched in a command and then looked at the computer screen expectantly. A confused look crossed his face. "It's not shutting down."

The brightness of the detector's glow ramped up.

Hans raised his hands. "Cut the power. Kill it!"

Sampson bent over his console again. His fingers blurred as they flew across the keyboard. A moment later, he shook his head. "It's not responding."

Hans eyed the large red button inset into the console's white surface. He fingered its clear cover, momentarily reluctant to lift it. Pushing the kill switch would activate several non-conductive, mechanical cable cutters. They would sever electrical feeds at multiple points along the supercollider's twenty-seven-kilometer circumference. The entire collider would be shut down for months, and the repair costs would run in the millions.

Suddenly the ground quaked. Hans raised widening eyes and stared at ATLAS.

Had the detector just rippled?

Beside him, Sampson shot to his feet. "Oh shit!" Pale-faced, he turned toward Hans. "Press the goddamn button!"

The ground lurched.

Another ripple radiated across the surface of the detector. This time, there was no questioning it.

Hans swallowed. His suddenly dry throat clicked in his ears.

He flipped the clear, plastic cover open and hammered the button.

Nothing happened.

The green LED next to the button cycled to red, indicating the wire cutters had activated, but the overhead lights didn't even flicker.

Hans pressed the switch several more times.

Still nothing happened.

The ground heaved beneath him.

This time, the entire detector assembly distorted.

Sparks shot out from the device.

Hans continued to pound on the big red button. "This … is not … possible!"

The reporter stepped up. "What's happening?!"

"I don't know!" Hans said, shouting over the din of the noise that was now coming from the ATLAS detector. "Vee must have lost cooling. I think there is a fire inside the detector, but that should not be possible." He pointed at the kill switch. "This button is hardvired to its own, dedicated power supply. It's a failsafe. There's no vay it didn't work, but vee still have power." He pointed at the overhead lights. "It should have killed everything, even the lights."

Sampson was back at his console. Again his fingers flew across the keyboard. Then he shook his head. "It's still running."

"Of course it's still running! I can see that vith my own two eyes."

Shaking his head, Sampson pointed at the display. "I mean the detector. It's not flatlined. It's maxed out. The energy coming through ATLAS is off the chart ... literally!"

"Vhat are you talking abou...?"

The words died in his mouth as Hans saw the value next to the single line: thirty tera electronvolts.

That couldn't be. Even after the upgrade, the collider wasn't capable of a center-of-mass energy level greater than twenty-five TeV, but there it was, pegged at the instrument's maximum displayable value. The fact that it wasn't deviating south of that number told him that the actual power output was likely even higher. As Sampson had said, the power level was off the chart.

The ground lurched, nearly knocking Hans and everyone else in the room from their feet.

The cacophony emanating from the detector reached ear-splitting levels, setting his teeth on edge.

Then everything stopped.

All noise ceased.

Even the omnipresent electrical hum of the collider's powerful magnets seemed to evaporate.

In the suddenly quieted control room, Hans exchanged pensive glances with Sampson and the reporter.

The postdoctoral candidate breathed a sigh of relief and pointed at the red button. "Finally, it worked."

Looking up, Hans shook his head. "The lights are still on." He pointed at the idle emergency lights. "Those should be on. They should be the *only* lights on."

The idiot cameraman followed his every move, first pointing the lens of his device at the overhead lights and then at the dark emergency ones.

An incredible wrenching sound shattered the silence.

All heads snapped to front.

The videographer aimed his camera through the observation window again.

Hans stared with widening eyes as the large, cylindrical body of the ATLAS detector began to crumple. It collapsed inward like a water bottle having its air sucked out. "No, no, no! This can't be happening."

The reporter looked at her cameraman. "Are you getting this?"

The man looked at her and gave a single nod.

She turned her attention back to Sampson and shook her head. "What can't be happening?" She gestured to the window. "What is it doing?"

Sampson pointed at the shrinking device. "The MBH didn't evaporate. It's a stable black hole, a singularity."

Miss Preston looked from the still shrinking device back to Sampson and Hans. "I thought you said that wasn't possible."

Hans shook his head. "No, it's not supposed to be. This can't be happening."

Sampson ground his teeth together and turned on Hans. "You keep telling yourself that, jackass!" He extended a hand and pointed toward the shrinking ATLAS detector. "In the meantime, you've killed the whole damn planet."

"Vhat!?" Hans shouted as he turned toward Sampson and poked the taller man's chest. "Oh, so it vas *vee* up until it goes wrong? Now it's me?"

The reporter stepped between them and pushed the two men apart. "Now is not the time! Shouldn't we be doing something?"

The two men glared at each other angrily. Then they looked at Miss Preston and shook their heads.

Sampson gestured at Hans. "Thanks to him, there is nothing we can do."

Hans bristled. He stepped up, ready to punch the man.

The reporter pushed him back again. She looked from the men to the slowly shrinking device and then at the room of dumbstruck scientists. She raised her voice above the cacophony of the ATLAS detector's continuing collapse. "Well, then, why is everyone just standing around?! We need to get the hell out of here!"

Hans's head dropped. Defeated, he stared at the floor. "No one is running because vee all know that there is nowhere to run to."

"Uh, yes there is. Anywhere but here would work for me right now."

Sampson shook his head. He pointed at the now van-sized clump of metal. "Soon, that's going to lose its attachment points. When it does, it's going to fall, and it's not going to stop until it reaches Earth's center. Then it's going to start gobbling up mass, and it won't stop until the entire planet, including everybody on it, has been sucked into the singularity."

Nodding, Hans looked up at the still glowing device. He tilted his head. "Vhat attachments? It has pulled away from everything."

Shaking his head, Sampson pointed at the ruined detector. "Something must be ..."

Miss Preston stared at the men, a confused look on her face. "What is it?"

Hans looked at her and then back at the indistinguishable mass of the detector's remnants. It now looked like a beach ball-sized orb of bright orange, molten metal. "Vhy is it just hanging there? It should have fallen already."

Sampson nodded. "You're right. And look, it's not shrinking anymore."

No sound emanated from the sphere.

A hush fell across the control room as all occupants stared in dumbstruck silence.

As they watched, the ball of liquid metal began to dim. Then the glow was gone completely. It appeared as if someone had suspended a perfectly round polished metal sphere where the ATLAS detector assembly had been.

Hans saw a fisheye reflection of half the facility painted across its curved surface. If not for the protective coating on the control room's window, he likely would have seen himself in that reflection. The film on the far side of the glass created a mirror effect, so a reflection of the orb hovered at the center of the image. It looked like a real-world version of an M.C. Escher spherical mirror painting.

Everyone in attendance winced as a loud ping rang out.

At the same time, the solid metallic sphere suddenly looked liquid as a ripple emanated from its top. Concentric rings radiated downward as if someone had dropped a large stone into the now mercurial ball. When the waves reached the bottom of the sphere, they rebounded and began to circle its round surface, creating undulating peaks and valleys of interference patterns across the ball of liquid metal.

Hans broke from his paralysis. He returned to his computer console and sat down.

Sampson pulled his eyes from the incredible scene and looked at him. "What are you doing?"

"I'm going to use the robotic arm und see if I can interact with it. Maybe I can disrupt it somehow."

"What good will that do?"

"I don't know. Probably nothing, but vee have to try."

Sampson started to say something else, but then the reporter shoved him aside and stepped up next to Hans. "Shut up, and let the man work."

Hans looked at her and nodded.

After activating the manipulator arm's software, he grabbed its actuator with his left hand and began to extend the long, mechanical device toward the still undulating sphere. He slipped his right hand into a gloved-shaped interface. It allowed him to control the robotic grasper at the end of the arm. He flexed his fingers and watched the remote hand mimic his movements. The grasper's white fingers waggled in unison with Hans's.

Approaching from the right side of the sphere, the grasper moved to within a meter of the mercurial orb's tremulous surface.

Hans stopped the arm.

What was he going to do? Slap the sphere with the actuator's hand? Punch it? Maybe this wasn't a black hole after all. If he could break it up, perhaps he'd disrupt whatever was happening.

Hans nodded. "Screw it!"

He balled the remote hand into a fist and then raised the arm. He'd just hammer the sphere and see what happened.

The orb suddenly stilled. The waves vanished in the blink of an eye.

Once again it looked like a solid sphere of polished steel.

Then the orb flared, its surface becoming as bright as the sun.

The blindingly bright light vanished before Hans could even raise a shielding hand.

Trying to blink the afterimage from his vision, he exchanged confused glances with Sampson and the reporter.

Then new movement drew their eyes.

Turning, Hans watched as the top of the once again mercurial sphere began to distort.

Then something emerged from the mass, extending almost a meter toward the ceiling.

Hans blinked. "Vhat the hell is ...?"

A hand opened up. It looked mechanical.

Just as Hans registered the fact, a second one extended from the top of the sphere. The two white arms probed the air for a moment. Then the metallic hands reached down and buried themselves in the equator of the beach ball-sized orb.

They heaved, and then Hans and his fellow observers gasped as two additional arms, as well as shoulders and a torso, emerged from the top of the sphere.

The being appeared to have its back turned toward the control room. Hans couldn't see the thing's head.

As it continued to rise, more of the torso slid into view. It tapered down to an extremely narrow waist.

Then it stopped rising.

Releasing the outside of the orb, the being extended all four of its arms out to the side. With only its upper extremities visible, the thing looked like a robotic version of a man, standing in waist-deep water, arms held wide, albeit with four of them instead of two.

The reporter bent over and whispered into Hans's ear. "Is that your robot? Was it inside the detector?"

Hans shook his head slowly. "I have no idea vhere that came from. Vee don't have anything like it here." He nodded toward the robotic arm and the controls still clutched in his hands. "Closest thing is this."

Remembering the device was still active, Hans started to lower the manipulator arm, pulling it back to avoid striking the being.

Apparently detecting the movement, the robotic interloper turned right and held up its right two hands defensively, but then it paused.

Hans stopped moving the manipulator arm. Then he saw that the robot did have a head: a flat, disc-shaped protrusion that rested atop its shoulders. It appeared to have no neck. However, he thought he could see two eyes inset in the edge of that disc.

Hans glanced sideways, intending to say something to the reporter, but she and Sampson had left.

Outside, the robot stared at the manipulator arm with apparent interest. It almost looked curious. Tentatively, it extended one of its arms toward the device.

Hans relaxed his hand, unclenching the grasper so that it no longer looked like a threatening fist. Then he extended an index finger toward the being.

Still reaching toward the manipulator arm, the robot extended a finger of its own.

Just as the two mechanical digits were about to touch, a door opened on the left side of the facility.

Hans halted the actuator as he saw Sampson and the reporter walk into the chamber.

The robotic being lowered two of its arms and grasped the equator of the sphere as it spun to face the new arrivals.

The idiots were holding their arms out to their sides, mimicking the previous pose of the robot. Both Sampson and the reporter appeared to be saying something, but he couldn't hear them.

Standing beside Hans, the cameraman continued to film. "This is incredible!"

Hans ignored the man and stared through the window. Looking at the being that was protruding from the top of the sphere, he thought he saw anger flare in the thing's eyes. It leaned menacingly toward Sampson and Miss Preston, pointing at them accusingly with its two free hands.

Both humans backpedaled, pressing hands to ears as a high-pitched, siren-like wail pierced the air.

The robot raised four clenched fists overhead and then dropped out of sight, disappearing back into the metallic orb and taking the high-pitched howl with it.

Hans and the rest of the control room's occupants stared through the window in stunned silence.

Sampson and Miss Preston lowered their hands and stared at the now calm surface of the mercurial sphere. Even from this distance, Hans could see the confusion on the faces of the damned fools. What the hell were they think—?

Hans winced and threw up a hand defensively as a brilliant beam of white light shot out from the orb. This time it wasn't the entire surface of the sphere fluorescing. It was a narrow fan of light that swept over Sampson and the reporter.

Then it vanished, leaving the orb as it had been.

Hans looked from it to Sampson and Miss Preston and then shot to his feet.

"Son of a bitch!" the cameraman said as he took a backward step. Forgotten, the small video camera clattered to the floor at the man's foot. "They're ... They're gone."

Hans knew the man was right. Sampson and the reporter hadn't left. They hadn't run away. He would have seen the movement.

They had simply ... vanished.

Hans flinched and stepped back as another white beam shot from the sphere. "Scheisse!"

It was a wider fan of light this time. Forming a wedge, it swept across the left wall of the facility. Then it began to move toward the control room.

Hans had just enough time to register the movement before it washed over him and the cameraman at his side.

Then the light vanished again, disappearing just like the occupants of the control room.

For a long moment, the becalmed, metallic sphere hung motionlessly at the center of the silent and now emptied ATLAS detector facility.

Then another beam burst from the orb.

This time, the white light looked like a laser beam shooting straight up into the ceiling. It passed through the intervening two hundred-foot span of earth and rock like light through smoke. The narrow thread of brilliant energy shot up through the roof of the building that occupied the ground above the ATLAS detector. It didn't stop until it reached the upper edge of the atmosphere.

A nearby farmer looked up from the side of his tractor. Standing at the center of his family's small parcel of land, he turned and stared at the strange light.

Through slitted lids, the wizened old man watched the beam, wondering why the scientists at CERN would be firing a laser from their building, but then the thin ray of light began to widen. The movement was barely perceptible where the rays emerged from the structure. However, as the farmer looked up, he saw that it no longer looked at all like a laser beam. Overhead, the thing had taken on a cone shape. The rapidly spreading fan of white light now looked like a mountain-sized megaphone with its wide end directed at the heavens.

Looking down again, the farmer took a backward step.

The base of the light had begun to move in earnest now.

The building from which it had originally emerged had vanished behind it, and now the light appeared to be coming out of the ground. It swelled rapidly, coming straight at him.

The farmer turned and tried to run, but before the old man could take two steps, the light washed over him.

The man vanished, leaving nothing in his wake but the dust kicked up by his well-worn and now absent boots.

The ring of sterilizing white light continued to spread, sweeping across fields and streams and then cities, mountains, and oceans.

Like its creators, the uncaring, energetic wave had no empathy. It didn't care about the life that it scoured from the planet.

It just was.

Until it was not.

CHAPTER 2

The bright lights of the control room vanished, and the ground heaved violently.

Hans's knees buckled.

He stumbled and nearly fell. Then he felt something moving underfoot.

"Get the hell off me!"

Hans peered down. In the wan light cast by the emergency lights, he saw two moving forms.

He took a backward step. "Sampson? ... Miss Preston?"

As Hans's eyes adjusted to the low light level, he saw that dust now covered their faces and clothing. "Vhat happened?"

Shaking his head, Sampson stood, helping Miss Preston up as he did. "Hell if I know. We were standing here trying to figure that out for ourselves when you suddenly landed right on top of us. You knocked us on our asses."

"How did you get back in the control room so quickly?"

Miss Preston looked at him with raised eyebrows. "Doctor Garfield doesn't know."

Hans furrowed his brow. "What don't I know?" Then he wrinkled his nose. "And vhat is that smell? Did something die?"

Sampson stopped brushing the dust from his lab coat. He grabbed Hans's shoulders and turned him around. Then he pointed up. "Look. We're not in the control room. We're not even inside!"

Hans opened his mouth to ask what the damned fool was talking about. Of course they were inside. However, the words died before he could form them as he stared at a tan-colored disc that hung high overhead. Then he blinked with sudden recognition.

They *were* outside.

That wasn't an emergency light.

It was the sun!

Hans stared at it. His heart raced as he tried to understand how he'd gotten there and what he was seeing. The sun looked too dim as if seen through an atmosphere choked with dust.

Lowering his gaze, he looked around. All of the other occupants of the control room were out there as well. They were standing around him. Several of them were also staring into the sky, although a few of the people had fallen. They were climbing to their feet and knocking dust off themselves.

Turning slowly, Hans scanned the hazy horizon. In every direction he looked, the ground fell away. They appeared to be standing on top of a broad hill. It was impossible to discern the height of the terrain as the hazed atmosphere obscured everything beyond two or three kilometers.

As Hans continued to turn, familiar terrain rotated into view.

He froze.

"Oh, mein Gott ..." He swallowed and shook his head.

The unmistakable outline of Geneva's surrounding Alpine peaks peered down on the mulling group of white-coated scientists. The wide bases of the mountains were lost to the dusty atmosphere, but their denuded, craggy peaks stared down on them without their normal cap of glacial snow.

How could all of that ice disappear?

"Vhat have vee done?"

Someone slammed into Hans, bowling him over and knocking

him from his feet. The impact caused his breath to burst from his lips as he careened down the arid slope.

The person landed on top of Hans and then rolled off of him, all the while cursing in French. The male voice sounded gravelly, like that of an old man.

Something on the ground crackled beneath Hans as he rolled across it.

It sounded like snapping twigs.

Or bones?

His lab coat snagged on a protrusion and tore.

White-hot pain erupted from his forearm as something gashed Hans and yanked him to a stop.

He scrambled back to his feet. "Vatch vhere you're going!"

The old man stood, not bothering to knock the dirt from his soiled overalls or the stained plaid shirt beneath.

Tilting his head, Hans reached out and flicked the worn denim of the man's clothes. "Vhere in the hell did you come—?"

The Frenchman batted away his hand. "Ta gueule!"

Hans's eyes flared angrily. "Don't tell me to shut up, dummkopf!"

The evident farmer bellowed loudly. He bowed up, raising his hands as if to strike Hans.

Then another body slammed into the old man, pounding him into the ground.

Multiple startled cries rang out as four more people and a cow suddenly appeared right in the midst of the group of scientists.

Hans stared wide-eyed, unable to comprehend what he was seeing.

Before he could utter a word, he fell to the ground again as someone else slammed into him.

He tried to stand, but something was pinning his legs.

Another person fell on top of Hans. He banged his head painfully. He'd hit a sharp-edged stone. Blood flowed freely from the point of impact. It dripped onto the rock. Looking at the now bloodied outcropping, Hans realized it wasn't a stone at all. It was the broken claw of a long-dead lobster. Hans shook his head, releasing an arc of red droplets. No, it couldn't be a lobster pincer. The thing was a meter long. It was too big to be a—

Someone else dropped onto Hans, slamming his head into the claw again. This time the weight was too much. He couldn't raise any part of his body.

He was pinned to the ground!

The weight pressing down on Hans continued to ramp up.

Then it became too great even to draw breath.

With his last conscious thought, Hans finally understood it all.

He had died.

And this was Hell.

He was right on one account.

Sometime later, the unending crush of new arrivals squeezed the last vestige of life from Hans, and he became correct on both.

CHAPTER 3

"You're from the future?!"

Commander Angela Brown stared into the lens of the video camera and nodded soberly. "Yes, Director McCree."

As Angela watched the reactions of Bill and Teddy, she tried to decide what to say, what to do.

Questions raced through her mind.

Had Vaughn survived?

Was he still alive?

Had he made the jump with her?

Was he back in Cleveland just as she was back on the space station?

She looked at her ISS crewmates.

Angela was certain that she could save Bill and Teddy, but what about people on the planet?

Could she save anyone else?

During her passage through the airlock, Angela had considered taking the Soyuz module down over Europe and land it behind the wall of light in Eastern France's farmland. She could go there now and try to shut down the collider before it could wipe all animal life from the planet. However, she had quickly abandoned the idea. If Angela went in there half-cocked, without a plan, she'd likely end up inside the growing pile of dying life in the version of Earth that she and Vaughn called Hell.

Angela would happily trade her life if it would save billions, but if she died without stopping the Necks, she'd seal the fate of Earth's biosphere.

Even if she somehow managed to make it in undetected and shut down the collider, she would be writing off half the world's population, maybe more.

No. Angela needed a plan to stop the Necks permanently, one that reset the timeline and stopped the robots from ever coming to this dimension. She was already working on that plan, but she needed people to help her execute it.

Angela had figured out all those things before she and Major Peterson had completed the airlock cycle. However, she still hadn't worked out how to save anyone else in the here and now.

"Commander Brown!"

Angela held up a hand. "Give me a sec."

"What do you mean you're from the future, Angela?"

She ignored the director as she worked through the problem.

If Vaughn was back, he was too close to the light wave to save more than himself and Mark Hennessy. To survive the passage of the life-stealing wall of energy, they'd have to be hovering the Q-drive flight module in the vacuum chamber when it flashed through their region.

Angela's eyes widened.

That was it!

She pointed into the lens. "Director McCree, you need to get everyone you can suited up and into Chamber A."

Back before the world had gone to hell, Angela had read an update about Houston's vacuum chamber. Johnson Space Center had modified Chamber A in support of the James Webb Space Telescope test program. The Apollo-era facility now had a high-vacuum pumping system.

"Commander Brown ..." The director hesitated. When he resumed, confusion and frustration twisted his words. "You want me to get people in spacesuits? And then put them in a vacuum chamber?"

"There's a lot more to do than that, but it's a start. We'll need a mix of military and computer specialists. And if you happen to have—"

"Angela! Why on Earth would I do any of that?"

She blinked and stared into the lens. Then Angela understood. She hadn't told them what the light was, what it was doing. She looked away from the camera, suddenly unable to meet anyone's eyes as the gravity of what she was about to say, what it would mean to all three of the men and their families, sank in.

Finally, Angela gathered her courage and looked Bill and Teddy in the eye. Then she gazed into the camera lens again.

"Director McCree ..." Angela paused and swallowed. Then she gave a short nod and continued. "If you are physically connected to the planet when that light passes your location, you die." She pointed toward the ground two hundred and fifty miles beneath them. "That wave of light is killing everyone it touches."

Teddy had been looking off to the side, but then his eyes snapped to hers. Moments ago, Director McCree had informed them that they'd lost contact with Moscow. Angela's heart broke all over again as she watched the ginger Russian cosmonaut's freckled face pale, turning lighter than his strawberry-blond hair. His Adam's apple bobbed, and his eyes lost focus as his gaze drifted off to the side again.

The director's voice boomed from the module's speakers. "What are you talking about, Commander Brown?" Randy's voice now sounded even more incredulous than it had at the prospect of her being from the future.

"Randy, that light wave isn't some anomalous northern light. It's not an aurora." She gave him a meaningful look. "I know you already suspect as much. You told me so last time."

She continued before he could interrupt her. "The only way to survive its passage is to be physically disconnected from the planet. You can't be attached to its ground, its water, or even its atmosphere." Anticipating their questions, she shook her head. "It doesn't matter if you're miles in the air or miles underground. It *will* find you, and it *will* remove you from this planet … completely."

All three men fell silent.

Major Peterson stared at her for a long moment. Angela watched him process the news. Bill looked from her drawn face to her suddenly longer hair and then to her too skinny figure. Then he shook his head. "That makes no sense."

Angela knew that the men had seen a plumper version of her a couple of hours ago. She had entered the spacesuit with shorter hair and her normal layer of subdermal fat, but now the matted mess of her hair rivaled Teddy's mane, filling a considerable portion of the Destiny module. The radical change in appearance buoyed Angela's claim, but Bill remained reluctant to accept what she was saying.

Angela didn't blame him. She was telling the man that everyone he loved, everybody he knew, was going to die in the next few hours. She had lived through it all, but now floating in the normal confines of the ISS, it was difficult even for her to believe what was about to happen … again. She shook her head. It wasn't 'about' to happen. It already was, and every moment they wasted here reduced the chances of saving anyone.

The sound of a phone ringing in the director's office came through the speakers.

Angela's eyes widened. Could that already be Vaughn calling?! Then she shook her head. It was too early for the light to have passed Cleveland. About now, the Necks' damned, life-stealing wave of energy was still crossing the Atlantic.

Director McCree's voice came through the speaker. "Stand by. I have to take this call."

Then Angela had an epiphany, and she remembered what the call portended.

Agonizingly long moments later, the director's voice returned. Randy sounded shaky and unsure. "I'm …" He hesitated and then sighed. "I'm back."

Angela spoke into the microphone, making sure to talk loudly enough that Teddy and Bill heard every word. "That was either the President or someone from the Joint Chiefs."

"It … It was." Randy stammered. "That was General Tannehill from the Joint Chiefs. How do you know that?"

Raising her eyebrows, Angela nodded. "He was calling to tell you that they lost the quick reaction force mid-flight."

"Yes … but how—?"

"And," Angela interrupted him. "They were watching a live video stream of the airplane's occupants when it happened."

Floating to the right of the camera, Major Bill Peterson tilted his head. "When what happened?"

Teddy snapped out of his fugue, suddenly becoming animated. "Da, what are you talking about, Commander Brown?"

Angela looked into the camera lens and spoke directly to the director. "You figured out that the light started at the supercollider under Geneva. The President ordered a strike team to CERN. They were going to the collider to shut it down, but they didn't make it."

Director McCree's voice issued from the speaker. "She … She's right, they didn't make it, but they didn't … die. They …" His voice faltered.

"They vanished," Angela filled in for him. "But trust me, sir. They're dead." She shuddered, and her eyes lost focus as she stared through the camera. "Or they soon will be."

Before the men could ask more questions, Angela shook the visions of Hell from her mind and continued. "Next, the President will order a massive nuclear strike on CERN, on Geneva."

"How do you know about …?!" The director didn't finish the question.

Angela opened her mouth to say more, but then Randy released a resigned sigh.

"Okay, Commander Brown. What do we need to do, and how does the vacuum chamber factor into it?"

Major Bill Peterson blinked. "What?!" Anger flared across his dark face. He yanked the camera from Teddy's hands and then turned it toward himself. He looked into the lens with evident incredulity. "You're not buying this, Randy, are you?"

"Bill, everything she has said has been one hundred percent spot on. The *only* way she could know all of those things is if she truly were from the future."

"But ..." The major faltered. He turned and stared at Angela's hair and then at her emaciated arms.

The last of the man's hope drained from his face. "Everyone? All of them will die?"

Angela gave a quick shake of her head. "No, not everyone. We'll survive, and I think we can save a few on the planet."

"Can we save my family?"

It was Angela's turn to falter. Her mouth clicked shut.

Major Peterson looked at her expectantly.

It took all the courage Angela could muster to meet his eyes as she slowly shook her head. "No, Bill. I'm sorry ... But—"

"But what?!" The major's voice echoed loudly as his question bounced down the long corridors of the station. "What good does it do for a few of us to survive? Why should we go on if there's nothing to live for?!" he scoffed. "We can't repopulate the planet by starting with—"

"Dammit, Bill!"

Angela's sudden outburst caused Teddy to flinch.

She took a deep breath and lowered her voice. "Listen for a moment, and I'll tell you how we can save everyone."

"There's nothing you can say that—!"

"We *can* save your family, Bill!"

Major Peterson's head snapped back, and he blinked. His voice lowered. "What?"

Angela shook her head. "I can't save them right now, not today." She held up a hand as Bill opened his mouth. "I don't have anything close to enough time to give you all the details, but suffice it to say that we *can* reset the timeline." She gestured at herself. "I already have once. That's how I got here, but I can't do it alone. To reset everything in a way that stops it from ever happening again, I need help." She sighed as the weight of everything pressed down on her. She pointed at Bill and Teddy and then into the camera lens. "I need *your* help."

Bill's mouth hung slack for a moment. He closed it and swallowed. The major looked over her tattered garments and her long hair once more. He glanced at Teddy. Then his eyes focused on hers, and he nodded.

The director's voice returned. "What happened? What's causing this, Angela ... or who? You said you have a plan for those bastards. Is it a terrorist group?"

Angela stared into the lens. "No, it's not terrorists." She paused, trying to decide what to tell them. Then she shook her head. "We can talk about that later."

Bill and Ted looked at her expectantly. "I promise, I'll tell you everything, but first, we need to save everyone we can."

Major Peterson nodded. "Okay ... What do you need? How can we help?"

Angela returned the nod. "You can start by getting the descent module ready and packing it with all of the rations and survival equipment you can fit."

Teddy emerged from his stupor like a man waking from a dream. "We're leaving?"

Angela nodded. "Yes, but not yet."

Bill's ebony face softened. "You think we might be alone for a while? Is that the reason for the survival equipment?"

Angela felt the passage of each lost moment as if it were a physical thing being ripped from her body. "I hope we don't need any of it, but if I don't get the director moving now, we might end up all by ourselves."

The two men needed no further prodding. Major Peterson exited the module first.

Teddy handed Angela the camera and microphone. He turned to depart.

Angela touched his arm. "I'm sorry for your loss, Teddy."

The Russian cosmonaut looked over his right shoulder, regarding her with his lips pressed into a thin line. Then Teddy gave her a short nod. He grabbed a handhold and pulled himself toward the exit.

"Oh, and Teddy."

The cosmonaut paused and looked over his shoulder again. "Da?"

"After you finish helping Bill, I need you to pull the two mice from their habitat and place them in a ventilated box."

He tilted his head and knitted his brow.

Angela gave him a weak smile. "Please, Teddy? I don't want to leave them up here to die."

Finally, he returned the smile and gave her a thumbs-up. "I'm on it, Command-Oh."

"By the way, we got their sex backward. It's not Mabel and Nate. They're Mack and Nadine."

"Oh … Okay. How do you know?"

Angela gave him a wan smile. "Because Nadine—the one we've been calling Nate—is carrying Nate Junior and his siblings in her belly right now."

He nodded slowly and turned to leave. Then he looked back and stared at her, an indiscernible look on his face. "You've changed. You're different now. That's why I never doubted your words. It wasn't your new look. It was you. You're harder, tougher, more like Russian now."

Angela stared at him. She couldn't tell if the man saw her change as good or bad.

Without further comment, Teddy turned and drifted out of the module.

Angela chewed her lip as she watched him leave. She wanted to call him back, wanted to hug them both, hold Bill and Teddy tightly and not let them go, but they all had work to do, and she had already let precious minutes slip away.

She turned the camera lens toward her face and held up the microphone. "Director McCree?"

"Still here."

Angela gave a short nod and then took a deep breath. "Okay, listen. You need to get as many people as you can suited up—"

"I'm already working on it."

Angela blinked in surprise. "Huh?"

"I just sent out a message."

"Good. Now you need to go meet up with them and get suited up as well."

"Yeah, uh … sure." Randy sounded distracted. A light tapping noise came through the connection.

Nodding, Angela continued. "Okay. Who are you pulling in?"

"Everyone I can. There's a good mix of military personnel and hackers."

Angela smiled inwardly as she remembered how McCree liked to refer to everyone on the technical side of the business as a computer hacker. It didn't matter whether or not they actually were programmers. At this point, Angela would take anyone she could get. There wasn't time to get too specific.

"He's right, you know."

"Good …" Angela hesitated. "Wait. What? Who's right?"

"Mission Specialist Petrovich—Teddy. He's right. You are different. I have no idea what you've been through, but whatever it was, it hardened you, matured you."

Angela frowned. "Focus, Director. Clock is ticking."

He released a low, mirthless chuckle. "Okay, Commander Brown. What makes you think that the vacuum chamber will help us?"

"Because at this very moment, Lieutenant Colonel Mark Hennessy and Captain Vaughn Singleton are preparing to hover the secret Q-drive test vehicle in Glenn Research Center's new vacuum chamber."

"Crap, Angela, how the hell do you know about …?" McCree sighed. "Never mind. Keep going."

Angela hesitated as she considered telling Randy to order Sandusky Control to stay on schedule no matter what happened. She shook her head. No, that wouldn't work. Anything she did might change something for the worse.

"What's wrong, Angela?"

"Nothing. I was trying to remember the details as I heard them," she lied. "Anyway, they were hovering the module when the light passed."

"The Q-drive worked? They managed to hover it?"

"Oh, it did a lot more than that, but I can tell you about it later. Anyway, we think they survived because they weren't attached to the planet or its molecular field."

"Okay. So you're saying Hennessy and Singleton survived because they were disconnected from the planet's molecular field? That's an awfully big leap of logic. Who came up with that?"

"Uh … You did, sir. You were the first one to speak with them afterward." Angela's eyes widened. "Oh, yeah! He's going to call you. Keep a phone on you at all times, and make damned sure that the office knows to forward all calls to you, especially anything that comes from Cleveland." She paused and then added. "You'll need to figure out a way to answer your phone once you're inside the chamber. Have them send it through a radio or something. Just do whatever it takes, but when the call comes, please patch me into it."

"Okay, but if I'm away from a radio, I don't know how to call the space station from a smartphone."

"Oh," Angela scoffed. "You'll figure it out."

"Let me guess: just like I did last time?"

"Yes, just like you did last time, but if you don't have enough time to call me, just tell Vaughn that we will meet them in Nebraska."

"Vaughn?"

"Yes, that's Captain Singleton." She shook her head. "I'll explain later, just tell him."

"Okay, got it. Nebraska. Are you talking about Soyuz's North American Emergency Landing Point Three?"

"Yeah, the one in the farmland east of Omaha."

"I'll tell him, but hopefully you can tell him yourself."

Angela nodded and then pointed into the lens. "You'll need a couple of things in the chamber before you seal yourselves in. Like I said, you have to be disconnected. You can't just be standing there when the light hits. Otherwise, you'll vanish just like everyone else."

"Okay," the director said. "So I imagine those two things are something to jump from and something to land on."

"Yes. Ladders, benches, whatever. Anything as long as it's tall enough to give them some free-fall time after they jump. They have to be falling when the wave passes through the chamber. I'll let you work out how to time that jump."

"I'll handle it." Again, the director sounded distracted. A series of clicks or taps came through the speaker.

"What's that noise?"

The sound stopped. Then Randy's voice returned, now tight and cracking. "That's me … I'm texting my wife."

The lump in Angela's throat seemed to swell to softball size.

She leaned toward the camera and peered into its lens. Angela swallowed hard as she considered her words. "Randy … I know you're worried about Betty and the kids, but I'll tell you the same thing I told Bill. The only way we can help them is if we live to fight for them, to have a chance to bring them back."

"I … I know. It's just …" He faltered.

"Don't think right now, Randy. Just get your butt to Chamber A. You'll be doing more for them that way."

An uncomfortable and too long silence poured from the speakers.

Angela was thankful for the chamber's recent high-vacuum upgrade. If not for its faster pumps, they wouldn't be able to pull a deep enough vacuum before the light reached Houston.

"Come on, Randy," Angela said softly. "The chamber upgrade bought us some time." Her gaze had drifted off to the side. She refocused on the camera lens and gave the director a meaningful look. "But still, it's going to be a near thing. I know this is a lot to take in." Her forehead furrowed into a peak. "And I know what it means for your family, but if we're going to have any hope of saving them and everyone else, you need to go now, Randy."

A moment later, the director's voice returned now sounding solid, resolved. "Okay, Angela. I'll do whatever it takes to make this happen."

"Thank you, sir."

She was about to terminate the call when Randy spoke again. "I don't know where or when you went to, Angela, but ... thank you for coming back for us."

CHAPTER 4

Vaughn felt as if insects were crawling across his chest. He tried to scratch the area, but his gauntlet-covered hand met the unyielding surface of his spacesuit.

"Shit!"

From inside his helmet, Mark gave Vaughn a sideward glance. "What's wrong?"

Lowering his hand, Vaughn shook his head then remembered that Mark couldn't see his face. "Nothing."

The last thing he wanted was another potential interruption to the scheduled lift-off of the module. He'd already thwarted one count-down delay.

Apparently, the doctor assigned to the test still had a hard-on for Vaughn. The man had already threatened to halt operations because of perceived glitches with Vaughn's health. Of course, the bastard thought he was still overweight and out of shape, ready to have a coronary at any moment. The doctor might have been right a couple of hours ago, before a half-year-older and significantly skinnier version of himself had replaced the suit's previous occupant: the chubby Vaughn who had squeezed himself into this suit this morning.

Was this really the same day?

Why could he remember everything from that original trip through the chamber even though he was now reliving it all in the first person? His mind now had competing memories of some of the same events.

And what had happened to fat Vaughn, the one who had climbed into this suit today? Where had that version of himself gone when he —the skinny one—had shown up?

Was he back in his home dimension, or was this merely a reasonable facsimile of it, a neighboring but slightly different version of home?

Vaughn gnashed his teeth. He had to stop. The unending loop of repeating questions wasn't going to keep him alive.

There was only one question that truly mattered: had Angela's reset afforded her enough time to stop the Necks' invasion? Had she been able to get word to her friends at CERN, prevent them from creating the micro black hole that opened the door for the robotic invasion?

Either she had, or she hadn't. Regardless, Vaughn had to make sure that the Q-drive module launched on schedule. There wasn't time to find out one way or another without jeopardizing the timing of the experimental flight. His and Mark's very lives depended on it.

Vaughn had agonized every minute since his arrival about whether or not he was doing the right thing. Should he have tried to save more people? Maybe he could have convinced them to load up the vacuum chamber with as many people as they could, have them all jump when the light passed.

He shook his head.

No. No one would have bought it.

This was the government, after all. They would want to start an investigation, find out how an apparent imposter got into his spacesuit.

The creeping sensation marched across the skin of Vaughn's chest again.

The doctor's nasal voice crackled through the helmet speaker.

"Team Sigma, we're seeing anomalous readings on Captain Singleton's EKG again."

Vaughn shook his head and tapped the chest of his spacesuit. "It's nothing, Sandusky. Feels like some of the leads are peeling up, that's all."

"Shouldn't be possible, Captain. The technician shaved those spots to prevent that from happening."

Vaughn frowned. That explained the problem. Those areas were anything but cleanly shaved now. His body hair had filled in those bald patches months ago.

Mark looked at him and then waved at the video camera that was monitoring them. "He's fine, Sandusky. I'd know if Captain Singleton was in distress."

A long pause greeted the astronaut's proclamation. Finally, the doctor's annoying voice returned. "Okay, Colonel Hennessy, but if I see anything else, I'm pulling the plug."

Mark held up a thumb. "Thanks, Control. We're all set in here. Let us know when you're ready to continue."

After receiving a response, Mark isolated their communications. He spoke to Vaughn without turning toward him. "Please tell me I didn't just lie to Sandusky Control."

Like Mark, Vaughn spoke without turning his body. He didn't want the safety Nazi in Sandusky to 'pull the plug' on them. "I'm fine."

"Then why is your mirrored visor still down?"

Vaughn reached up, intending to raise it but then remembered why he'd left the helmet's reflective visor in place. The last thing he needed now was for either Mark or Sandusky Control to see his bearded and too thin face.

Diverting his hand, Vaughn tapped the side of his helmet. "Told you, I have a bitch of a headache." He pointed at the lights that were bathing the chamber's interior in brilliant shades of white. "This place is bright as hell."

Vaughn winced inwardly. Disturbing images and memories flowed through his mind as he thought of the dead land where the Necks

35

deposited unwanted life forms. No, Hell wasn't bright at all. It was dark and dusty and had a well-earned stench of death.

Thankfully, Mark's voice pulled Vaughn out of his dark recollections. "I just hope your headache isn't related to those errant EKG readings."

Chuckling wryly, Vaughn held up the checklist that he was holding in his other hand. "Nothing that dramatic. More likely it's tied to last night's cocktails." He wiggled the booklet. Its thin pages moved oddly fast because of the chamber's near perfect vacuum. "This checklist ain't gonna finish itself."

Mark waved a dismissive hand. "We have time. Have to wait on Control now."

Vaughn tried to keep his voice calm as he looked at the module's chronograph. "They haven't delayed the countdown, have they?"

Mark's head shook side-to-side in his helmet. "They have to finish their checks before we move on. No worries, though. It's all built into the schedule."

Closing his eyes, Vaughn breathed a silent sigh.

Blissfully ignorant of the coming apocalypse, Mark patted Vaughn's knee and continued. "While we're sitting here, there's something I've been meaning to talk to you about."

"I'm all ears, Colonel."

Mark opened his mouth to speak but then closed it. Finally, he sighed. "I have to admit, you're doing better than I thought. Figured this would be more of a struggle."

Vaughn furrowed his forehead. "What are you talking about?"

The shoulders of Mark's spacesuit rose and fell. "I don't know. Guess you've always been a hard-headed son of a bitch, always had to do things your way. It's nice to hear a less combative version of you."

Vaughn's eyes flew open as a haunting sense of déjà vu washed over him.

Mark had said something similar last time they'd been here. The ensuing argument had haunted Vaughn for months afterward. He'd agonized over it, wishing for a chance to take it all back.

And now he had it.

Vaughn sat up and slowly turned to face Mark.

Could he change this conversation without changing the timing, without losing everything?

He could.

Mark had already said that they were waiting on Sandusky to finish their scheduled checks.

Vaughn nodded, a movement his friend couldn't see through the helmet's mirrored visor.

"Mark, before you tell me what's been on your mind, there's something I'd like to say."

His friend cocked an eyebrow. "Uh-oh. Did I speak too soon?"

Smiling, Vaughn shook his head. "No, Mark. You were right. I can be a hard-headed son of a bitch."

"*Can* be?"

"Yes, but that was the old me."

"Old, my ass? That was this morning, pal."

"What are you talking about?"

Mark pointed at his helmet. "Remember the incident with the sweatband?"

Vaughn did. When they had suited up on that day ... this day, Mark had told him he was putting it on wrong, and because he thought he knew better, Vaughn had spent the rest of the morning with the constant irritation of salty sweat streaming into his eyes. Even now, he could feel the thing bunched up in his hair. If not for the fact that his hair had grown significantly, he'd likely be experiencing the same thing now.

He chuckled self-consciously. "Okay, I *am* an asshole, but I'm ready to turn all that around."

"Oh, really? Why the sudden change of heart?"

Vaughn wagged his head side-to-side in his helmet and looked down. If Mark only knew how *not* sudden the change had been...

After a moment, he sighed and then continued. "Well, you already know what I went through with my ex."

Mark nodded.

Vaughn pointed at the chest of his own spacesuit. "I know that was my fault. When things went south between us, I didn't do anything to make it better. I didn't even try."

His friend stared at him wordlessly, evident surprise on his face.

"And I imagine you saw that I was passed over for promotion again."

Mark blinked. "Oh shit! I'm sorry to hear that, man."

Vaughn stopped and stared at Mark's face. "You didn't know?"

"Me?" Mark looked off to the side. "No. Didn't have a clue."

Vaughn laughed inwardly in spite of the dire situation that was at that very moment rushing toward them.

Mark was lying to him.

The man had told him that day—*this day*—that he'd seen the results of the promotion board. The fact that Mark had known of it had been one of the things that had set off Vaughn.

Letting it go, he bobbed his helmet up and down. "Okay. It is what it is. My military career is over, and I know that was my fault as well. I never applied myself."

Having intentionally used Mark's words from that long-ago conversation, Vaughn watched surprise march across his friend's face. While it felt good to get a small payback for Mark's lie about seeing the promotion board results, it in no way diluted his belief that his friend had been right. It had been all Vaughn's fault. He had never truly tried his hardest at anything, had never applied himself. Everything had always come too easily for him, so he'd gotten lazy.

Vaughn placed a gloved hand on Mark's arm. "That stops today. I'm ready to turn over a new leaf, start a new life." He paused and pointed a finger at Mark. "And I have you to thank for that. It was your example and your words that got me through …" Vaughn paused and swallowed down the lump in his throat. "It was your words that got me through the darkest hours and days."

Mark stared at him for long moments. Finally, he cocked an eyebrow. "Not sure what I said, but I'm glad it helped." The astronaut leaned back in his seat and faced forward.

Behind his mirrored visor, Vaughn tried to blow away the tear that was rolling down his cheek. "What was it you wanted to talk to me about?"

Raising a hand, Mark held up a thumb. "Nothing ... nothing at all." He patted Vaughn's knee again. "Oh, and don't worry about that career thing. I think we can find you something."

Vaughn knew the man was speaking of his desire to help him get a job at Lockheed. Pressing his lips together, he shook his head. Unfortunately, he was becoming more and more certain that the light was on its way, coming to erase all of them along with their hopes and dreams.

The radio crackled back to life. "Okay, Team Sigma. We're ready on this end."

Vaughn felt his pulse quicken.

The time for the light's passage was near.

Swallowing hard, he looked at Mark and raised the checklist. "I believe we have some work to do."

Smiling, Mark nodded and switched the communications selector to external. "Roger, Sandusky. We're ready on this end."

"All systems are a go," the controller said. "You're cleared for the first hover test."

Sitting in the capsule's right seat, Mark pointed to Vaughn. "Next checklist item, Captain."

Vaughn's respiratory rate doubled. His raspy breath sounded loud and harsh in his helmet.

His heart pounded in his ears.

He swallowed again and then read the next item on the checklist. "Gear ... Gear locks."

Mark flipped a switch.

Just as he had last time, Vaughn felt a soundless, metallic clunk radiate through the module's seat.

"Unlatched."

The module rested on the scaffolding. Only gravity held it in place. Overhead, the previously disconnected hoist hook finished retracting. Now a hundred feet of vacuum was all that separated the top of the skinless module's frame from the domed ceiling.

The controller's voice returned. "Stand by for launch."

Another EKG lead slipped from its mooring point. Vaughn felt its insect-like movement as it danced across the skin of his abdomen.

The doctor's annoying voice burst from the speakers. "That's it, Team Sigma. I'm pulling the plug. Captain Singleton's vitals are all over the board, and we just lost another signal on his health monitor."

Vaughn's eyes went wide. "No. No. No!" He sat up and held a hand toward the video camera. "Wait! I'm fine. Don't stop the countdown!"

Mark placed a hand on his arm. "Calm down, Vaughn. It's no big deal. This kind of thing happens all the time."

The nasal voice broke through the speaker again. "This is exactly what I was talking about, Colonel Hennessy. Now the captain's heart rate is through the roof. I told you he wasn't in good enough shape to take part in this experiment."

Mark gave him an embarrassed glance, but Vaughn couldn't give two shits less about his own pride at the moment.

Suddenly, several indicator lights on the console shifted to red.

"Crap!" Vaughn looked at Mark. "We don't have time for this!" He paused and stared at the console, shaking his head. "We have to take off now!"

Mark changed the communications selector back to internal. "Calm the hell down, Vaughn! Come on, man, I vouched for you!"

Ignoring Mark, Vaughn looked from the collective control stick that sat between them to the red lights on the module's instrument panel.

"Shit!"

He leaned forward and reached across his friend with his right arm.

As Vaughn started to toggle switches, Mark suddenly batted his hand away. "What in the hell are you doing?!"

"I don't have time to explain it right now, but if we don't take off right this goddamn minute, we're both going to die."

Vaughn reached for the control panel again.

Mission Control was squawking on the radio.

Mark grabbed his hand. "Stop this, buddy. You're losing it."

"You don't know how much I wish you were right." Vaughn shook his head.

He pulled his hand free from Mark's. Reaching up to his helmet, he unlatched the mirrored visor. "Hopefully, all of this is for nothing, but I promise you there's more going on here than you know."

Turning to face his friend, Vaughn retracted his visor, exposing his now bearded and too-skinny face.

Mark frowned as he turned in his seat. "You're not making any—!" Surprise and confusion suddenly contorted his face. "What ...? ... Who ...?" He started to shake his head slowly.

Seeing his friend stunned into inaction, Vaughn reached across him. "Sorry about this, Mark, but we're taking off right freaking now!" He toggled several switches and then entered a series of commands on the panel's touchscreen.

All the while, the voices of the controller and the doctor in Sandusky raged on.

After Vaughn entered a final command, several of the lights on the panel cycled to green.

Beside him, Mark continued shaking his head. "How are you doing that?"

"The module was locked out just like this the last time I flew it. Took me a while to figure out the workaround."

Mark stopped moving. "What are you talking about 'last time'? This thing has never flown before, not with anyone aboard it anyway."

"At this point, I think it's safe to say that I know more about this module than you do, but I'll explain that later."

Mark leaned forward and looked at Vaughn's face. "What happened to you? How did you get like this?"

"Later, Mark. For now, just grab the cyclic stick."

Vaughn clutched the collective control with his right hand. Anchored at its rearmost end, the stick protruded from the floor between him and Mark. It was tilted forward like a handbrake.

Applying upward pressure, Vaughn started to raise the stick slowly.

Mark's hand slammed down on top of his again. "No, Vaughn! We can't do this!"

Suddenly the tone of the conversation coming over the radio changed, becoming more animated. However, they were no longer focused on the actions inside the chamber. The doctor's nasal voice rose above the din. "What the hell is that?"

It was all Vaughn could do not to punch his friend in the chest. Instead, he stopped struggling and looked the man in the eye. "Hear that, Mark? They've seen it."

"Seen what?"

"Right now, there's a wall of light out there, and it's rushing right at us. If we are on the ground when it hits, we will die. We have to take off *now*!"

A female voice suddenly blared from the speakers. "Team Sigma … uh … Shut it down."

Maddeningly, Mark didn't release Vaughn's hand. Still pushing down, the stronger man kept it clamped onto the collective control stick. He tilted his head as he listened to the woman. "That's the local director."

Her voice returned, suddenly urgent. "Terminate the test, Mark! We need to get you out of there."

Vaughn's eyes widened. "Oh shit! That's exactly what she said last time!"

He tried to pull the stick up.

It wouldn't budge.

"It's almost here, Mark! Let go! We have to go *now*!"

"No, Vaughn! We need to—"

"What the hell is …?!" the director blurted over the radio, cutting off Mark. The woman's words trailed off mid-sentence. Vaughn could hear her quickening breath. In the background, several voices raised, some screaming.

Mark's face went pale. He looked at Vaughn and finally released his hand. He gave a short nod.

Vaughn returned the gesture and then pulled up the collective. He knew Mark could do this without his help, but there was no time to wait.

The familiar vibration of the Q-drive's ramping up power transmitted through Vaughn's seat.

He pointed at the center joystick. "Grab the cyclic! Keep us away from the walls!"

The power reading rolled rapidly through fifty percent.

Then the module lifted off the scaffolding.

Suddenly, the director's voice returned. "What the hell is that?!"

The now hovering module began to drift sideways.

Vaughn's eyes went wide!

The woman's voice echoed in his helmet. "Oh God! No! ... No—!" Her words died, and then she was gone.

"What are you doing, Mark?!" Releasing the collective control, Vaughn reached across the astronaut and grabbed the top of the cyclic. "You were so much better at this last time!"

Vaughn pulled the stick to the left, guiding the craft away from the side of the chamber. At the same moment, he reached across his own body with his free left hand, groping for the falling collective stick, but came up short as the shoulder harness kept him pinned to the seat back.

He couldn't reach the control!

Suddenly, a visible wave passed across the chamber's wall. The aluminum surface appeared to flex.

At the last moment, Vaughn remembered to close his eyes just before the wall flashed brilliant white like burning phosphorus.

An instant later, the dazzling radiance that was streaming through Vaughn's squeezed shut lids faded.

Then he was thrown against the harness.

Opening his eyes, Vaughn saw that the module had crashed down onto the edge of the scaffolding.

He released the cyclic and reached for the collective, intent on yanking the vertical control stick up, but it was too late.

The module began to topple, falling backward.

"Crap!"

CHAPTER 5

"Oh shit …" Vaughn coughed. "That hurt!"

Blinking, he stared up at the distant ceiling as he fought for breath.

Beside him, Mark groaned and nodded. "Yeah, it did."

Lying on his back, Vaughn rolled his head to the right and looked at Mark. "You okay?"

The astronaut's head bobbed up and down inside his helmet. Mark looked around at the toppled structure of the module and then shook his head. "There goes my career."

Leaning forward, Vaughn began to power down the vehicle. "I'm sorry to be the one to tell you this, truly, but it's a helluva lot worse than that."

Even though the flight module had crashed onto its back, all of its systems were still running.

Watching him work, Mark shook his head. "What happened? How did you get this way?" He paused and then knitted his brow. "And what the hell was that light? Why was everyone in Sandusky screaming?"

After flipping a final switch, Vaughn reached down and began to release his harness. "I'll tell you all about it, I promise, but right now, we have a phone call to make."

"We don't need to do that. I'll just call them on the radio."

Vaughn glanced at his friend as he continued to climb from the module. He pointed through the chamber wall. "There's no one out there to answer, Mark."

The astronaut stared at him wordlessly for a long moment.

Waving for his friend to follow, Vaughn continued to climb through the open architecture of the vehicle. A moment later, he slid through a wide gap in the tubular frame and stepped onto the chamber floor.

Looking back, he saw Mark disentangling himself from the harness and climbing out of the prone captain's chair. The man toggled his suit radio. "Control, this is Team Sigma, over."

Vaughn frowned. "Wasting your breath."

Climbing through the module, Mark shook his head. "What are you saying? What was all that about we're going to die?" He suddenly stopped and looked up at Vaughn, his eyes widening. "Was that a nuke?"

Vaughn shook his head again. "No. I almost wish it had been. That wouldn't be as bad as the truth."

Mark continued to stare at him.

Waving for him to follow, Vaughn started walking toward the red emergency phone that was mounted to the chamber wall. Fortunately, the module hadn't damaged it during the crash. Somehow, the falling ship appeared to have missed all of the electronics. Most importantly, the radio rack was still intact.

"What are you doing?"

"I told you. We need to make a phone call."

"Vaughn, we are in vacuum. That thing isn't going to work."

Undeterred, Vaughn pulled the phone from the wall and set it on a nearby bench just as Mark had done the first time. A moment later, he finished prying off the cover, revealing the hidden rotary dial beneath.

While he worked, Mark had continued his attempts to raise

someone via the radio in spite of Vaughn's assertion that it was wasted energy.

The calls went unanswered.

Mark now stood silently next to him.

In Vaughn's peripheral vision, he saw the man staring at his face. Then his friend looked down and saw what he had done to the phone. "How did you know about that dial?" He paused and then raised both hands, palms up. "About *all* of this?" He turned and stared at Vaughn again. "And what did you do to your face? Is that makeup?" His eyes lost focus. Looking through Vaughn, Mark shook his head slowly. "How did I miss that? I was there when you suited up."

Vaughn pressed his lips together and then shook his head as well. "Mark, anything I tell you is just going to lead to more questions." He pointed at the red phone. "Right now, I need you to connect this to the radio so that we can call Director McCree in Houston."

Mark did a double take. He opened his mouth to speak, but Vaughn cut him off.

"I know you can because I've seen you do it before."

Still the astronaut continued to stare at him.

Sighing, Vaughn placed a hand on Mark's arm. "I can tell you this much for now. This is the most important phone call you'll ever make. There is someone that the director can put us in touch with that might be able to undo all of this, but if we don't talk to McCree before the light reaches Houston ..." Vaughn paused and then shook his head. "Things will get much more complicated."

Mark looked from him to the phone and back. Then he nodded and pointed to a nearby toolbox. "Hand me that."

Vaughn grabbed the toolset and placed it on the bench next to the phone. Then he walked across the chamber.

"Where are you going?"

He pointed at an assembly mounted to the aluminum wall. "Going to start working on the manual pressure release."

"How do you know...?" Mark paused and then sighed. "Never mind."

Smiling wryly, Vaughn walked up to the red box. Just as it had the first time, the assembly sported a transparent front panel. Evenly spaced white chevrons covered the three-foot-tall, vertically oriented glass rectangle. A network of pipes protruded from the top and bottom of the fixture. A small tool hung from a chain on its right side.

Vaughn grabbed the bronze hammer and struck the clear panel. Like it had that first day, the safety glass shattered into pebble-sized shards and fell to the floor in surreal silence. Not wanting to risk a torn glove in the room's vacuum, Vaughn reached cautiously through the opening and extracted a steel pipe from the enclosure. He stuck one end of it into the metal sleeve that protruded from the box's plumbing. After twisting the tube a quarter turn, he grabbed the end of the handle and began to pump it up and down like a man trying to jack up a car.

Mark's voice came over the speaker in his helmet. "That's going to take a lot of pumps."

Nodding, Vaughn continued to cycle the handle up and down. "Oh, believe me, I know." He could already feel his energy waning, having long ago burned through the meal he and Angela had eaten another world ago.

As Vaughn worked, thoughts of his mother and Angela paraded through his mind.

Had Angela survived? What if the explosion or some piece of flying debris had gotten her before the reset could send her back?

No. Vaughn made a quick head shake. He couldn't think that way. She had to be alive.

Otherwise ...

He shook his head again. Stop it! She's going to be there.

The thoughts persisted.

What if she didn't remember him, didn't know him?

Vaughn had no idea what to expect. There was no manual for this, no instructions.

And what about his mother? Was she at this very moment standing in her backyard watching the approaching light?

As he continued to move the lever up and down, Vaughn closed his eyes and ground his teeth.

It was too much.

Another tear inched its way down his cheek.

Vaughn sighed.

He had to keep going. That's all any of them could do right now.

Clenching his jaw, he tried to focus all of his thoughts and energy on the pump's handle.

It almost worked.

Sometime later, he released the lever and bent at the waist, resting with hands on knees as he tried to catch his breath.

"I told you, you need to start working out."

Panting, Vaughn shook his head. Sweat dripped onto the inside of his visor. He gave his friend a sideward glance. "Dude, that is so not the problem."

Mark pointed at him. "Come on, man. Look how your suit is stretched out."

Vaughn peered down and smirked. He did look like the Michelin Man.

Standing upright, he twisted a valve on his suit's controls. His ears popped as the internal pressure of the spacesuit dropped to its nominal setting. He had increased the pressure earlier to disguise his new body form.

No longer pushed out by his belly or overpressurized, the suit shrank back down to its normal shape.

Vaughn turned to face Mark, arms held wide. He now looked significantly skinnier. "I told you, my friend. There is a lot more going on than you could ever imagine."

Standing next to the radio rack, the astronaut stared at him, mouth hanging slack.

Vaughn lowered his arms and pointed at the phone. "Got that thing working yet?"

Mark looked at him for a moment longer and then nodded. "Just attached the last wire. I connected it to our internal communications system."

Walking over to stand next to the man, Vaughn studied his work. "What are you waiting for? Fire it up."

He looked over to see Mark staring at his face again.

Vaughn sighed. "Dammit, dude." He pointed at the phone. "Focus!"

Mark flinched and looked away. "Sorry."

"Just make the call, already."

The astronaut nodded and then reached out and flipped a switch.

A dial tone began to stream through the intercom.

Releasing a breath he hadn't known he'd been holding, Vaughn closed his eyes and nodded. "Thank you."

CHAPTER 6

Standing outside of the building that housed Chamber A, Randy looked toward the parking lot and clicked his key fob button. When the lights of his four-by-four truck flashed, he pointed at it. "That one." He threw his keys to the intern. "It's Rourke, right?"

The young man snatched the keys from the air and nodded. "Y-Yes, Director."

"Okay, Rourke, take my truck over to the gym and grab some rubber mats."

"Mats, sir?"

"Yeah, you know, those flat ones, the ones that people lie on in the gym."

"Oh, you mean yoga mats."

Randy waved a dismissive hand. "Yeah, whatever. Just bring them. And hurry!"

Rourke gave a quick nod and then turned to leave. He'd run a few steps toward the parking lot across the street from the chamber facility when he stopped and looked at Randy. "Is this about that thing in Europe?"

"How did you hear about that?"

"It's all over Twitter, sir. Something about a weird aurora." He shook his head. "But nobody seems to know for sure."

Randy nodded somberly. "Yeah, son. It's about that ... but it's no aurora."

The man's already pale face turned a lighter shade of white.

Randy could relate. After finishing his discussion with Commander Brown, he had pulled up the video shot from inside the planeload of commandos. He had needed to see the event for himself. Just as General Tannehill had reported—and as Angela had known they would—all of the plane's occupants vanished, disappearing the moment the aircraft had passed through the light. Later, when the nukes had reached Geneva, they, too, had vanished. The entire fleet of nuclear reentry vehicles had winked out of existence a moment before reaching their targets.

"How many mats, sir?" Rourke said, snapping Randy from his thoughts.

"All of them!" He waved for him to continue. "Hurry! Don't stop for anyone, not even Center security."

Unmoving, the man stared at Randy.

"Go!"

Rourke flinched. "Yes, sir!" He spun on his heels and then sprinted toward the truck.

Randy turned and looked at the front of the vacuum chamber facility. He'd walked there from Mission Control. The two structures sat across a parking lot from each other.

His truck's turbodiesel engine roared to life behind him. Its tires barked as the young man hammered the vehicle's accelerator. Then it sped around the corner and was gone.

Still looking at the facility, Randy shook his head. "You guys picked a helluva day for a convention."

This week was the thirty-third annual Planetary Congress for the Association of Space Explorers or ASE. Astronauts, cosmonauts, and space explorers from all over the world had gathered in Budapest, Hungary. Every one of NASA's current and qualified astronauts was there. Which meant they'd had a front-row seat to the event that was sweeping across the globe, and it also meant that nobody with adequate knowledge of spacesuit operations was anywhere close to Houston ... or even alive.

If he'd had more time, Randy would have had his chamber techs rig up a Bigelow Expandable Activity Module, a BEAM. They could have loaded the BEAM with as many personnel as it could hold and then drop the vacuum-rated, expandable habitat from the ceiling when the light was about to pass. Its inflatable double walls would have absorbed the impact with the floor, protecting the occupants if they were properly secured.

However, there were two problems with that plan. The hoist had been removed because the folks from the James Webb Space Telescope program hadn't wanted the greasy thing hanging above their billion-dollar project during the current vacuum tests. The other problem was that the nearest Bigelow module was at the company's home base in North Las Vegas.

Then Randy had realized that there was a small pool of personnel who should be in the area, people who should have a modicum of spacesuit knowledge: the current class of ass-cans or astronaut candidates.

After a quick scan of their personnel files, Randy had identified several candidates that had skills that would be beneficial for what may lie ahead. He'd tried to reach all of them, but the phone systems were jammed. As Rourke had demonstrated, word was getting out. Everyone must have been trying to talk on their phones at the same time, creating a telephonic traffic jam. It had locked up the system, so Randy had sent texts to each of the astronaut candidates on his list.

Only five had responded.

That had proved to be a fortuitous number.

The spacesuit techs had decided that the event of the ASE Planetary Congress made this week an excellent time for annual overhauls. When Randy had called to tell them to prep the candidates' suits, they had informed him that all of the spacesuits were in varying states of disassembly. The tech on the phone had unhelpfully indicated that they could have a few ready in a couple of hours.

Randy had found five people to send into the chamber, but he had no spacesuits in which to send them.

A few frantic phone calls later, he had found a cache of serviceable spacesuits. The neutral buoyancy training facility had a few, and guess how many they had?

Yep, five!

Five goddamn spacesuits that weren't even onsite.

The pool was at the annex over on Ellington Field, a good fifteen-minute drive from Johnson Space Center. He'd texted the astronaut candidates with instructions to head to the facility. They were to grab those training suits and hightail it back to Chamber A. There was a van at the pool that they could use to change into their suits on their way to the chamber. As he'd done with Rourke, Randy had instructed them to stop for no one.

They'd each responded in the affirmative. Some had joked that it sounded like another ass-can initiation ritual.

Randy had decided to let them think that. They'd be motivated to take part, to outdo their predecessors.

Presently, he scanned the streets around the vacuum chamber facility. The astronaut candidates still hadn't arrived. Shaking his head, he walked back into the building. After passing through a narrow corridor, he entered the expansive room that contained the actual vacuum chamber. Its wide, round door stood fully open. Inside, several technicians were still fiddling with the device that currently occupied a large portion of the chamber.

Grinding his teeth, Randy ran up to the opening. "Goddammit! I told you to get that thing out of here!"

All of the personnel jumped and turned toward him.

Randy shook his head. "And why in the hell did you put on your bunny suits?"

The closest tech shrugged. "Sir, we have to wear our cleanroom suits. This is the James Webb Space Telescope. It can't be exposed to any—"

"I said to get it out of here. Not in an hour! I needed it out ten minutes ago!"

"But Director, this is a billion-dollar—"

"It's a billion-dollar paperweight now, and it's in my way!"

Shaking his head, Randy turned and scanned the area outside the chamber. Spotting something that he thought might help, he turned and ran toward it. Randy jumped behind its steering wheel and soon had the electric vehicle moving. He turned it toward the chamber in time to see four of the astronaut candidates emerge from the long corridor in their spacesuits. They each held a helmet under an arm.

Yanking the wheel to the right, Randy brought the vehicle to a skidding stop in front of the small group. "Wing Commander Bingham, why are there only four of you? Where's Johnston?"

All four ass-cans stood transfixed, mutely staring at him. Then, with evident confusion, they looked past Randy at the technicians working in the chamber.

Wing Commander Chance Bingham, a British pilot from the Royal Air Force, served as the senior candidate. The tall, thin man looked from the chamber and regarded Randy with a cocked eyebrow. "Sir? … What are you doing?"

"Chance! Focus. Where is Johnston?"

Wing Commander Bingham blinked and then shook his head. "I don't know, sir. We can't reach him. Something's amiss with the phone lines, and he's not answering our texts." The man paused and then pointed toward the front of the building. "But we brought his suit. It's out in the lorry."

"Lorry? You mean truck?"

Chance nodded. "Yes, right."

Randy frowned. "Okay, you four will have to do for now." He pointed at some nearby scaffolding. "I want all of you to grab that and roll it into the chamber."

The two men and two women looked at him, their evident confusion deepening.

Sighing, Randy shook his head. "I really don't have time to explain right now. I just need you to trust me. I'll give you all the details once you're in the chamber. But we have to get the vacuum cycle running now." His eyes lost focus as he stared through the candidates. "Otherwise, all this will be for nothing."

Wing Commander Bingham was craning his neck to look inside the chamber. He regarded Randy with knitted brows. "Okay, sir, but I don't think there's room in the chamber for the scaffolding. Not with the telescope in there." He paused and then a grin spread across his face. "Are you taking the piss, sir?"

"Taking the piss?"

The man rolled his eyes. "Bloody yanks ... Is this some kind of joke, a prank you pull on ass-cans?"

"Candidate, does this look like a joke?" Randy released the brake and guided the vehicle toward the vacuum chamber. The wheels bumped as it rolled over the lower door seal.

One of the cleanroom suit-clad technicians moved to stand between the vehicle and the telescope, hands held up and gesticulating wildly for him to stop.

Randy waved the man aside. "Move, jackass!"

At the last moment, the idiot jumped out of the way.

The massive, heavy-duty forklift slammed into the James Webb Space Telescope with a tremendous crash. Several of its polished beryllium mirrors crumpled under the impact. Randy didn't stop the vehicle until he had pushed the thing against the far wall.

He could hear people shouting behind him.

After several failed attempts, Randy found the lever that tilted the forklift's tines back. Then he pulled another handle, and the forks lifted the space telescope off the ground.

The beep-beep-beep of the reverse alarm echoed surreally through the metal cavern. As he backed the vehicle out of the chamber, the technicians and astronauts, now mute, stared at him with open mouths.

The ruined telescope trailed components. Shattered equipment and tangled wiring dragged along the metal floor of the chamber emitting a loud screech.

Randy slowed the forklift as he passed through the exit. He didn't want to damage the door seal. A moment later, he unceremoniously dropped the junked, billion-dollar space telescope onto the facility's concrete floor.

Randy jumped down from the large vehicle and ran over to the scaffolding. He started unlocking its wheels.

Looking up, Randy waved for the awestruck audience to join him. He employed the command voice that he'd developed during his thirty-plus years as a Marine officer. "Move it! We're running out of time!"

Careful not to drop the helmet pinned under his left elbow, Wing Commander Bingham held up his hands, palms facing out. He looked from the crumpled telescope and back at Randy. "Bugger that, sir. I'll have no part of it." Behind him, the other three astronaut candidates were similarly shaking their heads as they each backed away from him.

Randy sighed. He closed his eyes for a moment and then nodded. "Listen. I promise you, I haven't lost it. There's something happening, something that's going to hit us before too long."

The stocky Asian candidate, Rachel, he thought, began to nod. She spoke with a barely perceptible accent. "Chance, he's talking about that thing in Europe."

The four of them stopped backpedaling as they exchanged nervous glances.

Wing Commander Bingham glanced at Rachel. Then the color drained from the British man's face. "Blimey ... I thought that was nothing." He looked at Randy. "What is it?"

"I can tell you it's not an aurora. It's some kind of wave ... a light wave that's knocking out communications. It's not slowing, and it doesn't appear to be losing any of its energy." He hesitated and then shook his head. "But beyond that, we don't know much," he lied.

The senior astronaut candidate eyed Randy warily. "What are you not telling us, Director?"

"Listen, Chance. We're not exactly sure what it's doing to the people in its wake. We haven't been able to contact anyone."

"What about Britain?"

Randy shook his head. "We haven't been able to raise anyone there either."

Bingham opened his mouth to speak, but Randy held up a hand. "Like I said, we don't know what the light is doing, but we do have some damned solid intel that if you're in the chamber when the light passes, you won't be affected." He pointed toward the chamber. "That's why I need you four in there when it gets here. Afterward, you can come out and help the rest of us, but if you're still out here when it hits ... Well, I don't know what happens then."

Wing Commander Bingham's eyes darkened, and the muscles in his square jaw worked. He fixed Randy with a cold stare. His voice lowered, taking on a menacing tone. "What about our families? Mine is here in Houston."

Looking at the man, Randy nodded toward Chamber A. Lowering his voice, he matched the man's tone. "If you want a chance to help your family, you'll get in there."

The commander opened his mouth to say something else but then thought better of it.

Randy looked at the other three candidates. "I'll explain more once you're inside the chamber, but first, we have to get this scaffolding and you four in there with the door closed. We have to start the vacuum cycle ASAP."

Major Rachel Lee looked from Randy to Wing Commander Bingham. "Come on, Chance. What if he's right?"

Looking from her and then back outside toward the exit, Bingham finally nodded. "Okay."

A few moments later, the five of them, along with assistance from the still stunned technicians, finished wrestling the scaffolding into the chamber.

Randy heard a door burst open behind him. Then a voice rang out. "Oh my God. What have you done?"

Turning, he saw Rourke standing in the open hall door. The young man was staring at the crumpled mess of the telescope, a blue, rubber mat clutched in each of his hands.

Looking at the intern, Randy tilted his head. "How tall are you?"

Rourke blinked and looked at him. "What?"

"It's a simple enough question, son."

"Uh … five-nine …" He looked at the telescope and then back at Randy. "Wh-Why?"

Giving Bingham a sideward glance, Randy tilted his head at Rourke. "Think he'll fit in the suit you brought for Johnston?"

The commander gave Randy a double-take. "Yes, but so would you, Director." Chance pointed to his spacesuit. "And you have experience with these bloody things, a lot more than we do, for that matter."

Randy shook his head and looked down at the ground. "No … that was a long time ago." His eyes lost focus as he stared through the floor. "This is a job for younger people than me." He shook his head and then looked at Bingham. "Besides, I have to coordinate things out here."

Before anyone could raise further protests, Randy pointed to the tall female astronaut candidate that was standing behind Rachel. "Monique, you and Doctor Andrew take Rourke outside and help him get into the spare suit. While you're at it, bring the young man up to speed on what we've been talking about and our plan."

In spite of looking as if she, too, were in shock, the tall, dark woman put on a brave face. Monique nodded and then led an equally stunned Rourke from the chamber. Doctor Andrew gave Randy a nervous glance and then nodded and followed after the two.

Watching the man go, he shook his head. Doctor Andrew looked as nervous as a long-tailed cat in a square-dancing contest. Hopefully the man's nerves would settle down.

Gesturing at the other two candidates, Randy pointed at the exit. "Go with them, and bring in the rest of those blue mats."

A short time later, they returned with armloads of blue foam rubber.

Randy directed the candidates to line the floor of the chamber with the rubber mats. Along the way, he told them how the light wasn't affecting anyone disconnected from the planet. Several times they had inquired as to how Randy had come across this information.

He'd repeated that he would tell them everything he knew once the vacuum cycle had started.

Randy rechecked his phone. Before the mobile networks had gridlocked, several calls had come: the President, the Joint Chiefs, various department heads. He'd rejected them all. It didn't matter who. Johnston, the missing astronaut candidate, had finally gotten word to them that he was trapped behind impenetrable traffic, so Rourke was it. That left only two calls that mattered. One would come from Cleveland. The other ... He eyed the idle screen of his smartphone. The other call should come from a location much closer than Cleveland.

His wife and two children were on their way to the Space Center, but Randy couldn't reach them. It had been a while since he'd been able to place a mobile call, and now his outgoing texts were failing as well.

Randy shook his head. As he watched the crews work, he pulled out the wireless handset for his office landline. That phone still worked just fine, but it had no more luck reaching mobiles than had his smartphone. Still, he tried her number again and again got an 'all circuits busy' message.

Sighing, Randy stared at the mute devices clutched in his hands. "Where are you, Betty?"

In her last text, she had said that they were stuck in traffic. That had been twenty minutes ago.

Randy closed his eyes. He had to believe that Angela was right, that this wasn't the end of everything. He did believe it. Hell, he was betting everything on her claims: his career, his life, his family ... all of it. He was all in. If not, he would've left right then, taken his four-by-four and gone to find his family, damn the consequences, but if there were the slightest possibility that his actions here could save Betty and the kids, then he'd do whatever it took to see it through.

"We're done, sir."

Randy looked up from the two phones and saw Rourke staring at him. "What?"

"We finished laying out the mats."

Nodding, Randy tucked away his phones and walked into the chamber.

He gestured at their helmets. "Let's go. Get 'em on."

They exchanged nervous glances. Rourke's face paled. He fumbled with his helmet. He had it turned sideways.

Wing Commander Bingham looked at the young intern and rolled his eyes. However, Rachel, the tough Ranger-turned-Army attack helicopter pilot, took pity on the young man. After locking her helmet into place, she stepped over and helped Rourke with his.

Randy pointed at the intern. "Are you going to be okay, son?"

Rourke's too white and now sweaty face shook from side to side. "N-No ..." The now-closed helmet muffled the young man's words. "No, I'm not."

Rachel held up a thumb. "He'll be fine. I'll keep an eye on him."

Walking around the group, Randy did a quick inspection of their equipment. As he passed behind them, he dug a folded-up sheet of paper from his pocket. He pulled up a flap on the back of Rourke's suit. "I'll just tighten up this strap." He tucked the paper under the fold and then laid it flat. The Velcro held fast. Then he patted the young man's shoulder. "Looks good. You'll do just fine."

Stepping in front of the five of them, Randy pointed up at the scaffolding. "You need to climb up there. When the light gets here, you're going to jump down onto these mats."

Rourke looked from Randy to the top of the twenty-foot-tall scaffolding. His eyes went wide. "From the top?! It's too high! These mats aren't thick enough."

Rachel patted his arm. "Don't worry, Rourky." She used the nickname without malice. "The mats will be a lot thicker once we suck all the atmosphere out of here. They'll make good cushions."

Randy nodded. "Exactly. And we need to start that vacuum cycle right now."

Chance regarded him with a cocked eyebrow. "How do we know when to jump?"

"I'll let you know when." Nodding somberly, he pointed toward the exit. Then he held up a suit communicator and spoke into it. "I'm going to stand outside and watch for the light."

He saw more questions forming on their lips, but Randy held up a hand. "Later." He backed through the chamber's massive and now slowly closing door. "First, we get this thing sealed up." He pointed over their heads. "In the meantime, I suggest you start working your way up that scaffolding."

Standing outside the chamber, Randy watched the door continue its plodding swing.

Unmoving, the five space-suited individuals—two women and three men—stared at him through the narrowing gap with varying states of fear and confusion painted across the visible portions of their faces.

Then Randy flinched as the door closed with a deep, metallic thud.

CHAPTER 7

S tanding in the middle of the road, Randy looked at his watch.
Then he gazed at the two phones clutched in his left hand. They
had fallen ominously silent in the last half-hour.

Earlier, he couldn't take any of the calls from Washington. He had
even rejected those that had come from his boss: the Director of
NASA. He simply hadn't had time to brief them or discuss the
problem before closing up Chamber A.

And now that he was outside, the calls had ceased.

All Randy had was time.

Time to think about what was coming.

Time to wonder about his family and where they were.

Time to agonize over every decision he'd made in the last few
hours.

One decision he felt good about was letting each of the five individuals in the chamber place a short phone call. After he had initiated
the vacuum cycle, Randy had dialed each of their homes with varying
levels of success. Holding the Chamber A communicator to the office
phone's wireless handset, he'd listened in on more than one tear-filled
conversation. In each, the caller had assured the distressed family

member or friend that everything would be okay and that they'd be there for them after the situation had passed.

While he hated holding back the worst of the news, Randy didn't think it would do any good to tell them the true nature of what the light was doing. Hell, he didn't really know what it was doing, although Angela had stated the end result quite clearly.

Everyone the light touched died.

But knowing that fact would give no solace.

So he felt no qualms about withholding the truth.

Yeah, right…

Shaking his head, Randy looked up from the now quiet devices. He stood in the center of Second Street, the road that connected to both Mission Control and Chamber A. From where he stood, the street continued northeast, offering Randy an unobstructed view as he gazed in that direction. He knew that soon, bright light would likely obscure that horizon. That was the direction from which the white, aurora-like curtain of energy would approach. However, for the moment, the only thing visible at the road's far end was the trees that lined Mud Lake beyond the Space Center's northeast boundary.

Standing in the center of the road, Randy was in no danger of being run over. An eerie silence had descended over Johnson Space Center. He'd released all non-essential personnel, told them to go home, be with their families. The parking lots had emptied in a bevy of frenzied activity and roaring engines, but now, not a single car haunted its grid of lonely streets.

Randy's wandering thoughts went to his many friends who had been in Budapest, Hungary. Had he not been assigned as the current director of Mission Control, he likely would've been at the Planetary Congress with them. He didn't know whether to pity his friends or himself. At least they'd had the bliss of ignorance. It had likely ended before they knew it had started.

The street's oppressive silence weighed heavily on Randy. It seemed to press down upon him.

His pulse raced loudly in his ears.

Aside from the lack of vehicles on the street, everything else appeared normal. Houston's oppressive humidity was turning the early spring day muggy. However, the scattered clouds that dotted the otherwise blue sky meant that he would have a good line of sight for the coming event.

"Front fucking row."

Dragging his eyes from the horizon, Randy looked at the handheld radio clutched in his right hand and the two phones grasped awkwardly in his left. He used a free finger from the side that held the communicator to press a button on the face of his smartphone.

"Please, ring."

He closed his eyes and sighed as the damned three-tone all-circuits-busy jingle blared from the thing's speaker again.

"Shit!"

He turned and looked toward the entrance of Johnson Space Center. In the distance, he could see cars racing down NASA Road 1, the thoroughfare that ran along the southern boundary of JSC. However, none of the vehicles were turning to enter the main gate. All the cars were running in opposite directions, their occupants madly dashing about in hopes of going anywhere but here, he guessed.

"Where are you, Betty?"

He tucked the chamber communicator into his back pocket. With his hand freed up, he began to peck the screen of his smartphone, typing out a quick message. Then he pressed send. A blue progress bar marched from left to right across the top of the screen but then froze three-quarters of the way through the motion. A moment later, he got a message-failed announcement.

Hanging his head, Randy closed his eyes.

The handheld communicator stuffed in his back pocket sparked to life. Wing Commander Bingham's muffled voice shattered the street's odd silence. "Vacuum cycle shows ninety percent complete. Any chance we can get that briefing now, Director?"

Randy sighed. After giving his phone another longing glance, he dug the communicator from his pocket and raised it to his lips. "Roger. Sorry for the delay, guys. Been a little distracted out here. Are you all set in there?"

"Yeah. Rourke had a bit of trouble getting up here, but Rachel has him squared away now."

The young man's plaintive voice broke into the conversation. "No, I didn't. I just had a little trouble with my balance. This thing weighs a ton."

"Anyway," Bingham said, "what do you say you fill us in, Director?"

Randy nodded. "I've been waiting on a phone call—"

The wireless handset for his office phone suddenly rang. Seeing the area code, Randy raised his eyebrows. "Hang on. I think this is it."

Releasing the communicator's press-to-talk button, he reached over and accepted the call. "Director McCree here ... Is this Lieutenant Colonel Hennessy?"

A long, static-filled silence greeted his question.

"Mark, is that you?!"

"Uh ... Y-Yes, it is, Director."

A second voice chimed in. "Oh, thank God. He must've spoken with her."

Randy nodded. "Yes, Captain Singleton. I have." Pausing, he swallowed hard and then gave a short nod. "I-I take it the light hit Cleveland?"

Captain Singleton's voice returned. "Yes, sir. I'm afraid it did. We've lost contact with everyone on this end. Just ... Just like last time."

Closing his eyes, Randy released a long sigh. After a moment, he nodded again. "Okay, then. Standby. I'm going to conference in Commander Brown from the station."

Just as Angela had predicted, Randy had indeed found a way to use his smartphone's camera to place a video call to the space station. One of his hackers had shown him an app they'd been working on. It used the Center's Wi-Fi network to create a secure video conference with other NASA locations as well as the space station. The app hadn't been released yet. It was still in beta, but they had assured him that it would work for his purposes today.

Randy had already queued up the app. He activated it, and a few moments later, Commander Brown's anxious face filled the device's screen.

"Director McCree?"

Looking into the lens, he pressed his lips together and then nodded. He moved the two devices closer to each other. "I have someone that I think you're going to want to hear from."

"Vaughn?!"

"Angela! Oh, thank you." The man's voice cracked with emotion. "I was worried that I had ... had lost you, or that you wouldn't remember any of it ... or me."

"I'm here, Vaughn." Emotion choked Angela's words as well. Even though the only thing she could see through Randy's phone was the wireless headset, she reached toward the camera lens as if to touch it, a sad smile on her face. "And I remember everything."

"Me, t—" Vaughn's voice hitched. Then he coughed. "Me, too, Angela." He released an unsteady breath.

Her forehead furrowed, and her eyebrows peaked. "It didn't work. I couldn't stop it from happening again."

"It's not your fault, Angela. We're lucky to be alive, to be here ... now."

Randy watched her slowly shake her head. "Maybe, but I saw something in that computer. It gave me an idea, but I'll tell you about that later."

"Oh ... Okay." Vaughn paused for a moment and then continued. "Sure ... Later. It's so goddamn good to hear your voice. Are you okay?"

"Ha." She released a short, humorless laugh. "Same as I was last time you saw me."

"Yeah, me, too. Still in my spacesuit over here, but everything feels the same." He chuckled. "Still got this beard, and it smells like something died in my suit."

"I hate to interrupt the family reunion," Randy said. "But I kind of have a pressing issue here."

Angela blinked and then looked at him through the lens. "Sorry, Randy. How are things going there? Are you in the chamber?" She paused, and then her eyes went wide. "Wait. Why aren't you in a spacesuit?!"

"There's been a change of plans."

Randy paused as he stared at the smartphone. His hackers had told him that while the app was in use, it would block messages and phone calls, so if Betty managed to get an open phone line, she and the kids wouldn't be able to reach him.

"I'm putting all my faith in you, and from what little you've told me about what might lie ahead for you, I think the last thing you need is a busted-up, old test pilot slowing you down. I won't be going with you on this."

"No, no, no, you can't do this, Randy!"

He held the communicator so she could see it. "I found a group of people that I think can help you. They are in the chamber now. The vacuum cycle is almost complete."

"But, sir—"

"It's done, Commander," Randy said, cutting her off. As he stared into the camera lens, he softened his gaze. "What do you say we use the little time left to make some introductions. You need to brief the candidates on what you've seen and where you want to meet up."

"Candidates? … You got ass-cans in there? That's all you could find?"

Randy frowned. "Yes, and yes. But I really don't have time to go into the why and the how right now. Besides, I know somebody who was an ass-can herself not too long ago."

He checked his watch. "If the light hasn't slowed, we only have another twenty minutes or so before it reaches Houston."

Seeing more protests forming on her lips, Randy held up the communicator again and shook it. "It's time for you to brief them, Angela. They really don't know much yet other than that there's some type of light heading this way and that it won't affect them if they're in the chamber. They're standing on scaffolding, and we've padded the floor to cushion their landing."

Angela furrowed her brow. "How will they know when to …?" She faltered. Then understanding dawned on her face. "Oh God, Randy."

Her eyes darted as she studied the Cupola's monitor screen. "You're outside ... you're going to—?"

"Yes." He cut her off. "I'm going to watch the light approach and give them a countdown."

Angela stared at him, her face awash with emotions.

Randy gave her a wan smile. "You being back here after all you've obviously been through gives me hope, Angela, hope for my family, hope for the world." He glanced northeast and then held up the communicator. "But it's time to brief your team."

Her face now pale, Angela stared at him for a moment longer and then nodded. "Okay, let's do this."

CHAPTER 8

Activating the Chamber A communicator, Randy spoke loudly enough to ensure that his voice registered on all three of the devices in his hands. "Listen up, folks. I've opened a three-way conference call. I have Commander Brown on the horn from the space station. Also, Lieutenant Colonel Mark Hennessy and Captain Vaughn Singleton are with us. They are in the vacuum chamber up in Cleveland at the moment. Here in Chamber A, I've assembled a team of five individuals headed up by Wing Commander Chance Bingham. First things first. Let's make sure everyone is hearing me. Commander Brown?"

"Got you loud and clear."

Randy nodded. "Colonel Hennessy? Captain Singleton?"

Mark Hennessy's thin voice came through the office telephone wireless handset. "Five-by-five, Director."

"What about you guys here in Chamber A? All of you reading me alright, Commander Bingham?"

"Uh, yes, sir." The man sounded thoroughly confused. "Getting a little feedback, but you're readable."

"Okay, Commander Brown." Randy tilted his head toward her image on his smartphone. "You have the floor."

Angela chewed her lip for a moment. Then she nodded at Randy and cleared her throat.

"I'm Commander Angela Brown aboard the International Space Station. I know you don't have a lot of time, so I'll cut to the chase. We are under attack. I'm sure you've heard that there's something coming, but you probably don't know that it started in CERN, at the supercollider. What you also don't know is that it's no accident. An external operator is trying to wipe life from our planet."

Randy drew in a sharp breath. After some of Angela's earlier statements, he'd had his suspicions, but this was the first time she'd said definitively that they were under attack.

The wing commander's voice erupted from the communicator. "Commander Brown, how could you know that? I mean ... bloody hell, McCree ...! That's one giant leap."

Randy raised the communicator. "Chance—"

The man cut him off. "Please tell me you didn't junk the telescope and jam us in here based on the word of a nutter. External operator?! Utter bollocks!" he scoffed. "What the bloody hell is she talking about?!"

Angela's voice returned, cold and hard. "Listen, Commander. I don't have time to go into all of it, but you need to trust—"

"Director McCree! The woman has obviously lost the plot—!"

"Bingham!" Randy said through clenched teeth, cutting off the man. "Hear her out."

"No! I'm sorry, Director, but you're out there, intent on riding out this thing, while we have to leave our—!"

"Riding it out?!" Angela blurted over the smartphone. "He's not *riding out* anything. The man is going to die just like everyone else!"

"Ah, shit," Randy muttered under his breath as he shook his head. He hadn't told them that yet.

Angela continued her rant. "McCree could have taken one of your spots, but he's sacrificing himself to give you a chance to survive this, to give *us* a chance to fight for him and his family."

Sudden quiet fell across all of the devices clutched in Randy's now white-knuckled hands.

After a moment, Rourke's unsteady voice came from the communicator. "Everyone? … Everyone is going to die, ma'am?"

Angela blinked and then nodded. "Yes, the light that's sweeping across the planet … it … well, it's sending everyone it touches somewhere … somewhere else." She held up a hand. "I know how crazy that sounds, but trust me, if you're connected to any portion of the planet when that light passes your location …" She paused for a moment and then shuddered visibly. "Suffice it to say that if you don't jump when the Director says jump, you'll end up in a place that isn't compatible with life." Staring off into the distance, she shook her head. "Not for long anyway."

Beneath her thousand-yard stare, Angela's too skinny face turned another shade paler.

Randy felt his do the same. His insides suddenly felt like Jell-O as thoughts of his family crowded out all others. "Oh God," he said in a hoarse whisper.

Angela's eyes refocused on the camera. "I'm so sorry, Randy."

Before he could reply, Commander Bingham's increasingly annoying voice returned. "Are you having me on, McCree?! You didn't tell us that everyone is dying!"

Randy heard the rustle of movement coming through the man's microphone.

Rachel Lee's channel activated. "Where are you going, Chance?"

"I'm getting out of here. Going to spend what time we have left with my family."

Randy's eyes widened. "No, Bingham! Even if you use the airlock, you'll let in enough air molecules to endanger everyone!"

Angela held up her hands. "Wait, Commander Bingham. You didn't let me finish."

"You've already told me all I need to know."

"No, I haven't. We *can* save your family."

The sound of movement coming through Bingham's line ceased. "What? H-How?"

"We can't right now, but we can stop the invasion. Once we've done that, I'll reset the timeline. And before you ask, I know I can because I already did a partial reset once."

"You reset time." Bingham's voice dripped with sarcasm. The sound of movement resumed. "Oh, sorry, didn't realize NASA had a time traveler on the payroll."

Major Rachel Lee's voice exploded from the communicator's speaker. "Goddammit, Bingham." She sounded ready to pummel the man. "Get your uptight, British ass back up here before I jump down there and shove a fifty thousand-dollar spacesuit boot up it and turn you into a human popsicle!"

A deep, male voice came from the speaker of Randy's smartphone. "Chance, this is Bill Peterson." The major's ebony face drifted into the image as he floated into the Cupola and pulled up next to Angela. "You and I go way back. Now, I don't know all the details, but I can tell you that Commander Brown is one hundred percent on the level."

The rustling sound ceased. "Bill ...?" Labored breathing filled the Commander's channel. Finally, his voice returned. "Bill, it's good to hear you, but you don't understand. We've left our families alone based on what—"

"Dammit, Chance! My family is there, too. Listen, I felt just like you do. I had my doubts. You know me, and you *know* I'd have a damned good reason to believe Angela! And I do! I've seen the proof. I mean, salt my nuts, after a two-hour spacewalk, the woman came out of her suit with hair a foot longer than when we started, and she'd lost twenty pounds!" He looked at her and shook his head. "Wearing clothes that weren't even on the station!" The major wrinkled his nose. "And don't get me started on the smell. If those clothes had passed within a mile of this space station, I'd have smelled the damned things."

Major Peterson stared back into the camera lens and lowered his voice. "Chance, bottom line: I believe she's offering us the possibility to do something about this and maybe save our families, but if you don't shut up and listen to her, you're going to piss it away."

After a moment, the sound of movement started to come through the communicator.

Randy raised it and opened his mouth to speak, but then Chance's voice returned.

"I'm climbing back up. Commander Brown, please ..." He sighed. "Please, continue."

"Thank you, Commander Bingham. There's not nearly enough time to go over everything we've learned, so I'm just going to tell you what you need to know so that you can survive the light's passage and its aftermath, although, for that last part, I'll let Captain Singleton in Cleveland brief you on what to expect and what to avoid. We'll save the rest for after we link up."

Rachel Lee's voice returned. "You have our undivided attention, Commander."

Angela gave a melancholy smile. "Thank you. It's good to hear the voice of another woman ... It's been months. Who is this?"

"I'm Army Major Rachel Lee. There's one more of us in here, but we can wait on the introductions. Please, continue, Commander Brown."

Angela gave a short nod. "Alright, listen, you're only going to get one chance at this. Timing is paramount. The energy wave apparently propagates through our planet's molecular field. It's already passed Cleveland. The only reason Vaughn and Mark survived was because they were hovering a secret thruster module inside the new vacuum chamber up in Glenn Research when the light passed. No one else survived."

"Nobody in Cleveland?"

"No, Rachel. Nobody else on the planet. Only Vaughn and Colonel Hennessy survived. They were testing a reactionless thruster, so the two of them were disconnected from the planet in a way that no one else had ever been. That's why we know that no one else survived, and it's why we believe you *will* live if you're in free fall inside the vacuum chamber when the light hits."

Colonel Hennessy's voice came through the wireless handset. "What's she talking about, Vaughn?"

"She's right, Mark. You and I were the only ones that survived the first time I went through this."

"I don't understand. If I didn't die ... why don't I remember any of it like you do?"

"That ... That was my fault ..." The Captain's voice wavered. "But I'm not going to let that happen this time, Mark."

Vaughn paused for a moment and then coughed. "Listen, folks, when you come out of the chamber, be careful. The light itself doesn't damage anything, but after everyone disappears, all hell is going to break loose. With no one left to monitor things, a lot of shit is going to go wrong. There'll be massive crashes followed by big, goddamn fires. Don't go running into a burning house, don't try to rescue anyone. They're not there. They are *gone*! Watch out for one another, and for God's sake, stay away from airports for a few hours." His voice cracked again. "They're not safe."

He paused for a breath and then kept going. "Actually, Ellington Field by you guys wasn't too bad. That'll be a good place to un-ass the city. Oh! Hey, Angela, where are we meeting?"

Randy nodded. "I'll take that one, Commander Brown." He raised the communicator. "Rachel, I take it you're still standing next to Rourke?"

"Yes, sir, I am."

"Good. Take a look under the cover of his suit's rear equipment compartment. You'll find a folded-up map. I placed it there just before we closed up the chamber."

The intern's nervous voice piped up. "Wait ... What?"

"Just turn around, Rourky."

Randy listened for the tearing sound of separating Velcro but then remembered that they were in near vacuum. There was no air to carry the sound waves.

He cast a nervous glance at the northeastern horizon. The usual layer of Houston haze tinted the sky above the distant trees. It still looked perfectly normal, but Randy knew that would change soon enough.

"Okay, got it. Is that Nebraska?"

Angela rejoined the conversation. "Yes. There should be a mark on the map east of Omaha."

"Yeah, there is."

"Good. That's Soyuz North American Emergency Landing Point Three. I guess it's self-explanatory. We'll plan to make our descent into the area twenty-four hours from now. That'll allow enough time for the light to finish ... for it to go away, and it should give you enough time to get to the landing zone."

Looking up from the devices, Randy blinked and canted his head.

Had the sky above the horizon just brightened?

"Major Lee, this is Captain Singleton in Cleveland. Mark just told me you're an Army pilot, too."

"Yeah, Apache attack helicopters. Been staying current by flying part-time with First of the One Forty-Ninth Air Cav at Ellington."

"Okay, good. You have any time in utility helicopters ... like Black Hawks?"

"Yes, got a few hours in a Seahawk when I was in the Navy Test Pilot program. They're basically the same. Why?"

"I saw a couple of Black Hawks last time I was at Ellington Field."

"Yeah, they have two assigned to the unit."

Randy's heart threatened to burst from his chest. Over the last few moments, the northeast horizon had brightened significantly.

Captain Singleton continued. "Like I said, airports aren't safe. You can't count on having a useable runway at your destination. I visited Ellington last time. It's not too bad there. I think the Black Hawks were okay. Check 'em out. You'll need to fly everyone to Nebraska in one of them."

Randy looked at his phone. He wanted desperately to try Betty again, but ...

"Avoid industrial areas and large cities, especially the Houston Ship Channel and downtown. That area was so bad that it looked as if it had been nuked. Everything had burned."

Randy's respiratory rate redoubled as he watched the horizon's glow increase. Then a bright, white line began to rise from behind the distant trees. He lifted all the devices to his mouth. "Uh ... F-Folks, we need to wrap this up!"

Angela leaned toward the camera. "Oh no, Randy. Do you see it?"

Looking at her, he pressed his lips together and gave a short nod.

"Oh, shit, shit, shit!" Angela lifted her hands. "Everyone listen. I need you to memorize this." She gave them her CERN email address and then rattled off a string of numbers and letters. "That email and password will get you into the computer network at the collider. If all else fails, if I don't make it and you need to reset the timeline, work your way in and overload the collider's power circuits. There's a lot more to it than that, but if for some reason I'm not there, you'll just have to figure it out. Captain Singleton knows what to do."

"Uh ... No. No, I don't."

Randy jumped in. "I'm with Angela on this one, Vaughn. There's enough talent in this group. You'll figure it out if you have to." He swallowed. "We're about out of time here. The light is filling half the horizon now. Everyone has their assignments. I'm going to end the calls with the station and Cleveland."

Angela wiped tears from her eyes and then nodded. "I'm so sorry, Randy."

"Don't be. Just do your best. Set this right, and maybe none of us ever remember this. It'll be like it never happened."

Chewing her lip, Angela nodded again. "Will do, Director. ISS, out."

Randy ended the video call and then raised his office handset. "Captain Singleton, thank you for everything you've done and what you're about to do."

"I wouldn't thank me yet, Director. You haven't seen what's on the other side of that light."

"Ah shit, Singleton." He shook his head. "Make this go away, or I swear to God, I'll come back and haunt your ass!"

Randy jammed a thumb into the keypad and ended the call.

Staring at the approaching wall of light, he tried to estimate its speed. It still looked quite distant, but nonetheless, the curtain of energy already towered over the city. He felt as if he were standing near the base of an impossibly tall cliff, one made of brilliant white light instead of rock.

The upper reaches of the light now extended straight up to the limit of his vision. The advancing left and right peripheries of the energy curtain gave a better indication of the speed of its approach than did its now indiscernible height.

"I'm going to do a three count like this—and for God's sake, don't jump right now—three-two-one-jump. As soon as you hear the first part of the word 'jump' coming out of my mouth, you had better be leaving the platform! Got it?"

They all acknowledged his instructions.

The light drew closer.

Randy's heart pounded in his chest.

His suddenly dry throat refused to swallow.

As he spoke, his words came out as a croak. "It … It's almost here."

He finally managed a swallow.

"You heard Commander Brown and Captain Singleton. Do what you can, stay alive, and … and make this count."

"Yes, sir." Commander Bingham said, his voice heavy with emotion.

Rachel's voice broke through the speaker. "We got this, Director, even if I have to kick their asses myself."

"Of that, Major Lee, I have no doubt."

The light had now devoured nearly half the sky.

Watching the left and right sides of the advancing wall, Randy tried to estimate the time left. It was mere seconds now, but he had to get this perfect. He figured that their falls to the mats would take barely more than a second.

Thoughts of his family percolated to the surface. Inhaling deeply, Randy closed his eyes. "I'm so sorry, Betty. We'll be together soon, one way or another."

Randy opened his eyes. "Oh shit."

The apparent movement of the light suddenly looked incredibly fast. It had drawn damned close, but still it made no noise.

He raised the communicator to his lips.

"Here it comes! Get ready!"

After watching it a moment longer, he nodded.

"Three!"

He waited a beat.

"Two!"

The plastic housing of the communicator squeaked in his grasp.

"One!"

The light suddenly raced to envelop him with unimaginable speed. Randy's eyes went round.

"Jum—!"

The wall of energy washed over him.

Randy's final utterance echoed off the nearby buildings. However, in the wake of the light's otherwise silent passage, neither human, animal, nor even insectile ears remained to detect the reverberating sound waves.

PART II

"There are no great people in this world, only great challenges which ordinary people rise to meet."

—William Frederick Halsey, Jr.

CHAPTER 9

Vaughn continued to move the pump lever up and down. What had started as a stitch in his side now felt like an ax buried in the base of his ribs. He'd also achieved a new level of exhaustion, having long ago burned through the last of the meal that he and Angela had shared in Corsica a seeming age ago.

Mark's voice pulled him out of his thoughts. "So these robots had long necks?"

Vaughn released the handle and bent at the waist, resting with hands on knees. "No ..." He paused for a breath. "They didn't have any at all. We started off calling them No-Necks, but after a while that just seemed too long." He shrugged. "You said it. I'm a lazy man. If I can shorten a task, you know I will." He pointed at the lever. "I just wish we could shorten this one."

Mark pushed him aside. "Here, it's my turn anyway."

"Be my guest."

As Mark began to move the lever up and down, he looked at Vaughn with raised eyebrows. "How long? ... How long were you gone?"

After taking a couple of breaths, Vaughn stood up. "I'm not really sure. It took me almost two months to figure out that Angela was trapped on the space station."

Mark winced. "Two months? Ouch."

"Yeah, not my finest hour. I was a little slow on the uptake on that one." Shaking his head, Vaughn looked at the floor. "Anyway, we lost track of the days when we were trapped in the time loop. Felt like years, but it was probably another couple of months, so maybe four in total."

Mark nodded thoughtfully and then looked at Vaughn with an inscrutable expression. "You still haven't told me why I wasn't with you through all of this." His pumping arm paused. "I died, didn't I?"

Vaughn felt his insides twist. He nodded slowly.

His hand slowly lowering from the lever, Mark stared at Vaughn for a long moment. The dark skin of his face paled. His Adam's apple bobbed. "What happened? Did I get sick?"

"No … It wasn't that." Vaughn regarded Mark from beneath peaked brows. "Just promise me that if you hear an explosion or see the aftermath of a crash, that you won't go rushing in. Like I told everyone else, there's no one there."

"Is that how it happened? Is that how I … died?"

Vaughn nodded mutely.

"What did I do? … When did it happen?"

"I … I can't." Vaughn glanced at the chamber wall nearest to Cleveland Airport and shook his head. "Maybe someday, but not right now."

After staring at Vaughn for a moment, Mark nodded and grasped the handle again. His labored breathing echoed through the intercom connection as he worked it up and down.

Sometime later, Mark looked at Vaughn. "Those amphibians … they looked like Admiral Ackbar?"

"Yeah, I started calling that version of Earth Mon Calamari."

Mark nodded. "Of course, *Star Wars*."

"Exactly! Thank you. Angela had no clue what I was talking about."

Grinning, Mark raised an eyebrow. "Did you really say 'It's a trap'?"

"You know me. Of course I did."

A red light began to flash in the upper corner of Mark's helmet visor. Then the same indicator began to strobe in Vaughn's helmet.

"That's the CO2 alarm." Mark paused and then nodded. "Never mind. I'm sure you already knew that."

Vaughn grinned as he checked the atmospheric pressure. Seeing that it had finally risen to a safe level, he unlatched his helmet. In his peripheral vision, he saw Mark doing the same.

Vaughn dropped his to the floor and then winced as he remembered Mark's previous reaction to his dropping the helmet. However, when he looked at the man, his friend had a shocked look on his face.

"Oh shit, Vaughn." Mark's face suddenly flushed. "Sorry ... It's just that ..."

"I know. It's a big change."

Mark shook his head. "It's not just a change. You ... you're emaciated. Look at your neck ... You look like something out of a World War Two concentration camp photo."

Vaughn chuckled. "Stop, you're making me moist."

Mark smiled self-consciously and then shook his head. "Well, at least you didn't lose your sense of humor with all the weight."

As it had last time, the steam rising from each of their suit necks became a torrent.

As an icy chill ran down his spine, Vaughn stepped back up to the pump. He grabbed the handle and started to move it up and down. "We better hurry. I don't have the meat on my bones that I did last time. Don't want to freeze to death before we get this damn door open."

Before a minute had passed, the room seemed to spin.

Vaughn wavered and nearly fell.

Mark rushed to his side. He placed a stabilizing hand on his shoulder and guided him toward the large door.

Vaughn's vision narrowed. He turned, intending to lean on the wall, but his knees buckled. He would have fallen hard on his ass if not for Mark's assistance. Panting, he gave the man a nod. "Thanks. Think I'll just rest here for a moment."

His friend patted him on the shoulder and then jogged back toward the handle.

As he watched Mark work, Vaughn massaged the temples of his pounding head. His peripheral vision ebbed and flowed with each labored breath.

Sometime later, the loud, metallic clunk of the last lock retracting echoed through the chamber. Then a narrow shaft of light from the room beyond sliced through the vacuum chamber as the door began to slide open.

Closing his eyes, Vaughn rolled toward it and basked in the warmth that trickled through the narrow opening.

A moment later, he felt someone patting his face. From the residual stinging pain there, he realized it hadn't been the first slap.

"Vaughn! Wake up!"

His eyes fluttered and then opened. He winced against the bright light that burned into them.

Through slitted lids, Vaughn studied his surroundings.

He was propped up against a wall in a large room that he now recognized as the garage outside the chamber entrance.

Kneeling next to him, Mark stared at him intently. "You scared me there, buddy. Was starting to think I'd lost you."

"What happened?"

"You passed out. At first, I thought you were asleep, but when you didn't respond, I came over and found out you were unconscious."

Vaughn's eyes began to adjust to the room's light. He looked around.

His stomach growled.

He extended a hand toward Mark. "I'm awake now. Help me up."

Mark assisted him to his feet. Not waiting for his friend, Vaughn headed toward the doorway that led into the facility.

"Where you going?"

"Just try to keep up."

A moment later, Vaughn walked into the already stinky break room. Burned eggs and melted spatula adorned the stove top once again.

As he turned off the burner, he heard Mark enter the room behind him and then pull up short. "Oh shit. You're right. They ... They are gone."

Raising his eyebrows and nodding, Vaughn stepped up to the vending machine and unceremoniously jammed his boot through its front. As it had before, the glass broke and fell to the floor.

"Hey! What the hell are you doing?!"

Vaughn waved a dismissive hand at him and then reached through the opening and grabbed a bag. He tore it open with his teeth and began to devour the Funyuns within. A moment later, he pulled the now empty bag away from his mouth.

As Vaughn crunched the last of the golden rings, he rolled back his eyes and sighed. "Now I know how Angela felt."

Suddenly, a deep rumbling explosion rocked the building.

Vaughn opened his eyes in time to see Mark running from the room. "Wait!"

It was too late. The man was gone.

"Goddammit!" Mustering what energy he could, Vaughn ran after him.

"Mark!"

A moment later, Vaughn emerged under a too bright sky. Wincing again, he held up a hand to shield his eyes. As it had the last time, columns of gray smoke dotted the horizon.

Mark stood transfixed in the center of the quadrangle-shaped courtyard. He scanned the horizon just as they had done last time. Turning back toward Vaughn, he looked skyward. His eyes widened as he saw the ball of orange fire rising above Cleveland Airport, the same one that had lured them before.

Breathing heavily, Vaughn held up his hands. "Just wait one ...!"

The world began to spin again. His knees buckled, almost sending Vaughn back to the ground.

Mark ran past him, heading toward the airport.

Panting and bent at the waist, Vaughn managed to hold onto consciousness. "Dammit, Mark! ... Stop!"

It was no good. By the time Vaughn could raise his head, Mark had already disappeared around the corner of the building.

"Shit!"

Taking another deep breath, Vaughn stood upright and went after his friend.

A moment later, he rounded the corner at a pace barely faster than a walk and was relieved to see Mark right where he had expected.

The man stood between the two buildings, staring through the perimeter fence at the pile of mangled and burning passenger jets, the Boeing-fed bonfire.

Vaughn stepped up to stand next to his friend.

Mark looked ill, his face suddenly ash-white. His mouth worked, but no words came at first. Then he found his voice. "I … I remember this."

"What? What do you remember?"

"Standing here. Seeing that pile of burning wreckage."

Vaughn's stomach churned. "Do you …" His voice hitched. "Do you remember what happened next?"

Mark shook his head. "Just this. Not real clear, though. More like déjà vu." He turned pleading eyes to Vaughn and pointed at the wreckage. "You're sure …? You're sure no one is in there?"

Vaughn nodded somberly.

Mark's vacant stare returned to the burning aircraft. "I need to see it … see it for myself."

He took a hesitant forward step.

Vaughn put a hand out and grabbed Mark's shoulder.

"Hennessy!"

The man blinked. Finally stopping, Mark looked at him.

Vaughn held his gaze and canted his head toward the wreckage. "This …" He took a breath and then sighed. "This is where it happens, Mark."

He looked confused. "What the hell are you talking about?"

Panting, Vaughn raised an arm and pointed toward the end of the runway closest to the mangled pile of burning jets. "That … is where you died, Mark."

His friend stopped trying to pull free of his grasp. The blood drained from his face. "What happened?"

Vaughn closed his eyes and sighed. Then he gave a short nod and hitched a thumb, pointing over his shoulder. "Help me back to a picnic table in the courtyard and grab some more food from that break room, and I'll tell you as much as you want to know."

An hour later and already feeling better, Vaughn finished the last of a microwave dinner that Mark had found inside the break room's refrigerator. Vaughn had spent the time briefing his friend on the events of that day. He'd told him how the tumbling engine had taken his life, although he'd left out the goriest details. Then he'd told Mark about the hellish events that he'd encountered as he headed toward Colorado.

Finishing the last bite of the meal, Vaughn set the fork down. Closing his eyes, he tilted his head back and soaked in the warm sunlight.

As they often did during quiet moments, thoughts of his mother resurfaced. He knew there was nothing he could do for her, that the light had likely already passed through Boulder. He also knew that the best thing he could do was to help Angela find a way to stop the invasion from ever happening, but that didn't erase the knowledge of the literal Hell she had likely gone through, or the fact that she might still be going through it at this very mo—

"You know, it wasn't your fault."

"Huh?" Vaughn opened his eyes. Blinking, he stared into the surreally blue sky. "What are you talking about?"

"My death. Back in the chamber, you said that it had been your fault."

Vaughn opened his eyes and looked at his friend. "Did you remember more?"

Mark shook his head. "No. I just know it wasn't your fault. It was an accident, plain and simple."

Blinking, Vaughn looked from Mark to the table top and then back to his friend.

He suddenly felt as if a softball had lodged in his throat.

Vaughn tried to speak. His mouth worked, but no words would come.

A knot in his gut—one that he hadn't known existed until that moment—seemed to loosen a notch.

Mark gave him a crooked grin. "Hey, and this time, you saved my life."

Vaughn's vision blurred.

Looking away, he tried to wipe the moisture from his eyes. However, the nonabsorbent sleeve of the spacesuit merely spread it across his face. He looked down and then, smiling self-consciously, gestured at his chest. "Let's get the hell out of these things."

A while later, the two of them walked up to the NASA hangar. They had changed out of their spacesuits. Mark had donned his dark blue NASA one-piece flight suit.

After taking his first decent hot shower in months, Vaughn had tried on his two-piece camouflage Army flight suit, but it had been way too big. It had been like wearing a small tent. Fortunately, Mark had found a NASA flight suit that fit him. Attached by Velcro, Vaughn's green name badge contrasted sharply against the suit's dark blue fabric, but he didn't give two shits about that now. He would've left it off, but they'd soon have more than themselves to think about … hopefully.

Carrying bags stuffed with the supplies they'd cobbled together, the two of them walked across the hangar's parking lot.

Vaughn stared at the UPS airplane that was still sitting on the tarmac beyond the Glenn Research Center perimeter fence.

Seeing 'What Can Brown Do For You?' stenciled across the side of the wide-bodied jet, he wondered how things might've been different if he had understood the significance of those words the first time he'd experienced this day.

What if he'd connected the UPS slogan to McCree's last words about rescuing Commander Brown?

Shaking the thoughts from his head, Vaughn turned from the sight. He pointed toward the hangar entrance. "It's in there."

Mark nodded, and the two of them entered the large building.

Working together, they soon had the US Customs Black Hawk out of the hangar. They even found the aircraft key, so this time, Vaughn was able to forego the headache of bypassing the ignition lock.

As they worked, Mark continued to ask questions. Vaughn had already told him about Angela's theory that the Necks had locked onto a micro black hole created by the supercollider, so he briefed him on the time loops and Angela's idea about how they all linked back to the creation of the wormhole.

Mark tilted his head. "So that's how you reset the timeline? She dumped all the power they were channeling through the wormhole?"

Vaughn shrugged. "Yeah, I guess, but when she explained the details of her theory, I was just giving her a lot of nods and 'uh-huh's."

Mark looked at him with exaggerated surprise. "You? Mailing it in?! Psshaw!"

"Hey, I was doing well to understand half the words she used."

Raising an eyebrow, Mark just looked at him.

"Come on. The woman's a gravity-wave astronomer."

"Who happens to love you."

Vaughn gave him a double-take. After a moment, he grinned and shrugged. "What's not to love?"

Mark chuckled. "I think your ex could list a few things."

Vaughn frowned. "Yeah, she had good cause."

It was Mark's turn to do a double-take.

Nodding, Vaughn pointed at the pile of burning airplanes. "Nothing like spending a couple of months of introspection in this new world to put you in touch with your true nature." As he said it, Vaughn realized that things wouldn't have worked out if he'd connected the UPS slogan to McCree's words. He'd needed those months. The old him wouldn't have succeeded ... not that the new him had done a stellar job of the rescue.

"Introspection? Big word for a self-described cretin."

Vaughn smiled. "Hey, I paid good money for that word, dammit."

They both flinched, and their laughs faltered as an echoing report of an explosion shook the ground. They turned to see a small black mushroom cloud rising from the distant pile of wrecked airplanes.

Standing in front of the helicopter, they stared at the surreal image for a long moment.

After the sobering reminder of the day's events, the two of them finished their preflight preparations in silence.

Afterward, they both walked up to the right pilot door and then pulled up short.

Unlike airplanes, in helicopters, the aircraft commander usually occupied the right pilot seat.

Mark stepped back and held up his hands. "Sorry, buddy. You take it."

Chuckling, Vaughn shook his head. He extended an arm toward the door. "No, it's been a while since I've flown anything that doesn't fly itself. I sure as hell haven't flown a helicopter in a long time."

Hesitating, Mark looked at him, eyebrows raised. "Flew itself?"

Vaughn smiled wryly as he started to walk around the nose, heading to the left side of the aircraft. "Just get in. I'll tell you all about it on our way to Nebraska."

He could feel Mark watching him. Vaughn pointed at the cockpit and looked back at his tall friend. "Get in, Chewie, before your fur starts matting."

Mark scoffed and shook his head. "Damned entitled, rich kid."

Chuckling, they climbed into the aircraft.

Having flown together during flight school and through more than one combat deployment, they completed their final tasks wordlessly and soon had the aircraft running and ready for departure.

Vaughn had entered the coordinates for the Nebraska rendezvous point into the navigation computer. Presently, he pointed at it. "Landing zone is in the box." He looked at his friend. "You ready?"

Mark nodded. He keyed the radio transmit trigger but then released it. He gave Vaughn a sideward glance. "Old habits …"

"No worries. I did the same thing." Vaughn pointed into the wind, indicating the takeoff direction. Grinning, he said what he always had when Mark was the one flying: "Don't fuck up."

Smiling half-heartedly, Mark stared through the helicopter's windscreen. After a moment, he regarded Vaughn from beneath hoisted eyebrows. His sad smile morphed into a familiar grin. "Hold my beer."

He raised the collective control and soon had the helicopter accelerating into the wind. A moment later, Mark turned the aircraft toward Nebraska.

As the helicopter flew over the center of Cleveland Airport, Vaughn looked down on the swath of tortured earth that had been laid bare by the passage of multiple crashing airplanes. He spotted the area where Mark had fallen and blinked in recognition. There was still a small crater there. It took Vaughn a moment to realize that it was the impact point left by the careening engine that had killed Mark. After it had broken off of the sliding airplane, it must've followed its original trajectory. However, this time, no mangled corpse sat within that concave depression.

Dragging his gaze from the impact point, Vaughn stared at his friend. Then his words from that long-ago day echoed through his thoughts: 'I'll come back for you, Mark.' When Vaughn had returned to Cleveland with plans to convert the thruster module into an actual spaceship, he had lamented the fact that he'd never had the chance to keep that promise.

Looking down again, he watched the small crater pass beneath the helicopter and smiled to himself. He had come back for his friend, after all.

CHAPTER 10

Blinking his eyes, Rourke stared at the empty section of matting. "He's ... He's gone."

"What are you talking about, Rourky?"

He shook his head side-to-side slowly.

Doctor Andrew had been there just a moment before, but now he was gone. Rourke had been looking right at the man when he disappeared.

An hour ago, Rourke hadn't known the man existed, but now Doctor Andrew's apparent death had him unable to speak.

He stared at the mat with mounting horror, watching the fading impression left by the man's momentary contact with the engorged foam rubber.

When they had climbed atop the scaffolding, the doctor had taken up residence on the far right edge of the platform. Rourke had stood between the man and the rest of the group.

During the briefings they'd received from Commander Brown and then from Captain Singleton, Rourke had watched the doctor become more and more animated.

As the final moment had drawn near, the doctor's fidgeting had grown into pacing.

Earlier, the otherwise quiet man had expressed his discomfort with the whole situation, telling the group that he hadn't signed up for this. Then he had added that he was a geologist. "All I wanted to do was visit an asteroid."

Then Bingham had exploded on the director and nearly left the chamber. Doctor Andrew hadn't said anything, but Rourke had seen the man becoming increasingly agitated. His back and forth pacing became frenetic. He'd never said anything, but in the final moments before the countdown, his chest had started to rise and fall rapidly as if he were hyperventilating. Rourke had wanted to say something, but with the countdown and the moment rushing toward them, he never could get in a word.

As Director McCree's countdown neared zero, the doctor had been the first to step up to the edge of the scaffolding, doing so spasmodically.

In the corner of his eye, Rourke had seen the man's frantic breathing rate double and then treble.

The countdown inched to two and then one.

Doctor Andrew simply stepped off the top of the scaffolding. He didn't leap or jump as instructed.

He just walked off the deck like a man stepping off the end of a pier.

The sight of the doctor's erroneous dismount had startled Rourke so severely that he almost botched his own jump. The surprise of it threw off his timing, causing him to leap late.

The boots of Rourke's spacesuit had just left the scaffolding when McCree's final utterance cut off mid-word.

At the same instant, Rourke had looked down in time to see Doctor Andrew land on the swollen mat.

Then a blindingly bright wave of light had passed through everything.

Including the doctor.

The brilliance of it had washed out Rourke's vision, but not before he saw Andrew vanish, spacesuit and all.

One moment the doctor had been there, the next, he was gone, nothing left in his wake but the temporary afterimage of his white suit and the slowly fading bootprints he'd pressed into the blue mat.

"Rourky?"

Blinking, he pulled his gaze from the haunting image and looked at Major Lee. "He's gone."

The major looked past him. "What are you talking abou—?" Seeing the fading bootprints, she stopped, and her eyes went wide. "Shit!" Anger twisted her face. "Son of a bitch! We lost Doctor Andrew!"

Commander Bingham and the other astronaut candidate, Monique, Rourke thought, looked up from their hands. The commander tilted his head. "We what? How?" Then he looked down and started shaking his head. "Oh, bloody hell … the git jumped early."

Moving to stand in a semicircle, the four of them stared at the twinned depressions in solemn silence.

A moment later, the bootprints finally vanished.

The four survivors exchanged glances and then turned to look at the airlock.

Rourke felt his stomach churn as the reality of the situation sank in. Everyone outside had suffered the same fate as the doctor.

His family.

His friends.

McCree.

All … gone.

And it was still—

The wing commander shook his head. "This changes nothing." He started walking toward the exit. "We have a job to do, mates."

Monique, the tall African-American astronaut candidate, stared at him, anger flaring on her face. "What do you mean this changes nothing? A man died!"

Bingham spun on her. "A bloody hell of a lot more than that died, lassie!" He pointed at each of them in turn. "His family died. Her family died. Yours as well—if you have any besides your cats."

Seeing the look on her face, the man faltered. He appeared to deflate a bit, and the anger drained from his visage. He raised a hand, palm out. "Sorry, that was wrong." He pointed at his own chest. "I lost mine, too." He paused and stared at the ground. The muscles in his jaw worked. When he looked back up, his eyes glistened with unshed tears. "Yes, a man did die here, the first to perish in this offensive, this effort to take the battle to an unseen enemy." He looked into Monique's eyes. "Leftenant Gheist, the best thing we can do to honor his sacrifice is to carry on."

Monique stared back at him for a moment. Her anger appeared to wither. Then she nodded.

Bingham looked to Major Lee and then to Rourke, securing a nod from each.

"Very good. What say we get the hell out of this tin can?"

After clearing the airlock, they removed their helmets and exited the building.

The four of them walked out onto the street.

They turned and scanned the horizon.

An otherworldly silence lay across the land.

It was a mild day, so the normal strum of air-conditioners was missing, but there was more than that.

Or less.

The world seemed muffled.

Thinking that he needed to equalize the pressure in his ears, Rourke pinched his nose and blew.

Nothing happened.

His ears were fine.

He shook his head. "It's … too quiet."

Wing Commander Bingham slowly nodded. "It's the birds, mate. They are gone as well."

Lieutenant Gheist's eyes widened. "My cats, too?"

Anger again flared on Commander Bingham's face. "Cats?! We've lost our families, and you're talking about bloody pets?"

Monique glared at him.

Everyone flinched as the report of an explosion split the silence.

Rourke turned to see a small mushroom cloud rising above NASA Road 1, the highway that passed in front of the Space Center.

Commander Bingham started trotting toward it.

After exchanging glances, the other three members of the group followed after him.

A few moments later, they stepped up to the perimeter fence of Johnson Space Center.

Standing side-by-side in shocked silence, they stared at the after-effects of a multi-vehicle accident. A massive pile-up of ruined cars and trucks choked the major intersection in front of the facility's entrance. Several of the vehicles were burning. Flames fully engulfed the one that had exploded, its back end blown open and shredded where the gas tank had detonated.

Major Lee slowly shook her head. "It's just like they said."

Rourke nodded. Even from a hundred meters away, he could tell that the vehicles were truly empty.

As the four of them stared into the vacated cars and trucks, Rourke realized that this was the doctor's disappearance all over again. It removed any lingering doubts about the veracity of what they had been told.

He felt a pat on the shoulder.

It was Commander Bingham. "Come on, mate. We need to find a way to Ellington Field."

Turning, Rourke saw that the two ladies had already started to walk back toward the vacuum chamber. Major Lee had a comforting arm draped across Monique's shoulders. Rourke and the wing commander followed them.

Reaching the van, they changed back into their clothes in profound silence. The three astronaut candidates each wore their blue, one-piece flight suits while Rourke changed back into his tweed suit, electing to leave off the tie and lab coat.

Commander Bingham eyed the controls of the van. He shook his head. "I don't think this lorry has enough ground clearance to get us around what likely lies between here and Ellington Field."

Digging in his pocket, Rourke produced the keys to McCree's four-by-four. He held them up for the others to see. "I think the director's truck should get us there."

Bingham nodded appreciably. "Nice work, chap."

They exited the van and walked across the parking lot.

Major Lee pointed at the truck. "Rourky, you drive. You already have experience with this monstrosity."

After giving her a nervous glance, Rourke nodded.

They piled into the vehicle and soon had it through the Space Center's rear gate. The traffic had been lighter there, so they encountered fewer crashed cars. However, they soon came upon a completely clogged intersection. It took some maneuvering, but Rourke was able to guide the truck over the curb and around the worst of it.

They elected to stop by the living quarters they'd been assigned by NASA, ostensibly to collect some belongings for the trip ahead. However, Rourke believed that it was to get a measure of closure for those who had family in the dwellings—be they human or cat. Neither Rourke nor Major Lee had relatives in the area. The two of them returned from their apartments with bags packed. However, Wing Commander Bingham and Navy Lieutenant Monique Gheist emerged from their apartments sometime later. They returned to the truck with backpacks slung over their shoulders, their eyes glistening.

The four of them continued the trek to Ellington Field in shocked silence.

Usually, the trip would have taken less than half an hour, but with the need to circumnavigate multiple collisions and crashes as well as a few fires, it took more than an hour to get there.

Finally, they reached Ellington Field. On the way, Rourke learned that it was a retired Air Force base that had long ago been converted to a municipal field. It still housed multiple military units, including the National Guard unit through which Major Lee had maintained her helicopter proficiency. The latter part came in handy when they reached a barricade. Rachel entered her code, and it slid open.

Rourke drove through, and they soon passed between the last of the buildings and emerged onto the tarmac.

The vehicle coasted to a stop as each of them stared at a northern horizon choked with columns of churning, black smoke.

Wing Commander Bingham found his voice first. "That must be

the refineries that line the Houston Ship Channel. Singleton warned us to avoid the area."

Major Lee patted Rourke on the shoulder and directed him toward a pair of dark Army helicopters. He guessed that they were the Black Hawks that Captain Singleton had mentioned.

He stopped the truck between the two aircraft.

The major inspected one of the helicopters and its logbooks. She said it was already topped off with fuel.

They loaded up their gear.

Major Lee held up a hand. "Give me a few minutes. I'll be right back." She jumped into the truck and took off. A short time later, she returned.

"Rourky, help me with this stuff."

He nodded and jogged over to meet her at the back of the vehicle. Bingham and Gheist joined them as well.

Dropping the tailgate, Major Lee jumped into the bed of the truck. She opened a dark green crate.

Bingham whistled appreciably. "Hell's teeth, mate! Where did you get those bits 'n bobs?"

The major reached into the crate and extracted a gun. She handed it to the commander. "These *bits 'n bobs*, as you so eloquently put it, came from the unit's armory."

As Rachel finished handing out the weapons, Rourke looked at the rifle she had given him and gave her a questioning look. "Why do we need these things?"

"I don't know …" The major shrugged. "Zombies?"

Commander Bingham patted Rourke on the back and gave him an uncharacteristic smile. "'Tis better to have and not need than the other way round."

Monique pursed her lips and then said, "It's around."

"Pardon me, Leftenant?"

"It's the other way around not *round*."

The commander shook his head. "Damned Yank grammar Nazi." He gave her a grin. "You use your bastardized English, and I'll stick with the Queen's."

After loading a crate of munitions that the major had also brought from the armory, they started boarding the helicopter.

Once Monique and Rourke were strapped in, Major Lee climbed into the pilot's seat. Commander Bingham occupied the opposite one.

Rourke looked at Monique. "You're not a pilot?"

The tall, dark woman shook her head. "I am a nuclear engineer. I have a double doctorate in nuclear physics and in computer engineering." She smirked and cast a glance at Bingham. "With a bachelor's in English." Looking away from the man, she continued. "I started out in the Navy as a Nuclear Surface Warfare Officer, although my last assignment, before coming to NASA, had me working at DARPA."

Tilting his head, Rourke said, "DARPA? That sounds familiar."

"Defense Advanced Research Projects Agency."

Rourke nodded his understanding. "I remember now. If memory serves, it's the agency of the Department of Defense responsible for the development of emerging technologies."

"Yes, for use in future military applications." Pausing, the thin naval lieutenant regarded Rourke with a tight smile. "What about you …?" She raised her eyebrows. "Geller?"

Rourke nodded and extended a hand. "Yes, ma'am, Doctor Rourke Geller."

Keeping her eyebrows raised, she nodded appreciably and shook the offered hand. "*Doctor*? You look rather young. Wasn't McCree calling you an intern?"

Rourke smirked and canted his head. "He found me outside the vacuum chamber this morning. Guess he assumed I was an intern. I'm actually thirty, but a lot of people mistake me for someone younger."

"Why didn't you correct him?"

"Didn't seem important at first. I mean, I knew who he was. Everyone does, right?" He shrugged. "Figured anonymity was my friend. Better for the bigwigs not to know your name and all that." He gestured through the helicopter's side window, indicating a nearby fire. "Then he started talking about all this, and it no longer mattered."

Major Lee began to start the helicopter's engines.

Staring at a distant column of rising smoke, Monique nodded

thoughtfully and then looked at Rourke. "So, Doctor Geller, what were you doing before McCree wrangled you into this?" She said the last part while staring at the nearby burning remnant of a small airplane.

"I was part of the team that was testing the space telescope in the vacuum chamber."

The naval lieutenant looked at Rourke, understanding dawning on her face. "No wonder you were so shocked when you came back with the mats."

Rourke chuckled wryly. "Shocked doesn't come close to capturing the true sense of what I felt, but yeah, you got the idea."

The noise of the engines and whirling rotor blades rose to painful levels, so he and Monique donned their headsets.

Major Lee's voice suddenly crackled through the speakers. "Can everyone hear me?"

The three of them said they could.

Rachel glanced over her shoulder and smiled. "So it's *Doctor* Rourky, huh?"

He shrugged and stared out the window. "That suddenly seems a lot less important."

Wing Commander Bingham looked back. "A doctor? That's great! Good to have someone on the team to keep an eye on our health."

"Not that kind of doctor, Bingham." Monique patted Rourke's leg. "What is your field, Doctor Geller?"

"Astrophysics." He gave Monique a meaningful look. "My minor was in computer programming."

The woman gave him an approving nod. However, Commander Bingham's smile dissolved into a frown. He turned to face the front of the helicopter. "Wonderful, we have another certified nerd onboard. I'll certainly defer to you for all astrophysical calculations." His helmet shook side to side. "What the hell was McCree thinking, sticking us with this airy-fairy?!"

Major Lee's head snapped left. She gave the wing commander a hard look. "Watch it, Bingham. I may not have that fifty thousand-dollar boot, but I'll happily introduce you to the US Army combat boot suppository."

Bingham gave her a second glance. The self-assured, smug look evaporated from the man's face.

Monique looked at Rourke and winked. She covered up the microphone of her headset and leaned in conspiratorially. "He knows she can back it up, too. Major Lee was the first woman to complete Army Ranger training."

"I thought she was an Apache pilot."

Lieutenant Gheist nodded. "She aced Army flight training as well as Navy Test Pilot School *after* completing multiple combat deployments in Spec Ops."

"Spec Ops?"

"Special Operations. She was a Green Beret." Monique paused and glanced forward. Then she leaned in closer. "Word is, she has dozens of killed Tangos to her name, both in and out of the cockpit."

"She's killed terrorists?"

Monique nodded.

Major Lee looked back. As she did, her scowl changed into a broad smile. She gave them a thumbs-up. "You guys all secure back there?"

Monique returned the gesture.

Rourke held his thumb up and nodded. "Yes, ma'am. Good to—"

The helicopter rocked.

Rourke felt his insides shake. At the same moment, he felt pressure on his eardrums.

As one, they all turned to look to the north as a massive mushroom cloud rose above the roiling columns of black smoke.

Bingham pointed. "Something big just blew up in the Ship Channel."

Rachel nodded. "I think it's time we get the hell out of here."

Rourke shook his head. "The Ship Channel is miles from here. We should be safe."

Both pilots glanced back at him with indiscernible expressions.

The pitch of the helicopter engines changed as the major began to manipulate the flight controls. A moment later, the aircraft rose a few feet into the air. Then Major Lee had it accelerating across the tarmac.

Rourke stared at the still expanding mushroom cloud. Trails of smoke cut through the partly cloudy sky, arcing away from the blast point in every direction.

"Bloody hell!" Commander Bingham pointed. "Must have been an entire ship."

Rachel nodded. "Probably a tanker."

Suddenly, a massive chunk of red and black smoldering steel slammed into the pavement in front of the helicopter.

Rachel yanked the controls sideways, and the aircraft lurched, narrowly avoiding the hunk of metal. She continued to bank the helicopter left. "I'm going to put some distance between us and that shitstorm."

After she'd turned the aircraft one hundred and eighty degrees, the major leveled it out and continued accelerating, now heading southbound, away from the Ship Channel.

Another piece of smoking metal slammed into the ground a few hundred meters to the left, but after that, nothing else threatened.

A few moments later, Major Lee banked the helicopter to the right. "Going to head west for a little while. We'll circle around that side of the city and then head north for Nebraska. Should keep us clear of the worst."

Rourke glanced out the left window, and his eyes went wide. He pointed. "There's an airplane ...! Flying!"

Everyone turned and looked.

"Bob's your uncle! The token nerd is right."

As Rachel rolled the helicopter level again, the passenger jet flew ahead of them and continued flying to the northwest. It appeared to be descending.

Estimating its trajectory, Rourke glanced ahead and then realized where the plane must be going.

He pointed between the two pilots. "It's heading toward Hobby Airport. They're going to land!"

"The chap is right." The wing commander glanced at Major Lee. "Let's give it a see."

Next to Rourke, Monique shook her head. "What makes you think there'll be anybody in that thing?"

Bingham turned in his seat. "The altitude might have saved them. I think it's worth a look."

Rachel screwed up her face. "I don't know. Singleton was pretty adamant about staying away from airports."

Commander Bingham held up his hands. "We are in a helicopter, Major. Just stay sufficiently far away to keep us safe."

Rachel considered his words for a moment and then nodded reluctantly. She adjusted the controls and fell in behind the much faster aircraft.

As the helicopter rolled level, the wing commander pointed ahead. "Appears there's been a crash on the airfield."

Staring through the windshield, Rourke nodded. One of the roiling columns of smoke they'd seen earlier was coming from Houston's southern airport. Major Lee guided the helicopter low over the city. The large passenger aircraft continued its steady descent toward the airport. That's when Rourke realized something was wrong. He pointed. "Look. The landing gear is still up."

Rachel nodded. "I know." She glanced at Bingham. "I think it's empty, just like everything else."

The four of them fell silent as the passenger jet drew ever closer to its appointment with the airport's runway. A moment later, it pancaked into the concrete and slid down the paved surface in a spray of sparks.

Lieutenant Gheist placed a hand over her mouth, giving her words a muffled sound. "Hell's bells!"

Unable to look away, Rourke watched as the large airplane slammed into the piled wreckage at the far end of the runway and exploded. A boiling cloud of orange fire churned into the sky.

Rourke tried to work his suddenly dry mouth, but it took him a moment to get the words out. "This ... This is what Singleton was talking about."

The other three occupants of the helicopter nodded slowly.

Suddenly, an automated voice broke over the intercom system. "Traffic! Traffic!"

Major Lee looked down and stared at one of the displays. A yellow symbol drifted across its screen. "Where did that come from?"

The icon turned red, and the automated voice returned. "Climb! Climb!"

Rachel's eyes widened. "Oh shit!"

She yanked up on the control stick in her left hand.

The seat pressed into Rourke.

The engines screamed as their whining pitch amplified.

Then the computer-generated voice came back, now sounding even more insistent. "Increase climb!"

Rachel yanked the other stick to the side and started screaming. "Shit! Shit! Shit! It's right behind us!"

The G-forces increased.

Rourke felt his face sagging.

The world turned ninety degrees as the aircraft responded to Rachel's inputs and banked hard to the right.

Something big and bright zipped past just beneath the right window, too close for Rourke to see more than its metallic white skin.

Then it was gone.

Rourke slammed painfully into the shoulder harness as the helicopter spun like a falling leaf caught in a wind gust.

Monique screamed. Her arms flailed overhead.

Only their shoulder harnesses kept the four of them from falling to the ceiling.

The engines oscillated manically.

All the while, Rachel fought with the controls, struggling to rein in the gyrating aircraft.

The outside world spun around the helicopter. One moment, sky filled its windows, the next, buildings, streets, and green fields zipped past.

Rourke's heart pounded against his chest wall as he watched each rotation take them closer to the ground.

As the helicopter oscillated wildly, Major Lee continued to fight the controls, cursing all the while. "Come on, you piece of shit!"

One rotation later, she finally righted the aircraft.

Breathing heavily, the four of them exchanged horrified glances.

"Holy shit!" Major Lee shook her head. "That was a goddamn Antonov!"

As she spoke, Rachel turned the helicopter back toward the west. "I'm getting us the hell out of the way of any other aircraft."

Wing Commander Bingham was staring after the large airplane. "What in the hell was an Antonov doing coming to Hobby Airport? They don't land here."

Rachel shook her head. "Must have diverted here when the shit started hitting the fan."

Staring after the airplane, Rourke held his stomach and shook his head. He felt as if he were going to be sick. "What's an Antonov? And what happened to the helicopter?"

Next to him, Monique was holding her stomach as well and panting for breath.

Commander Bingham pointed at the aircraft. "That, Mister Geller, is the largest airplane in the world. And we got caught in its wake turbulence."

Monique leaned forward, her face pale and sweaty. She narrowed her eyes. "He is *Doctor* Geller, Wing Commander Bingham."

He waved a dismissive hand. "Whatever."

With its landing gear still retracted, the giant aircraft finished its descent and flew straight into the concrete runway. Its top-mounted wings snapped off. They each pinwheeled down the sides of the paved strip, leaving looping trails of fiery fuel in their wake.

The speeding and now wingless fuselage raced down the pavement. Twinned fans of sparks sprayed out from the point of contact. Then it rammed into the burning pile of airplane wreckage that blocked the end of the runway and blew through it without losing any speed. The impact launched flaming chunks of destroyed passenger jets into the air for short-lived final flights.

The Antonov's crumpled and now also burning fuselage traveled another quarter-mile. It crashed through the perimeter fence and plowed across a street intersection choked with mangled cars. Then it slammed into a building and detonated, launching a new conflagration into the sky.

Rourke saw several dark black items tumble away, bouncing like toys as they careened down the street beyond the building.

"I'll be a monkey's uncle!" Bingham pointed at the tumbling objects. "Those are bloody battle tanks! No wonder we got thrown around by its wake. The plane was loaded to the gills."

Looking a little green around the gills herself, Major Lee nodded. She pointed at the center console. "Plug the coordinates into the box for the Soyuz landing zone in Nebraska." She paused and then raised her brows. "And keep an eye on the moving map. Make damned sure we don't get close to any other airports."

CHAPTER 11

"I was able to talk to her this time, Vaughn." Angela released the mic key and dabbed a tear from her eye.

"Who?"

"Afia, the young African girl I used to chat with in Equatorial Guinea."

"Oh, on the radio?"

"Yeah, before it all happened ... the first time." Angela shook her head. "She sounded so frightened, Vaughn."

A long pause greeted her words. Then his voice returned. "What did you tell her?"

After taking a deep breath, Angela let it out in a sigh. "What I've been telling everyone: we're going to beat this. I told her not to be afraid."

Angela shook her head. "But ... we know what's going to happen to her." She shuddered involuntarily. "I lied to her ... I—"

"No, Angela!" Vaughn cut off her words. "You were right to tell Afia that. Like the director said, if we succeed, then none of this ever happened."

Angela dabbed another tear from her eye. She wanted to believe that, had to.

After a moment, she nodded and then keyed the mic again. "How are you guys coming down there?"

"We made it to…" Vaughn faltered. "Are you sure you're okay, Angela?"

She gave the radio a wistful smile. "I'm a long effing way from okay, but we'll get through this." She stared through the Cupola's window, watching as uncountable stars set behind Earth's retreating western horizon. "Anyway, where are you?"

After a slight hesitation, Vaughn's voice returned. "We are just outside of Omaha. Damn city is an inferno. How are things going up there? You guys all set to go?"

"Yeah. Major Peterson is wrapping up the last of the departure checklist. We'll be moving into the module soon."

Shifting her gaze, Angela looked down on North America. Over the last few hours, they had watched the wave of light complete its sweep across the planet. The ISS had passed over North Dakota a couple of minutes ago. Now the eastern seaboard was beginning to roll into view. By the time their Soyuz descent module returned to this side of the world, they and it would be deep into the atmosphere. In the intervening time, the Earth's rotation will have placed the land just east of Omaha beneath their descending module.

Angela toggled the radio again. "I'm not going to have line of sight with you much longer. We better say our goodbyes before we lose radio contact."

When Vaughn's voice returned, Angela could hear his smile in his words. "Hurry to me, Angela-Vaughn, I need my angel back here on Earth."

Unlike the first time she had conversed with him over this radio, Angela no longer had to imagine what that smile looked like. She snorted as she recalled the time she'd said, 'Call me Angela, Vaughn,' and the smart aleck had responded with that same name mashup. She held the mic close to her mouth. "I'll hurry every chance I get, smart ass."

He chuckled. "I'm glad you still remember that. I'll see you on the other side. Safe flying, Commander."

"I'll see you there, *Captain*."

She terminated the connection and then shouted over her shoulder, "How are we coming, Teddy?!"

She turned around to see him floating into the Cupola, a plastic box clutched in his hands.

"Major Peterson has the module prepped, and your little furry friends are ready for the journey."

Smiling, Angela reached out and took the offered box. She opened the lid a smidge and peeked inside. Two pairs of beady little eyes gazed at her from within its blue confines. Pink noses twitched in front of long, white whiskers.

She resealed the container and then inspected the lid and the holes that Teddy had cut into it. Then she nodded to him. "Thank you. I can't tell you how much this means to me."

The cosmonaut smiled, and his SoCal surfer boy persona reemerged for the first time since he'd learned of the fate of the world. "No problemo, Command-Oh."

They left the Cupola and headed toward the Soyuz module. It was attached to Zvezda in the Russian portion of the station. They joined the major. The three of them strapped into the descent module and then completed departure preparations.

Major Peterson soon finished the last checklist item and then gave everyone a questioning look. "Ready to go?"

Angela nodded. "If I *never* see this place again, it'll be too soon."

The two men gave her odd looks but then both nodded.

Bill flipped a switch.

A loud clunk followed by a slight jolt transmitted through the module.

"We're away." Reaching for the thruster control, Bill regarded Angela with a questioning look. "Are you sure about this? If I activate the thruster this close to the station, it's going to torch a portion of it."

Pursing her lips, Angela hitched a thumb toward the ISS. "I told you, the whole thing is already toast. It's going to die when those solar panels show their true nature." She pointed at the countdown timer. "Besides, it's too late to have second thoughts. We didn't allot time for the usual two and a half hours for pre-reentry maneuvering. It's time to start. Otherwise, we're going to overshoot Nebraska."

Peterson slowly nodded. After hesitating a moment longer, he toggled the command.

Another jolt passed through Angela's seat. Then Bill made two quick attitude adjustments. He looked at both of them, raising a thumb. "Ready?"

Extending their hands, Angela and Teddy responded in kind and spoke at the same time. "Ready."

Major Pearson nodded and then leaned back in his seat.

He pressed the final command.

Angela felt the welcome pressure of G-forces pushing her into the contoured crew seat. Months of malnourishment had her weak, but she was still in much better condition for the return to gravity than she had been the last time she'd descended from the station. This trip into zero-G had lasted hours not months, so she would have much less trouble with the return of gravity than she'd had last time.

Even Bill and Teddy should be okay. Neither of them had been in the station long when the light had swept across the planet.

Over the next thirty minutes, the reentry went as planned. All systems remained nominal, working as advertised for a change. Her crewmates seemed to be doing as well as could be expected. Occasionally, she would see one of them staring through the solid surface of a bulkhead, their eyes distant. Angela wished there was something she could tell them, some words that would alleviate their mourning, but she knew it was a path that each of them would have to negotiate on their own.

Heavens knew she had her own issues. Living through the eradication of most of the planet's biosphere a second time didn't come without its pains, its heartache. Her thoughts went to her lost family and friends. The knowledge that her and Vaughn's group of survivors might be able to undo it all provided her only solace.

Angela blinked and looked at her lap. She was feeling the first hint of gravity's return. Once Bill had completed the de-orbit burn, they had become weightless again. However, now the Soyuz module was beginning to encounter the upper atmosphere.

Her body settled deeper into the seat.

Then Angela heard the first wisps of air caressing the module's skin. Soon, the G-forces increased significantly, pressing her body into the thin cushions of the chair.

The whispering atmosphere crescendoed into a roar. The flickering orange glow of burning plasma shone through the descent module's small window.

After referencing his checklist, Major Peterson flipped a couple of switches.

Angela glanced out the small port window at the strobing orange light and then looked at Bill, her eyebrows raised. "E-Everything okay?"

He gave her and Teddy another thumbs-up. "All systems nominal."

Nodding, Angela stared at the flickering plasma. To keep her thoughts from dwelling on the incinerating forces that were excoriating the bottom of the module, she considered what might lie ahead for all of them.

How were they going to get to Europe?

Vaughn was pretty adamant that airports weren't an option, but it wasn't like they could travel via helicopter the entire way. An ocean-going ship would take too long as well. They needed to get to Geneva before the Necks got too entrenched.

They didn't lack for pilots. Teddy was a mission specialist, but she knew that Bill was a pilot, although she wasn't sure of what type aircraft.

Angela glanced over at the major. "How do you know Wing Commander Bingham?"

"He and I served together in a joint task force while I was in the sandbox."

She nodded slowly. By sandbox he meant the Middle East. "What kind of operation was it?"

"It was a heavy-lift op staffed by US and British transport pilots."

Angela twisted her face as she tried to form her question.

Bill gave her a knowing grin. "Yes, he is a bit of an asshole."

Angela raised her eyebrows. "Oh, no, I ... I wasn't thinking that." She felt her face flush as she heard the overly defensive tone in her words.

Major Peterson smiled. "Then you'd be the first." He waved a dismissive hand. "Don't worry, it's common knowledge, but he is a good man, extremely intelligent as well."

"So he commanded an entire wing of airplanes?"

Bill gave her a confused look for a moment and then understanding dawned on his face. "No, wing commander is just a rank in the Royal Air Force. I mean, he might have commanded a wing, but you wouldn't know that just by the title of his rank."

The conversation withered as the force pushing Angela into her seat increased to oppressive levels.

A few moments later, the G-forces began to relent.

Outside the window, the flickering gold light began to diminish as well. In the gaps, Angela saw that the sky had shifted from black to a deep, indigo blue.

She flinched as a loud, metallic report shot through the module.

Teddy pointed toward the window. "That's the drogue chute."

Over the next couple of minutes, Angela watched as the sky shifted to lighter shades of blue. When she looked at it again, the altimeter indicated they were descending through fifteen thousand meters. Angela knew that was about fifty thousand feet, higher than a passenger jet's cruising altitude.

They were still descending rapidly. The drogue hadn't slowed them much. Its primary purpose was to keep them aligned in preparation for the release of the main chute.

Just as Angela had the thought, the parachute deployed in a cascade of waving white and red fabric. She watched it inflate overhead.

The lines went taut.

The module yanked upward. It felt as if they had hit the end of a long rubber band.

Angela's vision narrowed as the sudden increase in G-forces

threatened to rob her of consciousness. However, a couple of short bounces later, everything settled down, plunging the module into relative silence interrupted by her brief spat of staccato coughs.

Teddy looked at Angela and smiled. "You okay, Command-Oh?"

She gave him a weak grin. "I'm fine."

The module now sat at a thirty-degree angle. This was a design feature. The harness held the Soyuz like that for a few moments, allowing the passage of the air over its bottom shield to dissipate the heat of reentry.

As expected, the module soon righted itself. Then the outside world turned white as they descended into a layer of clouds. A few moments later, the wispy vapor took on an ominously dark hue.

Angela's eyes widened as the module began to heave up and down.

Bill waved a dismissive hand. "We'll be fine. It's probably just a layer."

Nodding, Angela activated the radio. "Nebraska Ground, this is Soyuz One, over."

"Angela-Vaughn! Is that you?"

Smirking, Angela keyed the radio again. "Hello, *Captain*." She emphasized his title. "How are you reading me?"

After a slight pause, Vaughn returned, now sounding serious. "We are reading you five-by-five. What's your location?"

She nodded to Major Peterson.

Bill toggled the radio. "We were on course when our star plotter lost lock, so we should be pretty close to the target area."

Angela looked at the altimeter. "We are under the chute and descending through ten thousand meters now. Can you see us yet?"

Bill shook his head and pointed toward the window. The outside clouds had darkened further.

Vaughn's voice returned. Now Angela detected a nervous tone in his words. "Yeah, about that ... I can't believe I forgot this."

"Uh, forgot what?"

"Well, he-he. Remember that tornado I told you about?"

Angela's eyes widened. "Oh no! The system that nearly flipped your helicopter? Please tell me that's not the weather we're in."

"Yep, 'fraid so, but it's still a good way to the west. We have plenty of time to recover you and head out before it gets here."

Angela glanced back outside. Rivulets of rainwater cascaded across the glass portal. "It may be far to your west, but we appear to be right in the middle of it."

"Don't worry. I'm sure that's just an upper-level layer."

The module surged upward as a vertical gust yanked it skyward. Angela pressed her lips into a thin line. She keyed the mic. "That's easy … ugh." Another bout of turbulence forced a grunt from her. "That's easy for you to say." She shook her head. "Soyuz One, out."

She released the radio key and exchanged nervous glances with her crewmates.

They could only hope that the energy of their reentry had carried them past the worst of the storm.

Closing her eyes, Angela wrapped gloved hands around her shoulder straps.

The module continued to surge and swing. She could almost imagine they were floating in a small raft atop an angry sea.

They spent the next several minutes in silent anticipation. Every time the module twisted or turned, Angela was certain they had descended into the top of a funnel cloud. Fortunately, it settled down each time.

Craning her neck, Angela peered up into the concave belly of the single parachute. Its concentric rings of red and white flexed and pulsed, looking like a giant jellyfish as it expanded and contracted, appearing to breathe in the storm.

She glared at their Russian cosmonaut. "One parachute?! Really?!" She jabbed a finger toward the ceiling, pointing upward. "There should be three!"

Looking up with wide eyes, Teddy nodded. "Da!" His surfer boy persona reemerged. "But, don't be hating on the token Russian. It wasn't my fault. I didn't design this thing."

The three of them laughed nervously.

Another vicious vertical surge cut short their chortles.

Angela activated the radio again. "Anything yet? Do you see us?"

"No, but the ceilings are really low." The sound of beating rotors came through his radio transmission.

"Are you in your helicopter?"

"Yes. We won't be able to see you until right before you touch down—if at all—so we wanted to be ready to make a quick search pattern if needed."

Angela felt her heart rate increase as she considered what would happen if they were to descend into the helicopter's rotor blades.

"Well, I certainly hope we don't end up dropping in on top of you."

"Don't worry about that. It's the whole big-sky-little-bullet thing."

Angela gnashed her teeth. "What the hell does that even mean?"

"It means that there are probably bigger things that you need to be worrying about than running into me."

Next to her, Bill was nodding. He pointed towards the altimeter. "We just descended below three hundred meters. You need to brace for landing."

Nodding, Angela stared through the window again. She wished she could see down, but the angle was all wrong. As the ground rushed up toward the module, she worried about what might lie beneath them.

What if they were about to plow into a house?

Then she thought about the wind.

Angela looked at Bill. "How's our sideward drift?"

He pursed his lips. "Within limits ... just."

Looking up, Angela stared at the rain-soaked parachute. Under it, they were descending at a rate of twenty-four feet per second. She knew that, just before touchdown, six small rockets would ignite for a split second, cushioning their impact with the ground.

Hopefully, it was ground beneath them.

Angela tightened her shoulder harness again.

She had heard from fellow astronauts that the landing could be quite traumatic.

The radar altimeter continued its digital countdown.

Angela could feel her adrenaline ramping up with each lost meter of altitude.

Teddy began to read off the numbers.

"One hundred meters."

"Fifty!"

"Forty!"

Bill shook his head. "Shit! Sideward drift just red-lined!"

Teddy continued his countdown. "Thirty!"

"Twenty!"

"Ten—!"

A loud boom rang the module like a bell as the landing rockets fired.

Soyuz crunched into the ground, and it felt as if a speeding truck had slammed into the back of Angela's seat. The whole thing left her ears ringing and her body stunned.

Suddenly, the module tilted.

At the same moment, Bill reached up and swung his hand at the parachute disconnect button.

The capsule yanked sideways, and the major's glove missed its target and impacted the panel beside the switch.

Soyuz slammed onto its side and then began to shutter and skip as the parachute dragged it across the ground.

Their arms and legs flailed as the module bounced violently, lurching back into the air.

Bill tried to hit the disconnect button, but his hand missed the target again.

"Son of a—!"

As he cursed, Major Peterson swung at the button a third time, but a painful jolt cut off his words and knocked his hand aside. A tremendous report resonated through the module. It sounded as if they'd crashed into something.

The force of the impact launched the craft back into the air.

Angela's abdominal muscles clenched as she became weightless again.

Major Peterson took advantage of the drop in G-forces to reach up and smack the release button.

Another loud report rang out as the parachute finally disconnected.

The module dropped.

Bill's eyes went round. "Oh shit!"

Soyuz slammed into the ground.

The three of them whipped around as the craft tumbled end over end.

Checklists swirled around the interior of the cabin.

In a moment of dilated time, Angela watched as the box that contained the mice tumbled through the air as if in slow motion.

Her eyes went wide.

"No!"

She tried to reach for the box, but then her head snapped back and forth within her helmet, sending sharp pains down her neck.

Everything stopped with a final lurch, all movement ceasing.

The module fell quiet. Only the sound of Soyuz's spinning gyros and the raspy breaths of its three human occupants remained to fill the sudden void.

In the surreal silence, Angela stared at the now mud-covered glass portal.

After doing a mental inventory of her body and not feeling anything that seemed worse than the rest, Angela looked at Teddy and Bill. "You guys alright?"

The two men looked at her and nodded.

"Me, too."

She grabbed the box-o-mice. Lifting it to eye level, Angela peered into one of the air holes. She released a held breath when she saw Mack and Nadine stirring within. They appeared to be unhurt by their momentary return to zero-G and its violent end.

Angela and her crewmates removed their helmets and began to disentangle themselves from their seat harnesses.

Teddy opened the hatch.

Moving slowly, struggling with the returned gravity, Angela set aside the mice and climbed through the opening.

She dropped awkwardly onto the ground.

Having landed on all fours, Angela stood and looked across the field of waving golden wheat stalks. It seemed as if they had fallen into a sea of the stuff.

In the distance, the discarded parachute lumbered across the plains like a giant, red and white tumbleweed.

Angela turned to inspect the exterior of the module. She blinked in surprise and guffawed. "Where on earth did that come from?"

Bill was watching the slowly tumbling parachute. "What?"

Teddy turned, and a short laugh burst from his lips. Then he tilted his head as he read the words scrawled across the wooden plank. "Wilson's Seed and Feed?" He looked at Angela, confusion twisting his face. How did that get attached to the outside of Soyuz? Is this an American practical joke?"

Shaking her head, Angela leaned in and studied the board. The stub of a broken antenna protruded from the center of the sign. She pointed at it. "Looks like it got impaled on this."

Angela stood upright and stepped around the heavily damaged module, inspecting its exterior as she did. Mud covered the outside of the thing, and shredded, yellow stalks of wheat protruded from its every nook and cranny.

Looking up, Angela stopped in her tracks. "Oh my …!"

Bill and Teddy walked up and stood next to her. The three of them stared in shocked silence at the trail of carnage wrought by the tumbling passage of the Soyuz.

"Guess we know where the sign came from."

"Da, Command-Oh."

A highway and a roadside billboard sat at the far end of the trail of savaged earth. The large, wooden sign now sported a new, Soyuz-shaped hole. The module had passed through the panel, leaving a cut-out silhouette like Wile E. Coyote riding an Acme rocket.

Bill shook his head. "Well, if that don't beat all …"

Dragging her eyes from the surreal image, Angela searched the sky but could see no helicopter.

The south wind whipped her matted hair.

Looking right, she watched the dark storm clouds that lined the distant western horizon, but at the moment, only a steel-gray pall hung low overhead.

Clad only in their thin-skinned Soyuz environmental suits, the three of them crossed their arms, hugging themselves against the worst of the cold, damp wind. They stooped as if pressed down by the low ceiling of clouds.

Teddy stepped back to the module. When the man returned, he handed each of them a parka. Then he patted Angela on the shoulder. "Here you go, Command-Oh."

He placed a small radio in her hand. It looked like a walkie-talkie.

Angela had trained on its use. She raised it and pressed the appropriate button. Then she saw movement on the southern horizon and released the transmit key without saying anything.

She pointed. "Here they come."

The three of them watched as the helicopter slowly approached, its noise growing louder with each passing moment.

Angela placed hands over her ears as the sound rose to painful levels. Nervous anticipation had her stomach doing loops. That was silly. She had been apart from Vaughn for barely a day. So why was she so nervous?

The large, dark helicopter approached to within a couple of dozen meters and then set down.

Angela tilted her head as she realized there were more than just two pilots in the aircraft. The silhouettes of two additional occupants lined the interior of the helicopter.

The roar of the turbines died a few moments later, and the rotor blades coasted to a stop.

The three spacesuited crewmates exchanged confused glances.

The doors of the helicopter flew open. Four people that Angela had never seen exited the aircraft.

Major Peterson shook his head. "I'll be a son of a bitch." He started to walk toward the group. Glancing over his shoulder, he pointed ahead. "That's Chance Bingham."

CHAPTER 12

Before Major Peterson could complete two steps, his legs buckled, and he fell to his knees, nearly disappearing in the waist-high wheat.

The thin, tight-faced man that Angela took for Commander Bingham ran up to Bill and helped him back to his feet. "Easy there, mate. Give yourself a moment to get reacquainted with gravity."

As he helped Bill, Bingham looked past him. Staring at the crumpled Soyuz, he winced. "Are all of you okay?"

Angela rubbed the back of her neck. "Tomorrow, we'll probably feel like we've been hit by a Mack truck, but nothing's broken."

Breathing heavily, Bill smiled and nodded. "Nothing damaged but my pride."

Bingham dipped his head and backed up a step. He extended an arm. "Good to see you, Major Peterson."

Bill batted away the offered hand. "Get the hell out of here with that."

Surprise supplanted the confused look on the Brit's face when the major wrapped the man in a hug and slapped his back.

"Come on, you uptight, old fart. Loosen up." Releasing the man,

Peterson patted the wing commander's shoulder. "Good to see you, Chance."

Bingham recovered from his apparent shock, a tight smile returning to his face. He nodded. "I only wish it could have been under different circumstances."

Bill's smile faded.

Everyone fell silent and stared at the ground.

A moment later, the sound of another helicopter insinuated itself into the funereal quietude.

They turned to see a black dot traversing the northern horizon.

Remembering the radio in her hand, Angela raised it and then saw that its volume was down. She twisted the knob. Vaughn's voice crackled through the speaker. His words had a panicked edge to them. "—Come in! Repeat, Soyuz One, this is Nebraska Ground! ... Come in, Angela!"

Raising the device to her lips, Angela pressed the transmit key. "Captain Singleton, you're flying in the wrong direction."

"Angela?! Where are you?"

She started to squeeze the walkie-talkie's button but then flinched as a loud pop came from her right side. Turning toward the sound, she saw Teddy lowering a wide-muzzled gun as a bright, red flare arched overhead. Looking up, he chuckled. "Yippee-ki-yay, mother effers!"

The aircraft banked left, turning toward them. "I see you. We'll be there in a ... Wait, is that another helicopter?"

"Yeah, the Houston team just arrived."

A few moments later, the aircraft landed nearby, joining the odd collection of crafts in the center of the angry sea of wheat stalks.

Even with her limited knowledge of helicopters, Angela could tell that this one was of the same make and model as the aircraft in which the Houston crew had arrived. However, the one that Mark and Vaughn were in had a glossy black and gold paint scheme with US Customs markings instead of the flat-finished, dark olive drab sported by the Army model.

Angela felt her heart racing again as she craned her neck, trying to spot Vaughn. However, both pilots were wearing flight helmets with dark visors.

The emotions and anticipation that coursed through Angela made her realize that one very important fact had escaped her during their weeks and then months of traveling through alien worlds and dimensions: she had fallen madly and deeply in love with Vaughn Singleton.

The two men emerged from the helicopter and began to remove their helmets.

Spotting Vaughn, Angela smiled. A warm glow filled her.

Wide-eyed, Vaughn gaped at the destroyed sign and then at the trail of blasted wheat stalks. Finally, he stared at the hammered Soyuz module. "Oh shit!" He looked at her. "Are you okay—?"

A grunt burst from the man as Angela crashed into Vaughn and threw her arms around him. Standing on shaky legs, she rained kisses on his scruffy cheeks. "I missed you, Vaughn."

He pulled her tight to him and kissed her deeply. Then Angela buried her face in the crook of his neck and breathed in his scent.

Vaughn kissed her cheek. "I …" He swallowed. "I missed you, too."

They held each other for a long moment.

When the two of them finally peeled apart, Angela turned and blushed as she saw the other seven survivors staring at them with mixed emotions. She instantly felt guilty as a palpable sense of loss poured from each of them.

After exchanging embarrassed glances, she and Vaughn released each other's hands. Then they walked over and joined the group.

They spent the next few minutes making introductions and sharing stories of what they'd seen while en route to this field. The described condition of the cities and countryside matched too closely with what Vaughn had encountered the first time he'd traversed this freshly vacated vision of the apocalypse, eliminating Angela's faint hope that her and Vaughn's return had somehow ameliorated or changed the event. The cities were again burning, and there was no evidence that even the smallest insect had remained in the wake of the light's passage.

The Houston team included only four people—three astronauts

and one civilian—instead of the anticipated five. When Angela had asked about the missing crew member, they told her that they'd lost the person in the chamber, but they didn't go into details. The looks on their faces had told her all she needed to know.

Peaking her brows, Angela stepped over to the two other women. The tall African-American woman extended a hand. A warm smile suddenly blossomed on her previously severe visage. "Hello, Doctor Brown. I am Doctor Gheist, but you can call me Monique."

Angela shook the proffered hand. "Please, call me Angela."

"I shall. It is a pleasure to make your acquaintance."

Monique articulated her words precisely and didn't appear to use contractions. The woman's mannerisms and formal way of speaking at first seemed at odds with her warm smile, but Angela sensed that Monique had a heart warmer than her tone would imply.

Tilting her head, Monique continued. "I must admit to being a bit of a fan. I have followed your work on gravity waves with rapt attention. Your thesis on the parallels between electromagnetic waves and gravity waves was inspired."

Feeling her face flush, Angela nodded. "Thank ... Thank you, Monique."

The stocky Asian woman stepped up. She had a bright smile that seemed to light the air around her.

Angela decided she liked the woman before she even opened her mouth.

Returning the grin, she extended a hand. "I'm Angela Brown."

The lady's smile went supernova. Stepping up, she hugged Angela, wrapping her in arms that felt as hard as lumber. "I'm so goddamn glad to meet you."

Angela's feet left the ground as the slightly taller woman lifted her as if she were made of paper.

Sensing Angela's current frailness, the lady gently placed her back on the ground and then backed away. "Sorry. Got a little carried away."

The woman shook her hand firmly but without inducing pain. As she did, the muscles in the visible portion of her forearm rippled. "Hi, Angela, I'm Rachel."

"Pleased to meet you, Rachel. Since you were the one flying the helicopter, I take it you're Major Lee."

The woman dipped her head.

They all looked west as the sound of distant thunder rolled across the plains.

After a moment, Angela looked back to see everyone staring at her. "What?"

The group exchanged furtive glances. Then Wing Commander Chance Bingham shrugged. "I'll say it." He fixed Angela with a steely stare. "What is your plan, Commander Brown?" He gestured at their surroundings. "How do we stop all of this from happening in the first place? How do we reset the timeline and bring back our families?"

The wind blew Angela's hair across her face. She swept it aside and then looked each of them in the eye. "I saw something the last time I was logged into the collider's computer system. Right before I started the overload that sent us back in time, back to the beginning, I saw the last dataset for the final run of collisions, the ones that led to the Necks invading."

Bingham shrugged. "So?"

"I found something, something that gave me an idea."

Lieutenant Gheist nodded encouragingly. "What was it?"

"There were at least two black holes formed that day."

"What do bleeding black holes have to do with this?"

Angela blinked and stared at the Brit for a moment. Then she scanned the faces of the team. She knew Bill and Teddy understood. She'd already told them how micro black holes tied to the invasion. Mark Hennessy was nodding, so Vaughn must have filled in the man on her theory. However, confusion clouded the faces of the four members who'd come from Houston.

"Sorry. Guess I left out that part." Angela spent the next several minutes telling them about her and Vaughn's journey. She limited the briefing to the highlights, telling them about the machine city and its robotic citizens. She spoke of being trapped in a repeating time loop that carried them across multiple versions of Earth, of Hell, and of truly alien species. Then she briefed them on the Necks and the Taters and how the latter broadcast a light that had beamed them to Hell on numerous occasions. She steered the conversation away from the subject before anyone could connect the dots and ask if that light had anything in common with the one that had swept life from the planet. Not ready to reveal to the group the true fate of their family and friends, she purposely left out anything about the mountain of the dead they'd discovered in Hell.

For most of her impromptu briefing, the group had listened in rapt silence. When someone would start asking too many questions, Vaughn would cock an eyebrow and point a thumb at the approaching storm. "Later."

After casting a furtive glance at Vaughn, Monique raised a hand.

Angela pointed at her. "Go ahead."

"This is all … incredible."

"I assure you, it's all true—"

"No, no, no. Sorry. I believe you." She looked across the land. "Once you have seen a world wiped clean of life by the mere passage of a light wave, it is not difficult to accept all manner of things. No, I simply wanted to ask how all of this ties into your discovery in the dataset? What is the significance of the black holes?"

"I was coming to that, but I wanted you to understand what we had seen and experienced first."

Monique nodded and held out a hand. "Sorry, please continue."

After seeing Vaughn cast a wary glance at the encroaching weather, Angela turned back to the group. She told them of her theory that the Necks used the micro black holes generated by powerful proton collisions to open links to dimensions outside their own. She gave them a quick class on the theory that black holes bridged the multiverse, touching all dimensions equally. Then Angela told them how they had discovered that the Necks used that bridge to lock onto parallel universes and anchor stable, transdimensional wormholes to them. Finally, she explained that she and Vaughn had seen the proof of it across multiple dimensions while they had been trapped in the time loop.

The four arrivals from Houston stared back at her with varying levels of comprehension. After a moment, Monique hoisted her eyebrows. "And the significance of there being two micro black holes that day?"

"At first, I didn't think much of it, but then later, after we had reset the timeline, I had an epiphany. The Necks hadn't locked onto the first MBH. That black hole had evaporated in the expected burst of Hawking radiation. The fact that the dataset continued on to a second set of collisions and then ends the moment the collisions reached the required energy level told me that the Necks hadn't used the first one. The Hawking radiation indicates the first one evaporated, but there isn't any sign of the radiation in the second peak."

Doctor Geller suddenly looked very excited.

Bingham shook his head. "What is the significance of that? How does that knowledge help us?"

Rourke spoke before Angela could answer the man. "It gives us a starting point. That first MBH will have left an imprint on the quantum field." Doubt clouded his features, and he shook his head. "But that doesn't do us much good. We don't have the ability to sense things backward in time."

Angela grinned. "We do now."

Monique's forehead furrowed. "How?"

"I saw one other thing on that computer. The Necks uploaded their own code onto CERN's mainframe. The program appears to help keep this end of the wormhole stable."

Wing Commander Bingham's face darkened. "They're using our own computers against us?"

"Yes, they are."

Rourke's eyes lost focus as the man stared at the horizon. Then he slowly nodded and looked at Angela. "To keep it stable, they must be able to maintain the wormhole across every portion of space and time that it touches."

"Yes," Angela said. "And since they must've sensed the first MBH in order to latch onto the second one the instant it formed, there should be data about it in their control program as well."

Monique's eyes widened. "You can use that data to link to that first micro black hole?"

"Yes!" Angela beamed. "Using spatial and chronological coordinates, I'll initiate a wormhole overload that is tuned to disrupt the formation of the first MBH."

Some of the men exchanged confused glances, but Rourke nodded his understanding. "We'll be returned to the places we were when the first MBH formed. Just like you and Vaughn were, but a few minutes farther back in time."

"Yes, but actually, I'm trying to come at it from two different directions. Last time, there was just the reset. This time, I want to improve the odds. I'll try to do a reset aimed at the first MBH, but I'll also try to prevent its formation. If we're sent back farther in time, perhaps we can give him a warning and stop them from forming the second black hole, but if the first one never forms, the Necks don't find us, and the wormhole collapses. That alone should reset the timeline and return us to the starting point."

Confusion clouding his face, Mark Hennessy raised his eyebrows. "This water is getting awfully muddy."

"I want to go back to the alien software you found," Bingham said. "How were you able to read it? Shouldn't it be … alien?"

"I wondered about that too, but I guess they must have tailored their code to work on our system. I just know it wasn't there before, and its math was unlike anything I'd ever seen."

Rourke looked at the man and then turned his attention back to Angela. "How are you going to prevent the formation of the first MBH?"

"I think I can use the alien software to insert an interference pattern that'll disrupt the stream of protons. The first micro black hole shouldn't even form. Doctor Garfield will be so confused by the readings that he'll halt the experiments until they can process the data. That should uproot the far end of the wormhole and collapse it." Seeing confusion on several faces, she added, "If either approach works, we'll all return to our starting points, the places we were when CERN's first high-energy collisions started to occur."

Vaughn's eyes cleared and he nodded. "And this time, it won't be just the two of us trying to convince them not to continue." He gestured at the group. "It'll be all of us."

Bingham gave her a dubious look. "Seems like a bit of a reach."

Angela pressed her lips together and then dipped her head. "It is. It's a huge leap, and it won't be easy." She gestured at herself and then Vaughn. "I don't think we could've made it in there again. Not by ourselves. We need your help. But you're right, even with all of us working together, it might be a long shot. Make no mistake: we have a long, hard road ahead of us."

A smile crept across the wing commander's face. "The Royal Air Force specializes in long, hard roads. If it were easy, they'd let everyone do it. So Bob's your uncle. Where do we go from here?"

Angela grinned and then nodded thoughtfully. "Geneva, of course, but not yet. There are some things we need first, like supplies and weapons." She paused and then shrugged. "But not just any weapons. We need some specialized stuff."

Bingham's face twisted. "Stuff, ma'am?" He pointed back toward their helicopter. "We brought some kit, but it's nothing more than guns and ammunition. Could you please be a bit more specific, Commander Brown?"

The corner of Angela's lip curled up. Digging in her bag, she produced the shiny weapon that had accompanied her when she'd reset the timeline and returned to the here and now.

After glancing at the western horizon with evident unease, Vaughn turned and looked at her. Seeing the device in Angela's hand, he smiled. "You still have it!"

Major Peterson looked at her with mounting confusion. "What the hell is that, and where did that come from?"

"Where?" Angela shrugged. "The future. The past. Another version of Earth … Hell." She held the palm of her free hand toward the sky. "I guess it's a matter of perspective."

Bill gestured at the gun. "How does that thing fit into all of this?"

When Angela described how the weapon had disabled the robots, Monique's eyes had widened. "It caused them to shut down?"

Vaughn nodded. "Yep, it kills Necks and Taters alike." A shadow crossed his face. "At least, it did. We have no idea how it's powered or if it has any charge left. We found it in Hell. Didn't think it worked until Angela saved my life with it … twice." His eyes suddenly looked distant. He rubbed at the now bandaged wounds on his right wrist.

Angela knew that he was thinking of the nearly tragic encounter they'd had with the scavenger bot in Geneva. For the two of them, that event had only occurred a couple of days ago, but to Angela, it now felt as if a lifetime had passed in those intervening hours.

Vaughn shook his head. "Anyway." He gestured at the gun in Angela's hand. "We think it fires an electromagnetic pulse, an EMP."

Monique nodded, but she looked lost in thought.

Bill's face twisted. "But how did it get here?"

Shrugging, Angela pointed at Vaughn and herself. "Same way we did. It came through the wormhole with us. I had it tucked in the waistline of my pants."

They continued to stare at her without comprehending.

Angela pointed at Vaughn. "When we were trapped in the time loop, we discovered that anything we were wearing or holding at the moment of the jump would go through with us. The same holds true if you're sent to Hell by a Tater."

As understanding blossomed on their faces, Angela waved a dismissive hand. "But don't count on that helping us this time. If we're caught by one of those things and beamed to Hell, we'll be stuck there forever." She swept a hand in an arc, pointing at all of them. "If that happens, all of this will have been for naught … We'll have lost."

Angela scanned the collected faces and then nodded somberly. "That's why we need weapons." She gave Bingham a meaningful look and held up the EMP gun. It rocked in her open palm. "Specialized weapons like this."

She looked at the rest of the group. Then her eyes locked onto Monique's.

A smile had blossomed on the naval lieutenant's face. "I know exactly where to find something that might fit the bill."

All eyes shifted from Angela to the wiry woman.

"Wright-Patterson Air Force Base. DARPA has …" Her face darkened and she shook her head. "… *had* a large contingent there."

Bingham frowned. "DARPA? Isn't that your government's advanced concepts division?"

Monique nodded.

"How would a naval leftenant know about it?"

"Because DARPA is not specific to one branch. It is Department of Defense." Monique pointed a thumb at herself. "And this nuclear and computer engineer spent a couple of months on assignment there."

Angela's eyes widened. "Computer engineer! That's perfect." She smiled inwardly as she remembered the director's words. 'I found a group with skill sets that might come in handy.' Good job, Randy.

Vaughn cast another nervous glance at the western horizon. The dark clouds that lined that portion of the sky had acquired an ominous, green hue.

He looked back at the rest of the group members. "Wright-Patterson sounds good to me." He pointed at the approaching storm. "We need to get the hell out of here before the tornadoes start." He extended a palm toward Bingham. "I know … because this isn't the first time I've dealt with that storm."

The Wing Commander's mouth snapped shut. Then he nodded. "Wright-Patterson it is."

They elected to keep the group split in two. As much as Angela wanted to ride with Vaughn, she decided to join the Houston group. It wouldn't be wise to put the only two of them with first-hand knowledge of what lies ahead in the same helicopter.

The young man that had been with Monique in the back of the aircraft, Doctor Rourke Geller, asked to join Vaughn, so Angela volunteered to take his seat in the Houston crew's helicopter. Bill offered to ride with them as well while Teddy agreed to join Vaughn, Mark, and Rourke in the US Customs aircraft.

Hands were shaken and hugs exchanged, but as everyone started to part ways, Angela held up a finger. "Wait! There's something I have to do first."

She returned to the Soyuz. A moment later, she emerged holding the plastic box and a small shovel. After a few minutes, Angela finished digging out a niche for the mice. She placed the plastic box on its side. It provided a measure of shelter. Then she stripped the tops of several stalks of wheat. Rubbing them between her hands, she allowed the grain to fall to the ground. They formed a small pile in the overturned lid. Then she broke a wheat stalk into several pieces and stacked them up in the other half of the cover. Lastly, she poured water into a small bowl she'd brought for the purpose.

"Alright, Mack and Nadine. This is your new home. There's enough food here for a million lifetimes, and I know you'll find water and more shelter." She batted away a tear from the corner of her eye. "Your ancestors have been doing it for thousands of years."

Looking up, she saw the entire group staring at her. Most of them had confusion written across their faces, but Vaughn was dabbing at a tear of his own.

Angela looked back at the mice. Mack had already started to nibble on a kernel of wheat. Nadine was looking at her, her little nose sniffing the air. "If we do this right, the next time we see one another will be back on the station, you know, like it was before all this crap happened. If not ..." She sighed. "Well ... if not, I hope Nate Junior and the rest of your descendants become a serious pain in the ass for those damned Necks."

Standing, Angela swiped the back of her hand across her cheek.

The last eight humans on the planet stared at her wordlessly.

Setting her jaw, Angela narrowed her eyes. "Let's go kick some robot ass."

CHAPTER 13

Vaughn craned his neck to look around Monique. The tall woman was blocking his view of the door. "Are you sure you're doing that right?"

Lieutenant Gheist nodded and kept working on the keypad.

They had arrived at Ohio's Wright-Patterson Air Force Base early that morning, having overnighted in a palatial Indiana farmhouse. Unlike the vast majority of the cities they'd encountered while en route, the airbase remained largely intact. A few small fires had broken out, but it appeared that the sprinkler systems had minimized the damage.

Fortunately, the base still had power.

The chiming report of another failed attempt rang out, and it occurred to Vaughn that still having electricity might not be such a great thing after all.

Monique released a rare curse word.

Wing Commander Bingham shook his head. "We should skip this. Why all the fuss over an EMP gun when we have an entire nuclear arsenal at our disposal? Let's go to DC and get the launch codes. If that doesn't work"—the man pointed at Monique—"the leftenant is a nuclear engineer. Hell, she used to work on Navy nuclear weapons. With her help, we can loft a missile over the robots' beachhead."

"That won't work, Chance," Bill Peterson said. "Angela already told you what happened when the President tried to nuke them. They beamed out the warheads before they could even hit the ground, all of them."

"The nukes won't need to get close to the ground. If we detonate just one of them high above Geneva, the EM pulse it generates should fry all of the Necks," he pointed at Angela, "just like her handy little ray gun, but all at one time, not by the ones and twos!"

Angela gave the man her best 'you're an idiot' look—a look Vaughn knew well. She made air quotes. "Their 'beachhead' is in the ATLAS facility. It's under almost a hundred meters of soil and rock. It doesn't matter how good a nuclear engineer Monique is. There's no way the nuke's EMP reaches that deep."

"You don't know that it won't affect them. At least we can stop the ones that are trying to build the machine city you've been warning us about."

"We don't know if they've started that city yet. They might all be underground still. Besides, this is an all-or-nothing proposition. If something we do shuts down the wormhole, then we are stuck here in this timeline." She jabbed a finger toward the ground to emphasize her words. "This here. This now. They'll be no bringing back anyone." She paused and pointed at Bingham. "Including your family." Angela shook her head. "And there's another thing to consider. If we try and fail, they'll know that someone survived. The Necks could just as easily pull back and send that light through again. They'll swipe-left the entire human race."

That finally shut up the wing commander.

The quadruple chime of another failed attempt rang out from the door's electric lock.

Monique shook her head. "I do not understand why my code is not working. I still have DARPA access. My assignment was never withdrawn."

Vaughn stepped up beside her. "I'll give it a shot. What's the code again?"

Giving Vaughn the stink eye, the woman stepped aside and spouted off a short string of numbers. "But I do not see how you will have any more luck than have I."

The corner of Vaughn's mouth twisted up. "Oh, I have a way with these things."

He pulled the shotgun from the holster he'd strung across his back. Lowering the muzzle, he aimed it at the area between the lock mechanism and the jamb.

Several voices rose behind him.

Vaughn pulled the trigger.

Fire belched from the muzzle, and the targeted area disintegrated.

An alarm rang out, its warbling report echoing off the walls of the nearby buildings.

Bingham shouted above the din. "What the bloody hell are you doing, mate?!"

Vaughn reared back and kicked the door. It flew open, vanishing behind the churning smoke left by the shotgun blast.

Smiling, he turned and held the weapon across his body and then nodded approvingly.

Monique appeared to be in complete shock. The remainder of the group members stared at him with a mixture of anger and surprise. Only Major Lee had a smile that matched Vaughn's.

He extended a hand toward the destroyed door. "Behold the wondrous destructive power of the four hundred-grain, twelve-gauge slug, the key of choice for discriminating apocalyptic pirates."

Angela pursed her lips and then sighed. "Captain..."

Commander Bingham rubbed an ear. "How about next time you give us a bit of a warning, Captain Singleton?"

Rolling his eyes, Vaughn walked over to the still blaring siren. Attached to the wall overhead, it looked like a megaphone. He cocked the shotgun, chambering another round. Then he fired it into the metallic speaker. The loud squeal ceased.

Giving the weapon another appraising look, Vaughn nodded. He was really beginning to like the gun. He'd found it while they were raiding the armory for standard armaments and munitions. After loading their booty into the truck they had procured for the purpose, they had followed Monique to the DARPA facility.

Returning to the door, he slid the shotgun back into its holster and then gestured through the opening. "You're welcome."

Several members of the group shook their heads, but they all proceeded into the DARPA facility.

As she walked by, Major Lee smiled and gave him a high-five. "Strong work, Singleton."

Grinning, Vaughn fell in behind the group and followed them into the facility and down a long hallway.

Monique passed several rooms that appeared to hold interesting devices and equipment of unknown purposes. A moment later, she stopped in front of a door.

This one had a lock similar to the last. And like that one, it proved just as resistant to Monique's efforts.

Vaughn smiled again as everyone looked at him. "Would you like me to try my code?"

Nodding reluctantly, they backed up and placed hands over ears.

Monique looked at him. "Please avoid hitting anything inside the room."

"You got it, Lieutenant."

Vaughn raised the muzzle of the shotgun to the area between the lock and the jamb. Aiming downward to comply with Monique's request, he pulled the trigger.

The weapon discharged. Its loud report in the narrow confines of the hallway set his ears to ringing.

This time, the door opened without the need of an assist from his boot. It swung out of the way, revealing an interior that had several gun-looking devices hanging from its walls and a couple resting on tripods.

Monique walked past him. As the rest of the group followed her, Vaughn reholstered his weapon and stepped into the room.

The naval lieutenant extended an arm. "These are the EMP guns I've been telling you about."

Vaughn scanned the room, studying the weapons. Several of the devices looked like rifles, and one of the larger, tripod-mounted ones even looked like a cannon. However, they all had one thing in common. Each of them had a large block attached by a flexible cable.

Pointing, he looked at Monique. "Batteries?"

She glanced up from the one she was showing Rourke and Rachel and nodded.

Walking over to a particularly cool-looking one, Vaughn pulled it from the wall. The cable that led from that one disappeared into a backpack. He grabbed the bulky battery. The heavy ass thing nearly hit the floor. With a grunt, he slung it over a shoulder and then, stringing his other hand through the opposite strap, placed it on his back. Holding the weapon across his body as he had with the shotgun, he turned to face the group. "What do you think?"

Monique looked up from her conversation and shook her head. "I fear the only thing that will do is anger a Neck."

Vaughn screwed up his face. "What do you mean?"

"That is a DroneShield. It is designed to disrupt drone controls as well as the GPS signal they receive." She shrugged. "It will not fry any of its electronics."

Frowning, Vaughn looked at the weapon and then back at Monique. "Then why did you bring us here?"

Everyone looked at her expectantly.

Monique smiled and pointed toward the central, tripod-mounted weapon. "For this."

The large black EMP cannon formed the centerpiece of the room. The heavy-duty tripod that supported it sat atop a sturdy, three-foot-tall workbench. All rakish angles and mean lines, the futuristic-looking cannon sported long, cooling fins that ran the length of its inky black barrel.

Lieutenant Gheist moved to stand behind the weapon. "It will stop a truck dead in its tracks from greater than one hundred meters."

Shrugging off the backpack, Vaughn placed it and the attached DroneShield rifle on the floor and then joined Angela.

They moved to stand behind the group.

Angela slipped her hand into Vaughn's.

They exchanged a look that spoke volumes.

As he stared into her beautiful smile, a warm joy wrapped itself around his heart.

It was the same joy he'd felt when Angela had thrown her arms around him in the Nebraska wheat field. That singular moment had chased away the last of the doubts and insecurities that had haunted him during their first weeks together.

For a moment, his thoughts ventured back to his lost dream of plying the world's oceans with her.

Vaughn pushed out the notion. One thing their many journeys had taught him was to live in the here and now, to cherish the moments ... like this one. He squeezed her hand and then turned his attention back to Lieutenant Gheist.

Everyone was studying the EMP cannon in silence.

Unlike the other weapons, this one did not have an attached battery pack. The thick cable that ran from the gun ended in a hefty, four-prong plug that sat in a holster on the side of the tripod.

Vaughn squeezed Angela's hand again and then released it. He worked his way through the group and stepped up to the weapon. He tried to pull it off of the tripod, but the thing wouldn't budge.

After looking up self-consciously, he adjusted his grip and tried again.

This time Vaughn managed to lift it an inch or two. The veins in his arms pulsed. The healthy diet of the last couple of days had gone a long way toward restoring most of his strength, but he still couldn't raise the gun all the way off of its mount.

The cannon dropped back onto the heavy-duty tripod with a loud thud.

Vaughn looked at Monique. "This thing weighs a ton. How on earth are we ever going to carry it?"

Major Lee pointed at the plug on the end of the cable. "And where is the battery pack?"

"It does not have one. This weapon gets its power from the vehicle to which it is mounted."

Vaughn looked at her and shook his head. "We can't take a vehicle where we're going, not all the way, anyway. Remember that part about tunnels and narrow alleyways?"

An odd smile suddenly blossomed on the woman's face. She stepped over to a nearby desk and picked up a thin, black device. It looked like a small remote. She spoke into it. "Bob, please join me in room Eighteen Bravo."

Vaughn exchanged confused glances with the other members of the group.

Had the woman lost it?

Nobody was around to answer radio calls. He opened his mouth to say as much, but then it clicked shut as the sound of footsteps echoed down the outside hallway.

Vaughn's blood ran cold as he heard the heavy report of all-too-familiar footfalls. The sound of them engendered a vision of Necks spilling into the corridor in CERN.

The room's partially closed door suddenly swung open.

Everyone but Monique took an involuntary backward step.

Then Vaughn glimpsed the narrow waist and bulbous hips of a Neck.

Angela placed hands over her mouth. A stifled scream escaped her.

The robot stepped through the opening.

Vaughn pulled the shotgun from its scabbard.

Monique yelled something.

Jamming a finger into the trigger guard, Vaughn raised the weapon and readied to send the bot to its maker, but then he yanked his finger back.

It wasn't a Neck, wasn't even the right color or shape.

The robot's knees bent the correct way, not like the backward-bending ones on the Necks. Its upper body was completely different, more humanoid, and it only had two arms. Also, unlike a Neck, this robot did have an actual neck. The gray head that sat atop it turned and stared down the muzzle of Vaughn's shotgun.

Finally, Monique's words pierced his frantic thoughts. "Don't shoot! It's one of ours."

Staring back at the machine, Vaughn lowered his weapon. Careful not to point the shotgun's muzzle at anybody, he turned and glared at Monique. "Jesus Christ, Lieutenant! Next time warn us before you do something like that."

Monique flinched at the sharpness of his words. She pressed her lips into a thin line and then nodded. "Sorry. I should have considered your potential reaction."

"Ya think?!" Vaughn blinked several times. His adrenaline level lowered, and his anger ebbed. Finally, he sighed and shook his head. "Sorry I yelled. It's not your fault. You-You couldn't have known." He pointed at the now motionless robot. "It was the legs and its hips." He glanced at Angela and then back at the naval lieutenant. "Beyond the fact that they didn't have necks, we didn't tell you what they looked like. But from the waist down, they looked a lot like that but with backward-bending knees."

Tilting her head, Angela stared at the robot's upper torso.

Vaughn followed her gaze. As he studied the robot's chest plate, he saw a rectangular tag occupying the space where a name tag would sit on a military uniform. It was a small plaque with BOb engraved into its surface with an uppercase B and O followed by a lowercase b.

Angela looked back at Monique. She pointed at the name tag. "BOb? Is that an acronym?"

The robot's head dipped.

Vaughn blinked in surprise as the thing spoke with an inflected, reedy voice that sounded almost human.

"Yes. I am a T-Eight-Fifty, Model One-Oh-One Battle Operations bot." The machine paused and then canted his head. "Or BOb, for short."

Vaughn hoisted an eyebrow. A T-850 Model 101? He chuckled. "They should've called you Arnold."

BOb nodded. "Only an enemy combatant would see me as a Terminator."

It looked as if the thing had smiled, although, considering the rigid construction of its face, Vaughn thought it unlikely.

"Bloody Yanks!" Bingham shook his head. "I just hope this thing doesn't decide one of us is the enemy someday."

The Russian cosmonaut smiled and waved at the robot. "No enemy here, BOb. I'm Teddy, your friendly Russky ginger."

"Hello, Teddy."

Vaughn's smile faltered as he spotted a symbol that he recognized. He took a backward step and then glanced at Monique. "Does that mean what I think it does?"

"Captain Singleton, my doctorate affords me many abilities. However, mind-reading is not amongst them."

Vaughn frowned and pointed at the symbol. "Is that an RTG?"

"No."

He chuckled self-consciously. "Whew."

The woman gestured at the labeled part. "That is an SRG."

The smile fell from Vaughn's face when he saw Angela do a double-take and then take a backward step.

Major Lee tilted her head. "SRG?"

"BOb is powered by a Stirling radioisotope generator."

The group members stared at her with blank looks.

"It's nuclear-powered."

Everyone but Monique backed away from the robot.

Rolling her eyes, the lieutenant held up her hands. "It is perfectly safe. The SRG is combat-rated. Its radioactive core is encased in a hardened shell. Even a direct mortar strike would not split the case."

Vaughn looked from the robot to Monique. "What is the difference between an RTG and an SRG?"

"Hear that faint, purring sound?"

Vaughn had. He'd thought it must be coming from a hydraulic pump. He nodded.

"That is a Stirling motor. The heat of the nuclear core is driving it.

It is about four times more efficient than the thermoelectric couplings of an RTG."

As he nodded, Vaughn saw Angela staring at him. "What?"

Her nostrils flared, and she pursed her lips. "Do you have to know how everything works?"

He shrugged. "I'm a pilot. It's what I do." Looking left and right, he received confirming nods from Mark, Rachel, and Chance.

Angela looked at them and then shook her head. "God help me, I'm surrounded."

Commander Bingham stepped forward and addressed Monique. "How is this thing going to help us, Leftenant? I doubt it can do anything worthwhile for our mission."

The robot looked at Bingham and said, "Don't you hate it when someone answers their own questions? I do."

Chance did a double-take and scowled at the bot.

Ignoring the exchange, Monique pointed at the large, tripod-mounted EMP cannon. "BOb, please pick up the BFG."

Vaughn guffawed. "BFG?!"

The lieutenant looked perplexed by his outburst. "Yes, it is the weapon's technical designation. I am not sure for what it stands."

He cast a second glance at the naval lieutenant. "Really?"

The robot looked from Vaughn to the lieutenant. "The acronym stands for Big Fu—"

Angela's hands shot out. "That's okay, BOb."

Monique's eyes widened, and her mouth formed an O. Then she covered it with a hand. "Oh my word."

After a moment, she recovered from her embarrassment and pointed at the EMP cannon. "BOb, please pick up the … the weapon."

The robot nodded. "Yes, Lieutenant Gheist." It stepped between them and walked toward the tripod. Each step the thing took sent a tremor through the floor.

BOb was taller than an average-sized man. Of all the members of the group, only Mark Hennessy stood higher than did the robot.

It stopped in front of the tripod and grabbed the EMP cannon as if it weighed less than ten pounds. Lifting it free, BOb turned and looked at Monique. "Would you like me to connect the power, Lieutenant?"

"Yes, please. Thank you, BOb."

Bingham rolled his eyes and scoffed. "Now we're saying please and thank you to a robot?"

Major Lee grinned at the wing commander. "Care to find out what it's like to be on its enemy list?"

Unfazed, Monique nodded toward Rachel and then addressed the group. "This is no ordinary robot. Just a couple of years ago, we would have considered its brain to be a supercomputer."

As the Lieutenant spoke, BOb opened a port on the side of his narrow waist and plugged in the power cable.

Rourke looked nervously from the gun to Lieutenant Gheist. "Are you sure that is safe? What if he shoots someone?"

"First of all, he is of no threat to any of us. We have not been designated as an enemy combatant. However, even if he accidentally shot one of us—a highly unlikely event—you would feel nothing and would suffer no lingering effects."

She turned from Rourke and addressed the entire group. "Anyway, as I was saying, BOb has a level of artificial intelligence that is like nothing you may have previously encountered. While he does not have emotions, we have noticed that he responds more readily and eagerly when we use a modicum of tact and politeness."

Bingham rolled his eyes again. "Wonderful."

The bot looked up. "Uh, I am still in the room, folks. I said I was a robot, not deaf."

Everyone exchanged shocked glances. Then they burst into laughter.

BOb looked from the wing commander to Lieutenant Gheist. "It has been some time since I was last summoned. Where is everyone else?"

The laughs faded, and an uncomfortable silence fell across the lab. After a moment, Monique coughed and looked up from the floor. "There is no one else, BOb. Everyone is gone. We are the only remaining humans."

The robot nodded. "Okay." Then it fell silent, apparently having no further questions on the matter.

It occurred to Vaughn that being an emotionless robot may not be so bad after all.

When the uncomfortable silence became unbearable, Vaughn coughed and then gestured to the robot. "So, BOb, if that's not a hydraulic pump I hear, what's driving your actuators?"

"I don't have actuators, as you say. They're synthetic muscles, made of a flexible polymer that contracts when an electrical current runs through it."

Hearing the robot use contractions, Vaughn had to stifle a grin. Apparently, BOb was more comfortable with the use of words like *don't* and *they're* than was Lieutenant Gheist.

Angela looked from the robot to Monique. "Is there anything else we can get? Do you have other surprises for us?"

The naval lieutenant shook her head. "Nothing better than the munitions we already procured from the armory."

They had amassed an impressive collection of weapons, including grenades and machine-guns of varying sizes and capabilities. They'd also loaded up on shoulder- and tripod-fired rockets and missiles.

Vaughn hoped they wouldn't need any of it.

He looked pointedly at Major Lee and Lieutenant Gheist and then gestured toward the exit. "It's time you show us the ride to Europe that you promised."

Rachel and Monique shared a knowing look and then nodded. The two of them had obviously discussed the matter, but whatever idea they'd cooked up, they hadn't yet shared the details with the rest of the group.

Gesturing toward the door, Rachel indicated for Monique to lead the way. "I'll take over once we get there."

Vaughn held up a hand and looked at the robot. "BOb, how about you take point? ... Please." He left out the part about not being comfortable with having an armed combat bot walking behind them, regardless of the type of weapon.

The robot nodded and stepped eagerly toward the door. "I'm on it, Captain. Where would you like to go?"

Vaughn turned raised eyebrows to the conspirators. "Care to enlighten us?"

Monique looked past him and addressed BOb directly. "Take us to Building Eight-Two-Eight."

The robot nodded his mouthless head and then walked out of the room, each of its footfalls again sending a silent tremor through the floor.

Vaughn looked at Angela and shrugged. Then they and the rest of the group followed BOb.

A short time later, they stopped in front of the expansive doors of a large hangar.

Lieutenant Gheist held up a finger. "Wait here. I will be right back." Then she jogged toward one end of the building and disappeared around its corner.

Looking at the size of the hangar, Vaughn knew it likely contained a large cargo jet. He turned toward Monique. "What's in there, a C-17?" Not waiting for her reply, he shook his head. "I told you an airplane won't work. We can't count on having a place to land. You've seen the airports here." He pointed in the direction of the Air Force Base's runways. "Even this tarmac is littered with wreckage."

Major Lee didn't answer. She simply gave him an indiscernible smile.

A loud beeping noise rang out from the hangar. It sounded like the bleating alarm of a large truck's back-up warning horn. Then the massive hangar doors began to part.

Moving to stand side-by-side in a rough semicircle, the eight of them stared into the dark interior as the doors continued to roll open.

Vaughn glanced at BOb. He was pleased to see the combat bot had taken up a defensive stance. It had the BFG trained in a direction that covered the most obvious avenue of attack. Not that Vaughn antici- pated one, but it was good to see the bot taking its duties seriously.

Turning to look in the building, Vaughn saw something large sitting in the center of the expansive hangar.

Standing under a bright sky, he blinked several times, trying to resolve the apparent aircraft in the building's comparatively dark interior. Then his eyes widened with recognition. "An Osprey?"

A smile spread across the face of the Russian cosmonaut. "So cool!"

Rachel gave a smug nod and then smiled. "Can't get anything past you, Singleton."

He released a snort. "Ha-ha, but I don't think that tiltrotor airplane has the legs for a transoceanic flight."

Vaughn looked at Mark Hennessy for confirmation. Like Major Lee and many of the astronauts who'd come before them, the man had attended the Navy's Test Pilot course.

Mark shook his head. "No way."

Confusion clouded Rourke's features. "What's a tiltrotor?"

Bingham's face soured. "Did you never pull your nose out of your books?" He pointed at the aircraft. "*That's* a bloody tiltrotor. They call it that because its rotors can tilt, allowing them to work like both the rotor blades of a helicopter or the propellers of an airplane. The Osprey can take off and land vertically, but it can also cruise at more than three hundred miles an hour."

Vaughn nodded. "But like I said, it doesn't have enough range to cross the ocean."

Monique walked into the light and hitched a thumb, pointing over her shoulder. "This one does. It is a CV-22B."

The designation tickled a faint memory, but Vaughn couldn't quite recall it.

Rachel sighed. "Geez, Singleton."

Vaughn scanned the faces of the other members of the group. Seeing blank stares, he turned back to Major Lee. "Looks like I'm not the only one in the dark on this one."

With her fingers laced together in front of her, Monique moved to stand at the center of their semicircle. Walking backward, she led them into the hangar. "This is the Air Force Special Operations version of the Osprey."

Raising his eyebrows, Vaughn nodded slowly as the memory fully surfaced. An Army friend in Spec Ops had mentioned that the Air

Force would soon start transporting them into their clandestine operations in a new version of the Osprey, the CV-22B.

Vaughn gestured at the aircraft. "Extended range tanks?"

Monique grinned. "Exactly. They are built into its wings."

Commander Bingham shook his head. "Even with those, I doubt this thing could cross the pond in one hop."

Rachel walked to one of the craft's wide doors and opened it. After looking inside, she smiled at Monique. "Just like you said."

Responding to Bingham's words, Vaughn tilted his head equivocally. "If we can find this thing's auxiliary tanks, we wouldn't have to do it in one hop. They'd be additional tanks that ride in the plane's cargo area. Then we could make stops in St. John's, Newfoundland, and Reykjavík, Iceland."

Major Lee turned her grin toward Vaughn. She pointed inside the aircraft. "Auxiliary tanks like these?"

They walked up to the open door and gazed in.

Vaughn nodded appreciably. He could tell by the plumbing and the straps affixed to the tanks that they were already connected to the aircraft's fuel system and ready for flight.

He was happy to see they weren't too big. Even with the tanks in place, there remained plenty of room for the team and the supplies they had procured.

Wing Commander Bingham looked from face to face. "Now, all we have to do is find someone who knows how to fly the bloody thing."

Major Lee walked over and stood next to Mark Hennessy. "Did we mention that the Navy Test Pilot Course has a mandatory tiltrotor curriculum?"

PART III

"Do not go gentle into that good night ... Rage, rage against the dying of the light."

—Dylan Thomas

CHAPTER 14

As he gazed upon the living hell that was Paris, Rourke wondered if this was what awaited them in Geneva.

He shook his head. If only this were all that awaited.

Leaning closer to the window, he craned his neck, trying to see a bigger slice of Paris through the tiltrotor aircraft's small portal.

The City of Light now glowed in flickering orange hues as it burned beneath a mantle of black smoke propped up by uncountable roiling columns of the same. Thousands of scattered fires punctured Paris's smoke-filled night like burning embers glowing in the bowels of Hell.

The scene was just another installment in the serialized apocalyptic shitshow they'd been absorbing over the last five days of travel.

Had it really only been five?

It seemed as if he'd been trapped in this damned aircraft for a lifetime.

Turning from the window, Rourke glanced at the exposed pipes, ducts, and wiring that apparently passed for interior design amongst military planners. Over the last several days, he'd spent countless hours staring at the tiltrotor's complex interstices. Rourke now felt as if he knew every nook and cranny of the aircraft.

Shaking his head, he dragged his eyes back to the window.

As Commander Brown and Captain Singleton had predicted, massive fires were doing their utmost to scour humanity's legacy from the planet. A week after the event, infernos still engulfed many of the towns and cities that they had seen while en route. Even as they had crossed the Atlantic, the haze in the atmosphere had limited visibility to a few miles.

A moment ago, as Major Lee had guided the tiltrotor southeast over Paris, she'd directed them to the left side of the aircraft by shouting over the intercom, "Shit on a shingle! You're gonna want to see this."

Unstrapping from his seat, Rourke had activated the microphone on his flight helmet. "What is it?"

"We're coming up on downtown, Rourky. I'm going to fly along its south side, so look out one of the left windows."

Now at the window, and still not seeing anything new in the shit-show, Rourke shook his head. "What am I looking for?"

Major Peterson's deep voice came through Rourke's helmet speakers. "Oh, you'll know it when you see it."

Looking back inside, Rourke saw that Commander Brown had remained seated. She appeared to be sleeping. Considering everything the woman had been through in the last several months, he wasn't surprised. Angela had a significant sleep deficit to work off. During the previous five days, she'd eaten well and gotten lots of rest. Her appearance and apparent health had improved dramatically.

After peeking outside again and still see nothing exemplary, Rourke glanced ahead, looking through the door into the cockpit. Anchored to their pilot chairs, the silhouettes of Major Lee and Colonel Hennessy leaned left and right, cutting black voids in the burned orange and smoky black mural painted across the aircraft's windshield.

Just behind them, in the tunnel that led to the flight deck, sat Major Peterson and Captain Singleton. Their silhouettes framed the left and right side of the opening, both of them staring at something off to the aircraft's front left.

Vaughn had also benefited from the last few days of recovery. The man looked significantly better than he had five days ago, standing in that Nebraska wheat field.

Major Lee and Colonel Hennessy were flying the aircraft tonight, but as they had crossed the ocean, the other pilots had taken turns rotating onto the flight deck, spelling one of the formally trained tiltrotor pilots for several hours at a time. However, this was to be their final leg, so Rachel and Colonel Hennessy had opted to fly this one themselves, although they all hoped the two pilots wouldn't need to apply their skills in any meaningful way tonight.

They'd met in a Nebraska wheat field five days ago, and now they were two short hours from finally seeing Geneva: Ground Zero for the event that had wiped life from the planet.

Rourke's chest heaved, and his pulse raced in his ears as he contemplated the coming events.

What if ...?

Rourke sighed, willing himself to calm down.

What if, ha!

Frowning inwardly, he shook his head. Major Lee had taught him the futility of that line of thinking a couple of days ago. He'd been feeling sorry for himself, lamenting that he'd have saved himself all of this misery if he had turned and run when McCree had spotted him outside Houston's vacuum chamber. Rachel had cut off his whining, right at the knees. Putting her usual subtle touch on it, she had shouted back from the flight deck, "Can someone get Doctor Geller a nice cup of *suck it the fuck up*?! He's not in Kansas anymore. This shit is real!" Then she'd leaned over and looked back at him with a humorless smile. "If!? Ha! *If* my aunt had balls, she'd be my uncle." Seeing the shock on his face, she'd nodded, but a measure of the kindness she usually reserved for him had returned, her look softening. "We're all in this together, Rourky. It is what it is, and it doesn't do anyone any good to wonder what might have been."

Rourke nodded then as he did now.

He could do this.

Tonight, they planned to pass south of Geneva and land on the back side of the same ridgeline that Commander Brown and Captain Singleton had used to get their first glimpse of Geneva. It was Mont Salève, a small mountain above the city known as the Balcony of Geneva. It was there that Vaughn and Angela had first seen the Necks' Machine City.

This time, they planned to get their first sighting of the area as the sun rose on the seventh day of an Earth devoid of life, wiped clean but for the nine of them ... and two mice in a Nebraska wheat field.

The tiltrotor aircraft heaved as it churned through the tumultuous atmosphere.

Rourke bumped into Monique's shoulder. "Sorry."

Standing beside him and staring through the same small window, she waved off his apology. The naval lieutenant frowned as she continued to study the scenery that was scrolling past the portal, a deep sorrow evident on her face. "I never imagined I would see Paris like ... like—" Her head snapped left, eyes widening. "Oh my word!"

Following her gaze, Rourke blinked as he saw what had drawn Monique's awe.

Above the burning embers of the ruined city sat a surreal image of a listing Eiffel Tower. Two of its four curved legs had buckled. Most of its now tilted upper reaches lay hidden within the low-hanging mantle of black clouds. However, strangest of all, the Cupola and the tower's top antenna hung upside down, protruding from the ceiling of smoke. Evidently, that portion of the structure had snapped when the steel monstrosity had tilted. It hung by a virtual thread, a tenuous connection that lay hidden within the churning, black mantle.

Illuminated by the city's myriad fires, the inverted top of the Eiffel Tower now pointed straight down from the clouds like the accusing finger of a dark god.

A stifled cry escaped Monique.

Rourke turned to see her holding a hand over her mouth as she looked not at the tower but the city beneath. Orange light glinted off a tear rolling down her cheek.

The sight of it pulled Rourke out of his thoughts.

Peering back through the portal, he saw the tragedy from a fresh, raw perspective. For the first time in days, he allowed himself to truly see it.

He had grown numb to the scale of the loss they had all suffered, but now he looked upon row upon row of burned-out apartment homes and businesses as they scrolled past the left side of the V-22 airplane. Ceilings and roofs had collapsed, leaving jagged walls that outlined the spaces formerly occupied by innumerable Parisians.

Tears began to cloud Rourke's vision as he contemplated those families: the parents, the kids, and even their pets banished to a place, to a Hell so dark that Vaughn and Angela still wouldn't discuss it in detail.

Rourke's thoughts went to his own lost family and friends. Swallowing, he pressed back the emotions, reminding himself that, if they succeeded in the coming day, they'd reset all of it and bring everyone back.

A few heart-wrenching minutes later, they finally left the last of Paris behind them, the tiltrotor continuing its low-level southeasterly course across the thankfully dark French countryside.

Leaning back, Rourke peered through the door into the cockpit. In the faint green glow of the instruments, he could see Major Lee and Colonel Hennessy scanning through the windshield. Twinned tubes of night-vision goggles—or as they called them, NVGs—now hung from their helmets. Their heads pivoted side-to-side, but since he had no NVGs, Rourke had no clue what they saw in the inky void ahead of the aircraft.

The silhouettes of Major Peterson and Captain Singleton still buttressed the left and right side of the opening. They were also wearing night-vision goggles and appeared to be acting as a third and fourth pair of eyes. They craned their necks, peering into the darkness ahead of the onrushing V-22.

Looking over the crates of munitions and weapons that occupied the center of the narrow cabin, Rourke saw the sleeping form of Teddy, the Russian cosmonaut. Next to him sat the equally motionless robot. Before departing England, they had strapped BOb into the aftmost of the seats that lined each side of the cabin.

153

Movement drew Rourke's eyes back to the front. In the shadowed green glow of the night-vision goggle-friendly lights that illuminated the interior of the cargo bay, he saw Wing Commander Bingham massaging his temples. It was no wonder that the man's head ached, considering the amount of alcohol he had consumed the night before this final leg.

The thought brought back the events of that last day of rest. As the sun had set on a chilly evening of last-minute preparations, the group had gathered around a campfire. They had been discussing the details of what they would do today. Everything had gone south when the wing commander returned to his mantra about nuking the robots. He'd brought up the subject several times over the last few days, but this time, alcohol lent a level of vitriol to his words.

"While you twits sit here arguing amongst yourself, Her Royal Majesty's nuclear arsenal is just sitting here doing nothing." He tilted his half-empty bottle of whiskey toward them. "Give me a couple of days, and I'll pop one over those bastards' heads."

Commander Brown had sighed heavily. "I told you, Chance. If we try to hit them with an EMP, we'll just as likely wipe out our computer network as shut down the Necks."

"Pfft!" Bingham had scoffed with drunken exaggeration. "You're always going on about how it's two hundred feet underground." He'd spread his arms out, sloshing whiskey from both the cup in his right hand and the bottle in his left. "Ought to be enough to protect the network."

Angela nodded. "Yeah, and it'll be enough to protect the robots down there as well."

Bingham sat bolt upright. "Maybe, but it won't be any protection for all of the bastards on the surface, the ones we'll have to go through to get anywhere close to your bloody computer console."

At that point, Captain Singleton had moved to the edge of his seat, leaning into the sightline between Bingham and Brown. "What the hell good is that going to do, Bingham?"

"It will give us a helluva lot better chance of getting to ATLAS. It was pure luck that the two of you ever got in there at all."

Vaughn held up two fingers. "Twice! We made it all the way in there *twice.*"

"Well, you bloody wanker, if we don't cull the herd, we don't stand a chance of making it a third."

Captain Singleton's eyes flared, but Angela had placed a hand on his arm and shaken her head.

Then Monique's soft voice had broken the stalemate. "Why are you so intent on attacking our enemy with nuclear weapons, Wing Commander?"

Bingham hadn't replied. He'd just glared at the ground as if trying to burn a hole through it.

"Chance ..." Major Bill Peterson paused, appearing to search for the right words. "Chance, all the nukes in the world won't bring them back."

Raising the bottle, Bingham had stared at the sloshing whiskey. Filtered by the amber liquid, the fire cast wavering ocher light across the man's tortured visage. Then the wing commander threw the bottle into the fire. It shattered and the whiskey within combusted in a hot flash. The man dropped onto his butt and lowered his head. Emotion twisted his words. "They have to pay!" Voice dropping, he appeared to shrink as if pulling into himself. "They have to pay for what they did."

Surprising Rourke, Rachel Lee had walked over and plopped down next to the wing commander. She draped an arm across his shoulders and held up a glass of whiskey and clinked it against the one still clutched in Bingham's right hand. "Oh, we'll make them pay, alright, Chance. We are all going to make sure those no-neck-having mother fuckers pay dearly for ever showing their ugly little heads in our dimension."

An uncomfortable silence followed. Then Teddy had pointed at a nearby bike. "My dog used to chase people on bicycle. He did it a lot."

Rourke looked at the man through knitted brows. In his peripheral vision, he saw the other members of the group doing the same.

Teddy pursed his lips and nodded. "Da. The dog chased people so much, I had to take bike away."

Everyone stared in shocked silence for a moment. Then they had dissolved into fits of laughter.

After Teddy had broken the tension of the moment, they had spent the rest of the evening laughing and sharing jokes. Near the end, even Bingham had added a couple.

At one point, Major Lee had nodded at the robot. "You know any other good jokes, BOb?"

Over the last few days, their mechanical friend had proven to be quite humorous at times, so it was a reasonable question.

Sitting cross-legged, the robot pointed at the campfire. In its flickering light, BOb almost appeared to grin. "Sherlock Holmes and Doctor Watson go on a camping trip. They pitch their tent under the stars and go to sleep."

BOb had surprised them then by lying back and staring up at the sky. After lacing his fingers behind his head, he'd continued. "Sometime in the middle of the night, Holmes wakes Watson and says, 'Watson, look up, and tell me what you see.' The doctor says, 'I see millions and millions of stars.' 'Yes, Watson, and what do you deduce from that?'" BOb extended an arm and pointed at the sky. "'Well, if there are millions of stars, and if some of those have planets, it's quite likely there are many planets like Earth out there, so there might also be life.'" The robot had stopped for a beat. Then his head had lolled to face the group, and Rourke could've sworn he'd seen a glint in one of the machine's eyes. "'Watson, you idiot, it means that somebody stole our tent!'"

Rourke had guffawed, and the rest of the group had dissolved into fits of laughter again.

That had been last night. In the days leading up to it, they had traveled through Newfoundland and Iceland with overnights in St. John's and Reykjavík. Exhausted, they had decided to get an extra day of recovery time when they stopped along the United Kingdom's eastern coast.

After two days of rest at a helicopter base that had supported oil exploration operations in the North Sea, they'd woke this morning with varying levels of hangovers. The wing commander seemed to have suffered the most. Rourke had heard him throwing up on more than one occasion. However, the man had gone out of his way to apologize for the previous night's words.

Presently, Bingham rubbed his temples again. Seeing Rourke looking at him, the man dipped his head. "Think it'll take more than another round of bangers and mash to quell this mindquake."

Monique handed him a bottle of water and then extracted a pill from a small pack she pulled from her pocket. "Take one of these. I use them for my migraines."

Accepting the water, Bingham took the pill and held it up, studying it in the dim light. "This won't fog my brain, will it?"

The lieutenant shook her head. "Quite the opposite, it has a good shot of caffeine in it as well."

The Wing Commander nodded. "Thanks, Leftenant. You're alright for a bloody grammar Nazi."

Rachel's voice came across the intercom, a smile audible in her words. "Don't make me come back there, Chauncey-Baby."

Bingham scowled. "I've told you I don't like that. It's Chance, not Chauncey."

"I'll try to keep that in mind, Chauncey-Baby. Now settle down and take your medicine."

Bingham held up a hand in surrender. "Yes, my Asian-American princess." He took the pill and washed it down with a long draw from the water bottle.

Angela stirred in her seat. "Pipe down! You people are making it impossible for a woman to get any sleep around here."

Rachel laughed. "Suck it up, buttercup."

Commander Brown smiled and appeared to go back to sleep, although Rourke doubted she was actually getting any shuteye.

The bot's voice broke over the intercom. "Did Lieutenant Gheist tell you the creators originally designated me as a Corps Operations Combat - Robotic Invasion Neutralization Gunner?"

Rourke looked back. "BOb, why did they change it to Battle Operations bot?"

The robot pointed to Monique. "Lieutenant Gheist was vociferous about it not being appropriate. She was quite adamant my name be BOb."

Sitting up, Teddy looked from the bot to Monique. "Why? Was the other name too long?"

A guffaw burst from Bill. "Wait, wait, wait! ... They called you a Corps Operations Combat - Robotic Invasion Neutralization Gunner?"

BOb nodded. "Yes, Major Peterson."

Through barking laughs, Bill asked, "So ... the acronym ... the acronym ... would've been ... Ca ... Ca ... COC-RING—?"

"William!" Monique shouted, cutting off the man. "That is quite enough."

Vaughn and several of the others snorted loudly over the intercom.

"Suffice it to say," she added, "I was having none of it."

Bingham scoffed. "Of that, I have no doubt."

Rachel had been laughing, but she looked back and gave the Brit a hard look.

The man's mouth clicked shut, although the snickers continued.

Covering his lower face, Rourke looked everywhere but at Monique.

Major Lee's voice cut through the giggles. "Everyone strap in. It's about to get rough. First ridgeline is dead ahead."

The laughter evaporated, leaving cacophonous silence in its wake.

Dropping his hand, Rourke looked forward and swallowed hard. "Shit, shit, shit, shit ..."

CHAPTER 15

R ourke scrambled back to his side of the aircraft.
As he finished strapping himself into the seat, he could feel his heart racing.

Rachel was right.

This shit was getting real.

Up to this point, it had all seemed like a remote possibility, disconnected from reality, but now that Major Lee was preparing to go tactical, using the tiltrotor's terrain-following laser radar to keep the aircraft low and masked from enemy detection, it suddenly seemed very real indeed.

Staring at his console with mounting trepidation, Rourke eyed the video game-like controller that currently rested in its cradle.

Captain Singleton had assigned him to the crew chief's jumpseat. That station came with the responsibility of controlling the aircraft's belly-mounted Gatling gun.

After leaving Wright-Patterson Air Force Base, they had taken turns firing the Osprey's two machine guns. The one on the ramp was actually an automatic grenade launcher that rained smart grenades onto a target at an impressive rate of fire. Mounted to a pedestal, it had a dedicated seat. In spite of its high-tech electronics, it still required you to fire it the old-fashioned way: by hand.

However, the other weapon, a belly-mounted, swiveling Gatling gun rigged to extend and retract through a bay in the middle of the floor, was controlled and fired by a video game-style controller, the device that Rourke was still staring at with increasing unease.

What the hell had he gotten himself into?

Why on earth had he thought this a good idea?

A long-time gamer, Rourke had proven to be the best shot with the camera-equipped Gatling gun, regularly able to nail passing cars and buildings with ease, even when Major Lee had been turning the aircraft from side-to-side to simulate combat conditions.

Rourke had even taken a measure of pride in his success. It had been the first time he'd received an approving nod from Wing Commander Bingham.

He extended a trembling hand toward the controller and then shook his head and snatched it back.

What if he had to use the gun?

That would mean they had been seen, that someone was chasing them, maybe one of the Taters.

Shit! Again with the reality thing.

His Adam's apple bobbed as he swallowed and his ears began to ring in response to the massive load of adrenaline dumping into his system.

The interior of the V-22 seemed to darken as his vision narrowed.

A hand touched his arm.

Looking left, he saw Commander Brown staring at him with concerned eyes. She covered up her helmet's microphone and leaned toward him. "What's the matter?"

Rourke pivoted his mic boom away from his mouth. "Oh, I don't know." Heart still pounding, he paused to draw a breath. "Maybe the idea that we're about to fly into a nest of killer robots?"

Angela's eyes softened, and her words took on a soothing tone. "We'll be okay. The idea is not to be seen." She pointed toward the front of the Osprey. "And we have some of the world's best military pilots making sure that doesn't happen. They're used to covert ops, especially Rachel. She spent an entire combat tour in Afghanistan flying in a unit that made a ton of incursions into enemy-held territory, and no one ever knew they were there, at least, not until they wanted them to know."

Rourke swallowed again and then nodded.

His breathing rate subsided. He looked at the console. Knowing Commander Brown was watching him, he finally summoned the courage to act. He grabbed the gun controller. Smiling self-consciously, he turned to the commander and held up the device. "*This* is a video game I'd rather not play."

Angela nodded toward the belly cannon's monitor screen. "I doubt you'll ever have a chance to even glimpse a robot on that thing."

"I hope you're right." Rourke furrowed his forehead as another consideration troubled him. "What if they don't send any robots? What if they see us and just send out another wave of light?"

"I don't think they can do that. They spotted Vaughn and me a bunch of times back when we were trapped in the time loop, but they never sent out the entire wave again. It was always just a Tater."

Rourke nodded. Feeling his pulse rate subsiding, he took another deep breath and let it out in a long exhalation. Then he looked at the commander and grinned sheepishly. "Tater, huh? Who came up with that name?"

Angela smiled and then removed her hand from her microphone. "That was Vaughn. He thought they looked like eggs, but I always thought they looked more like a boiled potato, so he started calling them Taters."

BOb spoke up, his voice taking on a Southern drawl. "They call me Tater Salad."

Rourke laughed in spite of the uncomfortable churning sensation in his gut. BOb's head cut a comical silhouette. The helmet strapped to the robot's otherwise skinny head made the bot look like a life-sized bobblehead. Initially, BOb had been able to broadcast his voice directly through the airplane's intercom system without the need for a headset or helmet. However, at Captain Singleton's insistence,

Monique and Rourke had deactivated and removed all of the bot's wireless interfaces. Vaughn had reasoned that, should the enemy robots become aware of their existence, he didn't want them to be able to reprogram BOb remotely, hijacking the armed robot and using it as a weapon against them.

Laughing, Vaughn turned and looked back. "Thanks, Bobblehead BOb." He shifted his gaze to Angela. "Did I hear my name being used in vain?"

Angela nodded. "Was just telling Rourke how you said the flying things looked like a potato."

Rourke twisted his mic boom back into place and tilted his head toward Captain Singleton. "He also says you're the theory savant. Got one on why they wouldn't just send the white light through instead of a Tater?" He said the last part with a Southern drawl, mimicking BOb.

Screwing up her face, Angela shrugged. "Not sure. I think they're sentient, so maybe the light can damage that part of them, but I don't know. There's another thing, though. They seem almost nonchalant about life. I mean, once they've swept the planet clean, they never go out of their way to watch for us. It's like they see any remaining life as a pest, something to be squashed like a bug, but only if it rears its ugly head. Otherwise, they don't bother to actively look."

Rourke nodded slowly as he leaned back and stared through the far side of the airplane. Then he looked at the commander. "So essentially, a Tater is just a giant can of Raid?"

Angela smirked. "Yeah, albeit a floating, egg-shaped can that sprays out white light that'll send you to Hell, but you've got the idea. Bottom line is I don't think they can be on this side of the wormhole when they send the light through."

Vaughn had followed the conversation since first hearing his name. Now he leaned over and looked at Rourke. "Yep, she's the theory savant alright."

Smiling, Angela rolled her eyes. "Aww, stop it. You're getting me all hot and bothered."

Vaughn grinned. "Beautiful, too, but if it's all the same to you, I'd rather not put this particular theory to the test."

"Okay!" Major Lee interrupted. "Let's adjourn the mutual admiration society before you make Chauncey-Baby throw up again."

Bingham massaged his temples. "Hear! Hear!"

Rachel laughed and then gave them a meaningful look. "We're almost to the first ridge. If you're not already strapped in, do so now."

The robot jumped from the bench and belted himself into the rear ramp's gunner seat. Looking toward the cockpit, BOb extended a thumb and his voice changed to that of a serious-sounding, deadpan male. "I want to tell you both good luck. We're all counting on you."

"Ha!" Vaughn laughed. "Leslie Nielsen. Airplane! Love that movie." He slapped his forehead. "Oh, shit. That reminds me." He leaned in and patted Colonel Hennessy on the shoulder. "Don't fuck up."

"Thanks!" Mark said, drawing out the word. "No pressure."

Looking back with a smile, Vaughn saw their confused faces and shrugged. "Tradition."

Rachel shouted over the intercom. "Brace yourself, folks. First ridgeline in three … two … one!"

CHAPTER 16

Rourke's face sagged, and his spine compressed.

He clutched at the sides of his seat.

His heart began to hammer in his chest again.

A moment later, the aircraft reached the top of the ridge and pitched over, generating negative G-forces and causing his body to press upward into the shoulder straps.

The Gatling gun's wireless controller lifted from the table. He'd forgotten to secure the damned thing in its cradle.

Rourke's eyes widened. *Oh crap. Way to go, dumbass.*

He reached out to grab the surreally levitating device.

The V-22 pitched over further as Rachel urged the plane down the far slope.

The levitating controller lurched upward and disappeared into the ceiling's cluster of ducts and conduits.

Ah shit!

A moment later, gravity began to reassert itself, and the device reappeared. It fell from the ceiling and accelerated toward the floor. Lurching for it, Rourke managed to grab it before it would've slammed into the deck.

He plugged it back into the charging cradle. Looking around, he released a held breath. It appeared no one had observed his screw-up, but then he saw Wing Commander Bingham glaring at him.

Wonderful.

Two heaving gyrations later, he saw Monique doing a little heaving of her own. Fortunately, she managed to catch the remnants of her previous meal in a bag designed for the purpose.

BOb's voice came over the intercom in a passable impression of C-3PO. "Thank the maker I'm not cursed with a stomach."

Everyone started to crack up, including Monique as she wiped the back of a hand across her mouth. Then the airplane did another gyration, cutting short their laughter.

This time, even BOb grabbed the side of his seat.

His voice returned, now sounding like Lloyd Bridges. "Oh … I picked a bad day to stop doing acid."

The aircraft lurched upward and then just as quickly reversed direction.

For the first time—that day, anyway—Rourke began to seriously fear for his life.

"Yee-Haw!" Rachel shouted, her voice so loud Rourke was certain he'd have heard her even if she hadn't transmitted the shout over the intercom system. She laughed hysterically. "It's getting real now!"

"She's enjoying this," Bingham said, shaking his head. "That woman is an absolute nutter."

This elicited another round of laughter from the front. "Oh yeah, I'm crazy alright, crazy 'bout you, Chauncey-Baby."

For a moment, Rourke wondered if the major had gone off the deep end, but when he looked around, he saw everyone smiling between G-induced grimaces. Then it dawned on him: they were whistling past the graveyard.

Rourke doubted Rachel's machinations were accidental. Considering her history as a badass special forces operative, he imagined this was just another one of her finely tuned abilities.

And it had worked…

For a moment.

Now that he had seen through her psychological warfare, his thoughts returned to what lay ahead of them.

Rachel turned and looked at him, her head tilted back so that she could see under her night-vision goggles. "Rourky?" she called, drawing out his name. "I can feel you thinking. Cut it out. You're not paid for that anymore." She nodded toward the Gatling gun's control module. "Go ahead and activate the cannon. Focus on your new job. Keep us safe."

Rourke swallowed and then gave a short nod. "Yes, ma'am."

"We're getting close to Geneva now. Don't worry. I'm not going off-script. Still planning to land on the back side of Mont Salève, but it's better to be ready and not need it than …" She left the rest unsaid. Lowering her helmet, Rachel looked at him through her night-vision goggles and dipped her head.

He returned the nod and then activated the cannon's control system.

Major Lee turned her attention back to the outside world. "You're doing great, Rourky. You'll be fine."

Rourke sighed. He toggled a final command. The sound of rushing air filled the cabin as the bay door on the belly of the aircraft opened.

Colonel Hennessy called back from the flight deck. "You ready, BOb?

Strapped into the tailgunner's ramp seat, the gray robot adjusted the mic boom on its helmet. "Yes, Colonel Hennessy, I am in position."

"Good. When I open the ramp, you are cleared to engage any enemy combatants you see."

"Roger, Colonel. Does that include airborne assets?"

Captain Singleton's head spun to face the robot. "*Especially* airborne assets. If you see a goddamn Tater following us, I want you to blow the bastard from the sky."

"Yes, Captain Singleton."

Mark nodded at Vaughn and then looked back at the robot. "I'm going to open the ramp now."

Barely visible in the dark, BOb raised a thumb. The machine's voice lowered an octave and acquired a British accent. "Make it so, Number One."

At first, Rourke didn't see anything change, but then he saw a horizontal sliver of a lighter shade of black appear beyond the robot. The thin line soon became a fat bar. A moment later, he saw fields and tree lines through the expanding gap, all of the features dwindling as they fell behind the onrushing aircraft.

For now, BOb was manning a grenade launcher instead of his EMP cannon. The latter weapon had proven capable of killing a truck's engine from better than a hundred meters. When they'd tested the EMP cannon, it had permanently fried the electronics of everything they'd aimed it at. However, Monique had worried it might not have the range it needed to be effective from the back of a flying aircraft, so they had mounted an MK47 Striker 40mm automatic grenade launcher to the ramp pedestal. It was a beast of a weapon that could shoot a shit-ton of grenades downrange at a high firing rate.

Like the belly-mounted Gatling gun, the Striker had a dedicated camera and display. It also afforded the gunner the ability to fire programmable grenades designed to airburst at a user-specified range.

Rourke had helped Monique adjust the robot's code so that it could program the smart munitions through its hardwired connection, changing the detonation timing on the fly. This eliminated the need to enter the data manually as a human operator would.

During aerial target practice, the robot had proven very proficient with the weapon. It had even used the delayed-detonation feature to hit targets that were concealed behind cover. BOb would program them to air burst directly over the mark. The code that Rourke and Monique had written into the robot's programming allowed BOb to dynamically adjust the range on every round, even at the weapon's high firing rate. Coupled with the fast speed of the aircraft, the ability made for a highly effective, deadly combination.

"How's the view on the gun camera, Doctor Geller?" Bingham asked sharply.

Rourke flinched. Turning, he saw the wing commander giving him a hard look.

"Focus, young man."

Rourke grabbed the controller and pulled the device from its cradle. Glancing up, he nodded at Bingham.

The Brit tilted his head toward the screen. "As the good Major said, concentrate on that, and you'll be fine."

Rourke sighed again. He wished everyone would stop telling him that.

Frowning to himself, he stared at the screen as the cannon and its dedicated camera slewed to the front. He scanned the area ahead of the aircraft.

Over the next several minutes, Rourke swept the cannon side-to-side, searching the bit of land visible from the bottom of the V-22. Most of the time, he couldn't see more than a few hundred meters. The underside of the aircraft blocked a large portion of the camera's upper field of view. Their ridiculously low altitude didn't leave much to see except terrain that was scrolling past so quickly most of it was rendered a blur.

Periodically, Major Lee would bank the aircraft, revealing a wide swath of rapidly scrolling fields, trees, and hills.

The aircraft heaved as it flew up the side of another steep embankment. A moment later, it reached the apex. Just before the V-22 pitched over, Rourke glimpsed a broad valley ahead. A long, low mountain lined its far side. His eyes widened, and he looked toward the flight deck. "Is that the Balcony?"

The aircraft pitched over, causing Rourke to float up out of his seat and pressing him against his shoulder harness again. He grasped desperately at the sides of his workstation. Then gravity returned and pushed him back into his chair. The nose of the airplane pitched up, but this time, he didn't feel like they were climbing up the side of a hill.

"That's right, Rourky. It's dead ahead. I'm slowing the aircraft in preparation for our approach."

No longer feeling like his insides were about to exit through his mouth—or the other end—Rourke turned his attention back to the screen. The tiltrotor was flaring, pitching up its nose while the rotors tilted back. As the aircraft transitioned from airplane to helicopter, the gun camera had an unobstructed view forward. Mont Salève filled the lower two-thirds of the display.

They had completed their circumnavigation to the backside of the ridgeline that Commander Brown and Captain Singleton had been on when they'd gotten their first glimpse of Geneva and its new machine city.

Before leaving Britain's eastern coast, they had found a map of the Franco-Swiss border region. It had revealed the geologic feature was named Mont Salève, although they'd also learned that it was popularly known as the Balcony of Geneva.

Reasoning that the geologic feature's high precipice would give them a safe observation point from which to recon the city, they had opted to return to the same location. Angela had assured them that the petals of her so-called Gravity Flower hadn't formed until at least a month from now, so they shouldn't be in danger of being knocked from the top of the ridge by any levitating steel structures.

Searching the air above Salève, Rourke saw that it was indeed clear. Neither planes, trains, nor automobiles traversed the sky above the mountain.

Wing Commander Bingham sat up in his seat. "Any indication we've been spotted?"

Looking up from his monitor, Rourke saw Major Lee shaking her head. "Nothing, no threat radar, no lights even. Haven't seen anything moving."

"Of course, dude," Teddy said, his SoCal surfer boy persona drawing out the words.

Rourke looked up to see the crazy man jump onto the cargo that occupied the center length of the cabin.

"That's 'cause Charlie don't surf!" Standing sideways with his arms held wide and swaying, the Russian cosmonaut crouched on top of a crate of munitions as if he were riding a surfboard.

Monique's eyes widened. "Theodore, get down from there before you kill yourself."

Winking at Rourke, the Russian cosmonaut deepened his crouch and wagged his butt at Monique. "Don't be hatin', Lieutenant."

Commander Brown sat up. "Teddy! Get your ass down! Right now!"

The man flinched. He looked at Angela and smiled.

She jabbed a finger toward his seat.

Teddy began to climb down from his perch. "Da, Command-Oh."

Looking across at Monique, Rourke saw her laughing and dabbing tears.

Smiling in spite of his knotted-up innards, Rourke returned his focus to the gun camera's screen and scanned the area ahead as the tiltrotor continued to decelerate.

Major Lee and Colonel Hennessy soon had the aircraft in a stationary hover.

Rachel pointed ahead. "Our landing zone is a few miles off the nose. I'll start heading that way. Gonna keep it low and slow till then."

Angela and Vaughn had described their hike up the backside of the mountain. From hearing them speak, Rourke had expected to see more treacherous terrain, but from this perspective, it looked reasonably tame. On the satellite imagery, they had noticed that the backside of the ridgeline offered a sufficiently flat area where they could approach and land much closer to the top of the low mountain without exposing themselves to the city beyond.

A few minutes later, the tiltrotor flew over the last of the trees, arriving over the broad expanse of grass that was their landing zone, or LZ as military people liked to call it.

The major glanced over her shoulder. "Go ahead and stow the gun, Rourke. There is enough room to leave it out, but I don't want this long grass gumming up the works."

Nodding, he activated the retract mechanism. The gun camera shut down, and the Gatling gun drew back into its bay. Then the belly hatch slid shut.

Looking up from the mechanism, Rourke saw everyone shifting in their seats. Suddenly, he felt as if he might get sick. No longer distracted by the Russian's antics or his own gun duties, he became acutely aware of their proximity to Ground Zero, the point where the alien robots had invaded their planet. Not far from where they now sat, the light that had swept life from Earth had first emerged.

Blinking, he stared at the now inert computer display, a realization sinking home: they had been right. He had lost himself in the work.

The aircraft touched down with a gentle bump.

Major Lee and Colonel Hennessy began to throw levers and flip switches. Soon they had the aircraft shut down.

Everyone stood and began to collect their equipment.

Standing as well, Rourke looked around. "Wh-What now?"

Wing Commander Bingham looked at the faintly glowing face of his watch. "Sunrise is in an hour. Should give us just enough time to hike to the Balcony. We'll get our first view of Geneva." Looking up, the man must have read something in Rourke's face. He smiled and patted his shoulder. "Not to worry, my boy. The rising sun will be at our back. We'll be invisible to anyone … or anything … looking in our direction."

Major Lee exited the flight-deck. Having already grabbed her rifle, she walked through the group, heading toward the back ramp. She had doffed her flight helmet, replacing it with a camouflaged baseball hat. Her eyes glowed behind the tubes of the night-vision goggles.

Rachel moved with a stealthy grace. She looked like a finely tuned killing machine. Pausing, she glanced back and waved them on. "Move it, folks. Get your battle rattle on, and get the hell off my airplane."

Rourke swallowed and then picked up the weapon they had assigned him while in England: A US Army M4 assault rifle with an attached underslung M320 40mm grenade launcher. It was one of his favorites. He'd fired it thousands of times. Angela's initial excitement upon hearing that news had faded when he'd clarified that it had all been while playing a video game named *Call of Duty*.

He'd never touched an actual assault rifle or a grenade launcher until they'd hit the impromptu range they'd set up at the British helicopter base. After initially fumbling with the mechanisms, Rourke had adapted rather quickly to the real weapon. However, his first shots had gone high and wide. He hadn't adjusted his aim to compensate for the recoil.

Several suppressed snickers had erupted after that initial attempt, but they had all ceased when he'd nailed the target on the next shot. Afterward, he'd proven to be an expert with both weapons. Rourke remembered turning to see their surprised faces.

He had looked at Major Lee and shrugged. "Don't flight simulators make you a better pilot?"

Presently, Rourke felt the heft of the weapon and nodded nervously. He grabbed a bandolier of grenades and slung them over a shoulder. Looking down at himself, he felt like a complete fraud.

Around him, the others were donning their gear with varying levels of grace. All of them looked way more comfortable than he felt, and unlike him, none of the members of the team appeared to be shaking either.

Climbing out of the ramp-mounted gunner's seat, BOb doffed his flight helmet and grabbed the bulky pack of munitions and strapped them to his back. The makeshift backpack was considerably larger and heavier than one a human would typically wear. The military officers had stuffed it full of extra rounds for their rifles and grenade launchers.

The robot bent over and opened a wide case and extracted the BFG from it, easily lifting the large Electro-Magnetic Pulse or EMP cannon. After plugging the weapon into the power socket on its side, the robot stood and looked at Rourke. BOb held out the cannon as if flexing. "Say hello to my little friend!"

Still walking, Rachel pointed ahead. "Outside, Al Pacino!"

"Yes, Major Lee." BOb turned from Rourke and headed for the exit, following close behind her. The aircraft shook with each of the robot's footfalls. Moving with apparent ease, the bot effortlessly supported the heavy gun and the large backpack with its cache of munitions.

Rourke stared at BOb's back, warily eyeing the overstuffed bag. He sure as hell hoped they never needed any of it.

A few moments later, the ten of them—nine humans and one robot—gathered in a circle behind the aircraft.

Major Lee looked at Vaughn and held out a hand. "We're on the ground now. It's your command, Singleton."

The captain nodded.

Even though Vaughn was the lowest-ranking military member, the other officers in the group had insisted he lead the task force. They had reasoned that he had first-hand experience with the enemy and knew the situation on the ground far better than did any of them. Rachel had told him Spec Ops forces regularly placed the person with the most onsite experience in charge of a mission, especially if it was an international task force like theirs. After initially declining their request, Captain Singleton had finally agreed to lead them into Geneva.

Rourke watched as the man studied each of them in turn. He had his night-vision goggles tilted up so they didn't block his line of sight. When the captain looked at Rourke, he smiled at him and winked.

"Okay, here's the plan." Vaughn hitched a thumb at the tall silhouette of Colonel Hennessy. "Chewie and I are going to take BOb and scout ahead. We'll recon a couple of hundred meters ahead of the group." He gestured at Rachel. "Major Lee is going to bring up the rear with the rest of you. No radios, folks. As much as I'd love to have them, we don't know what the Necks can or can't detect. Can't take a chance that a radio we think is off is actually still working in the background."

The captain cast a wary glance at the robot. Then he looked at Rourke and Monique. "You sure he's completely disconnected? There's no way the Necks can hack into him."

Rourke shook his head. "No, not wirelessly anyway." He glanced at Monique.

She nodded. "I agree."

"Okay, good enough for me." Captain Singleton pointed at the robot. "BOb, you are still cleared hot. If you see anything moving that isn't one of us, you're cleared to engage it with the BFG only. I don't want you accidentally blowing up one of us. Understood?"

The robot's head bobbed up and down. "Yes, Captain Singleton. Understood. I am only to engage the enemy with the Big Fu—"

Angela's hand shot upward, cutting off the robot mid-word. "That's good, BOb."

Vaughn grinned at her and then nodded at the robot. "Do you still have the coordinates for our overlook?"

BOb tilted his head in an oddly human manner, but Rourke knew it was merely an affectation built into the robot by its programmers. "I'm sorry, Captain. Please define 'overlook.'"

"Observation Point One. The destination we set for this first leg."

Nodding, BOb pointed northwest. "Affirmative, Captain Singleton. We are currently two-point-five kilometers from O-P-One."

"Okay."

Under the haze-muted starfield, Vaughn looked at the assembled group. "Everyone ready?"

Scanning from face to face and making eye contact, the captain tilted his head at each, wordlessly demanding and receiving an affirmative nod from every member of the group.

He glanced at the robot and gestured toward the far side of the ridge. "BOb, you take point. Lead the way."

A short, warbling whistle came from the machine as it began to walk toward the ridgeline.

Bingham blew air through his nose. "Great! Now the bloody robot thinks he's R2-D2."

CHAPTER 17

For the fourth time in as many minutes, Vaughn slid open the chamber of his grenade launcher. In the dark, he ran a finger across the smooth metal back of the casing within, verifying the round was still present and accounted for.

Yep, still there, just as it had been during the previous three checks.

"You're going to wear that thing out before you ever get a chance to use it," Mark said.

Peering through the night-vision goggles, Vaughn looked at his friend's green silhouette and shrugged. "If we do this right, I'll *never* get to use it."

The tubes of Mark's NVGs bobbed visibly as he scanned the woods ahead. "Hope you're right." Pausing, Vaughn held the M4 assault rifle across his body with both hands and lifted it appraisingly. The corner of his mouth twisted upward. "But I can tell you one thing for damned sure. I'd have given my left nut to have one of these bad boys last time Angela and I were here."

Stepping between two trees, Vaughn followed the path that BOb had taken ahead of them. Even looking through the goggles, he could barely see the robot. The thing was nearly invisible in the pitch-black forest.

BOb's dark gray skin appeared to be made out of a material that didn't reflect light, and it barely registered in the spectrum visible to the night-vision goggles. If not for the bobbing pack strapped to the robot's back, Vaughn wasn't sure he would've been able to see the machine at all. As it was, he could just barely make out the large EMP gun held across its torso.

Before entering the woods, Vaughn had glanced back toward the other party and the aircraft behind them. The eastern sky had just started to glow with the sunrise's first light. However, now that he and Mark had progressed a full kilometer into the forest, Vaughn could no longer see any evidence of the coming day. Even above the well-worn trail that they were following, the thick canopy of the forest blocked light from reaching the ground.

Lifting the muzzle of the EMP cannon to vertical, BOb stepped through a narrow gap between two trees. Then the darkness again swallowed all but the swaying backpack.

Mark stumbled into a low-hanging branch. "Son of a bitch," he said, cursing under his breath. "It's dark as death's shadow in here."

Smirking, Vaughn glanced at his tall friend. "You're probably the first Sasquatch to walk this trail."

"Go to hell."

"Been there. Got the bumper sticker to prove it."

"Oh shit. Sorry."

Raising a hand, Vaughn waved it off.

After a while, Mark spoke again. "The silence … I've never heard anything like it."

Vaughn nodded. "Eerie, isn't it? Wish I could tell you it gets better, but I still haven't gotten used to it."

"Guess I never realized how much background noise life makes."

"Yep."

Earlier, Vaughn had placed BOb in tactical mode, dictating no unnecessary talking. Following the now mute robot, they continued deeper into the inky void of the deathly silent forest.

Mark held out his rifle. "I hear you on the weapons. They're definitely a comfort." Pausing, he looked sideways. "What about the team?"

Vaughn tilted his head. "What about them?"

"What's your read on them? How do you feel about them being here?"

Vaughn thought about the question for a moment and then returned his friend's gaze. "It is what it is. I could wish we had a dozen more Rachels, but that won't get me anywhere." He grinned lopsidedly. "I got you and Angela. That's all that matters to me. Either we'll make it work ... or we won't."

Mark nodded slowly. "If it comes to action, I'd definitely like a few more of her."

They walked in silence for a few beats. Then Vaughn shrugged. "If the shooting starts, I have no idea what happens next. Angela and I never had a chance to fight them directly, although it came close at the end there."

"From what the two of you said, it was *damned* close. They were already in the Control Room, right?"

"Yeah, bastards attacked en masse." A chill snaked its way down his spine. "If it gets that bad, I'm not sure a battalion of Rachels would make a difference."

"Guess we need to make sure it doesn't come to that, then."

Vaughn nodded. As a group, they'd already discussed all of this, ad nauseam. "Yep. Bottom line: we need to get in there without being detected. Otherwise, we'll likely be overrun, regardless of the armament we carry." He sighed. "In that way, we're multipliers more than combatants."

Mark regarded Vaughn with a puzzled face. "Huh?"

"All of us know how to reset the timeline now." One corner of his lips curled up. "Well, Rourke and Monique do anyway. I don't like our odds if it comes down to one of us non-nerd types."

Releasing a short chuckle, Mark dipped his head. "I know that's right."

Vaughn held up an open hand. "It's not for lack of trying. I've memorized the password and all of the steps Angela has drilled us on, but I have zero confidence that I'd know what to do if, no, *when* I hit a snag."

"Me neither."

"I saw Angela power through glitches both times she overloaded the wormhole. Her fingers were a blur on that keyboard." Vaughn shook his head. "Don't know about you, but if it comes down to me, we're probably all screwed."

"Same boat here. Pretty sure all of us pilots are in it."

"Anyway," Vaughn continued, "like I was saying, we're multipliers, extra chances to complete the mission should one of us fall, additional opportunities to push that button or buttons ... keyboard keys, whatever. You know what I mean."

Mark nodded again. "I do."

They walked in silence for a time. Vaughn contemplated what might lie ahead for them. One way or another, things would soon come to a head.

And now it was all on him.

The group had elected him as the leader of this expedition. He had said it needed to be Rachel—she was a Ranger, for God's sake—but she had shaken her head, saying that she'd take over if and when it came to a hot fight. They'd reasoned that he and Angela had the best knowledge of the situation on the ground. That, coupled with his military training and combat experience, made him the ideal person for the job.

Yeah, right.

Vaughn shook his head.

He'd reluctantly agreed to lead in spite of his lingering doubts about the decision. The last thing they needed was one of his screwed-up—

"What's wrong?"

He blinked and turned to look at Mark. "What?"

"Come on, Vaughn. I've known you for years. We've been through more than one combat deployment together. I know when something's bothering you."

Following the robot around a bend in the trail, Vaughn shrugged. "I don't know. Guess I'm not sure I'm the right person for the job."

Mark stopped walking and held up a clenched fist. "BOb," he called out, still keeping his voice down. "Hold up."

The robot halted and matched Hennessy's low volume. "Yes, sir."

Lowering his hand, Mark turned and looked at Vaughn. "What the hell happened to the old Vaughn, the snarky asshole that we all followed since the early days of flight school?"

"You happened."

Confusion twisted Mark's face. "Come again?"

Slinging his assault rifle over his shoulder, Vaughn turned to face his friend. "Remember how you were going to have that discussion with me when we were in the vacuum chamber, the one where you were going to tell me to quit doing things half-assed, to apply myself?"

"How did you know...?" Mark paused. Understanding dawned on his face. He nodded. "I take it that discussion went differently the first time."

"Yeah, it did. I blew off your advice at first, basically told you to pack sand." Vaughn's gaze fell to the floor of the forest. "Later, I had plenty of opportunities to regret that." He shook his head slowly. "Nothing like a couple of months of solitary introspection to help you see the error of your ways."

"What the hell did I say?"

Smiling crookedly, Vaughn shrugged. "All I heard at the time was, 'Blah, blah, blah, you're fat, blah, blah, and lazy.'"

Mark winced. "Really?"

"Nah. I mean, yeah, that's what I heard, but it wasn't what you meant. It took a bit longer for that to sink in."

"How much longer?"

Vaughn gave him an embarrassed grin. "About as long as it took you to get killed by a tumbling jet engine."

"Ouch."

"Yeah. It wasn't like that got me going all at once, though. You know me. A little slow on the uptake sometimes."

"Pfft. Sometimes?"

Vaughn smiled.

They began to walk again. BOb needed no prompting. The machine resumed its point duties.

"Anyway, your words made me take a hard look at my life. You were right. I'd been coasting through life and hadn't applied myself to anything since before flight school."

Mark nodded appreciatively. "Nice to know I can have that much of an effect on you. Have to file that away for later. Hopefully, next time, I won't have to get flattened like Wile E. Coyote to drive home my point."

"Dude! That's harsh."

Shrugging, Mark continued. "So, you were slow on the uptake, huh?"

"Ayup."

"What got you going?"

"What do you mean?"

"What was the catalyst? If seeing me get squashed like a bug didn't draw you completely to the light side of the force, what did? There must have been a moment, an epiphany."

Staring at the ground, Vaughn repressed a shudder as he recalled gazing down from the edge of the Royal Gorge Bridge. He shoved out the memory of his narrowly failed suicide attempt and looked at Mark. "The end of the world has a way of … of rounding off your rough edges." He sighed. "Once I got past myself, I realized you were right. I needed to …" He shrugged. "I don't know, apply myself, I guess." He blew air through his nose. "Of course, by then, I figured it was just for me, for my own sanity. Didn't know about Angela yet, but even after I did, it still took a few more screw-ups for me to get fully on board with the applying myself thing."

They walked in silence for a moment. Then Mark gave him a sideward glance. "That's great. Truly, it is. I'm glad you found it within yourself, but …" He paused as if searching for the right words. Then he nodded. "I think you may have gone a bit overboard on the introspection thing."

"What are you talking about?"

"I've been watching you, Vaughn. You're agonizing over every decision. You need to get back to flying by the seat of your pants. Quit doubting your instincts."

Vaughn rocked his head equivocally. "I don't know about that. Flying by the seat of my pants didn't work so well in the *Aurora*. Damned near killed myself and Angela with me. If I had died, she wouldn't have survived." He made air quotes. "My *instincts* would've killed her, too."

Mark stared into the woods for a moment. He looked back at Vaughn and pointed ahead, jabbing an extended finger toward Geneva. "In situations like this, your instincts are good. When we were in the sandbox, your intuition kept us from getting our asses shot out of the sky or blown up alongside a road more times than I can count. You kept us alive simply by flying by the seat of your pants, whether you were in the air or on the ground."

Mark placed a hand on Vaughn's arm and gently pulled him to a stop. He studied his face for a moment and then lightly tapped Vaughn's forehead. "It's time to start trusting those instincts again, find a happy medium. Quit second-guessing yourself."

When Vaughn opened his mouth to counter, Mark held up a hand. "When the situation permits, buffer your instincts with wisdom ..." He paused, and then in the shadowed depths of the forest, a barely visible smile spread across the man's face. "Wisdom and some of that 'applying yourself' thing."

Staring ahead, Vaughn nodded. Mark was right. Since agreeing to lead the expedition, he hadn't let his concerns seep into his words or his actions, not around the rest of the group, not even in front of Angela—especially in front of Angela. He knew that a military unit— regardless of the makeup of the individuals within it—needed unwavering leadership. He'd seen the effects of both ends of that spectrum during his multiple combat deployments. He'd watched strong leaders guide their people through hellish action, prevailing against seemingly insurmountable odds, and he'd seen ineffective leaders yank defeat from the jaws of victory.

"I'm serious," Mark said, pulling Vaughn back into the discussion.

Apparently misreading his continued silence as disagreement, Mark continued. "These people are counting on you."

Vaughn nodded. "You're right, Mark. I'm on it." He smiled self-consciously. "Thanks. I needed that."

Mark grinned. "I know." He pointed ahead. "Lead the way, Captain."

Three steps up the trail, Mark smacked the back of his hand against Vaughn's upper arm. "You know, if you don't feel up to leading, I'm sure Bingham would be happy to take over for you."

"Oh, *hell* no!"

"Good to hear." Mark unslung his rifle and held it across his body. "It's your command, Captain. Just remember: Don't fuck up."

Chuckling lightly, Vaughn shook his head.

Several minutes later, he realized he could see faint light between the trees to his front.

Slowing their advance and stooping, the trio crept forward. The winding canyon of conifers slowly parted, revealing a haze-filled, dimly lit sky.

They had reached the trail's far end.

A ten-meter span of treeless earth sat between them and the precipice of Mont Salève's rocky cliff: the Balcony of Geneva.

Crouching at the edge of the woods, Vaughn whispered to the robot. "BOb, continue tactical mode." He pointed at the ground beneath the machine's feet. "Hold position here. Watch our six."

"Roger, Captain Asshole," the robot responded, speaking softly.

Mark did a double-take. "What did he call you?"

BOb looked at him, head canted comically. "Is that not correct, Colonel?"

Scoffing, Mark said, "Oh, it's correct, alright. I'm just surprised to hear it coming from your mouth ... er, speaker, whatever."

"I told him to call me that."

Mark looked at Vaughn as if a mushroom had sprouted from his forehead.

Vaughn shrugged. "Long story. Just a way to make sure I don't get

too full of myself. Anyway," he pointed ahead, "let's see what we see."
He looked at Mark. "Ready?"

"Aren't we going to wait for the others, for the sunrise to blind any
instruments that might be looking our way?"

"We're reconning, right?"

Looking pensive, Mark nodded.

"Then, let's reconnoiter, Colonel. We'll hang back far enough so
that we're not visible from CERN. I just want a feel for what the area
looks like."

"Okay," Mark said, drawing out the word. He slowly lowered to his
belly.

"Captain Asshole, how should I alert you to approaching combatants? You ordered my radio removed."

"Can you whistle like a bird?"

"Yes, sir." The robot tilted its head. "But aren't they all gone?"

"Guess we'll know it's you, then."

The robot stared at Vaughn for a moment and then dipped its
head. "Okay, Captain Asshole."

Vaughn nodded and started to turn away, but then he looked back
at the robot. It almost sounded like the son of a bitch was enjoying
calling him that.

Shaking his head, Vaughn turned back toward the cliff. He lay
prone next to his friend.

Mark looked at him. "I hope he knows not to call you that in front
of the crew."

Vaughn waved dismissively and began to low-crawl toward the rocky
ledge. "Yeah, I instructed it to only use that name around the two of us."

The dew-covered grass soon soaked through the camouflaged
cloth of his uniform.

Every member of the team was wearing urban digital camouflage,
or digicam as they'd called it in the Army. Vaughn had reasoned that
its blotchy pattern of dark charcoal, light gray, and off-white speckles
would serve best for their ingress into CERN, especially if they had to
work their way through the burned-out city.

The short, wet grass clung to him as he inched forward. Last time he'd been atop this low mountain, Vaughn had crawled through thigh-high foliage. However, this soon after The Disappearance, the grass still had the manicured look of a well-maintained park.

The dirty sky above Geneva Valley glowed with the light of the coming sunrise.

As Mark and Vaughn crept closer to the edge, an ever-widening span of the valley slid into view.

Vaughn stopped a couple of meters back from the ledge. "That's close enough for now," he whispered.

"My thoughts exactly. Can't see the middle of the valley from back here, but then again, nothing down there can see us either."

Peering through the relatively short vegetation and resisting the urge to raise his head, Vaughn studied the small slice of Geneva Valley visible from their safe vantage point. The floor of its far side lay hidden, lost beneath an obscuring layer. He frowned. "I can't see shit."

"Me neither. Can't tell if it's fog or smoke, but it's blanketing the whole area."

When he'd emerged from the dark forest, Vaughn had flipped up his goggles, but now he rotated them back into place. He stared into the valley's low obscuration and then nodded. "Lots of bright spots. Still stuff burning down there."

After glancing at Vaughn, Mark flipped his goggles back into position and then nodded as well. "Sure the hell is."

Night-vision goggles amplified light, but they also detected near-infrared energy, a temperature-based spectrum of light otherwise invisible to the human eye.

Still peering through the goggles, Vaughn swept them side-to-side, scanning the far side of the valley—the only portion of it visible from their current vantage point. Hidden within the obscuring layer, dozens of hotspots shone through the smog, their higher temperatures glowing like a street light under a blanket of fog.

"Dammit," Mark whispered under his breath. "I sure hope this fog or smog, whatever the hell it is, burns off when the sun comes up."

Vaughn frowned. "Me, too. Daytime heating should whip up the winds, blow some of it out of the valley."

Mark continued to study the visible portion of the valley. "At least it's not as bad as Paris. I don't see nearly as many hot spots here."

"Not as many still burning anyway. When Angela and I came here, the part of the old city that remained was burned to the ground. Looked like something straight out of a World War Two—"

Green light suddenly flashed in Vaughn's goggles. "What was that?"

"Not sure." Mark shook his head. "I was looking beneath the goggles when it happened. Only saw the light through the tubes. Otherwise, I wouldn't have seen it at all."

Trying to figure out where the light had come from, Vaughn gazed across the valley. A range of mountains lined its far side.

The sky above the distant peaks flared phosphorescent green.

Vaughn blinked in sudden recognition. "That was lightning."

"Yeah, it was," Mark whispered back.

Staring at the horizon, Vaughn saw the far hills beginning to glow in the early morning light.

Sunrise was closer than he'd thought.

When they'd emerged from the forest, Vaughn had mistaken the dark sky over the far horizon for the last vestiges of the fading night.

Mark pointed at the darkening horizon. "A storm's coming. Must have followed us here overnight."

Pressing his lips into a thin line, Vaughn shook his head. "Well, shit. That's gonna make things fun."

"What is?" asked a female voice inches from his ear.

Vaughn barely contained a scream as his entire body spasmed. He turned to look at Rachel. The woman had crawled up right between him and Mark.

Panting, both men began piercing the cool morning air with rapid-fire shots of steamed breath.

"Jesus Christ, Major! I've told you a million times not to sneak up on me when I'm trying to sneak up on an alien horde."

"And I've told you a trillion times not to exaggerate, Captain."

Vaughn closed his eyes and tried to rein in his racing heart.

Then he looked at Rachel and whispered harshly. "Where in the ever-loving hell did you come from?!"

"Uh ... from behind you. Duh."

Looking over his shoulder, he tried to scan the woods, but light from the coming sunrise burned through the dense forest canopy and washed out his goggles.

Vaughn flipped the NVGs out of the way and saw BOb and the rest of the group crowding the trailhead.

Glaring, Vaughn raised a hand toward the robot in a what-gives gesture.

The bot held out its hands, palms up. A short, sorrowful birdsong whispered from its lipless mouth.

Peering from behind BOb, Angela smiled and waved over the machine's shoulder.

Vaughn glared at the robot.

"Not his fault," Rachel said. "I told BOb to keep quiet."

"Thanks," he said, drawing out the word. "How many more minutes do we have till the sun hits the valley floor?"

"Just a few more now."

Vaughn nodded and then scrambled back to the waiting group. He stood and hugged Angela. Then he turned and whispered, addressing the entire team. "The sun will be fully risen soon." He gestured at the ledge, sweeping his arm in a wide arc. "I want you to spread out. No sense in all of us bunching up." Seeing nervous looks on a few of their faces, he added, "I don't think they'll even be looking, much less be able to see us, but there's no sense in making ourselves an easy target."

Bingham pursed his lips. "Remind me again of what we hope to accomplish here."

Cocking an eyebrow, Vaughn nodded tightly. "We're looking for a way to get into CERN without being observed. Might be able to use the same subway entrance that Angela and I used the first time. But I'd like to have eyes on it before we go charging in there." He held up a hand. "And before you ask, no, we're not going to come back and nuke them, regardless of what we see."

Not waiting for the asshole to respond, Vaughn looked at the rest of the group and continued. "Once you are in position, low-crawl toward the edge, but don't go any closer than Mark is right now. Don't move past that point until you receive the okay from one of us."

He looked at Angela. "And remember to keep your asses down."

She rolled her eyes.

Vaughn looked at and received a nod from each of the other team members. Motioning for them to spread out, he dropped to the ground and lay prone. Then he crawled toward the cliff and stopped abeam Mark's position.

Emitting grunts and squeaks, the remaining members of the team low-crawled toward the cliff's edge. Rourke and Monique complained about the dew soaking their uniforms, but a moment later, they all reached their assigned positions and stopped, holding back from the precipice of Geneva's Balcony just as had he and Mark.

Angela crawled up next to Vaughn.

He gave her a crooked grin. "You don't follow orders so well."

"You ain't the boss of me."

"Uh, yes I am, young lady."

"Pfft." She pointed toward the valley. "Less talking, Captain, more looking."

Vaughn rolled his eyes but did as instructed. Over the next several minutes, he watched the sunlight creep down the valley's far side. As it did, he inched forward, closer to the edge, and motioned for the others to do the same.

Each advance brought more of the valley into view.

Silently, he and Angela studied the land with rapt attention. Splayed across the Balcony, the other members of the team murmured amongst themselves as they also scanned the visible portions of Geneva.

Vaughn could feel his heart rate quicken with each shift closer to the precipice.

Beside him, Angela was breathing heavily as she experienced the same sensation.

Her hand worked its way into his.

He squeezed it, and they exchanged nervous glances before returning their attention to the now partially obscured city.

Fortunately, Vaughn could see portions of the valley floor. A light breeze had begun to perturb the early morning air. Diffusing the fog, the breeze slowly broke up the obscurant and revealed patches of burned city blocks.

Angela pointed to their front left, gesturing toward the northwest. "The ATLAS experiment should be over that way. Can't quite see it from here yet. We're still too far back, but I think the sunrise is getting close to the area. We should be able to see the collider's main entrance soon."

Vaughn nodded. "Our next move up will bring the area into view." He raised his eyebrows. "I just hope we can see more there than fog."

Angela tilted her head toward the valley. "Looks like the wind is thinning it."

"Yeah, you're right. It's already better than it was a few minutes ago when Mark and I first got here."

The dark clouds above the far horizon suddenly flickered with a blast of internal light.

Angela looked up, seeking the source. Then her eyes widened. "Is that a storm?"

"Yep. Looks like it followed us here."

"Wonderful."

"My sentiment exactly."

CHAPTER 18

V aughn raised his head and peered down over the ledge. Nodding, he dropped back to the ground and regarded his team. "Light's hitting the target now. You're clear to move up, but stay low. We don't know how far they've advanced. There may be enemy bots outside of the central point."

Not waiting for a reply, Vaughn crept the last few feet toward the Balcony's precipice. Beside him, Angela and Mark, along with the rest of the group, did the same.

A moment later, all nine of them stared out from their lofty perch. Foggy streams of nervous, raspy breaths shot from each as their bodies reacted to the prospect of imminent discovery combined with the pulse-quickening proximity of the thousand-foot drop.

Digging out his tactical binoculars, Vaughn raised them and scanned the area above ATLAS's entrance. The lenses of the military-grade field glasses had a special coating that minimized reflections, reducing the chance that an enemy might see light glinting from them. Beside him, several of the others did the same, although Rachel used the CQBSS scope she'd mounted to her assault weapon. The DDM4 ISR had an integrally suppressed rifle and attachments that even he had never seen, and he had no idea what most of them did.

Vaughn swept his binos side-to-side, scanning the approximate location of the collider's aboveground entrance. It was still quite far away. The distance made it difficult to determine if he was looking at the right area. Without reference points, he couldn't be sure. However, that entire portion of Geneva still had a blanket of fog covering it.

Lowering the field glasses, Vaughn shook his head. "Crap. Smog's still obscuring the ground above ATLAS."

"Bloody hell!" Bingham said as he peered through his binoculars, scanning the eastern end of Geneva. The slowly thinning fog in that portion of the valley was revealing patches of the underlying city. "There's nothing left."

Rachel nodded as she studied the area through her scope. "Looks like a firestorm swept through the whole thing."

Vaughn and Angela exchanged knowing glances.

"It appears some places are still burning," Monique said, using her overly concise English. "I see streams of black smoke embedded in the haze."

Looking sideways, Vaughn watched his scattered teammates as they scanned the valley. "Anyone see anything moving?"

A chorus of 'No's rang out as everyone shook their heads.

Rourke suddenly became animated. "It's still running."

Vaughn's pulse quickened. "What is?" He turned to see the young man pointing to the right side of the valley, near the point where the tapered west end of Lake Geneva invaded the city's east side. Drier air was blowing off the water, pushing the fog from right to left. The receding obscuration had revealed a towering column of spraying water.

Monique nodded. "That is the Jet d'Eau. It literally means water jet. I cannot believe it is still running."

"It looks so tall," Rourke said. "Even from up here."

"It should." Monique nodded as she raised her binoculars to look at the feature. "The fountain shoots water five hundred feet into the air."

Shaking his head, Vaughn continued to scan the valley with his binos. "Focus, people. We're here to reconnoiter, not sight—"

"What is that?!" Monique said, cutting off Vaughn as she extended a finger and pointed toward the fountain.

"Blimey!" Bingham said as he studied the area through his field glasses. "It's an Airbus, an A380, the big double-decker one." He released a long, low whistle and then shook his head. "What's left of it, at any rate."

Vaughn shifted his binoculars and scanned the area around the fountain, at first not seeing what they were talking about. Then he spotted a wing protruding from the water at a steep angle. A moment later, he saw the nose of the thing sticking up as well. Initially, he'd mistook it for a massive boulder, but now he saw the broken-up and partially submerged remnants of the fuselage beyond the shattered radome and flayed cockpit. Twinned rows of black dots lined each section of the fuselage. The two lines of small windows revealed Chance was right. It was the giant, two-story-tall airplane.

They stared at it in silence. The broken, empty hulk served as a poignant reminder of what the Necks had stolen from them.

Angela had released his hand so that she could use her binoculars to study the scene. Now she patted his arm urgently.

Vaughn turned to see her looking at another part of the valley floor. "What?"

"I see something moving!"

"Where?" Following her line of sight, he swung his binos toward the area. The remnants of a cathedral towered over a destroyed city block. Its architecture reminded Vaughn of the Cathedral of Notre-Dame. The sight of its burned-out roof and partially collapsed steeple engendered memories of the tragic fire that had almost destroyed Notre-Dame back in 2019, although, during their flight over Paris, he'd glimpsed the cathedral in flames yet again.

Vaughn shook his head. "I don't see any movement. Where is it? Anywhere close to that partially collapsed cathedral?"

"Not far. Look a couple of blocks west of there."

Panning left, Vaughn scanned the ruined remnants of an apparent business district. The metal frames of its collapsed buildings extended from the rubble like the splayed ribs of a fallen giant. "I don't see any …" A glint of light drew his eye. Shifting his gaze, he zeroed in on the source. A bright, blue-white arc of light flickered to life and then died.

Vaughn blinked with sudden recognition. "That's a scavenger bot."

Mark looked at them. "Where?"

Pointing, Vaughn said, "A few blocks west of that chapel, about two klicks left of the lake."

In his peripheral vision, he saw everyone exchange nervous glances and then shift their gaze to study the area.

"It's a scavenger bot." Vaughn lowered his binoculars and looked at the still bandaged injuries on his right wrist. "Angela and I had a run-in with one of those bastards."

Monique lowered her field glasses and looked at Vaughn. "There is more than one." She tilted her head toward the city. "That business district is full of them."

Vaughn swept his glasses across the scene. The receding fog continued to reveal more of the ruined metropolis. It appeared there was at least one scavenger in each of the metal structures that occupied that portion of the city. Then he saw something larger move down one of the streets. Zooming in on the area, he watched a dump truck work its way down the cluttered roadbed, weaving between piles of debris as if a human driver were maneuvering it.

He looked at Angela. "Do you see that?"

She nodded. "Who do you think is driving it?"

Rourke's voice raised an octave. "Is that a truck?"

"A truck?" Rachel craned her neck to look over the edge and then aimed her rifle to scope the target. "Who's driving it?"

"No clue," Vaughn said as he continued to watch the vehicle.

It stopped in front of an object that was blocking the road. As if in answer to their questions, both doors of the truck flew open and two Necks emerged from the vehicle's cab.

Rourke turned wide eyes toward Vaughn. "Are those Necks?"

The muscles along Vaughn's jaw rippled as he ground his teeth. He nodded. "Ayup, sure the hell are."

As the group watched in stunned silence, the two robots walked to the front of their vehicle. Something long and dark lay across the road. The Necks moved to each end of the object and then, bending, picked it up effortlessly, each only using one of their four hands. Then they walked around to the back of the large vehicle. A moment later, they lifted the item into the air and tossed it into the bed. It wasn't until he saw the truck rock under the weight of the freshly deposited item that Vaughn realized how heavy it must have been.

In his peripheral vision, he saw Major Peterson's head snap back in surprise. "Son of a bitch! That was a street light pole."

Beside him, Teddy nodded. "Da. They lifted it like cardboard."

The members of the group turned and looked at Angela and Vaughn with varying levels of trepidation.

Rourke swallowed. His mouth worked a couple of times before he finally managed words. "You … You didn't tell us they were that strong."

Angela shook her head. "We didn't know."

Nervous chatter worked through the group.

"At ease, folks!" Vaughn said, whispering harshly to be heard. "This changes nothing. Hand-to-hand combat was never going to be an option. We already knew that much." He patted the weapons slung in an X across his back. "That's why we have these." He tilted his head toward Major Lee and smiled. "And our own spec ops badass."

Rachel grinned menacingly. "They come at us with one of those light poles, and I'll shove it right up their mechanical sphincter."

"Blimey!" Bingham said. "The woman is mad for arseholes."

Rachel looked at him and winked. "Especially for yours, Chauncey-Baby. You screw up down there, and I'll still be happy to shove my boot up that ass and wear you like a flip-flop."

Angela snorted, and a few nervous chuckles ran through the group.

"Now that we have that sorted," Vaughn said as he turned to look over the edge again, "let's get back to work."

Over the next few minutes, they watched as the fog slowly swept out of the city, leaving only trails of smoke in the hazy atmosphere.

The retreating obscurant revealed several additional vehicles. All over the business district, teams of Necks were filling trucks with scrap iron. Those that were fully loaded appeared to be heading west, toward the entrance to the supercollider, Vaughn assumed as he watched another one disappear into the fog that still blanketed that end of the valley.

He leaned toward Angela and spoke softly. "I haven't seen any movement within a mile of the lake."

Nodding, she pointed toward the cathedral they had spotted earlier. "Looks like the bots are focused on the central business district. Lots of steel in that area."

"Hey, Command-Oh. Why trucks? Why not just float the steel, levitate it, as you say?"

Monique looked at Teddy and answered for Angela. "They have likely not yet built the infrastructure to do so."

The cosmonaut's face twisted, the woman's overly formal English apparently confusing him.

"She's right, Teddy." Angela paused and pointed toward the still hidden entrance to the collider. "They probably haven't had enough time to build the equipment to manipulate gravity."

Teddy looked at Monique. "Why didn't you just say that?"

"I did, Theodore."

He smiled apologetically and then looked at Angela. "So they have to collect it manually?"

"Yeah, for now …" She paused, and her eyes lost focus.

Vaughn knew that look. Angela was working on another of her theories.

Angela nodded. "That would be specialized equipment. I'll bet they're still bringing parts for it through the wormhole."

Monique looked at her and then pointed at the line of westbound trucks. "Then, for what are they collecting all the metal?"

Teddy's face twisted as the woman's torturously rigid English further baffled the man.

Chewing her lip, Angela glanced at Vaughn and then shrugged as her gaze fell on the ruined city. "Guess we'll find out soon enough."

Major Peterson nodded slowly. Then he shrugged. "At least they can't use it on us."

Angela canted her head. "What do you mean, Bill?"

The dark skin of the man's forehead wrinkled. "Just that we won't have to worry about our guns or any other metal objects being yanked away from us."

Bingham's face soured. "Not yet, anyway. That can always change."

Giving up on the conversation, Teddy started scanning the valley. Then he raised a hand and pumped it wildly, pointing an extended finger toward the western end of the city. "What is that?"

As one, the group turned to follow his gesture.

It appeared Teddy was staring in the general direction of the ATLAS facility.

Studying the area with his naked eyes, Vaughn thought the fog might have thinned, but he still couldn't see the ground.

He raised his binoculars and saw a curving black line emerging from the top layers of the vapor. A moment later, it resolved as the upper extremities of a massive metal ring. His pulse quickened as the continued retreat of the fog bank revealed additional details.

Narrowing his eyes, Vaughn adjusted a knob on his binos and zoomed in on the area, focusing on the machinery beneath the base of the construct. Through the patchy haze that still clung to the ground, he saw several small lines snaking their way inward from the east.

Then the scale of it all became apparent.

Vaughn blinked several times. He peered over his binos and then looked through them again. He stared at what he now realized were three partially constructed city builders, the all-in-one machines that rode upon twinned, highway-sized mechanized tracks. One of the three had the beginnings of a stadium-sized cauldron emerging from its center. The circle he'd seen protruding through the fog was actually the top of the giant bowl.

"It's one of the cauldrons."

He heard a couple of gasps.

"It's empty and still has a few missing sections, but if we can't reset the timeline, it'll hold a few million gallons of molten metal soon."

Still gazing through the binos, he focused on the lines he'd seen streaming in from the east. Hundreds of dump trucks and eighteen-wheelers lined the streets that led up to the base of the cauldrons. The scale of the enormous machines dwarfed the vehicles that fed them.

"Are those the bloody lorries?" Bingham asked, sounding uncharacteristically humble.

Turning to look at the man, Vaughn nodded. "Yeah, those are the trucks we've been seeing."

Surprise broke through Monique's severe countenance. "Oh my word. The vehicles look tiny in comparison. I had no concept of the scale."

Beyond her, Teddy nodded. "Like ants walking under a laundry basket."

Mark stirred next to Vaughn. "Holy shit! So all that machinery … Those are the city builders you were talking about?"

Vaughn nodded. "The beginnings of three of them, anyway."

"Wait," Rourke said, turning toward Vaughn. "You said the buildings dwarfed the cauldrons."

"Yes, they did, and they will again if we don't stop them." Raising his binos again, Vaughn zoomed in on the ground beneath the machinery. "Looks like the whole mess is sitting right on top of ATLAS."

Major Bill Peterson scoffed. "Well, then, we sure as hell aren't getting in that way."

Vaughn turned a questioning look to Angela.

She raised her binoculars and began to scan the valley floor to the south of the ATLAS experiment entrance, closer to their current position. Then she nodded. "We'll just go in the same way Vaughn and I did the first time." Pausing, she pointed to an area of the burned-out city that lay between them and the entrance to CERN. "I think I see Marché Station."

Rourke craned his neck to see the area. "That's the subway entrance you two used to get in?"

Nodding, Vaughn raised his binoculars and scanned the area. "Yeah, the first time, anyway." Searching the rubble-strewn roads and still smoking hulks of gutted buildings, he soon identified the main thoroughfare that Angela had led them down the first time they had searched for the entrance. It was still quite far away, although significantly closer than ATLAS.

Spotting a familiar stone archway, Vaughn tried to turn the zoom knob, but it would go no farther. He narrowed his eyes and then nodded. "I see the entrance." He raised an arm to point. "It's right there along that main road, next to the … Wait." Seeing movement in an adjacent building, he shifted his field-of-view and saw a scavenger bot working inside the structure. Then he detected additional movement. Panning the field glasses, he slowly shook his head. "Crap," he said, drawing the word into two syllables. "We're not using it this time."

Mark looked at him. "Why not?"

"The area around the subway entrance is chockablock with scavenger bots."

"Shit, man," Teddy said, his surfer boy persona reemerging. "That's hella-thorny."

Monique spoke up as she continued to peer through her binos. "Is there another way into the subway, perhaps another station?"

"Yeah," Vaughn said. Looking over the edge again, he studied the land beyond Marché Station. "We passed through several of them on our way to the collider."

Panning upward, he inspected the burned-out remnants of the city, seeking another entrance. Block after ruined block slowly slid across the narrow field of view afforded by the zoomed-in binoculars. Then he spotted a cleared area where something had shoved aside the rubble, leaving the ground smooth. It was roughly rectangular and had a dark black square at its center. He tilted his head. "I think I see another entrance, but it looks like they've done something …"

The forgotten words fell from his mouth as a horse-sized, multi-legged black monstrosity emerged from the square black void that he now realized must be a vertical shaft.

Vaughn's pulse pounded in his ears as he stared at the robot that had emerged from the opening in the ground. With its many and frenzied legs, the thing looked like a giant mechanical caterpillar.

"Where?" Major Peterson asked as he raised his binoculars and started to scan the area. Then he flinched. "Slap my ass and call me a donkey! What the hell is that?!"

Having seen the same thing, Angela lowered her field glasses and looked at Vaughn with a face drained of color. "It must be one of those construction bots, the ones we saw climbing up the sides of the towers and working on their tops."

Teddy looked at her with widening eyes. "You have seen this before?"

Watching the monstrous insectile bot slither across the ground, Vaughn shook his head. "No, not this clearly anyway."

"Wh-Where?" Rourke stammered. "Where did you see them?"

Vaughn twisted his face. "I might have forgotten to mention these."

Bill looked at him accusingly. "How in the hell do you forget to mention ten-foot-long mother-effing caterpillars?!"

Rachel's head snapped toward the man. "Keep your voice down, Major Peterson."

He looked at her and nodded and then shifted his gaze back to Vaughn, eyebrows raised in a look that said 'Go ahead.'

"When we first saw the city, there were lines of black dots streaming from the industrial facilities. They were climbing the sides of the newer buildings, the incomplete ones. They covered the tops of the ones that were still under construction."

Teddy's brow furrowed. "There were many of these things?"

Raising his binos and staring at the menacing-looking machine, Vaughn tried to swallow. His suddenly dry throat clicked in his ears. He nodded. "Thousands of them."

As if on cue, several dozen of the caterpillar-like robots began to stream from the opening. Spotting additional movement near the top of his field of view, Vaughn shifted the binoculars upward and found a similar aperture. "I see another shaft."

Angela lowered her field glasses and looked at him. "Where?"

Raising his free hand, Vaughn pointed to the area. "It's a few blocks north of the first one."

As everyone else focused on the new shaft, Vaughn zoomed out and then blinked. "There are more openings. They're in a line that points toward the construction site above the ATLAS experiment."

Angela nodded. "Looks like they're following the rough outline of the subway's underground passage."

A realization struck Vaughn.

He lowered the binoculars and looked at Angela. "Those must be the shafts they'll use later to access the aboveground portions of the city. They're building the infrastructure to support it all."

"Uh ..." Major Peterson started but then paused.

Vaughn turned to see the man slowly shaking his head as he continued to stare through his binoculars.

Finally, Bill found his voice again. "So ... So you're saying the entire subway is ..." His Adam's apple bobbed. "... is full of those things?"

Vaughn slowly shook his head in disgust as he zoomed in on one of the machines. "Yeah, I think it is."

The caterpillar dug into a pile of debris, viciously extracting a large hunk of steel. It shook the item like a dog shaking a rag. Dust and debris flew off of it in every direction.

"Oh, hell no!" Bill dropped his binos and started backing away from the ledge. "Nope. Nope. Nope. I am not fucking with an army of ten-foot-long mechanical caterpillars."

Monique looked at Major Peterson, and her eyes narrowed. "Get your black ass back here, William."

Blinking, Vaughn lowered his binoculars and turned to look at Monique. It was the first time he'd heard her use anything close to a swear word. The tall African-American woman was leering at Major Peterson.

She pointed at the ground next to her. "Get back in position, and help us find another way!"

The man hesitated.

Monique glared at Bill as she tilted her head toward Rachel. "You think having your ass used as a flip-flop sounds painful? Try me, William. You will wish a metal caterpillar was your only problem."

The big man's visage took on that of a scolded puppy. He looked from Monique to the city and back to the woman as if trying to decide which was the greater threat. Evidently deciding the nearer of the two represented a more imminent danger, he slowly returned to the indicated position.

Still regarding the man with her lips pressed into a thin line, Monique nodded curtly and then looked at Angela. "As I recall, the collider has a circumference of almost seventeen miles. Is there another access point we may use?"

Angela nodded. "Yes, actually. There's one for each major experiment."

Raising his binoculars, Teddy started scanning the valley floor. "Where are they, Command-Oh?"

Vaughn looked at Angela, eyebrows raised. "Uh, yeah, Command-Oh, where?"

Angela looked at him defensively. "I never mentioned it because, at the time, it was already covered by the machine city."

"Oh … Guess you got a point."

Pursing her lips, Angela turned from Vaughn and started surveying the valley. "There are three other large scale experiments, each with its own entrance."

"Those are the only other entrances?" Mark asked as he, too, followed her gaze.

"No, there are dozens of smaller ones, emergency evacuation shafts, but I don't know the exact location of those. They only have small buildings at their exit points, but the experiments each have large aboveground facilities, buildings we should be able to see from here."

Peering through his binos again, Vaughn searched the region Angela was scanning but didn't see anything that stood out. "Where are they?"

"Picture the ring as a clock." Raising an arm, she pointed toward the alien construction site. "As seen from our current vantage point,

ATLAS sits at the collider's seven o'clock position." She shifted her gesture to point farther west. "The next experiment over is ALICE. Its ground-level access is at the ring's nine o'clock position."

As she spoke, Angela continued to search the indicated area.

Vaughn again tried to follow her gaze. She appeared to be looking at an area a mile or two northwest of the robot construction site. The wind had swept the last of the fog from the region.

Smoke streaked the valley floor like the septic veins of a dying world, hazing the otherwise relatively clear atmosphere.

Dark clouds pregnant with a coming storm still hung above the northern mountains. Other than an occasional flash of internal lightning, it didn't appear any closer. Not yet, anyway, Vaughn thought.

Angela pointed. "It should be over there, just beyond the western edge of the city." Blinking, she lowered her field glasses and peered over them. "They're gone."

Vaughn looked from her back to the edge of town. "What is?"

"The buildings. They're all gone."

"Maybe they burned up," Mark said.

"No." Angela squinted through her binos. "I'm looking right at the area. The ground is smooth, almost like it's been paved over."

Locating the indicated section, Vaughn saw what she was talking about. It was a large, rectangular patch of ground absent of any structures, burned or otherwise. Then movement drew his eye. A black dot crawled up from an unseen hole in the ground.

He realized it had to be one of the caterpillar construction bots.

Bill groaned. "That's another massive load of Nope!"

"Crud," Angela said as she shifted away from the region. She started searching the ground east of Marché Station. It appeared she was looking at a parcel just beyond Geneva's airport. "Maybe Beauty's access is still intact."

Raising his binos, Vaughn pivoted into position and searched the area.

"What beauty?" Teddy asked.

"It's the name for the experiment where we were trying to discern why the universe has more matter than anti-matter."

"Da," the cosmonaut said, nodding sagely.

When Vaughn looked at the man, Teddy stared back at him with a befuddled expression.

"Dammit!" Angela said and then released a frustrated growl.

"What?" Vaughn turned and squinted through his binos. "What is it?"

"Same thing. Paved over. Nothing but caterpillar bots."

Vaughn gnashed his teeth. They were running out of options.

Apparently, Rourke had the same concerns. When the young man spoke, his voice sounded an octave higher than usual. "What do we do if we're cut off, if we can't reach ATLAS?"

Still scanning the valley through her binoculars, Angela said, "Like I told you, we don't have to get to ATLAS. Part of the collider's High-Luminosity upgrade was an expanded intranet. They even called it the HiLumi Intranet. There's a firewall that prevents external access, but if I can reach a HiLumi-enabled computer terminal anywhere within the collider complex, I should be able to initiate the overload."

"Yeah," Rourke said, not sounding the least bit reassured. He pointed toward Geneva. "But how are we going to get in there with monster caterpillars crawling all over the place? They're cutting off all of your access points."

Angela lowered her field glasses and looked at Vaughn, a smile blossoming on her face. Then she leaned forward and addressed the entire group. "The CMS facility is still intact." She pointed across the valley. "It's on the far side of the ring, about the one o'clock position as seen from here."

Raising his binos, Vaughn studied the indicated area. "Where is it?"

"Just past the northwest side of the city."

Everyone else sighted in on the region.

Rachel used the scope on her rifle. Then she glanced at Angela and cocked an eyebrow. "Could you be a little less specific?"

Angela rolled her eyes. "You don't have to be a smart ass." Sighing, she raised an arm and pointed. "Okay ... see the ski slope on the far side of the valley?"

Vaughn did. Snow still clung to a few of its trails. Even through the hazed atmosphere, the small white patches glowed starkly against the otherwise dark mountainside.

Teddy's head bobbed. "Da, Command-Oh, I see it."

"Me, too," Mark said.

"Everyone else see it?"

"Good," she said after receiving an affirmative nod from the rest of the group. Angela shifted the aim of her gesture. "Now pan down from there until you see a broad patch of farm fields between two villages. You'll see the area below and just a tad to the right of the ski slopes."

"I think I see the facility," Rachel said. "Is it that group of gray buildings?"

Angela nodded. "Yeah. The ones right in the middle of that farmland."

Bingham lowered his binoculars and looked at Angela and Vaughn. "How in bloody hell are we supposed to get all the way over there? That's the far side of the valley."

Rachel raised her gun until it appeared she was aiming it at the top of the far ridgeline. Still gazing through her scope, she said, "Maybe we can fly the V-22 around to the back side of the ski slope and come in from there." Just as she finished saying it, a massive bolt of lightning struck the top of that mountain.

Bill Peterson shook his head. "Nope!" He pointed toward the far side of Geneva. "Besides, our entire ingress will be exposed. Every robot in the valley will see us all the way down the mountain and as we cross those fields."

Vaughn turned his attention back to the fountain and the eastern portion of the city that surrounded it. The area still looked clear. The robots hadn't ventured that far east yet. Recalling the topology of Mont Salève, he nodded. "I think I know a better way, one that won't expose us to observation or require us to fly into that line of thunderstorms."

Rourke looked at him with wide nervous eyes. "H-How?"

Vaughn grinned menacingly. "As our token Millennial, you're really not going to like this."

CHAPTER 19

Rourke stared at his endlessly swinging boots. The passage of each launched a small cloud of ash from the pavement. Their pendulous back-and-forth movements mesmerized him. He felt as if—

"Heads up, boy-oh," Wing Commander Bingham said, breaking his trance.

Blinking, Rourke looked up. "Huh?" His mind felt foggy as if he were coming out of a dream.

"It's bad enough you've been staring at your feet for the last three miles, but now we're close to the heart of the city, son. You need to keep your head on a swivel."

Vaughn looked back at him and spoke softly. "He's right. We're close now. Help us keep an eye out."

Rourke nodded and began to scan the ruined city around them visually. He had allowed his weapon to droop, but now he held it across his body, its muzzle pointing away from the center of the formation, mimicking the way the others carried theirs.

They'd been walking for almost three hours now. After backtracking through the woods that buttressed the mountain's balcony-like terrace, Vaughn had led them down a trail that descended the northeast end of the ridgeline. When they had reached the wooded foot of the mountain, they had emerged from the scorched periphery of the forest and stepped into the broken and burned city. Both business parks and residential neighborhoods alike had fallen to the all-consuming inferno.

Even now, broken remnants of burned-out structures stabbed into the smoky sky all around them. Row upon row of shattered apartments gnawed at the choked atmosphere like the fractured teeth of a giant's lower jaw.

Vaughn had guided them northeast for several blocks after they'd reached the streets of Geneva, making the detour to keep plenty of room between them and the robot-occupied portions of the city. Eventually, they had turned northwest and headed toward the towering column of spraying water that marked the lake's west end.

Presently, they walked up to a major intersection. Vaughn waved them to the near side of a mound of broken masonry. "Time to start tactical ops. We'll break up into two teams." He pointed at Major Lee, Colonel Hennessy, Lieutenant Gheist, and Wing Commander Bingham. "You five are Team One." He gestured at the other four humans and the robot. "We'll be Team Two. We'll advance through this part of the city five at a time. One team will cover while the other advances, taking turns. Cover then move. Cover then move. Any questions?"

Everyone shook their heads. Rourke hadn't expected any questions. They'd discussed the tactic in detail back in England and had even done a few practice runs around the facility. He'd also employed the same tactic for years while playing *Call of Duty* with his friends.

Vaughn peered around the corner and then nodded. "Looks clear." He gestured left and right. "Team One, take up covering positions. Scan your sectors just like we trained."

After the other team moved to cover them, Vaughn nodded to the robot. "BOb, take point." Then he motioned to Rourke and the rest of Team Two. "Let's move."

They spent the next half-hour leap-frogging their way across the city, each maneuver drawing them ever closer to the busy, broken heart of Geneva.

Ahead, the fountain still licked at the sky, although now they'd drawn close enough that Rourke had to tilt his head back to see its entire height.

Between maneuvers, while the two teams were gathered behind piled clumps of wrecked cars, Vaughn gestured at the tablet clutched in his hand. "We're only a few blocks away from the Mont-Blanc Bridge. It's just to the left by the fountain. That'll be our closest pass to the robots. I wouldn't be taking you that close, but the lake is forcing my hand. It's way too big to go around, and if we tried to cross it, we'd be completely exposed."

Each member of the group silently acknowledged his words with a nod.

While Team One advanced, Rourke heard a light scuffing sound followed by a muffled string of curse words behind him. He looked back and saw Bill Peterson grimacing as he massaged his right knee.

Seeing Rourke staring at him, the major released the leg and stood straight. He stepped forward in preparation for the next advance. As Bill moved, he waved a hand dismissively. Speaking so that only Rourke could hear him, he said, "Old football injury. Knee gets a hitch in it every now and again. It'll go away. Always does. I'll be fine."

The man didn't look fine to Rourke. Over the next few minutes, he watched as the major's limp worsened. During each advance, Peterson was covering their rear, following close behind the group. Because of that, none of the other team members had noticed the man's building discomfort.

At the next cover point, just as the other team joined them, Rourke surreptitiously glanced at Peterson and then extended a hand toward Vaughn. "My feet are killing me. Any chance we can take a break?"

Bingham muttered something about him being a *bloody uphill gardener*, whatever that meant.

Apparently, it wasn't good. Monique turned and glared at the man.

The Wing Commander held his hands out and smiled at the woman. "Lighten up, Colonel Klink. I'm just taking the piss, having the boy on."

Vaughn turned. "Keep it down, folks." He gestured at the wing commander. "Cut the shit, Chance." Then he looked at Rourke and pointed ahead. "There's a parking garage on this side of the bridge. We'll rest there."

"Thanks, Captain."

"Don't thank me. We all need a break. Besides, that'll be our closest approach to the occupied portion of the city. It'll give me a moment to recon and evaluate our situation."

They advanced in silence for the next several minutes. The bridge grew closer with each maneuver.

As the fountain started to slide off to their right, the towering column of water jetted hundreds of feet into the sky. They still hadn't drawn close enough to hear any of the alien robots, so the noise of the thing generated the only sound in a lifeless world.

A north breeze carried its mist along a path that paralleled theirs. It wasn't close enough to soak them, but it further cooled the air, and Rourke could smell the ozone generated by the spray. It was a welcome relief from the acrid and often foul odors that had assaulted his senses since they'd first emerged from the woods at the base of the mountain.

They closed to within half a block of the bridge. The road began to widen precipitously, forcing them to take longer sprints across wide-open spaces.

A few moments later, the last maneuver carried them to the southern end of the bridge.

Just as Vaughn had promised, a dark opening sat on its left side. The mouth of the subterranean garage entrance yawned skyward like a hungry bird.

Having reached it first, Rourke advanced a few feet down the ramp before pulling up short. A reflection of the sky shone on water that covered the sloping pavement ahead of him.

Vaughn walked past Rourke and extracted a flashlight from his belt. "Shit! Looks like the pumps failed. The water is the same height in here as it is in the lake. Guess it found a way in." As he spoke, he stooped further and directed the beam of his flashlight into the inky blackness. Only a couple of feet separated the top of the water from the garage's low ceiling. The light bounced crazily in the narrow darkness beyond, casting curling waves of light across the exposed rooftops of the few vehicles tall enough to protrude from their watery graves.

Scanning the walls of the ramp, Rourke did a double-take as he spotted a half-submerged poster plastered to the wall on one side. The turban-covered head of a gray-haired, bearded man peeked above the gently lapping water. Rourke tilted his head. "That's an odd slogan for a religious leader."

Mark glanced over. "Huh? What is?"

"Don't be a dick."

The dark skin of the tall astronaut's forehead puckered. "What the hell? I wasn't being a dick."

Eyes flying wide, Rourke held up his hands. "No, no, no." He pointed at the poster. "This guy said it … I mean, shit. That's what it says here, above his head."

Vaughn looked back. "We'll keep that in mind." He gestured at the depressed area formed by the ramp. "This is low enough. It'll work. We'll take a break here."

All heads turned and looked up the ramp as the high-pitched whine of a distant electric motor pierced the air, rising above the omnipresent sound of spraying water.

Crouching near the top of the ramp, Rourke could see a narrow sliver of the city to his west, the direction from which the sound was coming. A river-like finger of the body of water extended along his line of sight, delving another half-mile into Geneva. Its gently winding path carried it toward the occupied portion of the ruined metropolis. Roads paralleled each side of the channel. Several arcing bridges spanned the waterway, connecting the two roadways.

As the volume of the noise slowly increased, the members of both teams joined him near the top of the ramp.

The nine of them plus the robot gazed west, crouching along the sidewall, only the tops of their heads extending above ground level. A line of desiccated shrubs ran along the edge of the ramp, providing a measure of concealment.

Rourke peered between the narrow trunks of two leafless shrubs and stared down the waterway, seeking the source of the rising electrical whine. It sounded like a motor, a rather large one.

Several blocks to their west, a large truck rolled out from behind a building, emerging onto the road that ran along the south side of the shoreline, kicking up dust as it approached rapidly.

Rourke's breath hitched in his chest.

Had they been discovered?

Vaughn grabbed the back of Rourke's shirt and pulled him down the ramp. "Everyone take cover!" he whispered urgently. "They might be able to see heat."

Rourke nodded. He knew the man was right. If the eyes of the robots were sensitive to infrared energy, the heat of their human heads would shine like light bulbs.

Still crouched, they quickly descended the ramp, taking cover in the shallow space afforded by the entrance into the watery automotive catacombs.

Rourke's pounding heart was in his throat. Its pulse raced in his ears. He held his gun tightly in shaking hands.

Looking behind him, he considered whether or not to retreat into the water. It was still quite cool outside. It was early spring. There had not been sufficient time for the water to warm. Likely, it was barely above freezing. Then there was the smell. Oil and other liquids floated on the surface of the water, oozing noxious fumes.

As he began to back toward the polluted mass, Rourke felt a hand on his forearm.

He turned to see Rachel smiling at him reassuringly. "It's okay, Rourky. I don't think they saw us. They were still quite a way off."

After swallowing, he gave her a nod.

The sound of the whining electric motor grew louder. He realized it must be one of the newer electric trucks. Not that it mattered. Electric, diesel, or gas, it was likely occupied by a pair of robots capable of throwing light poles single-handedly … which didn't bode well for what they could do to the likes of him.

They exchanged nervous glances as the growl of tires on pavement joined the rising noise.

He looked at Rachel from beneath a puckered forehead. "It's still coming. Doesn't sound like it's slowing down either."

He saw concern in her eyes. She opened her mouth to respond, but Captain Singleton waved for her. "Major Lee. With me."

She nodded and stepped to his side.

Vaughn waved for BOb to follow. Then he motioned for the rest to hold back.

Eyes widening, Rourke watched as the odd trio low-crawled up the ramp. Reaching the top, two humans raised their heads and snuck a quick peek at the approaching vehicle.

Rourke swallowed. The dry click it elicited momentarily over-topped the cacophony of his pounding heart.

He exchanged a nervous glance with Monique.

Mark Hennessy leaned toward the trio. "What do you see?"

Angela peered over the colonel's shoulder. "Wh-What's it doing?"

Vaughn waved them back. Pressing his lips together, he shook his head. "It's still coming."

Rourke's fingers dug into the side of his weapon. He started to rock back and forth as he cursed under his breath. "Shit, shit, *shit*! This is *nothing* like *Call of Duty*!"

CHAPTER 20

Lying on his back at the top of the ramp, Vaughn gripped the stock of his M4 assault rifle tightly. Through sheer force of will, he managed to keep his breathing rate in check as he peeked over the wall and eyed the rapidly approaching vehicle again. "Nothing to see here. Turn around, you sons a bitches."

Rachel stared at him.

He looked at her and nodded. "Still coming." Then, looking at the robot, he pointed in the direction of the onrushing vehicle. "BOb, if that truck gets within fifty meters, I want you to disable it with your EMP gun."

Rachel looked at him sharply and then looked at the EMP cannon askance. "You going to put all your eggs in that thing?"

"We need to know what it does to them."

Rachel looked ready to say more, but Vaughn held up Angela's much smaller EMP gun. "If BOb's gun doesn't take them out, I'll shoot them with this."

"Does it have the range?"

After raising his head to check the vehicle's progress, he looked at Rachel. "Hell if I know, but at the speed they're going, their inertia will carry them close enough." He shrugged and held up the small gun again. "If their backward-assed-bending legs are still kicking, I'll finish off the bastards with this."

Rachel turned down the corner of her mouth and nodded. "Okay … Sounds like a plan." She pointed at the small gun. "Just be damned fast with Noisy Cricket there. Don't give them a chance to alert their friends."

Vaughn turned back to the robot. "When the time comes, hit 'em with max power. It'd be awesome if you took out both the truck and the Necks."

BOb nodded. His voice acquired a mildly lilted, pompous accent that almost sounded British. "Trust the awesomeness, Captain Asshole."

Vaughn did a double-take. He'd given the bot specific instructions. This was no time for the thing to start glitching.

Seeing Rachel smirk, he waved a hand. "Never mind that." He pointed at her M4. "I know your rifle has a silencer, but those rarely live up to the promise of their name. Don't open fire unless it's our only option."

She nodded and then guffawed. "Roger, Captain Asshole."

Vaughn gave her a pained look. "Et tu, Brute?"

"That'll teach you to program the robot when I'm in earshot."

Her smile faltered as the sound of the onrushing truck rose to new heights.

Vaughn didn't want to expose the heat signature of his head, so he gestured at the battlebot. "Your skin temp still maintaining background neutral?"

BOb nodded.

"Good." He pointed at the ramp's sidewall. "I want you to *slowly* move into a firing position there. Keep us updated on its distance."

Nodding again, the robot raised a few inches and peered over the wall. At the same time, it brought up its EMP cannon and aimed it at the vehicle. "Four hundred meters, sir."

"A quarter-mile," Vaughn said. "They'll turn."

Rachel cocked an eyebrow. "They better."

"They will, or they won't. Either way, we'll be ready."

Vaughn and Rachel exchanged nods. She looked like a coiled spring, ready to pounce.

Closing his eyes, Vaughn took a deep breath and then slowly released it. As always happened when potential combat drew near, he felt everything slow down. The pulse pounding in his ears seemed to subside, and his breathing rate halved. A Zen-like silence descended as a quiet calm fell over him. The ever-present sound of the fountain faded into the background. At the same moment, he became acutely aware of the noises generated by his surroundings: the shuffling feet and the heavy breathing of those behind him, the pop of small gravel launched from under the edge of the truck's tires, the tissue paper-tearing sound of sand and ash spraying up in its wake.

Metal clanked loudly as the rambling vehicle bounced sharply on its hard springs, sounding as if it had run over something in the road.

Other than a steady increase in its volume, the noises coming from the vehicle remained unchanged as it continued to close on their position.

"Two hundred meters," announced BOb.

Grinding his teeth together, Vaughn growled. "Turn, already."

"One hundred meters."

"Shit." Vaughn prepared to stand. He reached out to tap the robot and order it to fire.

The sound of the vehicle dropped precipitously and then vanished.

"Target has stopped ... Standby." BOb tilted his head curiously. "Vehicle appears empty."

"Wait ... What?"

He exchanged another glance with Rachel.

She shrugged.

BOb looked down. "What are your orders, Captain?"

"Hold your fire."

Rising slowly, Vaughn peered over the wall.

The truck sat motionlessly a couple of hundred feet from their observation point. Peering over the sights of his rifle, Vaughn stared into the vehicle's cab. "BOb's right," he whispered. "It looks empty."

Rachel eased into a firing position beside him. Aiming her rifle at the target, she studied the truck through her scope.

"See anything?"

She shook her head. "Looks like it's empty. Must be a self-driving truck. Judging by the way it's riding, I think the bed is as empty as the cab."

"Yeah, I saw that. The thing was bouncing like it had no suspension, like there wasn't enough weight to compress its springs."

They both twitched as the electric truck started moving again. It turned left onto a bridge and crossed the narrow channel.

When it reached the opposite bank, it turned left again and headed west, away from them.

Then it stopped once more.

Rachel continued to peer through her scope. She shook her head. "Still don't see anything."

BOb suddenly shifted the aim of the EMP cannon. "New targets."

Turning, Vaughn saw two Necks emerging from a side road. Each carried armloads of scrap steel. Reaching the truck, they tossed the metallic refuse into its bed. It landed with a tremendous crash, and the vehicle lurched under the weight of the impact.

Vaughn released the breath he'd been holding. It was just another scavenging run.

Hearing feet shuffling nervously behind him, he turned and gave the rest of the team a thumbs-up.

Beside him, Rachel blew out a long sigh and rested her head against the stock of her rifle. "Thank you, thank you, thank you."

For the next few minutes, they watched as the robots and their truck continued west, drawing farther away with each movement.

Finally, the vehicle and the two Necks passed out of sight.

Vaughn ordered BOb to hold position and maintain a lookout. Then he and Rachel eased back from the wall.

As they walked the few steps down the ramp and rejoined the group, Vaughn received a handful of questioning looks.

Angela held her hands out, palms up and mouthed, "What happened?"

Placing a finger over his lips, he waved them into a tight circle.

Rachel hitched a thumb, pointing back over her shoulder. Whispering, she said, "It was an empty self-driving truck."

"She's right. The thing was coming back for another load of steel."

Eyes widening, Rourke looked at him. "Self-driving? One of ours?"

Vaughn nodded.

"Son of a bitch." Rourke slowly shook his head. "They're using our own technology against us?"

"Nothing new, chap," Bingham said with an exasperated sigh. "The tossers have been doing that since they first latched onto our collider."

The distant crash of another deposited load echoed off the remnants of the surrounding buildings.

Vaughn gestured over his shoulder. "It's moved back into the city. There are a couple of Necks loading it up as it goes, but they've moved out of sight. We're clear for now."

Light flickered outside.

Vaughn glanced toward the top of the ramp and then looked back at the group. "Was that lightn—?"

The tremendous boom of a thunderclap cut off his words and answered his unfinished question with its rolling reverberations.

Vaughn motioned for everyone to hold fast. Returning to the underground garage's exit, he poked his head out and looked north.

The mountain range that lined the far side of the valley had disappeared, hidden behind a steel-gray curtain of rain. The downpour hung from the billowing black belly of the tumultuous clouds that were slowly invading the region.

Vaughn had been so focused on the bots and their truck, he'd forgotten all about the coming storm. Now he saw that its brassy glare had sapped the last vestige of color from a city already rendered in shades of coal by the inferno that had eaten it.

Lightning split the sky again, a blinding shock of white arcing down from the obsidian wall cloud. It forked silently and pierced the unsuspecting earth miles to his west. As usual, the thunderclap shouted its warning too late.

A moment later, the last of the rumble rolled away, and a new noise rose to replace it.

Vaughn ducked, thinking it the sound of another approaching vehicle, but peering west, he saw nothing moving.

Turning to follow the noise to its source, he looked north. At the far end of the Mont-Blanc Bridge, the charred stubble of a flag at the top of an oddly bent pole started to move. Initially, it fluttered lazily, but then it started flapping like a playing card jammed into the speeding spokes of a child's bicycle. Beneath it, the branches of a denuded tree began to sway like seagrass caught in manic waves.

The approaching wind front lifted ash and debris, generating a dust storm. Beyond the rattling flag remnant, flames sprang anew from a previously smoldering ruin, the winds of the storm front breathing life into the coals of the apocalypse.

Vaughn looked back at his team and waved urgently. "Time to go!"

CHAPTER 21

As she walked down the avenue with Vaughn at her side, Angela stared at her dust- and soot-covered boots. The military members of the group had raved about how comfortable they were, and they had seemed so ... *four hours ago*!

She glanced at Vaughn and pointed at her boots. "Didn't you say these were state-of-the-art and top-of-the-line?"

He gave her a knowing look. "You walk this many miles in a matter of a few hours, and it doesn't matter how well made they are. Your feet are going to hurt."

She pulled off her bandanna and goggles. "The winds have let up some." Continuing to walk, she took off her backpack and stuffed the items inside. "Don't think we need these anymore." She eyed the storm front warily and added, "I just hope we make it to CMS before the rain reaches us."

Vaughn nodded. "Now that the winds have died off, it looks like the thing has stalled out again." He checked the map. "Few more miles to go."

"I'm just glad we have the strength to do this. Can you imagine what this would've been like a couple of weeks ago?"

Vaughn blew air through his nose. "Nope."

They walked in silence as her words sent both of them into their own thoughts.

Angela's eyes lost focus as she remembered how she'd felt when the reset returned her to the ISS. It seemed an eon ago. So much had transpired since. She shook the memory and the dread it eschewed from her thoughts and looked back at Vaughn.

He smiled and nodded at her. "You look a lot better."

Angela smirked. "Oh, Captain. You really know the path to a girl's heart," she said wryly.

"I'm just saying that—"

Angela smiled and waved a hand at him. "Just screwing with you. You're right. We both do. Amazing what a week of good food and sleep can do."

They walked in silence again, continuing to scan the buildings around them.

Since leaving the shelter of the parking garage, they had progressed several miles across the city. Initially, they had followed Lake Geneva's opposite shoreline, hanging a right after crossing the bridge and staying low to keep out of sight of any potential enemy robots. Using Vaughn's tactical leap-frogging advances, they had followed the shoreline northeast until they were once again well clear of the mechanized infestation. Then they had turned left, heading to the northwest, toward the CMS experiment.

At that point, they had dropped the tactical maneuvers in favor of what Vaughn called a forced march.

As she continued the long hike on aching feet, Angela looked at Vaughn and grinned crookedly. "This reminds me of our first long hike up the back side of Mont Salève." A small laugh escaped her. "I can still see the look on your face when you realized how close you'd come to falling off that ledge on our way up."

"Ha, ha. Laugh it up."

Angela's smile withered. Giving him a meaningful look, she tilted her head toward the city center. "That was before we knew what waited for us on the other side."

Vaughn nodded somberly. "We sure as hell know now."

"Speaking of ..." Angela paused and scanned the road ahead. "Are we near the airport yet?"

"Yeah, about a half-mile from its northeast tip. This avenue should skirt its right perimeter fence."

"Good. If I remember right, it's pretty much a straight shot from there to CERN Entrance Five."

"Yeah, it would be, but we're gonna veer right in a few blocks. I don't want to get too close to the airport. That's a wide expanse of land. We'll be too exposed." He pointed off to the right. "So I plan to sidestep a block or two after we get closer."

"Why not do so now?"

"For the same reason. That wide expanse will give us a good, unobstructed view of the city. It's a good recon point, especially now that the dust has settled."

Angela watched Vaughn as he spoke. He had changed. She wasn't sure when it had happened, but gradually, over the course of the day, she had picked up on subtle differences in him. Good things. She liked the way he'd taken charge. He wasn't hesitating anymore. He seemed more sure of himself. The lingering doubts seemed to have vanished.

Vaughn looked at her and canted his head. "What?"

"Nothing. Was just thinking you look stronger now, like you did back in Tripoli."

He nodded. Pushing out his otherwise flat belly, he patted it and smiled. "Good food and good drink." He winked at her. "Company's not bad either."

Angela chuckled and held out a hand. "Whatever." She gestured at their fellow survivors. "I feel better that it's not just the two of us this time. Everything doesn't hinge on us. The world won't end, literally, if one of these buildings collapses on top of you and me."

Vaughn scoffed. "Not afraid of death now?"

The corners of her mouth flexed contemplatively, and she shrugged. "I have a healthy respect for it, but no, I don't fear death. I had accepted that we were going to die the last time I overloaded the collider. Guess everything after that is just borrowed time, a bonus."

Vaughn walked in contemplative silence. Then he gave her a sideward glance. "There's more than that. Now we have a big, red, easy button, a 'Ready Player Two' reset."

"What do you mean?"

Vaughn grinned. "Just saying, if it comes to it, and we have to, one of us can just overload the collider again as a last-ditch reset. We can start over."

Scoffing, Angela cocked an eyebrow as she gave Vaughn a knowing look. "God help us if you're the one left to push that button."

He gave her a double-take. "What are you saying? You're the one who taught me how to do it."

Angela blew air through her nose and kicked a piece of debris with her dirty boot. "Yeah, but I've seen you with a computer. I don't like our chances."

"Guess you got a point there," Vaughn said through a lopsided grin.

Angela looked ahead. Between two buildings, she glimpsed a long expanse of chain-linked fence. Raising a hand, she pointed at it. "I think we've found the airport."

Vaughn followed her gesture and nodded.

Ahead of them, BOb suddenly dropped to the ground and lay prone.

The rest of the team began to do the same.

She looked down and saw that Vaughn had also dropped to the ground.

He waved urgently. "Get down!"

A metallic squeaking echoed off a nearby wall. Then the roar of a distant engine filled the air.

Angela dropped down onto her belly and then low-crawled up next to Vaughn.

Giving her a sideways glance, he cocked an eyebrow. "Try to keep up next time."

"Very funny." She looked around, searching for the source of the noise, but from her new position lying on the street, she couldn't see anything beyond a few meters. "Where's that sound coming from?"

"Don't know."

After scanning their surroundings, Vaughn signaled for everyone's attention. Then he pointed at a structure on their left.

The one-story building was relatively intact and appeared to have been a small grocery store. It had a flat roof and had previously featured an all-glass front façade, although that had all blown out during the firestorm that had consumed the surrounding buildings.

Vaughn jabbed a finger at the store. "We'll take cover in there." He gestured at the robot. "BOb, cover our six."

The bot dipped its head. "Roger, sir."

Vaughn exchanged a silent glance with Rachel and then pointed a bladed hand toward the store.

The major nodded. Rising to a low crouch, she moved onto the building's front stoop. After a quick glimpse into the store's darkened interior, she disappeared inside. A few moments later, she reemerged and waved them in. "All clear."

Pointing ahead, Vaughn signaled for Angela to go first.

She nodded. Heart pounding in her chest, she crawled to her feet and hustled inside. The sounds of shuffling feet erupted from behind her as the rest of the group rose to follow her.

Shattered glass crunched underfoot as she trotted past the major and entered the store. Fortunately, the distant rumble of heavy machinery all but drowned out the sound.

Rachel pointed down an aisle. "Post up by those bottles."

Angela nodded. Avoiding the worst of the shattered bits of glass, she walked deeper into the building and stopped at the indicated position. Then she pulled a toppled water bottle from a nearby shelf. After wiping off the worst of the dust, she removed the cap and took a long draw.

Teddy stepped up next to her and grabbed a Coke. "Good idea, Command-Oh."

She turned and watched the rest of the team work their way into the building. Rourke and Monique followed by Bill and Chance joined her. Then Mark Hennessy walked up.

Finally, Rachel and Vaughn joined them with BOb in tow.

Following the examples set by Angela and Teddy, everyone grabbed bottles and started drinking.

Major Peterson took a long draw from an orange soda. He glanced toward the street and then back at the group. Light gray soot streaked the dark skin of the man's face. "Anyone see what's making that sound?"

They all shook their heads, even the robot.

After scanning the interior of the store, Vaughn pointed at the ground behind a rack of canned goods near the front. "BOb, take cover behind that and keep an eye out for any movement outside." Then he looked at the rest of the group. "Spread out. See if you can find roof access. This is the highest building in the area. If we can get on the roof, we might be able to see where that noise is coming from."

Rachel held up her water bottle and nodded to Angela. "Good idea." Turning to walk deeper into the store, she called over her shoulder. "Grab something to eat while you're looking. No sense in using up what we're carrying."

Heading off in a different direction, Angela pulled a bag of Funyuns off the shelf and opened it. Crunching the delicious rings loudly and not caring what fell to the floor, she soon found herself at the back of the store and still hadn't seen the roof access.

She followed the back wall for a few meters, holding her nose as she passed a display case full of rotted meats. Then she saw a pair of double-swinging stainless-steel doors.

She dropped the now empty bag and pushed through the swinging, silvery panels. In the gloomy space beyond, she saw a rectangle of white light outlining a framed opening in the ceiling. The dust-filled light cascading from it revealed a wall-mounted ladder.

Turning, she pushed her head through the doors and peered back into the grocery store. She whispered loudly. "I found it."

Vaughn's voice rose from the gloom. "Where is it?"

"Back wall. Through the double doors. Looks like a storeroom." Making a sour face, she added, "Just follow your nose."

Rachel was the first one to reach her. Completely unfazed by the rank odor, the woman stopped across from Angela and, using her teeth, pulled a chunk of beef jerky from the stick in her hand. She proceeded to chew it loudly, eyes rolling back in her head. "Mmmm."

Commander Bingham rounded a corner. He clasped an open Guinness stout in one hand and a bag of pretzels in the other. Chance held up the large bottle. "This'll calm the mindquake …" The man grimaced. "Oh, that's beastly! Pardon me, ladies." Holding the items in front of himself, he pushed past Angela and Rachel. "God save the beer." Then he stepped through the doors and disappeared into the storeroom.

Major Lee looked at Angela and rolled her eyes. Talking through a mouthful of half-chewed jerky, she grumbled something about Brits and beers and then followed him into the storeroom.

Seeing that the rest of the crew were on their way, and having had more than her fill of the putrid odors coming from the deli counter, Angela pushed through the doors.

The balance of the team soon filed in behind her.

Rachel tucked the remainder of her jerky into a leg pocket and then climbed up the ladder. A moment after she reached the top, light flooded the room as she turned the handle and raised the hatch. Initially, she only lifted it a couple of inches, but after a quick scan and apparently seeing no threats, she opened it fully.

Everyone winced as the hinges squealed. Fortunately, the engine noise that poured through the roof hatch more than drowned out the sound.

The major moved up a rung on the ladder and poked her head through the opening. Twisting her body left and right, Rachel peered around. Then she looked back into the room. "It's all clear. There's a parapet wall. We'll be covered." She waved for them to follow her. "Come on up." Then she climbed the rest of the way onto the roof and slid out of sight.

Angela and Monique exchanged nervous glances.

Mark Hennessy nodded to Vaughn and then headed up the ladder followed by Bill and Teddy. Next, Rourke and Monique crawled up after them.

Bingham downed the last of his beer and then tossed it and the empty bag into a utility sink stuffed with rags. Then he, too, followed them up.

Vaughn frowned at the man. Then he looked at Angela and gestured toward the ladder. "Ladies first. I promise not to stare at your butt ... much."

Scoffing, Angela glanced back toward the front of the building. Through a window in one of the storeroom's doors, she saw BOb standing vigil. She stepped over and started up. Looking back, she saw Vaughn staring right at her ass.

Angela grinned and rolled her eyes. "Really? We're in the middle of the apocalypse, and that's still all you can think of?"

"Was just thinking camouflage makes your butt look *huge*."

Angela guffawed. "Yeah, I wish. Thanks to our diet for the last few months, I'm suffering from a serious case of no-ass-at-all. Pretty much have to run around in the shower just to get wet."

"There you go, throwing images into my head."

"Oh goodness, that's enough, Captain."

"Yes, Commander."

A moment later, she emerged onto the debris-cluttered rooftop, and the smile fell from her face.

Crouching under a hazed sky that suddenly seemed wider and somehow more threatening, Angela fell back into her hellish reality. She felt exposed despite the four-foot-tall parapet wall that ringed the roof and hid them from observation.

On hands and knees, she watched as Vaughn climbed through the hatch.

Judging by the quantity of charred chunks of framing lumber and other bits melted into the roof deck's tar liner, she thought it a miracle that the structure hadn't burned with the rest.

Angela looked around. Every member of the team was squatting or kneeling so that their heads weren't visible above the top of the wall. "Uh ... we got a problem." She gestured at the parapet. "This is the highest building in the area. If we poke our heads above that wall, we'll stick out like a sore thumb."

Vaughn looked at her and nodded. "Yeah, we'll cut a silhouette. Any robot looking this way will see us."

As he spoke, Vaughn scanned the roof perimeter. Then he scrambled over to a collection of pipes that protruded from the face of the short wall. He started tugging at the foil tape that covered the point where the tubes passed into the parapet.

Realizing the wall faced the airport, Angela understood. She scrambled over to him and started helping. Teddy saw them and started heading their way. The rest of the team members soon followed suit.

Angela and Vaughn peeled off the last of the tape, revealing a large, rectangular, boxed-out opening that passed all the way through the parapet. She peeked through the wide gap between the frame and the pipes and saw that tape also covered the far side of the foot-wide passage.

She tried to reach through, but her hand wouldn't fit.

Growling, she shook her head. "Got anything we can poke through there?"

Vaughn pulled the Ka-Bar from its sheath and held up the long survival knife. "How about this?"

"That should be big enough."

A crooked grin spread across his face. "That's what she—"

"Captain." Cocking an eyebrow, Angela shot him a warning glare.

Vaughn's mouth snapped shut.

He bent over and started jabbing the knife through the opening.

The interior of the box-out began to glow as light entered from its far side.

Sawing and hacking, Vaughn worked for another couple of moments. Finally, he nodded and shoved the Ka-Bar back into its sheath.

He peered through the foot-wide opening. Light streaming through it illuminated his widening eyes. "I see movement."

Leaning in, Angela tried to look past him, but Vaughn was blocking her line of sight. She glanced over her shoulder and saw the rest of the group had collected behind them and were similarly blocked.

"What is it?" Mark asked.

"I don't know." She tilted her head toward Vaughn. "Captain Big Head here is blocking the view."

After giving her an annoyed glance, Vaughn fumbled for his binoculars.

Angela already had hers ready. She nudged him aside. "Here, lemme see."

He grunted and begrudgingly shifted out of her way.

She peered through the opening. "I see the airport. Looks like it dodged the firestorm. Most of the buildings are still standing. There's a bunch of wide metal ones just past the fence.

Vaughn leaned in. "Yeah, those are hangars. That's where I saw the movement."

Angela narrowed her eyes, searching the scene. "I see some empty foundations. Looks like some of the buildings are gone, but I don't see any ... Wait."

Something moved by a large dump truck that sat next to one of the hangars. "I see it."

"What is it, Command-Oh?"

"Hang on, Teddy."

She raised the binoculars and used them to pull the truck close. The movement resolved.

Her blood ran cold. "It's a Neck."

"What's it doing?" asked Monique.

"Just walking right now. Wait ... It's waving its arms."

Nervous murmurings came from behind her. "Has the bloody thing seen us?"

Angela shook her head. "No, Bingham. It's waving at something behind one of the hangars."

The engine noise they'd been hearing roared, and the warbling, metallic squeaking sound she'd heard earlier sprang back to life.

The Neck started walking backward, waving on the unseen progenitor of the noise as it did. A moment later, a large vehicle rolled out from behind the hangar. It had tracks like a bulldozer, but its body was making a slow rotation to the right as a long, articulated arm reached out from its center.

"What's making that sound?" Vaughn said beside her.

Still staring through her binoculars, Angela shook her head. "Not sure. Looks like some piece of construction equipment. There's another Neck inside, driving the thing."

"Let me see."

Angela stared at it a moment longer and then relinquished her position.

Peering over the pipes with his own set of binoculars, Vaughn studied the distant scene. "It's a trackhoe."

Angela tilted her head. "What's a trackhoe?"

Vaughn pointed through the opening. "That."

"Thanks, smartass. What's it do?"

"It's a hydraulic excavator. Usually, it digs trenches."

A loud, renting noise careened over the parapet wall.

Vaughn shook his head. "But they're using this one to scrap hangars."

Pushing Vaughn aside Angela peered through the opening. Through her binoculars, she saw dust rise from the corner of the building as the trackhoe took another large bite out of it. Looking like the leg of a person lying on their back, the machine's long arm bent like a knee and drew back, pulling the giant, sharp-toothed scoop at its end toward itself and dragging a chunk of the building with it. The metal squealed its protest as it tore away from the structure.

Light flashed from within the wounded building. Then Angela saw additional movement. Adjusting a knob on her binoculars, she zoomed in and spotted another robot through the new gap. A blue-white jet of light streamed from a tool held in front of the thing, and sparks began to spray out from the point where it burned into a metal beam.

"I see a scavenger bot. Looks like it's using a cutting torch."

The trackhoe turned and dropped the metal into the back of the dump truck. A loud crash rang out, and the vehicle bounced under the weight of the deposited material.

Angela shifted her gaze back to the Neck. The robot was filthy, its white carapace covered in soot. A shiver ran through her as she watched the thing effortlessly pick up a large I-beam and toss it into the truck. The vehicle rocked again as the heavy girder slammed against the inner side of its bed. "Geez!"

"What is it?" Rourke asked.

Angela shook her head. "Nothing."

The Neck waved the excavator on. Again, she was struck by how human its movements appeared. Stick a hard hat and a day-glow vest on the thing, and she could have easily mistaken it for a human construction worker—as long as she ignored the two extra arms and backward-bending knees.

Several new noises rang out.

She lowered her binos and craned her neck. Looking left and right through the opening, Angela saw the same scene repeated around several of the adjacent buildings. "Shit!" She shook her head. "There's more of them. This end of the airfield is teeming with the bastards."

Angela turned from the opening. Moving clear, she sat on the roof. The rest of the group members passed around her binoculars and took turns looking through the opening. Various curse words issued from them as they saw the events on the airfield.

Rourke looked at Vaughn. "How do we get past them?"

"Well, my precious little snowflake, I don't think you're going to like the answer."

The young doctor's face fell. "Ah, crap … More walking?"

"More walking."

CHAPTER 22

Looking left, Vaughn once again whispered a silent thankyou for the density of the tree line. In spite of their lack of foliage, the deciduous trees and shrubbery that lined that side of the road were sufficiently dense to obscure the team from the city center and any robots that might be looking their way.

Rachel maintained her point position stalwartly, her head pivoting left and right as she covered their advance.

They had been walking down this long country road for quite a while now. He looked at his watch. It felt as if they'd been going for days. However, only eight hours had passed since they'd left Mont Salève.

The sun had reached its zenith before the advancing storm had finally covered it. Now it was well past noon. The weather system had swept a couple of thin squall lines across Geneva's skeletal remains, but the brief rain showers and short spats of high-intensity winds hadn't been enough to hinder their advance. The rain had barely dampened their clothing. However, the main body of the storm now looked ready to attack in full force.

Tumultuous clouds of septic yellows and putrid greens filled half the sky. Periodic bolts of lightning striated the pall, their thunderous cracks shaking the ground beneath his feet.

The team would have to take cover if they didn't reach their destination soon, although Vaughn had no idea where they would find it. It had been more than a mile since he'd seen a structure.

He swayed as another blast of wind shoved him aside.

The branches of the trees along the road rattled against one another like the sticks of a drum corps staffed by an army of meth-crazed chihuahuas.

Looking past Rachel, Vaughn glimpsed something gray ahead, on the left side of the road.

He looked at Angela and pointed. "Do you see that? Is it CMS?"

She narrowed her eyes. "Where?"

Seeing that she was looking in the wrong area, Vaughn shifted his gesture. "Over there, just past where the tree line ends."

A wan smile blossomed on her face. "Oh, thank you! Yes, yes, that's it." She blew a strand of hair out of her eyes and looked at her boots. "Good thing, too. I don't think my feet could've taken another minute of this."

Vaughn placed a hand on her shoulder. "Hang on just a bit longer."

The facility ahead looked untouched. It appeared that neither the Necks nor their bots had even approached this side of the valley, and Vaughn hadn't seen so much as a scavenger bot in over an hour. Their remote location coupled with the clatter coming from the trees would mask a freight train's passage, so he raised his voice and addressed the entire group. "Almost there, folks."

Shouts of joy rose above the din.

"About bloody time," Bingham grumbled.

Teddy pumped a fist in the air. "Cowabunga, dude!"

"Thank God," Monique said with a sigh. "My feet are killing me."

Angela nodded. "Mine, too."

On the back right corner of the loose formation, Bill Peterson had started to limp again. He looked up with a relieved smile and said, "Not a moment too soon. My knee is starting to talk to me."

Rourke looked back at the major and gave him a thumbs-up.

Vaughn was proud of the young man. If they survived all this, he might even have to reconsider his opinion of Millennials. Not that he'd stop ribbing Rourke anytime soon.

He smiled at the thought. His mind began to clear, and his energy level started to rise as the prospect of their long forced-march's impending end pumped adrenaline into him.

He also felt hope inching its way into his soul.

It might all be over soon.

Apparently, Rachel was feeling the same things. At the front of the formation, she broke into a slow jog. One by one, the remaining members of the group exchanged smiles and also began to double-time.

A few moments later, they reached the end of the tree line. The open farmland beyond it afforded Vaughn an unobstructed view of the city.

In spite of the brief showers, wind-whipped dust still hazed the atmosphere.

Diagonal lines dashed the horizon as reborn fires spewed tilted columns of black smoke into the sky.

Staring at the far end of the farm field, Vaughn saw a listing, wedge-shaped, tan plume rising from the dusty plain. As he looked at its source, he blinked and then waved frantically. "Oh shit! Get down!"

He dove for a nearby trench. Landing hard in the still dry drainage easement, he turned back and continued to wave them off the street. "Take cover, *now!*"

Breathing heavily, they piled into the ditch around Vaughn.

"Were those …?" Bill Peterson paused for a breath as he massaged a knee. "Were those dozers?"

Vaughn looked at Angela and nodded. "Big ones. We've seen them before. They were preparing the ground ahead of the city builders. They're automated. I don't think there's anyone onboard, but that doesn't mean they can't see us."

Mark looked around and then pointed toward the CMS facility. "Let's follow the ditch. It'll get us close to the building. Then we can work our way in from there."

They all exchanged nods and then began to shuffle in the indicated direction.

A moment later they reached the end of the ditch and then low-crawled the last few feet to the facility's entrance.

Looking over his shoulder, Vaughn saw no indication that they had been seen. However, he took little comfort in the notion. The Necks and their machines of destruction may very well be coming for them at this moment. He knew this might not be random at all.

The thought sent his gaze skyward. He saw no Taters heading their way. Not yet, anyway.

Looking at his team, he said, "Stay low, but keep an eye out for flying potatoes."

Angela had already been casting a wary eye toward the tumultuous clouds. Now he saw the others looking up as well.

A high-pitched, oscillating squeak broke through the howling winds.

Several members of the task force flinched. Rachel rolled onto her back and aimed her rifle into the sky.

Vaughn shook his head. "That's not a Tater. It's the dozers getting closer." Jabbing a finger toward the building, he urged them forward. "All the more reason to keep moving, folks!"

Low-crawling at the front of the group, Mark finally reached the door a moment later. The entrance was hidden from the field by the building's corner, so when Rachel crawled up next to Mark, the two of them scrambled to their feet.

After a quick scan of the sky, Rachel motioned for Mark to try the door as she raised her rifle to cover him.

Mark slowly pried the door open an inch. When no alarm sounded, he pushed through it and peered inside. Leaning back out, he gave the all-clear signal.

Vaughn checked that BOb was still covering their rear flank and then waved for the rest of the group to enter.

Slithering like a line of caffeine-fueled lizards, he and the rest of the team members scrambled the last few feet to the stoop and then, rising to their feet, filed into the building's dark interior.

The coming storm had muted the day's light, giving the entrance foyer a haunted feeling. Vaughn felt a chill run down his spine as he looked into the dark corners of the shadowed building. He listened intently, trying to determine if they were alone in the facility. However, the metallic cacophony of the rapidly approaching heavy construction vehicles thwarted his efforts.

He turned and looked through a south-facing window just as the first of the dozers rolled into view. "Shit. They're coming fast. We don't have long."

Plastic clicks issued from behind him. Vaughn turned and saw Angela tapping the keys of a nearby computer terminal. She looked up at him and shook her head. "There's no power here. It's dead."

Pressing his lips into a thin line, Vaughn nodded. He ran over to a nearby elevator, and, against all hope, pressed the down button.

It stayed as dark as the rest of the building.

Of course. Why would anything ever be that simple?

Turning, he scanned the shadowed interior of the facilities entrance lobby. "Anyone see a stairwell?"

Several heads shook. No one had seen one yet.

"Spread out. Try to find a way down."

Angela held up a hand. "Wait!" She pointed toward a glass door at the back of the room. "There's a main hallway through there. The stairwell that leads to CMS is along it. I just don't remember which side it's on."

Vaughn nodded. "Perfect. Team One, take the left side. Team Two will take the right."

Rachel looked at him. "Maybe we should fall back." She pointed north through the wall of the facility. "We can regroup and try to find a new way to come at this."

Vaughn shook his head. "No good. There's too much open country around here. We'll be exposed. If they don't know about us yet, they will if we bust out of here. Our best option for both survival and success lies two hundred feet beneath us."

Twisting her face, Rachel glanced outside and growled in frustration. "This fucking sucks. I hate being backed into a corner."

Vaughn eyed the onrushing machines. "I'm more than happy to hand you the reins, Major Lee, but whatever we're going to do, it needs to be right fucking now!"

Also looking outside, Rachel shook her head. "No. No, you're right." She turned toward the glass doors. "Team One, with me!"

Vaughn waved to his group. "You heard the Major. Let's go!"

Everyone broke for the entry foyer's rear exit. Ahead, Team One passed through the double doors and soon disappeared into the gloom.

Reaching the same doors, Vaughn and his team passed into the corridor. Even in the dim lighting, he could see that it was wide and quite long. "Wonderful!" He pointed into the darkness. "Bill and Teddy, you take the far end of the hallway. Check all the doors on the right side, starting at the halfway point. Angela and I will check the ones on this end."

The men nodded and headed off to start their search.

Looking at Angela, Vaughn gestured down the corridor. "Start there!"

She ran toward the indicated door and shouted over her shoulder. "I'm on it!"

The sounds of opening doors and curse words echoed down the length of the passageway.

Vaughn ran down his side of it, throwing open door after door. All the while, the din of the coming mechanical horde grew louder. "Shit, shit, *shit*! Not finding anything here. Anyone else having any luck?"

"Nothing on our side," Rachel shouted.

"Bingo! Found it."

Vaughn tilted his head. "Was that you, Bill? Where are you?"

"Yeah! Far right side."

Vaughn hurried toward the man's voice. Coming in from his left and right, shadows and rapid-fire echoing footfalls converged on the same point.

The major manifested from the gloom ahead, holding open a door.

Peering through, Vaughn saw the top treads of a set of stairs. They descended into unlit depths.

He glanced back toward the entrance foyer.

From the sound of it, the bulldozers were showing no sign of slowing.

Turning back to the opening, Vaughn pointed through the door. "Everyone down the stairs."

Rachel held out a hand. "Hold up. We don't know it's clear down there!"

Vaughn hitched a thumb toward the coming tracked vehicles. "We *do* know that it's not going to be safe up here much longer. Even *if* they don't know we're here, what do you think they're coming to do? Think about it. What happened to all of the other CERN facilities we saw from the mountain?"

Rourke looked at him with widening eyes. "They got flattened." He glanced toward the doors and then back at Vaughn. "But what if they've already seen us?"

Vaughn frowned and then gestured at their surroundings. "Then up here is the last place we want to be. *Comprende?*"

The young doctor cast another nervous glance down the hall and then nodded.

"You're right," Rachel said. She moved to stand at the top of the stairs and waved urgently for them to follow. "Go down. I'll cover your six."

Shaking his head, Vaughn pointed down the steps. "No, Major Lee. I need you to take point. BOb and I will bring up the rear."

Rachel blinked. She looked ready to argue further, but then she nodded curtly. The major cast a final glance toward the corridor's far end and then disappeared down the stairs.

Vaughn gestured after her and looked at the others. "Go! Go! Go! Don't bother with the goggles. Use your flashlights, but wait until you're down a couple of flights."

Monique went next, followed closely by Bill and Teddy. Mark gave him a nod and then followed behind them.

When Bingham descended into the shaft, Vaughn turned to Angela and gave her a meaningful look. "Do you think there'll be power down there?"

She dipped her head. "Yeah, I think the Necks have to keep the collider running to keep the wormhole open." After casting a nervous glance in the direction of the approaching machines, she looked back at him. "If I'm right, there should be electricity along the entire ring."

"Then we'll just have to hope you're right."

Turning toward the foyer, he cupped hands around his mouth. "BOb! Get down here."

He turned back to her and pointed down the stairs. "Go, already. I'll be right behind you."

Angela raised herself onto her toes and kissed him. She looked into his eyes and hoisted an eyebrow. "You better be, Captain." Then she turned and disappeared down the stairs.

As he watched her go, Vaughn grinned in spite of the dire situation.

"BOb, I want you to ..."

The robot wasn't there.

Vaughn ran toward the far end of the corridor. "BOb!"

The robot jogged through the double doors. "Yes, Captain Asshole?"

Sliding to a stop, Vaughn waved over the bot. "Stay behind me and cover my back."

The robot dipped its head. "Roger, Captain Asshole."

Vaughn's momentary smile faded as he looked over BOb's shoulder.

Mouth falling open, he took an involuntary backward step.

The dozers were moving much faster than he'd estimated.

Rooster tails sprayed up behind the tracks of each giant machine.

He watched in stunned amazement as the enormous blade of the lead bulldozer reached the edge of the parking lot. The tractor trailer-sized steel plate peeled up the pavement like butter. The cars parked there flew into the sky, batted aside as if they had the mass of a beach ball. The resistance didn't even slow the dozer. Unfazed by the impact, the machine ran headlong directly at the building.

The ground quaked, and the floor lurched beneath his feet.

Long-dormant dust rained down from hanging fixtures.

Creaking loudly, the building swayed around Vaughn.

A tremendous crash erupted from somewhere behind him.

Vaughn flinched. "Oh shit!" He turned and ran toward the stairwell. Over the cacophony, he heard BOb hot on his heels.

Reaching the open door, Vaughn launched himself down the stairs. Just as he crashed down onto the first landing, the entire shaft lurched sideways.

CHAPTER 23

B reathing heavily in total darkness, Rourke pulled his flashlight from his kit and flipped it on.

Bingham winced. "Get your bloody torch out of my face."

"Sorry."

Running footfalls cascaded down from above.

Major Lee flipped on her light and shined it up.

Angela rounded the bend and held out a hand to shield her eyes.

"Where's Vaughn?" Rachel asked.

"He and BOb should be coming soon."

Rourke and Monique exchanged nervous glances.

"I don't hear him," said Bill Peterson. "We're three flights down. If the man is coming, he better shake a—"

The metal deck beneath Rourke's feet suddenly lurched sideways, and the handrail drove into his hip.

Peterson's arms flew into the air. "Son of a bitch!"

The entire stairwell continued to quake.

Raising her rifle with one arm and waving the other for them to follow, Rachel started down the stairs. "Move it now!"

Rourke turned to follow her, but then Captain Singleton burst into sight with the robot hot on his heels.

Seeing Rourke, the man waved his arms frantically. "Go! Go! Go!"

Someone grabbed the front of Rourke's shirt and yanked him down the stairs. Looking ahead, he saw Rachel dragging him.

"Move it, Rourky! Don't stop for anything."

He realized then that she must have backtracked to grab him.

The major was taking the steps two at a time, dragging him bodily. It was all Rourke could do to keep his feet under himself. She pulled him past the other members, resuming her place at the front.

Rourke batted away her hand. "I've got this!"

The deep rumbling crescendoed into bone-shaking thunder.

Rachel released him. "Keep up!" She threw her weapon across her back and, grabbing the handrails with both hands, began to hurl herself down the stairwell three and four treads at a leap.

Rourke mimicked her actions and rushed after her.

Dust rained down, filling the atmosphere with the acrid stench of dank limestone.

The whole world suddenly lurched.

Rourke flinched sideways as a foot-wide chunk of masonry slammed into the stair tread next to his boot.

Someone above him cried out in pain. Then a baseball-sized piece of debris fell past him. It looked like a chunk of asphalt. Had that come from the parking lot?

Looking back, Rourke saw Monique holding her shoulder. She looked at him and shook her head. "I'm okay. Keep going!"

At each landing, the stairway cut back, descending another flight into the dust-filled darkness.

Insanely gyrating flashlight beams cut sporadic patterns through the inky blackness.

The shaft they were descending was about the width of a small, one-car garage. Its zigzagging stairs filled all but a narrow gap along the outside of the handrails.

Suddenly, it felt as if a building dropped onto the top of the shaft. The entire stairwell bounced.

Rourke yanked his hand off the outer rail just as a torrent of gravel and rocks rained down through the gap between it and the wall. Overhead the rolling thunder ebbed, becoming muffled.

Staccato clangs rang out as rocks and boulders bounced off of metal treads and rails. Then they began to diminish as well.

Rourke looked back and then nearly fell as he ran into something. It was Major Lee. She had stopped her descent.

Standing on one of the landings, the stout woman grabbed his shirt and pulled him to a stop, preventing him from tumbling farther down the stairs.

He looked at her and felt his face flush. "Sorry."

She shook off the impact and righted him. Then she looked up the stairwell. "That was a cave-in."

Monique rounded the corner followed closely by Major Peterson and the cosmonaut. Hennessy and Bingham were right behind the two men. Dust covered all of them head to toe. Then Angela rounded the corner. She blinked as she stared into the beams of their combined flashlights.

Mark looked back at her. "Where's Vaughn?!"

Angela blinked "He… He was right behind me!" Terror took over her features. She and Mark started back up the stairs. The lieutenant colonel craned his neck to look up the central gap. "Vaughn!"

Rourke listened breathlessly. His ears rang from the cacophony of the cave-in. However, he heard a new sound.

He exchanged a nervous glance with Monique.

Angela paused at the landing above them. Her eyes went wide as she looked up the next set of stairs. She screamed, "Oh God, Vaughn!" Then she and Mark ran out of sight.

Rachel pushed past Rourke and sprinted up the stairs after them. "Wait!"

Then, holding Vaughn in his arms, BOb rounded the corner with Commander Brown and Colonel Hennessy following him. Shocked looks twisted their features.

Blood was leaking from the captain's head. It mixed with the dust, cutting muddy, ocher streaks across the man's slack face. Tears in his uniform exposed cuts on his arms and legs.

As they reached the landing, Rachel pointed at the floor. "Set him down, BOb."

The robot complied and gently placed Captain Singleton on the landing's metal deck. Major Lee and Commander Brown dropped to their knees next to the man.

Rourke looked at BOb. "What happened?"

"Enemy operatives attacked the building with heavy machinery. When it collapsed, I threw myself across the captain in an attempt to shield him. Debris fell upon us. When I extricated us, Captain Singleton was unresponsive."

Crying, Angela grabbed the man's shoulder and shook him insistently. "Vaughn, please! Say something!"

Rachel produced a rag and poured water over it. She wiped the dirt and blood from the man's face. Grabbing her flashlight, she inspected the lacerations on his forehead. "It doesn't look too bad. Not very deep."

She shifted the light to Vaughn's eyes and then raised one of his lids. Then she did the same to the other. Releasing a pent-up breath, she nodded. "His pupils are responding normally. I think he's going to be okay."

The major looked at the robot. "Any chance you were followed? Do we have any company coming?"

BOb shook his head. "Negative, Major. Judging by our depth, I estimate forty cubic meters of dirt and debris currently block the upper portion of the stairwell. No enemy operatives will be approaching from that direction."

Vaughn coughed and then opened his eyes. Blinking and squinting, he looked from Major Lee to Commander Brown. "Angela? What's wrong?" Then his eyes widened, and he sat up. "What happened?!"

Wing Commander Bingham bent over the man. "There was a cave-in, chap." He tilted his head toward the robot. "It appears the bloody toaster here saved your sorry arse."

Rourke looked up to see that Major Peterson and Teddy had taken up the position of rearguard. They were aiming their rifles up the stairwell, covering their six, as the military people liked to say.

Seeing the same thing, Rachel pointed at the robot. "BOb, go down a few flights and cover that end of the stairwell. Hit anything that comes up the stairs with your EMP cannon."

BOb dipped his head. "On it, Major." Then the robot stepped across them and descended the stairwell, disappearing into the darkness below. With its infrared vision, the machine did not need a flashlight. BOb could see just as well in the dark as they could in broad daylight.

The major turned her attention back to Captain Singleton. "Anything broke?"

Vaughn patted his arms and legs and then shook his head. "I don't think so." He touched one of the areas around a tear in his pants and winced. "But it feels like I've been run through a meat grinder."

Rachel dug into her kit and produced some first-aid supplies. She and Angela went to work on the man's wounds, cleaning and bandaging each of them. While they worked, the major gave the captain a meaningful look. "What do you think?" She looked up and nodded her head toward the ceiling. "Was this intentional? Are we under attack?"

Vaughn gasped as Angela applied disinfectant to a cut on his leg. Grimacing, he stared back at Rachel and shook his head. "I … I don't know. They came pretty fast and went straight at the building, but this could just be them doing the same thing here that they already did to all of the other access points."

Major Lee nodded slowly as she placed a bandage on the last wound.

Nodding his thanks, Vaughn stood, wincing again as he did. Angela kissed his cheek. "Sure you're alright?"

Vaughn nodded. "I'm fine. Just got my bell rung. That's all. He caressed her face and wiped away a tear with his thumb. Then he glanced down the shaft. "I just hope you're right about this going all the way down to the collider."

She nodded and gestured at their surroundings. "This is the emergency exit stairwell for the CMS experiment."

Massaging a temple, he returned her nod and then looked at the group. "Whether they know about us or not, we need to get the hell out of here. It's a dead-end vertical corridor with only one way out. If the Necks are coming for us, I'd rather have the seventeen-mile circumference of the ring to maneuver in than this shaft."

All of the military members nodded their agreement.

Angela shook her head. "We are fine going into the CMS experiment, but we can't use the collider tunnels."

Bingham cocked an eyebrow. "Why on earth not? I've seen pictures. There's a roadbed down there. It might just be a glorified walkway, but there's plenty of room for us to maneuver."

"Yeah, that works great when the collider is shut down. But not so much when it's running."

"Why not, Command-Oh?"

"Synchrotron radiation, Teddy." Looking at the cosmonaut, Angela pointed downward. "When the collider is in operation, particles are circling the entire seventeen-mile circumference eleven thousand times per second. We use powerful magnets to bend the protons into a circular path, but a fraction of their energy escapes laterally, like water flying from a spinning wheel. The radiation can be everything from low-frequency to high-frequency, visible light to hard x-rays. In this case, it's mostly the latter." She pointed at Bingham. "He's right. There is a walkway. It follows the inside circumference of the tunnel for that very reason. Additionally, there are motion sensors in the tunnel. If anything moves down there while the collider is running, it'll automatically cut the power."

Rourke instantly saw a flaw with her logic. "I don't think those are still active."

Turning toward him, Angela raised her hands. "What makes you say that, Doctor Geller?"

Everyone turned to look at him.

"I-I just remember you and Captain Singleton said a bunch of the Necks rushed you last time you overloaded the collider."

In his peripheral vision, he saw Vaughn nodding. "He's right. A lot of them came from the side of the experiment, but some of the Necks came from the tunnel itself. If the power had dumped, the collider would have shut down before you could've overloaded it, and we wouldn't be here now."

Angela considered it for a moment. Then she shrugged. "It really doesn't matter. We can't go in there. The radiation will kill us."

Bingham leaned forward. "I thought you said that the radiation sprays outward. If we stay on the inside passageway, we should be fine, right?"

Angela rocked her head equivocally. "The backscatter off the walls will still be enough to cause damage to our tissues."

Vaughn waved a dismissive hand. "None of that matters. For now, we need to focus on getting the hell out of this shaft."

Rourke felt his gut knotting up. He didn't understand how they could be discussing their options so calmly when they were so completely fucked. He raised a hand.

Bingham looked at him and rolled his eyes. "This isn't kindergarten. Spit it out, Doctor Geller."

Haltingly, Rourke lowered his arm. He felt his face flush as everyone stared at him again. Finally, he found his voice. "Aren't we forgetting something?"

No one spoke.

He pointed toward the ceiling. "We're trapped in here with no way out, and all the other access points are full of giant caterpillar bots."

Rachel gave him an understanding smile. "Rourky, that won't matter if we win. Once we reset the timeline, all of this gets undone."

"What if we don't win? What if this doesn't work? We're sealed in with what looked like hundreds of caterpillar bots."

Major Peterson shifted nervously.

Captain Singleton shrugged. "Guess we'll just have to succeed, then." Turning from Rourke, Vaughn addressed Angela and pointed toward the bottom of the shaft. "Still think you'll be able to overload the collider from down there?"

She nodded her head rapidly. "Yes, yes. This will take us straight to the CMS Experiment. Its computers are tied into the facility's intranet."

Momentarily setting aside his concerns, Rourke nodded with her. "I've read quite a bit about CERN's HiLumi network upgrade. I think she's right. If her credentials are still intact, any one of us should be able to do it."

The decking trembled beneath his feet as a low rumble cascaded down the shaft. Dust drifted from above, and he heard the clatter of falling gravel.

They all looked toward Major Peterson and Mission Specialist Petrovich who had been standing on the landing above them.

Both men had ducked and scrambled down a few steps, but then the sound faded, taking the tremors with it.

Returning to the upper deck, the cosmonaut and the major glanced up the previous flight. Teddy looked down on them and extended a thumb. "Hunky-dory. No robots here ... so far."

Rourke exchanged nervous glances with several of the team members.

Wing Commander Bingham shrugged. "They don't appear to be actively seeking us out. Either they think they've killed us or that they have us cornered."

Rourke raised hopeful eyebrows. "Maybe they don't know we're here at all."

Bingham looked at him as if he were staring at a piece of crap stuck to his shoe. "You go ahead and hope for rainbows and unicorns. We adults will be planning for reality."

Rachel gave the wing commander a sour look, but Angela spoke up before she could say anything. "He may be right, Chance. When the Necks discovered Vaughn and me, they always sent a Tater to do the job. They never sent heavy equipment."

Monique tilted her head. "I don't know. That could just be because they haven't had time to bring them through the wormhole yet."

"Whichever the matter," the Brit said, waving a dismissive hand. He gestured at Vaughn. "I agree with Captain Arsehole. It's high time we bugger on out of here. Otherwise, we may soon be up to our twigs and berries in robots."

Singleton frowned at the man but nodded. "Everyone locked and loaded?"

It took Rourke a moment to realize what he meant. The intent of his question only became obvious when he saw the other members of the team slide the bolt of their rifles back and verify a round was chambered.

After momentarily fumbling with the mechanism, he slid back his bolt and glimpsed the brassy glint of a live round.

Looking up, he saw Vaughn staring at him.

Rourke released the handle, and the bolt snapped back into position. He returned the man's gaze and nodded. "L-Locked and loaded."

Captain Singleton dipped his head. "Good." He stepped back and looked down over the railing. "BOb! Your EMP cannon hot?"

"Does a one-legged duck swim in a circle?"

One corner of the captain's mouth twisted downward. "I guess it does, but that's enough of that shit. Resume tactical mode, BOb. Stay a few flights beneath us."

"Roger, Captain Asshole."

The muscles along Vaughn's jawline flexed as he cursed under his breath. Shaking his head, he gestured at Angela. "You stay just ahead of Bill and Teddy. They'll cover our six in case an eager-beaver bot tunnels through all the shit behind us."

She nodded.

The major and the cosmonaut exchanged glances. Then Bill held up a thumb. "Knee seems better now." He flexed the leg and nodded. "Won't be a problem."

Vaughn dipped his head. "Glad to hear it." Addressing the entire group, he added, "If you've got a grenade launcher, use it first on anything that gets past BOb. If you wait till they're too close, the grenades won't be armed. They'll just bounce off the target. So keep them trained down the central stairwell. We'll need to hit anything before it gets too close. No matter what happens, one of us has to reach that terminal. Otherwise, all this has been for nothing."

"Thank you for your inspiring speech, Captain Obvious," Bingham said flatly.

Vaughn frowned at the man again and then looked over the railing. "Start down, BOb." Before the robot could respond, he held up a finger. "Not a goddamn peep! The only words I want to hear coming from your lipless mouth are 'enemy destroyed.'"

CHAPTER 24

As she rounded yet another landing, Angela struggled to draw sufficient breath. Her lungs starved for oxygen. Having lost track of the number of the flights they'd descended, she felt as if they'd been going down the stairs for an eternity.

She looked down as they rounded the next bend and saw a glow coming up from below.

She glanced at Vaughn.

He nodded and then held a finger to his lips. Then he gestured for everyone to turn off their flashlights as he did the same.

Angela struggled to hold in her building excitement.

The lights were on in CMS.

In spite of her insistence that the experiment's power would still be on, she'd held a deep-seated fear that the light here would be dead, that somehow the Necks would have found a way to power the mechanisms of the collider without energizing its surrounding circuits. She'd been half-certain that they would reach the bottom of the stairwell and find nothing but more darkness.

Glancing over the handrail, she saw the robot three flights beneath them, still leading the way. BOb had set a fast but steady pace all the way down the shaft.

Angela felt her pulse further quicken as the prospect of imminent discovery ratcheted up another notch. If the Necks or their minions had ventured this far into the ring, she and the rest of the team would likely cross paths with them soon, and she had no idea how that would play out other than with extreme violence.

As they continued downward, Angela began to hear the collider. The machinery generated a high-pitched whirring. If you were around it long enough, the sound would fade into the background, but now it was setting her teeth on edge.

Two flights of stairs later, they reached the bottom. A set of double doors stood between them and the CMS experiment's facility. The noise coming through the panels now seemed to have a physical property to it. The frequency and amplitude of it seemed somehow different. Angela didn't know if it was her imagination or if she was picking up on a change made by the robots.

BOb took up station to the left of the doors, Rachel to the right.

The woman looked no more winded then did the bot. On the other hand, Angela was still trying to catch her breath, and her legs burned with the exertion of having descended so many steps.

Panting as well, Vaughn pointed to Rachel and then extended two fingers toward his own eyes and then at the two small windows set into the doors.

Major Lee gave a single nod and then eased up to the window. Peering through it, she leaned left and right as she scanned the space beyond. A moment later, she gave the all-clear signal.

Angela released her held breath. Several of her teammates did the same.

Rourke gave her a sideways glance and then shook his head. "It felt like we were going down forever," he whispered breathlessly.

Between pants, Angela nodded. "Couple of hundred feet at least."

From behind her, Teddy patted her shoulder. "Where do we go from here, Command-Oh?"

"Like I said, we need to find a computer terminal."

Wincing, Vaughn held out a hand. "Keep it down, folks."

Rachel nodded and, keeping her voice low, said, "Get yourselves under control, people. From here on, we exercise extreme silence. Once we pass through these doors, I don't care how loud it is. Not a single sound. Got it?"

They did.

Vaughn frowned as he regarded the major through knitted brows. Then he appeared to shake off whatever was bothering him. He stepped up and looked at the group. "Take a moment. Catch your breath, and then give me a nod when you're ready."

Angela whispered a silent thankyou. She'd been struggling to rein in her adrenaline. With her heart racing, it was difficult to slow her respiratory rate. After a few moments, she finally began to gain the upper hand. Her pulse slowed, and she managed to draw sufficient breath.

Swallowing, she looked at Vaughn and dipped her head.

He smiled and returned the gesture. Then he winked at her and mouthed, "Almost done."

The other members of the group soon had their physiological responses under control as well. One by one, they nodded to Vaughn.

Standing beside him, Rachel drew something from one of the small pouches attached to her kit. Then she worked on some wires that extended from the frame of the double doors. When the woman stood to inspect her work, Angela saw she clamped a small, dark object over the wires.

Rourke leaned in and nodded. "You bypassed the door alarm, didn't you?"

Rachel gave the young man a crooked grin. "It wouldn't do having a klaxon announce our arrival."

The major looked at Vaughn. She raised her rifle and held it across her body. "Ready, Captain?"

He nodded.

Rachel slowly eased the door open. She peered left and right and then, moving lithely, disappeared through the opening, waving for them to follow.

One after the other, they each slipped through the open doors.

Vaughn signaled for BOb to cover their rear. Then he grabbed

Angela's upper arm gently, and they passed through the opening together.

When the two of them stepped into the light, Angela looked right and saw the near side of the CMS experiment.

She looked at Rachel and pointed.

The major nodded and then began to advance in the indicated direction.

Holding his rifle at the ready, Wing Commander Bingham followed close on her heels.

Angela was happy to see the man fully invested for a change.

Crouching and looking left and right, Rourke walked just behind the man's right side.

Positioning herself off the young doctor's right wing, Monique transitioned into full badass mode. Her visage morphed from librarian into that of a warrior queen. It was the same hard look she'd given Bill when he'd tried to bail on them.

Aiming her weapon off to the side, Monique covered the right sector of the advancing team while Mark Hennessy on her opposite side similarly covered their left flank.

At the center of the formation and cupping Angela's elbow, Vaughn guided her down the corridor while training his rifle up and to the left. At the same time, she covered the right sector, tilting her muzzle up as well.

She could feel Bill, Teddy, and the robot following close behind. Glancing back, she saw them walking backward, each of their weapons covering a discrete sector.

From above, the formation would look like a slowly advancing ring with ten weapons aiming out like the petals of an elongated, deadly flower, Angela and Vaughn forming the stamen at its center.

She looked right and saw something out of place.

A large set of pipes emerged from the wall only to end in a sharp, diagonal line as if they'd been cut. Thick cables extended from their open ends. Someone—or something—had cut them as well. Shattered pieces of the carbon fiber conduit sat mixed with short, thick strands of wire on the floor beneath the truncated assembly.

Staring at the severed lines, Angela realized they must be the supply couplings that fed power from the surface.

Or they used to anyway.

Smiling and releasing a silent sigh, Angela patted Vaughn's hand and pointed at the cut cables.

He followed her gesture and studied the scene. After a moment, he gave her a meaningful look. Then a smile spread across his face, and he nodded his understanding: the Necks had already switched the collider over to the power they were pumping through the wormhole.

This was crucial.

Angela had expected to find the power lines cut, especially considering the conditions on the surface. It was doubtful, in the extreme, that the collider would have remained energized if it had relied on Geneva's infrastructure. However, the critical part of the finding lay in the power required to overload the wormhole. If they had arrived too early, if somehow the collider was still powered by Geneva's grid, there wouldn't be sufficient energy to reset the timeline.

This was good.

It was fucking outstanding, actually.

A few steps later, they emerged into the CMS experiment proper. It had a similar layout to that of the ATLAS experiment, although it didn't have the large radiating network of pipes.

At the head of the slowly advancing group, Rachel spotted the control room. She pointed a bladed hand toward it and then redirected the ring-shaped formation.

A moment later and still crouching, they stepped up to the room's entrance.

Using hand gestures, Vaughn moved the team into a defensive perimeter. At its center, Rachel tried the latch.

The door didn't open.

After glancing back, she punched in the code Angela had supplied.

They all winced as a beep rang out with each keypress. Fortunately, the constant drone of the machinery all but drowned out the tones.

After the last beep rang out, the red light on the keypad shifted to green.

Angela released her breath.

Rachel grabbed the lever and slowly twisted it. This time it yielded, and the door unlatched. She swung it open.

Vaughn posted BOb as a sentry and then the rest of the team filed into the control room.

Rachel gently snicked the door closed behind them.

Angela watched Rachel and then turned to see everyone staring back at her expectantly.

She blinked. "Wh-What?"

Vaughn gave her a crooked grin. He pointed at a computer monitor that had a HiLumi logo floating across its screen. "We made it. This is it, this is what we've been looking for."

Angela's mouth went round as she stared at the logo. "Oh shit ..." Pausing, she smiled and looked at Vaughn. "You're right. I was so wrapped up in the race, I forgot about the finish line."

Her gaze returned to the workstation.

This was it.

This was her chance to set everything right, to push the bastards out permanently. She wanted to do so much more than that to the Necks. She wanted to make them pay for what they had done to Earth's life and for what they had done to the life of all the worlds that she and Vaughn had traveled through.

But she couldn't do any of the last parts. All she could do now was settle for denying the bastards this Earth.

No, it wasn't the vengeance she wanted.

But it would do.

Vaughn made a show of pulling the chair out from behind the computer terminal. "Madam, your coach awaits."

Swallowing hard, she stepped slowly to the seat and then, still standing, stared at the HiLumi Intranet logo.

Vaughn pushed in the chair, buckling her knees and dropping her into the seat.

This was where they would end it all, where she would reverse what the bastards had done to them and bring everyone back.

Permanently, this time.

If she didn't screw up.

Angela felt the other members of the team closing in. Standing behind her, they formed a semi-circle around the back of her chair.

Tentatively, she reached out for the space bar.

"Do it, Command-Oh."

Chewing her lip, she pressed the bar.

The screen turned black. A white segmented circle with an atom icon on its side spun at its center. The rolling symbol was the HiLumi equivalent of a spinning hourglass.

They all watched in breathless anticipation.

After intolerably long moments, a message popped up on the screen. To Angela's dismay, the customary sign-in block was missing. "What on earth?"

Mark leaned in. "What does it say?"

As she registered the words, Angela felt her stomach sink.

The lieutenant colonel read aloud. "There was a problem connecting to the server 'HI-LUMI Intranet.'" Bending closer, he read the small print beneath. "The server may not exist, or it is unavailable at this time. Check the server name or IP address, check your network connection, and then try again."

"Shit," Bill said through a growl. Several additional curse words rose from behind her.

Rourke leaned in. "Try rebooting."

Angela frowned. "Ya think?"

After throwing an annoyed glare at the man, she shut down the terminal.

She looked at Rourke and pointed to the back of the workstation. "Check the connections."

His face brightened, and he nodded.

While he inspected the wires, Angela had Monique de-energize the entire console.

After waiting sixty seconds, she looked at Rourke.

He held up a thumb. "All cables and connections look good."

Angela pointed at Monique. "Power it up."

A few moments later, the icon returned, but when the symbol completed its too long rotation, the screen displayed the same damned message: "There was a problem connecting to the server 'HI-LUMI Intranet.'"

"What does it mean?" Teddy asked without humor, his normal Russian accent supplanting that of the surfer boy affectation.

"It means," said Rourke, "that the ring isn't the only thing the Necks isolated."

"No," Angela said, shaking her head. "It means we have to go to ATLAS."

CHAPTER 25

Rourke puckered his forehead. "You said that would kill us."

Angela shook her head. "Actually, I said it would damage our tissues. And it will. Long-term, it might even kill us. But we have a lot more to consider than just ourselves." Her eyes lost focus as she stared through the wall. "That's all it's been about for quite some time now." She shifted her gaze to Vaughn. "But there's another problem, and it might be a deal-breaker."

Vaughn tilted his head. "What could be worse than killer radiation?"

"Going into this potential battle with no weapons."

"Why in bloody hell would we do that?"

"Because the ring is a damned big electromagnet. Any ferrous hardware," she pointed at Chance's rifle, "like your gun, will be yanked to the surface of the collider the instant you enter the tunnel. We're talking about a seriously powerful magnet. It'll crush anything caught in the middle."

Monique nodded.

Bill and Teddy exchanged nervous glances.

Angela continued. "Additionally, the magnetic lines will induce an electrical current through non-ferrous metals. They'll get damned hot." She extracted a magazine from one of her pouches and held it up and pointed to the bullets within. "Like, the rounds will start cooking in their casings and eventually explode, hot."

Eyes widening, Bill looked at Angela and pointed toward the collider tunnel. "You're saying we can't take any weapons with us, that we're going to go up against a fucking army of ten-foot-long mechanical caterpillars with nothing but our bare knuckles?"

Monique's eyes flared. "William! Keep your voice down. You will not shoot the messenger. No, sir!"

Bill looked at Monique. "I ...! I just—!"

"Think of your family, William. What would they want?"

His head rocked as if she'd slapped him. Myriad emotions streamed across the man's face.

Monique's eyes softened. "Commander Brown is simply relating the facts, William." She gestured at Vaughn. "It is up to Captain Singleton as to what we do with the information."

Bill deflated. "Shit." The man's shoulders slumped, and his gaze fell to the floor. "S-Sorry, Angela."

Angela waved it off. "It's okay, Bill. Believe me. I'm struggling with the same thing." She looked at the faces of their comrades. "We all are."

They sat in uncomfortable silence. After a few moments, everyone turned and looked at Vaughn. Even Major Lee seemed content to let him take this one.

As Angela, too, looked at him, she saw the leader Vaughn was becoming. These military members, some of them outranking him, respected his leadership. They were all ready to follow his orders.

Vaughn pressed his lips into a thin line. Finally, he nodded and pointed at Angela. "Like you said, we have a lot more to consider than just ourselves. Our entire world hangs in the balance." He regarded each of them soberly. "It's all or nothing, folks. We can't mail it in. We have to see this all the way through ..." Pausing, he gave each of them a meaningful look. "All the way through ... regardless of the cost."

His words hung in the air for a long moment.

Vaughn stood weightily. He walked over to a corner of the control room and propped his rifle against the wall. Then he started shedding his battle rattle. Metal components ran through all of it.

He looked back at the group. "Let's go, Team Two. Lose the metal." He peeled off his watch and looked at its face. "We roll in five."

Major Lee did a double-take. "Team Two? What about the rest of us?"

"I have other plans for you and BOb."

CHAPTER 26

Vaughn stepped into the security booth and glanced at the retinal scanner next to the opposite door. "I hope you're not going to be a problem."

He tried the latch.

It turned, and the door opened, revealing a more spacious booth beyond.

After seeing the cut power coupling, he'd expected these doors to be unlocked. There'd been no evidence that the Necks or their bots had ventured into CMS's aboveground facility—well, not until their massive dozers had shown up and flattened the place.

On the other hand, there'd been plenty of evidence that they'd worked their way into the below-ground portions of the facility. The Necks must have accessed the power conduits through the tunnel.

Fortunately, it looked like they had withdrawn from the area once they completed their modifications. Vaughn and the rest of the team had seen no further evidence of their presence, and BOb reported that he'd detected no sign of movement out to the limit of his passive sensors.

Stepping through the now open door, Vaughn passed into the

larger booth beyond. It was like entering an airlock, but instead of the vacuum of space, only hard radiation waited beyond the next hatch.

Vaughn bounced on his toes experimentally, seeing if he could sense any give. According to Angela, the floor of the booth incorporated a scale. The department responsible for safety and material control had used it to ensure nothing got left in the facility. They weighed everyone when they entered the tunnel and again when they exited. The department had to account for any weight changes before they could reenergize the collider.

Vaughn eyed the opposite door warily.

Angela had also warned him that passing through the next hatch would place him in the collider tunnel, radiation and all.

He looked over his shoulder. "Come on in. I ain't dead yet."

Mark entered the booth. "This sucks."

Vaughn frowned. "Yeah, it does." Pausing, he gave his friend a sidelong glance and hitched a thumb, pointing behind them. "You didn't have to come. You were part of Team One."

"Yeah, like I was going to let you hog all the glory."

"Glory?" Still staring at the far door, Vaughn shook his head. "Your lips to God's ears. We have to succeed for there to be any of that."

"Well, I sure as hell didn't want to be the reason you fell short."

Vaughn looked up at the taller man. "Chewie! Was that a double entendre?"

"If the elevator socks fit, wear 'em."

"Damned shaved Sasquatch."

Mark blew air through his nose. "Team One'll have BOb. Without weapons, all you have to throw at the problem is bodies. What if it comes down to a point where success is just one person away?" He pointed back toward the other members of Team One. They stood huddled against the far wall, just visible through the now open entry booth door. "You're right to have them hang back and try to find another way out, but we both know the Necks have likely sealed off all the emergency exits, too."

Vaughn shrugged. "It is what it is."

"Yeah, it's a desperate, last-ditch effort." Seeing Vaughn's face,

Mark held up a hand. "You're right to do it. It's a good decision, but I'll be more useful with you than with them."

Nodding slowly, Vaughn looked past Mark and saw BOb standing guard. The robot couldn't enter the tunnel. It didn't have much in the way of ferrous metals, but it did have plenty of circuitry and other components that would be affected by the collider's magnetic field.

Mark pointed at the bot. "Angela positioned BOb and the rest of Team One so they'll be safe when you open the door. She said something about their distance and angle from the collider's entrance shielding them from most of the radiation. Heard her also say something about it being out of the magnetic field, at least the part that could cause damage."

Standing just outside the entrance door, next to Angela and Bill, Teddy leaned over and peered into the booth. His Adam's apple bobbed. Then he held up an unsteady hand and extended his thumb. "We're ready, El Capitan."

Peterson looked in and dipped his head.

Angela gave Vaughn a weak smile. "Let's do this."

Vaughn nodded at his team. Then he turned to face the booth's opposite door and extended a tremoring hand toward its latch. Closing his eyes for a moment, he let out a short sigh. "Fuck it."

Grabbing the handle, he opened the door.

No alarms rang out.

A Neck didn't reach through the opening and grab him.

He didn't feel anything either.

The increased volume of the collider's electric thrum served as the only perceptible change.

Looking over his shoulder, he waved for Team Two to follow. Let's do this."

Before Vaughn could turn back toward the tunnel, he saw BOb look at him from the far side of the outer room and cant his head. Then the robot raised a hand. "Captain Singleton, something is wrong."

Vaughn felt his skin tingle as adrenaline dumped into his system. Instantly alert, he tried to listen for approaching enemies, but he couldn't hear anything over the electronic hum of the collider. "What's wrong? What are you detecting?"

"Nothing … That's the problem."

Angela glanced at Vaughn and then back at the bot. "What do you mean, BOb?"

The robot pointed past them, indicating the collider. "I'm detecting no radiation."

"Nothing? No x-rays?"

"No, Commander, I detect no significant increase within the range of my sensors."

Angela glanced into the tunnel. Then she held up a finger. "I'll be right back."

She darted out of the booth and ran back to the control room. A moment later, she emerged with a screwdriver.

Holding up his hands, Vaughn stepped into her path, blocking her from getting any closer to the collider. "What are you doing?"

"Working a hunch. Get out of my way."

He held his ground.

Angela narrowed her eyes. "I'm the one who told you about the danger. Now, move it, Captain."

Raising hands in surrender, Vaughn backed away. "Be my guest. Just don't get caught between that and the collider's surface."

Giving Vaughn a meaningful look, Angela opened her hand, allowing the tool to rest on her open palm. She pushed past him and stepped into the tunnel. As she moved, the screwdriver rocked gently, but otherwise, the tool didn't so much as twitch.

Angela looked back and smiled. "This thing should've flown out of my hands and slammed into the collider. It didn't even turn toward the ring."

"Tool might not be ferrous, Command-Oh."

Angela grabbed the handle and tapped the thing on the booth's glass panel. "May not be magnetic, but it's definitely metal." She gripped the silvery shaft and shook her head. "Still room temperature."

Vaughn looked from her to the three-foot-wide blue conduit that held the collider's guts. He entered the tunnel and walked across the narrow path that lined the inner circumference of the ring. He touched the casing tentatively, pulling it back quickly as if he'd been checking a hot iron.

"Didn't electrocute me."

Lowering his hand back to the surface, he let it rest there. He looked at Angela. "Just a light vibration, almost a hum."

Angela nodded and turned to face the rest of the group. "They've changed it."

Teddy looked at her, his face a mass of confusion. "The Necks? What did they change?"

She shook her head. "I ... I don't know, but they're not transmitting particles through it. The magnetics are offline."

"Then what's generating that hum?" Bill Peterson asked.

"I don't know." She looked at Vaughn. One corner of her mouth twisted upward. "But I do know one thing: we won't have to leave anything or anyone behind."

CHAPTER 27

Vaughn craned his neck and narrowed his eyes, but he still couldn't see the ALICE experiment. It sat three-quarters of the way from CMS to ATLAS, and considering how long they'd been walking, he knew it wouldn't be long now. They were close.

Thus far, they'd encountered no robots. Not so much as a mouse droid had crossed their path. However, from what he'd seen from Mont Salève, Vaughn knew the upper reaches of the ALICE facility were crawling with caterpillar bots.

Fortunately, they could now throw more than bare knuckles at the enemy.

After discovering the changes to the collider tunnel's environment, Vaughn had instructed the teams to retrieve their battle rattle and weapons.

Over the last thirty minutes, the reunited members of Team One and Team Two had circled a considerable portion of the ring's circumference.

The tunnel was large enough to permit the passage of a truck, but the three-foot-wide conduit that housed the collider's tubes, or dipole magnets as Angela had called them, ran along the outer half of the tunnel. Equipment and miscellaneous smaller conduits and cables cluttered the ceiling and walls, leaving only a narrow corridor along its inner circumference. The pathway featured a white centerline, giving it the appearance of a miniature roadway.

The tunnel's gently curving circumference afforded them a long sightline fore and aft. Unfortunately, that also meant they could be seen for quite a long distance from either direction.

Careful not to make a sound, Vaughn jogged ahead and caught up with the robot.

BOb continued to advance, but looking over its shoulder, the bot gave the agreed-upon signals for no changes in radiation or magnetism. Then the robot pointed a bladed hand ahead and signaled all-clear, meaning he'd detected no contacts to front.

Vaughn looked past the bot, inspecting the tunnel to the limit of his vision, and then extended a thumb.

Working his way back toward the rear of the long formation, he passed Major Lee at its center. She smiled at him and lovingly caressed her highly modified M4 rifle.

For their long advance along the ring's circumference, Vaughn had positioned BOb at the front of the formation while keeping the Army Ranger-turned-astronaut candidate at its center. Rachel's sniper skills would be best utilized there, giving her the ability to engage threats whether they approached from front or rear.

As Vaughn worked his way toward the back of the slowly advancing formation, he recalled the discussion they'd had before departing CMS.

He had gathered the two teams in the tunnel. Raising his arms, he'd pointed in both directions. "We have two choices. We can go east and travel clockwise around the ring, or we can go the other way and head west."

Angela had spoken up. "We should head west. It's shorter."

Mark looked in the indicated direction. "I thought there was another experiment that way."

She nodded. "Yes. ALICE is in that direction."

"Who's Alice, Command-Oh?"

"Not who, Teddy, what. Colonel Hennessy is right. An experiment named ALICE sits between ATLAS and us."

Bill Peterson's eyes widened. "Wait, wait, wait. Isn't that where we saw the giant caterpillars coming up?"

Angela shrugged and pointed toward the opposite end. "Yeah, and we also saw them coming out of the experiment that lies in the other direction." She gestured back to the west. "But this way is shorter, and ALICE is closer to the wormhole, so if we can't find a working network connection inside ALICE, it's also a shorter walk from there to ATLAS than it would be going the other way."

Rachel looked at Vaughn. "Why not split back into two teams and go in opposite directions? That'll give us some redundancy."

Wincing, Monique had shaken her head. "I am not sure that helps our situation. It will effectively double our chances of discovery."

Bingham scoffed. "I think that horse has left the barn, lassie."

Squaring on the taller man, Rourke stepped between him and the lieutenant. "You don't know that."

Sour-faced, the wing commander glared down on the young doctor. "Listen here—"

"He's right, Chance," Vaughn said, cutting off the man.

"What?"

"I said, he's right. We don't know that we've been discovered. The success of our operation depends heavily on the enemy not knowing of our existence. Anything we do to increase our chances of being discovered goes counter to that mission."

Bingham had frowned, but he'd said no more on the subject.

Vaughn had pointed down the tunnel. "We *all* go west."

Now he shook his head. None of that mattered at this point. They'd already covered three-quarters of the distance to ATLAS from CMS.

All remained quiet on the Western Front ...

So far.

After checking on Bill and Teddy at the back of the formation, Vaughn returned to his central position just ahead of Rachel.

Peterson's limp hadn't returned, so it appeared the knee issue had worked itself out.

Looking over Angela's shoulder, he saw a widening ahead.

They had reached the outskirts of the ALICE experiment.

Gaining everyone's attention, he pumped his hand in a slow down gesture.

All of the team members nodded, even the robot.

Stooping, they crept forward stealthily.

Vaughn hugged the wall that lined the inner radius of the gently arcing tunnel as he and Angela inched forward one small step at a time. They carried their rifles at the ready.

With the stock of his M4 pressed into his shoulder, Vaughn swept the muzzle left and right as he scanned the tunnel. Angela did the same a few steps ahead of him.

He saw nothing moving in his field of view.

Glancing back, Vaughn nodded to Rachel. The stealthy woman maintained her central position, hanging just a few steps behind him as they inched their way closer to the ALICE experiment.

He peered around Rachel and received a thumbs-up from Monique three car lengths farther back, just ahead of Rourke and Bingham.

Behind them, Bill and Teddy were bringing up the rear, just ahead of the point where the curvature of the corridor would have placed them out of sight of the main group. Vaughn had spread out the formation to prevent one enemy shot from taking all of them out.

Turning his attention back to front, he saw BOb crouching at the point where the tunnel widened to accommodate the ALICE experiment. Mark was leaning against the wall just behind the robot. The two of them were a good twenty meters ahead of Angela.

After craning its neck to scan the area ahead, the battle operations bot looked back and gave the all-clear signal.

Vaughn released a held breath and relayed the sign to Bill and Teddy at the back of the formation.

Turning back to front, Vaughn reached forward, but before he could tap Angela and signal for her to advance, a door just beyond her in the tunnel wall began to swing open.

The white carapace of a long, mechanical leg slid into view. Then the entire body of the Neck to whom it belonged emerged from the apparent side corridor.

The robot suddenly seized as it stared at Angela, its actions screaming surprise.

Then it did scream, releasing the same wailing siren sound that Vaughn had first heard when he and Angela had chanced upon a Neck in their Corsican nature reserve.

Unlike those bots, this one didn't settle for pointing while it screamed.

The Neck reached out with all four of its hands and grabbed her arms, yanking them wide and causing Angela to drop her weapon before she could fire it.

Vaughn raised his rifle and tried to aim it at the Neck, but Angela's writhing body blocked his shot.

He looked around the door and saw Mark and the robot running toward them. "Shoot it, BOb!"

The battlebot raised the EMP cannon.

A sharp report rang out.

Unfazed, the Neck continued swinging Angela like a shield.

The door the robot had exited through sat between BOb and the Neck.

Vaughn shook his head. "The goddamn door blocked the pulse."

"Let me go!" Angela shouted at the robot.

She kicked its chest plate.

The Neck yanked her violently.

Flailing, Angela screamed out in pain.

Remembering how the alien bots had thrown heavy-assed street lamps, and fearing what that kind of strength could do to a human body, Vaughn lurched toward the scrambling pair. He leaned around Angela and thrust the muzzle of his assault rifle toward the flat disk of the robot's neckless head and squeezed the trigger.

In the same instant, the Neck released Angela with all but one hand and triple-backhanded Vaughn.

It felt as if a freight train had slammed into his chest.

The shot went wide, punching through the door behind the alien robot.

The blow from the Neck knocked Vaughn from his feet and sent him flying backward.

As if moving in slow motion, he sailed over the collider's wide, blue conduit.

Hanging by one arm, Angela searched her beltline with her free hand.

Vaughn slammed painfully into a piece of equipment and then dropped to the floor.

Just as he landed, a familiar snap and subsequent whine rose above the collider's thrum.

Fortunately, it hadn't been his bones breaking.

The sound had come from outside of him.

Scrambling back to his feet, Vaughn saw Angela still dangling from one of the Neck's now motionless arms. In her free hand, she clutched the audibly whining alien EMP gun.

She kicked at the Neck's torso again. "Get this damn thing off me!"

BOb yanked the still open door off its hinges. Holding the EMP cannon in one hand and the steel panel in the other, the battlebot looked ready to both pummel the Neck and shoot it. Seeing that they'd already immobilized the alien bot, BOb lowered his weapon and dropped the door. Then he started prying at the Neck's frozen fingers.

Vaughn clambered over the blue section of pipe and wrapped his arms around Angela. "I gotcha." He supported her weight while BOb worked open the enemy bot's digits.

"Are you okay?"

The robot freed Angela from the dead Neck's grasp.

Breathing heavily, she looked at Vaughn. "Yeah. Set me down."

He lowered her gently to the ground.

Rubbing her left wrist, she turned and looked at the immobilized robot.

Mark peered around BOb. He looked at the Neck with wide eyes. It was the first time he'd seen one in person, up close.

This Neck looked like all the others. It had the same hips and lower legs as they'd seen before. They had the same basic design as had the two-legged walking tanks in the *Star Wars* movies.

The similarities ended there.

Where the body of the tank would have been, the Necks had a narrow waist topped by a widening white torso that featured four fully articulated arms. A white, disc-shaped head sat atop it all.

Looking around, Vaughn realized the entire group had collected around him and Angela. All of the members of the team stared at the Neck with open-mouthed amazement. Varying levels of horror twisted their faces, although Rachel's look also contained an analytic keenness.

Vaughn urgently pointed fore and aft, indicating each end of the tunnel. "Spread out!"

BOb complied instantly. He spun around and sprinted back to his position at the front of the formation.

Vaughn looked back at the gathered group. They were moving too slow. "Go! Go! Go!" He pumped his arm insistently. "We can't be this bunched ...!"

A new sound rose above the thrumming of the collider's mechanisms.

The words fell forgotten from his suddenly dry mouth.

An icy chill ran down Vaughn's spine as he exchanged a knowing glance with Angela.

The bit of color that had returned drained from her face. "A Tater's coming."

Rourke blanched. "Oh, no!" Eyes flying wide, he turned left and right.

A string of additional curse words sprang forth as the other team members similarly scanned the far ends of the collider.

The volume of the screaming banshee sound continued to rise.

Vaughn looked at the still motionless Neck. The damned thing must've gotten out a Mayday before Angela had killed it.

Looking past the robot, he scanned the tunnel ahead for the approaching, life-stealing bastard. "Sounds like it's coming from ALICE."

Angela nodded. "From the sound of it, it'll be here soon."

"We need to get the hell out of this bloody tunnel!"

"Thanks, Wing Commander Obvious." As Vaughn spoke, he glanced through the doorway from which the Neck had emerged. Racks of computers filled its cramped quarters. "Dammit! No good. It's a server closet, a dead-end."

He stepped back and looked around.

"Shit! There's nowhere to go."

The sound continued to climb.

Vaughn turned to face Rachel. "Time to fight, Major."

She gave a sharp nod and then, looking at the rest of the crew, gestured at the dead Neck. "We need to get away from this thing." She pointed down the tunnel. "Fall back a few meters and take cover."

Bingham looked at her incredulously. "Take cover behind what?"

"Anything, Chauncey-Baby." She swept a hand toward the machinery that lined the wall on the other side of the collider's main conduit. "Just get the hell outta sight."

The sound reached new levels.

Jumping into action, they each scrambled a couple of car lengths down the tunnel.

Rachel slid in behind a cabinet and waved the others past her.

Diving for concealment, Vaughn and the rest of the team members darted beneath and behind bits of machinery and tubing.

Leaping back over the conduit, Vaughn positioned himself behind a large cabinet.

Angela dove into the narrow crawlspace beneath the collider conduit.

Peering toward the noise, Vaughn saw BOb still standing in the open. The machine had followed his orders to spread out so quickly it hadn't heard Rachel's subsequent command.

Vaughn started to raise an arm, intending to signal BOb to take cover, but then he spotted movement at the far end of the tunnel, well beyond the battle operations bot.

A Tater slid into sight.

Vaughn worried the machine would see his thermal signature, but then he felt the heat coming off the cabinet he'd hidden behind. The collider's multiple heat sources should mask their presence.

BOb must have detected the Tater at the last moment. Just before the alien device had emerged, the battlebot pressed itself against the wall behind one of the rare cabinets that lined the inner circumference of the curving tunnel.

Apparently not seeing BOb, the Tater drifted forward. The levitating machine's long axis slowly swept left and right as if it were scanning the tunnel ahead. Then the sweeping motion stopped just as it lined up on the motionless Neck.

Locked on, the Tater angled straight at its immobilized comrade.

It flew past the battlebot.

Lightning-fast, BOb darted from behind cover and leveled the EMP cannon, aiming it at the back of the Tater.

"Take the shot!" Vaughn urged, whispering under his breath.

The high-pitched, penetrating eruption of the cannon's sudden discharge echoed throughout the tunnel, momentarily eclipsing the sounds of both the collider and the Tater.

The machine stopped.

It hung motionlessly in the air.

Vaughn held his breath.

Had it worked?

Had it killed the Tater?

The still levitating, potato-shaped machine turned toward the battle operations bot.

The thing appeared to study BOb.

After an eternal moment, the Tater turned from the bot and resumed its advance.

BOb raised his EMP cannon and fired again. The piercing report of its activation echoed through the tunnel once more.

The advancing Tater didn't slow or turn. It continued to fly straight toward the dead Neck, utterly ignoring BOb.

"Shit! Shit! Shit!"

Vaughn mentally ran through their options as he watched the machine close the gap. He had ordered everyone not to use grenade launchers in the tunnel, worrying that an explosion or shrapnel might take down the collider and trap them in this timeline.

The Tater continued to close on the dead Neck.

Vaughn shook his head. "Think, Singleton!"

The enemy machine moved to within half a football field from Major Lee.

Vaughn could already see the light wave emitter hanging from its belly. The sight gave him an idea.

"Rachel," Vaughn whispered urgently.

From her hidden position behind the next electronics cabinet, she looked back at him. "What?"

Vaughn extended a finger toward the Tater. "Can you hit the lens on its belly?"

Peering through her scope, Rachel gave a single nod. "Is a pig's vagina pork?"

Vaughn blinked. "Wha—?"

A faint crack split the air as her suppressed rifle spat a bullet downrange.

The clear glass emitter on the belly of the Tater flickered but remained intact.

Rachel fired another round, the rifle bucking in her hands.

Light glinted off the fixture again.

The major shook her head.

"What are you doing?" Vaughn whispered. "Did you hit it?"

"Of course I did!"

She fired again.

Light flashed from the belly once more.

Vaughn realized he hadn't heard the expected twang of a ricochet from any of the shots.

Growling, Rachel stepped from behind cover and switched to full auto. The silenced rifle danced in her hands, releasing a staccato stutter that sounded like a rapid-firing nail gun.

Dozens of lights shot out from the Tater's emitter. The damned thing was beaming out the rounds, sending them to Hell.

The machine turned and flew straight at Rachel. When it was still a good twenty meters away, a white fan of light shot out from the belly of the Tater.

Rachel disappeared.

Vaughn's eyes flew wide. "Son of a bitch!"

Cornered and out of options, he activated his grenade launcher.

"Fuck it!"

He leaned out from behind cover and leveled his weapon.

The weapon jumped in his hands when he pulled the trigger. A loud hollow-sounding thump belched from its muzzle.

Vaughn watched as the spinning round arced toward the nose of the Tater.

Another flicker of light flashed out from the emitter, and the grenade disappeared mid-flight.

The reports of several other barking launchers rang out.

The light wave emitter flickered frenetically, illuminating the walls of the tunnel like the strobing flashes of paparazzi cameras, each beam eradicating another grenade mid-flight.

The Tater adjusted its trajectory and flew straight at Vaughn. In the corner of his eye, he saw Angela roll out from under the conduit and raise to a knee, her arm extended.

Vaughn held out a hand. "No, Angela!"

She pointed the alien EMP gun at the Tater and squeezed the trigger.

Click.

Angela jerked the trigger several more times, but nothing happened. The tiny weapon hadn't finished recharging.

A fan of white light flickered over her.

Angela and the gun vanished.

Vaughn froze with his arm still held out, staring at the place she'd just been in. His jaw worked, framing a silent, unrealized scream.

As Vaughn stared at the bare, concrete floor, part of his brain registered movement beyond the potato-shaped vessel.

Scrambling stealthily, BOb sped along the ceiling of the tunnel, using the overhead ladder-shaped cable racks like monkey bars.

With insectile dexterity and preternatural speed, the robot raced toward the back of the menacingly advancing Tater.

Having perceived the movement subconsciously, Vaughn continued to stare at the section of floor where Angela had been a moment before.

The white light returned, striking the ground just in front of his feet.

Everything slowed.

Time dilated.

The curtain of light slowly swept toward Vaughn.

Part of him thought the Taters enjoyed tormenting their prey like a cat playing with a mouse before snapping its spine.

Then BOb slammed down onto the back of the levitating machine.

Disconnected and drowning in a silent cacophony, Vaughn perceived all of it as if in a dream.

The Tater bobbed visibly under the robot's heavy weight.

The fan of white light skidded past Vaughn.

A horrified scream erupted from behind him.

Was that Rourke?

Straddling the machine like a jockey mounting Seabiscuit, BOb raised a clenched fist and began to jackhammer it into the top skin of the Tater.

The now jittering fan of white light danced around Vaughn.

Angela's empty expanse of concrete seemed to scream.

No. That was him.

"Angela!"

Something plowed into Vaughn.

He stumbled backward.

Mark's face filled his vision. He was shouting something.

The man flinched and then looked over his shoulder.

Mark and Vaughn watched as a white chunk of the Tater's shell clattered to the floor.

BOb's arm sank elbow-deep into the machine's body. Then the battlebot heaved mightily.

Sparks flew from the top of the Tater, bouncing from the ceiling and showering down on the ground beneath.

The robot's arm emerged from the opening, clutching a handful of cables and hardware.

At the same time, the white light extinguished, and the Tater crashed to the floor.

Dropping to his knees, Vaughn stared into the empty space beneath the collider's large blue conduit.

He saw none of it.

A vision filled him, that of a hill covered in unimaginable sorrow and unspeakable horrors.

"No, no, no, no. No, Angela."

He closed his eyes, but the image of Angela alone atop a mountain of the freshly dead persisted.

A choked cry escaped Vaughn.

"No ... please ... no."

CHAPTER 28

Vaughn closed his eyes and shook his head hard. *Stop it, Singleton! You have to keep going.*

If he didn't get moving, Angela would be lost forever, trapped in a real Hell, not the proverbial one, but one that even Dante couldn't have envisioned.

Vaughn felt himself slipping back toward the abyss. The mere thought of Hell threatened to quit him.

The place had been bad enough—by a damned sight—when their interdimensional travels had thrust them upon it months after the initial event. At this point, scarcely more than a week since the Necks had deposited the whole of Earth's life upon that dusty rock, the dead would be … fresh.

The Tater hadn't beamed Angela onto a mountain of dust-covered bones.

The bastard had beamed her to …

A chill snaked down his spine.

This time, Vaughn shook his head so hard it caused him to stumble back a step.

Mark grabbed his shoulders and pulled him upright. "I'm so sorry, Vaughn. I … We …"

Pushing his friend away, Vaughn scanned the faces of the other team members. "We have to finish this!" His eyes narrowed. "And I mean to finish it right goddamn now!"

Rourke, who had been staring at the now empty space where Rachel had been standing just a moment before, dragged his eyes away from the void and stared back at him. The blood had drained from the man's face.

Vaughn knew that the young doctor had grown close to Major Lee. He watched the man collect himself and then swallow. Finally, Rourke looked at Vaughn and gave a short nod. Then he said something that caught Vaughn off guard. "We lost Wing Commander Bingham, too."

Looking around, he realized the young man was right. Chance was gone.

Behind Doctor Geller, Major Peterson nodded soberly. Angela's crewmates looked as shocked as Vaughn felt.

He realized that when the light had skittered past him, it must have taken out the wing commander. That's why Rourke had cried out. He'd been right next to the man.

Monique's look mirrored that of everyone else. However, she pressed her lips into a thin line and dipped her head. "You are correct, Captain Singleton. We need to finish this right now."

Mark nodded. "We're with you."

Vaughn glanced toward the ALICE experiment's facility. No new sounds had emerged above the steady drone of the still working collider. At the moment, nothing else appeared to be coming.

That wouldn't last.

He pointed at Monique and Rourke. "Lieutenant Gheist and Doctor Geller. With me."

Dropping all pretense at stealth, Vaughn turned and started running toward the widening end of the tunnel, heading for the ALICE experiment's facility. "There should be a computer terminal here somewhere, and the two of you are my best computer geeks." He left out: *remaining*.

Spotting a console next to an arcane piece of equipment, Vaughn darted over to its location. As they had seen back at CMS, the HiLumi icon was drifting across its screen.

Vaughn pulled out the chair and waved Monique into it.

She gave a short nod and slid into the seat. However, a moment later, they all growled in frustration as the same network unavailable message popped up.

The Necks had severed its intranet connection.

Vaughn looked around, desperately searching for another network access terminal, but then he shook his head. "We don't have time to waste. Nothing here'll be connected. Let's get to ATLAS."

"Agreed," Mark said. Then his face twisted. "But what do we do if, no, *when* we run into more resistance? Especially if it's another Tater. Nothing we threw at that thing worked, and I doubt we can count on them ignoring BOb anymore."

Vaughn turned from the far end of ALICE and nodded. "You're right." He looked at each of their rifles and sidearms and then shook his head. "We have to find a weapon that works. The bastard beamed out everything we threw at them." He pointed at the robot. "BOb's EMP cannon didn't even make the thing sneeze. And Angela's EMP gun... Well, it's gone." The thought almost sent him back over the edge.

Everyone stared back at him somberly, waiting for him to continue.

After taking a deep breath, Vaughn returned their gazes. "We need something that can hurt them."

"Maybe we improvise weapon." Pausing, Teddy gestured at their surroundings. "Use something from here."

Vaughn nodded as he recalled trying to attack the collider control pedestal in Mon Calamari with a large pipe wrench he'd found lying around the facility.

He scanned their surroundings. Nothing stood out. Aside from the dead Tater that still lay outside the far end of the facility, nothing looked out of place. There wasn't even a loose tool lying around this portion of the collider.

His gaze returned to the white ovoid. Taters seemed to serve as the Necks' alien police, their blue force, or white in this case.

Vaughn tilted his head. "I wonder ..."

Breaking from the group, he ran over to the dead Tater. He could hear the others close on his heels.

"El Capitan," Teddy whispered urgently from behind him. "What are you doing? You're going the wrong way."

Vaughn stopped in front of the fallen machine.

Aside from the gaping hole that BOb had made, the featureless construct sported only one protrusion from its otherwise smooth skin. When the thing had fallen to the floor, it had rolled onto its side, leaving its belly-mounted light wave emitter exposed. It now stared unblinkingly at them from the bottom of the Tater.

Vaughn felt vulnerable under its unwavering gaze. He half-expected to see white light shoot from it. After a moment, he decided it must be entirely dead.

He pointed at BOb. "Start peeling off the skin. Let's get a look inside."

As the robot bent to its work, the rest of the team stared at Vaughn.

Glancing back at them, he gestured at the fallen machine. "Maybe there's something inside the Tater, something we can use as a weapon."

Looking at the emitter, Vaughn tilted his head as he saw a new feature: a seam in the skin. It ran around the emitter lens, forming a circle roughly a meter wide. This was the first time he'd seen anything other than a smooth surface on a Tater.

Leaning in for a closer look, he studied the area. He ran a finger along the thin outline, trying to work a nail into the groove, but the skin wouldn't yield.

Standing, he waved the robot over. "BOb, see if you can pry open this part."

"Wait!" Rourke said. "He's just as likely to break it as open it."

"We don't have time for subtleties, Doctor Geller."

The young doctor held up a hand. "I see something."

"Doctor Geller, I said we don't—"

Extending a finger, Rourke touched a portion of the Tater's exterior just outside the outline. The shell around the emitter began to slide outward.

Everyone jumped back, raising their guns defensively.

Vaughn had his pistol out and aimed at the lens before he'd known he was moving.

No light came.

The receding skin divided into triangular-shaped sections and retracted like a giant camera shutter opening in slow motion. The pie-shaped pieces silently slid out of view, leaving the emitter and its mounting hardware protruding from the center of the opening.

Monique stopped backing up and leaned toward the Tater. "What on earth …? What is that doing in there?"

Confused, Vaughn looked from her to the emitter. Narrowing his eyes, he focused on the thing's mounting hardware and the wires and connections feeding into it. He holstered his pistol and looked back at Monique. "Wh-What?"

She slowly shook her head and pointed into the guts of the thing. "*That* should not be there."

"Lieutenant Gheist, what are you talking about?" Vaughn said with mounting frustration.

Monique leaned in closer and probed the area with a finger. "The mount, the connectors, the hardware, none of it should be in this thing."

"Oh my God," Rourke said, suddenly looking as mystified as Monique. He bent over and stared into the belly of the Tater. "Is that One Eighty-Eight hardware?"

Lieutenant Gheist nodded, her head bobbing up and down rapidly. "Yes. Yes, it is."

Rourke looked at her. "That's not possible."

Vaughn and the rest of the men leaned over the Tater, trying to see what they were talking about.

He and Mark exchanged a confused glance. Then Vaughn placed a firm hand on Doctor Geller's shoulder. "What's wrong with that hardware? Why shouldn't it be here?"

Dragging their eyes from the interstices of the machine, Rourke and Monique stared up at him. They looked as confused as he felt.

Lieutenant Gheist pointed at the hardware and connectors at the base of the emitter. "This is a MIL-Standard One-Eighty-Eight interface."

"MIL-Standard?" Teddy said, confusion crowding his face. "As in Military Standard?"

Rourke nodded slowly. "Yes, it's United States Military Standard hardware."

CHAPTER 29

Rourke watched as Lieutenant Gheist directed BOb. Using tools built into its appendages and moving quickly, the robot soon had the emitter and its hardware removed from the belly of the Tater.

Monique had been correct. The design of the connectors and the mounts were straight out of United States technical bulletins and design criteria. He'd become intimately familiar with the hardware when he was assigned to work on the James Webb Space Telescope at Johnson Space Center in Houston. MIL-Standard One-Eighty-Eight-compliant hardware, firmware, and software were utilized throughout the space-based telescope.

Now that they were digging into the thing, they discovered that, in spite of the mount's US mil-spec design, it had been manufactured using alien technology. The thing definitely followed the parameters set out by the standardization regulations. However, it appeared the Necks had constructed it via some type of advanced 3D printing.

Lording over them, Vaughn breathed heavily. He glanced down the tunnel and then back at them. "So you're saying the Necks likely built this?"

Monique nodded. "It appears so."

"Then why is it US mil-spec?"

The woman held up the piece and studied it intently. "I have no idea, Captain." She sounded distracted as she continued to stare into the emitter's connector. "I wonder ..."

Looking up, she waved the robot over. "BOb, please remove the transmitter assembly from the end of the Mark Twenty-Eight EMP cannon."

The bot nodded and wordlessly complied.

Looking like a robotic version of Edward Scissorhands, BOb extended tools from the tips of multiple fingers and began to probe the end of the large, electronic gun.

A moment later, the robot extracted the business end of the EMP cannon and set it aside. Then it regarded Lieutenant Gheist expectantly.

She held out the emitter. A short cable hung beneath its mounting hardware, swaying like severed entrails.

After retracting the tools back into its fingers, BOb took the device.

Monique pointed to the open socket on the end of the EMP cannon. "BOb, please attach the hardware and connect the cable."

"Yes, Lieutenant."

Using only its fingers, the robot snapped the device into place. Then it plugged the cable into the exposed harness on the end of the gun's chassis. BOb gently twisted the connector's outer sleeve.

Rourke heard it click home as the plug mated perfectly with the device.

Captain Singleton blinked. "I'll be a son of a bitch ..." He looked at Monique. "It fits perfectly."

She nodded. "It is a standard interface, designed for interconnectivity."

Bill Peterson slowly shook his head. "Then what the hell is it doing in an alien vessel?"

Monique mirrored his gesture. "I have no idea." Pausing, she looked at the robot. "BOb, run a BIT on the device."

The robot nodded. "Built-In-Test complete. Device is One-Eighty-Eight dash Two-Twelve-compliant."

Confusion twisted Vaughn's face as he glanced from the naval lieutenant to the robot.

Monique ignored him and addressed BOb. "Two-Twelve? TADIL B?"

"Affirmative, Lieutenant. Confirmed as Link-Eleven data communications."

"Tattle?" Vaughn asked.

Monique shook her head. "T-A-D-I-L: Tactical Digital Information Link. It is the interoperability and performance standards we use for land- and ship-based systems."

Bill Peterson looked ready to ask another question, but Monique held up a finger. "I told you, William, I do not know how it got there." Lowering her arm, she looked at Captain Singleton. "I can, however, venture a guess."

Glancing toward the ALICE experiment facility, Vaughn spun a finger in the air. "Quickly, please."

"Perhaps the aliens adapted technology they found on this side of the wormhole for their own purposes."

The captain nodded impatiently. "Sounds plausible, but right now, I need to know if it—"

"Lieutenant Gheist," BOb said, interrupting Vaughn. "I've located some data, although I am not sure of its purpose."

Alarm registered on Captain Singleton's face. The man stepped back and drew his pistol. Raising it, he aimed it directly at BOb's head.

The robot froze. Then it slowly turned to look at Vaughn. "Have I done something wrong, Captain?"

Singleton ignored the question. He looked at Monique and dipped his head toward the new attachment on the end of the EMP cannon. "Can that thing infect him?"

The robot shook its head. "Negative, Captain. The interface facilitates one-way transfers. I can access tabular data, but it will not permit incoming data streams or viral uploads."

Monique nodded. "BOb is correct. It is a safety built into the software interface for that very purpose."

Vaughn allowed his weapon to drop. He glanced toward ALICE

once more. "Go ahead, BOb." He rolled a finger again. "Hurry up and finish what you were saying."

"Thank you, Captain Asshole."

Vaughn scowled at the machine.

Rourke held up a hand. "I've got this." He yanked a small tablet computer from his backpack and quickly connected it to the robot using a USB cable. "Show me the data, BOb."

An instant later, numbers began to stream across the screen. Rourke could feel the other members of the team looking over his shoulder. Bill pointed at the tablet. "Some of those look like coordinates."

The robot nodded. "I believe you are correct, Major Peterson. They appear to be associated with this location and one other. However, I do not have sufficient information to extrapolate the significance of the additional datasets. They do not appear to be coordinates."

Teddy raised his eyebrows. "Maybe the second location is Hell."

"Yes ..." Monique nodded. "I believe you may be correct, Theodore."

"Son of a bitch!" Major Peterson paused and then pointed at the now modified EMP cannon. "You're saying we can beam things to Hell with this, Monique?"

"Yes. I believe so."

Captain Singleton's face darkened as an inscrutable look crossed it.

Colonel Hennessy saw it as well. The man shook his head. "Don't even think about it, Vaughn."

Mark's words pulled the captain from his thoughts. He looked up, his eyes suddenly pleading. "She's there all by herself. If I go—"

"No, Vaughn! Angela's best chance lies in us resetting the timeline. The Necks have already reduced our numbers. If you go there, too, we'll have even fewer redundancies. You'll not only be dooming yourself; you could also be dooming the entire human race."

Myriad emotions crossed the captain's face as he considered Mark's words. Finally, he shook his head. "Shit, shit, *shit!*"

Teddy looked from the two men to the emitter now mounted to the end of the EMP gun. "I still want to know how US military hardware ended up in alien device."

Vaughn waved a dismissive hand. "We can figure all that out later." Turning from the cosmonaut, Captain Singleton pointed at the robot. "Can you fire it?"

BOb nodded. "I believe so."

Hennessy looked at Singleton, fresh concern twisting his face.

Raising a hand, Vaughn shook his head. "Not at me." He pointed at the Tater. "Shoot that."

As BOb moved into position, Rourke spooled through the table displayed on the touchscreen. When he reached the top, he saw words and stopped. Then he looked at Monique. "It's in English."

Everyone fell silent and turned to look at him.

"What is?" Monique asked.

"The labels at the top of the chart."

BOb dipped his head. "Affirmative. However, I need more data to extrapolate their meaning."

Vaughn shook his head impatiently. "We don't have time for this!" He pointed at the Tater again. "Shoot the goddamn thing, BOb!"

The robot leveled the large gun at the target. White light extended from its end. BOb swept it over the Tater twice, but nothing happened.

The light died, but the white ovoid remained.

It hadn't been beamed to Hell.

Turning his attention back to the tablet, Rourke cycled through the menu items. While he was unable to determine the meaning of several titles, he saw checkboxes and radio buttons beneath some of them. It appeared they could be toggled off and on. One, in particular, drew his eye. It was labeled ORG. Touching the indicated area, he found he was able to cycle it from 'On' to 'Off.'

Looking up, he pointed at the Tater. "Try again, BOb."

The robot raised the rifle again and aimed at the machine. The fan of light arced over the Tater.

This time, when the light died, it left nothing behind but a depression in the concrete where the Tater had been. Not only did the light banish the dead machine, but it had also sent a scoop of the floor with it.

Monique looked at Rourke, surprise registering on her face. "What did you change, Doctor Geller?"

He showed her the tablet, indicating the cell labeled ORG. "I turned off this one. Thought maybe it meant organic."

"Whatever you did, it worked," Vaughn said and then smiled. "I'd say we have a weapon." He patted Rourke's shoulder. "Great job, Doctor! Hurry up and disconnect your tablet. It's time for us to get some payback."

CHAPTER 30

Captain Singleton pointed toward ATLAS. "Let's move, gentlemen."

The man grabbed BOb by the elbow and led the robot down the tunnel.

After exchanging a nervous glance with the rest of the team, Rourke stored the tablet and gathered his rifle.

Falling into formation, he and Monique began to trot toward ATLAS.

As they reached the far side of the ALICE facility, Captain Singleton released the robot and gestured into the tunnel. "BOb, take point again. Hit anything that moves with that light beam." He held out a hand. "Just don't hit the collider. We can't lose it."

Nodding, the robot turned and sprinted ahead.

Next, Singleton addressed Major Peterson and the cosmonaut. "Bill and Teddy, cover our six. I know these things don't work." He held up his weapon to emphasize his words. "But if a Tater approaches your end of the formation, fire as much as you can. Maybe you can overwhelm it. The main thing is to slow it down long enough for BOb to reach your position."

The captain turned and addressed the entire team. "Don't fire grenades unless we're about to be overrun, but don't wait till they're on top of you either."

Peterson rolled his eyes. "Are you going to tell us how many squares to use when we wipe our asses?"

"Just don't hit anything critical." Vaughn paused and pointed fore and aft. "Spread out."

Colonel Hennessy nodded and ran up to resume his position behind the robot.

Captain Singleton stood in the middle, a few meters ahead of Rourke and Monique. Looking up and down the line, Vaughn nodded. "Let's keep this spacing." Then he gestured forward. "Move out!"

As one, they began to run down the corridor at a brisk jog.

After several minutes, a stitch set up shop in Rourke's side.

Wincing, he massaged the area with a thumb. Then he froze as a screaming rush announced the approach of another Tater.

BOb raised his gun and sighted on an unseen target ahead. "Contact!"

The Tater was too far down the curving tunnel for Rourke to see.

Adrenaline dumped into his system.

He forgot the stitch in his side.

Pulse pounding in his ears, Rourke fought to draw sufficient breath.

The white light arced from the tip of BOb's weapon and disappeared into the distant tunnel.

The sound of the unseen Tater's drive vanished, but then two more raised to replace it.

A second beam and then another shot out from the robot's modified cannon.

"Keep going!" Vaughn waved the remaining humans forward. "We're almost to ATLAS!"

The sound of approaching Taters redoubled. The noise began to warble in and out of harmony like a pair of mistuned airplane engines.

Rourke looked over his shoulder, and the noise grew louder. "Oh shit!"

He felt the blood drain from his face.

Multiple Taters were approaching simultaneously from each end of the tunnel. The colliding sound waves of their combined engine noises generated the reverberation.

Then Rourke's heart threatened to burst from his chest as he saw two of the machines coming up from behind them.

Running forward while looking back, he watched the pair of cow-sized Taters round the gentle curve of the tunnel, speeding along unerringly, as if they were hanging from monorails. The alien ovoids raced side-by-side, their bellies six feet above the main passageway.

Vaughn shouted back to Bill and Teddy. "Too many Taters hitting us upfront! You're on your own back there. Hit 'em with everything!"

Bill Peterson stopped running. "No argument here." He raised his rifle, aiming it at the onrushing enemy vessels.

The cosmonaut slid to a stop just behind the man and shouted over his shoulder. "We're on it, El Capitan!"

Still running forward, Rourke watched the men as they aimed their rifles at the Taters.

The double womp of simultaneous grenade launches issued from their muzzles. Visible in spite of their speed, the rounds arced through the air.

Before the grenades had covered half the distance, twinned light beams radiated out from the bellies of the approaching Taters.

Both rounds vanished mid-flight.

Rourke and the lieutenant turned and ran several meters closer to ATLAS. He heard Bill and Teddy running behind them.

Monique hopped over the collider's conduit. Rourke instantly understood. The lieutenant's shift would give her a clear line of sight for the next engagement.

They all stopped running and turned back toward their attackers.

No longer having to worry about hitting Peterson or the cosmonaut, Monique pumped round after round into the approaching Taters. She didn't have a grenade launcher, but she was a crack shot with her rifle. However, none of her bullets reached their targets.

Blue-white light burned into every round she'd fired at the enemy machines.

Suddenly, all hell broke loose ahead, at the front of their running formation.

Rourke looked forward and saw Colonel Hennessy firing his rifle on full auto. Flashing fire belched from its muzzle, strobing the walls gold at that end of the tunnel.

Captain Singleton looked at Rourke and pointed a bladed hand toward the back of the tunnel. "Help Bill and Teddy. Go full auto with your rifle. See if you can overwhelm their defenses. Maybe one of those grenades will get through."

Beyond Captain Singleton, light from the battlebot's BFG added a blue-white hue to the tunnel walls as another beam burned into its farthest reaches.

Focusing on Vaughn, Rourke swallowed hard and nodded.

The captain returned the gesture. "Hurry! We're almost there!" Then he sprinted forward, apparently intent on shoring up the formation's advancing front.

Rourke looked at the side of his rifle's receiver and flicked the selector to fully automatic.

Running to stand between Bill and Teddy, he raised his weapon and aimed it at the enemy vessels.

His pulse pounded in his ears. Somehow it even managed to override the cacophony of the mounting battle.

Two more reports rang out from the muzzles of Bill and Teddy's grenade launchers.

The dark, wobbling rounds arced through the air with incredible speed. Then they, too, disappeared, vanishing just as the others had.

Rourke hesitated. He still worried what might happen if one of the rounds missed their target and hit the wide, blue tubing of the collider's conduit. Likely as not, that would collapse the field and shut down the collider.

They would be trapped in this timeline.

Shaking his head, Rourke ground his teeth together. Captain Singleton had been right. What else could they do? They were out of options. If the robots stopped them now, that was it, game over. Any chance they had of defeating the Necks would die and the whole of humanity with it.

Understanding there was no alternative, Rourke raised his assault rifle and began to spray and pray, firing dozens of rounds at the two Taters.

Lightning-like beams danced through the air, eradicating all of his bullets. None of them reached their target.

Looking around, Rourke realized he could no longer see Monique.

Where had she gone? The Taters hadn't gotten close enough to beam her out.

The alien machines pressed on.

Firing while falling back, Rourke, followed by Bill and Teddy, fought to stay ahead of the two Taters.

As the machines continued to advance, bluish-white light flickered from the emitters on their bellies.

Lieutenant Gheist popped up right next to the enemy ships.

She must have hidden, waiting for the Taters to overfly her position.

Rourke skidded to a stop and aimed at the onrushing vessels.

Monique fired twice in rapid succession.

At the same time, Rourke poured fire into the noses of the Taters.

The first few rounds vanished, but Monique's bullets found their targets. The emitters shattered and the twinned beams of blue-white light extinguished.

Bullets from the rifles of all three men tore into the Taters.

The two white ovoids fell to the floor and tumbled to a stop.

Monique looked at Rourke and pumped a fist into the air.

She never saw the third Tater round the corner behind her.

Rourke raised his rifle. "Get down!"

Before he could squeeze off a shot, a wide, white arc reached out from the new Tater and swept across Monique.

Rourke blinked, suddenly unable to breathe as he watched her disappear.

CHAPTER 31

Rourke's eyes flared. "No!" He raised his gun and began to fire it on full auto. "Die, you son of a bitch!"

None of the bullets reached the Tater.

Behind him, the high-pitched discharge of BOb's modified EMP cannon echoed off the tunnel walls, pouring over Rourke's shoulders like a crashing wave. The staccato reports of multiple rifle and grenade shots also peppered the air, echoing crazily within the confined space.

His gaze returned to the spot where Monique had been. Dragging his eyes from it, he looked at the now slowed advance of the third Tater.

In a sudden epiphany, Rourke understood that their counterattack was the only thing that had prevented the bastards from already beaming them all to Hell. From the descriptions relayed by Captain Singleton and Commander Brown, he believed they were already within range of the new one's light wave emitter.

Regardless, Monique's sacrifice had proven they needed to change their tactics. If not, they would fail. All of them would join her and the others in Hell.

Narrowing eyes and gnashing teeth, Rourke toggled his grenade launcher.

He moved to stand between Bill and Teddy. "We need to overwhelm its defenses. We'll fire our grenades in unison and then switch to auto."

The two men nodded.

"On one," Rourke said.

Major Peterson and the cosmonaut sighted down their weapons.

Accelerating, the third Tater closed to within fifty meters.

Rourke raised the launcher and aimed it.

"Three, two, *one!*"

The triple womp of simultaneous discharges concussed the air.

In the fraction of a second that it took for their gently arcing grenades to cross the narrowing distance, all three men loosed a fusillade of bullets.

In his dilated perception of time, Rourke imagined he could see the hundreds of 5.56mm rounds zip past the wobbling grenades.

White light flickered from the belly of the Tater, strobing manically.

Two of the explosives winked out of existence.

An instant later, the nose of the alien vessel burst open, rupturing as the third grenade found its target.

The explosion pushed all three men back and set Rourke's ears to ringing.

He watched in surreally muffled silence as the shredded remnant of the Tater slammed into the white-striped pavement. Its inertia carried the thing to a grinding halt a mere dozen feet ahead of them.

Someone grabbed him by the collar. Captain Singleton shouted into his ear. "Move it, Doctor Geller!" Then the man shoved him toward the opposite end of the tunnel, in the direction of ATLAS.

Rourke nodded and started running. Ahead of him, BOb was waving them on and shouting something, but Rourke couldn't discern the words over the ringing in his ears. The robot had stopped firing in that direction, and they weren't dead yet, so they had that going for them.

He released a short, manic laugh, surprised by his ability to joke at the moment.

Looking over his shoulder, he saw Captain Singleton urging Major Peterson and Cosmonaut Petrovich onward, the man's message clear even above the ringing. "Go! Go! Go!"

Rourke turned his attention back to front and soon caught up with Colonel Hennessy.

As they advanced down the tunnel, following the once again running battlebot, he saw divots dug out of the curved concrete ceiling. The light beam from BOb's cannon had also scooped out parts of the cables and racks that lined the top of the passageway. Their stunted raw ends, some of them sparking, terminated in sharp edges where the light beam had cut clean through them.

Seeing this, Rourke ran a hand across the top of the wide metal tube. The ringing in his ears made it impossible for him to hear whether or not it was still humming. However, the conduit thrummed smoothly under his sliding fingertips. Thankfully, the damaged cabling hadn't been part of the collider's power supply or control system. It was still running.

Looking up, Rourke saw that he'd fallen a few strides behind Colonel Hennessy. Ahead, the man followed the robot into a widening section of the tunnel.

Had they reached the ATLAS facility?

Captain Singleton pulled up next to him and confirmed it. Running, Vaughn pointed ahead and shouted breathlessly, "We're almost to ATLAS! You're my only computer geek." He paused for air and then added, "Be ready. First terminal I see, we're stopping."

The screech of another approaching Tater suddenly penetrated Rourke's muffled senses.

He exchanged a horrified glance with Captain Singleton.

The howling wails quickly rose to painful levels. Then the sound began to warble once more but with more intensity than last time.

The enemy vessels were coming from both directions again, but now, there were more of them.

Rourke couldn't see the Tater ahead, but when he looked over his shoulder, he saw three of the cow-sized alien vessels slide into view at the far end of the curving tunnel. Rapidly approaching from the team's six, each of the Taters jostled for position in the limited space afforded within the equipment-choked passageway.

BOb's cannon barked to life ahead.

Another howling drive fell silent.

Running with an awkward sideways gate, Rourke dragged his gaze from the Taters behind them and glanced forward.

Hennessy followed the robot deeper into the facility.

Running behind Captain Singleton, Rourke again saw damaged cables and pipes where BOb's gun had eaten into them.

Rourke's ears had recovered enough that he could hear the thrum of the still functioning collider.

BOb fired his cannon again.

Vaughn and Mark sprinted ahead.

Dropping back, Rourke added his gun to those of the major and the cosmonaut. Using the same tactic that they'd employed against the previous enemy vessel, they soon overwhelmed the defenses of the trio of flying bots, but not before the last one got dangerously close.

The final Tater collapsed to the floor. The smoking ruin slid to a stop at their feet.

Rourke turned and saw that they had reached the widening section of the tunnel. It appeared to delineate the beginning of the ATLAS facility.

Ahead, BOb's cannon fell silent, as did the last of the Taters. The robot must have cleared out the enemy crafts before Mark or Vaughn had needed to add their rifles to the effort.

Rourke continued deeper into ATLAS. He heard Bill and Teddy running a few meters behind him.

Craning his neck as he ran, Rourke searched desperately, trying to spot a workstation or computer terminal.

He saw none.

The tunnel opened further, revealing a starburst of large pipes radiating out from a central point.

They'd reached the backside of the ATLAS experiment's iconic works.

Even after being chased by a pack of killer robots, Rourke marveled at the scale of it. As he ran toward the back of the assembly, he stared at it with reverent awe.

The thing was huge.

Pictures had done it no justice. He'd heard it contained more metal than the Eiffel Tower, but that still hadn't prepared Rourke for this.

He followed BOb and the two Army pilots down stairs that hugged the floor of the widening tunnel.

Rourke felt his hopes rising at the prospect that they might be gaining the upper hand. They had reached ATLAS. Soon, he would activate the commands that would undo all of this, bringing back Monique, Rachel and the whole of humanity. They would—

The stairs deposited Rourke onto an exposed, elevated landing, and his short-lived hope suffered a quick death.

Standing motionlessly atop their lofty perch, Rourke, Mark, and Vaughn, along with BOb, stared across the open facility.

Breathing heavily, Teddy came running up behind them. "What are you waiting for, El Capi—?" The man seized and slid to a stop next to Rourke.

Bill landed heavily on the metal deck. "What the hell are we ...? Oh, fuck me ...!"

Transfixed atop the elevated landing, BOb and the five humans stared across ATLAS.

The wormhole hung suspended at its geometric center, directly across from them. It looked exactly as Vaughn and Angela had described.

However, the silvery sphere was not the source of their shared trepidation.

Behind the mercurial orb, hundreds of Necks lined the far side of ATLAS.

The enemy robots stood on catwalks, balconies, corridors, and walkways. They covered every surface of the facility's opposite side.

With ominous menace, the veritable army of multi-armed, white-bodied Necks silently glared at the last vestiges of Earth's life and their pet robot.

CHAPTER 32

U nlike Vaughn and Angela's descriptions, these robots were not waving their arms about or conversing animatedly. They simply stared back at the group.

However, the wormhole perfectly matched the accounts of Captain Singleton and Commander Brown. The sphere hung suspended at the facility's central focal point. The perfectly smooth surface reflected a fish-eyed, wide-angle rendition of the ATLAS detector's radiating network of conduits. Rourke knew his shocked visage hung somewhere in that image, but from a hundred meters away, he couldn't see more than the starburst pattern of the overall structure.

In the moment it took him to take in all of this, nothing moved. The opposing forces merely stared at each other in a surreally stretched out motionless stand-off.

The men winced, and, too late, Rourke threw up a shielding hand as brilliant light flared from the orb.

He had just enough time to register the fact that it hadn't beamed them to Hell, that the flash was instead the prelude to another arrival when the solid-looking sphere suddenly liquefied.

According to Angela and Vaughn, the flash of ethereal light seemed to precede the passage of something through the wormhole.

Concentric rings raced across its curved surface.

Rourke remained rooted in place. He worried the next thing to come from the sphere might be an arc of white light with designs of beaming them all to Hell. Angela had said she didn't think the Necks could fire the beam through the wormhole while they were on this side of it, but Rourke wasn't ready to bet all their lives on that unproven theory.

Yet, he still couldn't move his seemingly anchored feet. The utterly alien situation held him transfixed, trapped between fight or flight.

The top of the mercurial orb began to distend, stretching upward. Then the disc-shaped head and broad shoulders of a neckless Neck popped through the wormhole's oscillating surface.

Halfway through the act of emergence, the robot seized up as it appeared to see the biological interlopers.

It stopped rising. Only the upper portion of its white body protruded from the top of the four-foot-wide sphere.

Turning, the half-buried Neck joined its peers in staring at the humans.

Its hanging arms began to rise, drawing its four hands from the still undulating wormhole.

Behind the new arrival, each of the Necks in attendance raised all four of their arms and pointed at the team accusingly.

Rourke started to duck, thinking the Necks were bringing weapons to bear, that each hand surely clutched a gun. However, nothing but an accusingly pointed finger extended from each of the thousands of arms.

Most of the remaining team members flinched as a siren wail rose. Only BOb and Captain Singleton didn't react.

It took Rourke a moment to realize the sound was coming from the Necks.

"Enough of that shit!" Vaughn said through a growl.

The captain raised his weapon.

The rifle barked out a shot.

The disc-shaped head of the Neck protruding from the wormhole flew from its body.

Rourke watched it tumble backward like a flipped coin. In his time-dilated perceptions, the disembodied robotic head appeared to move in slow motion.

The siren wails stopped. The collider's thrumming cadence reclaimed its dominance over the enormous facility.

At the same time, the central robot's arms went slack. They dropped, pulling the Neck's now inanimate body forward. It toppled out of the wormhole and fell to the floor four stories beneath the levitating mercurial orb, crumpling into a heap and then moving no more.

On the floor some distance away, its disc-shaped head spiraled down noisily like a spinning dinner plate.

Finally, it, too, stilled.

Behind the robot's now lifeless remains, the crowd of attending Necks stared down at their fallen comrade with seeming incomprehension.

Then the bots erupted into action. Flailing their arms and gesticulating wildly, they shouted at the humans accusingly.

Narrowing his eyes, Vaughn smiled menacingly. "Goddamn, that felt good!" He gave Rourke and the remaining members of the team a sideward glance. "What the hell are you waiting for, gentlemen?"

The captain switched his assault rifle's selector to full auto and raised the weapon, aiming at the screaming crowd of Necks. "Light 'em up!" Before pulling the trigger, he gave the men a meaningful glance. "Just don't hit anything important."

Then Vaughn fired a short burst into a line of the Necks, strafing them from left to right.

Pandemonium erupted from the gallery. Finally understanding what was happening to them, the Necks began to crawl over each other as bodies fell like dominoes. Several leaped into the air, flying six feet or more over the heads of their brethren.

BOb and the other members of the team opened fire, raising the mechanical carnage another level.

Shattered carapaces and dismembered arms flew into the air.

Rourke raised his rifle. He still had full auto selected. He fingered the trigger and then hesitated.

The seemingly sentient robots were dying by the dozen.

It was a massacre.

Then images of his lost family and friends streamed through Rourke's mind.

These bastards hadn't hesitated, hadn't paused to consider what lives they were snuffing out when they'd swept the planet clean of all animal life.

Rourke added his weapon to the effort. Opening fire, he swept the jittering muzzle of his M4 across a scrambling swarm of the robots. Several dropped instantly. However, many stumbled as parts of their bodies flew off, exposing shadowed interstices laced with twinkling lights.

He took no solace in the act. It sickened him, but in Earth's bloody history, there had never been a more clear case of it's-us-or-them. Either Rourke and the Merry Band of Pirates would succeed, or humanity would cease to exist.

As equations went, it didn't get much more straightforward than that.

After firing another burst, Rourke watched as a group of the scrambling robots reached the floor on the right side of the facility. Instead of fleeing as he'd expected, the Necks turned and ran full-tilt straight at him and the rest of the humans.

"Oh shit!" He fired into them. "They're coming this way!"

Vaughn, who was shooting in a different direction, looked at Rourke and then followed his line of sight. The man spun right, shifting his fire toward the new threat. "Incoming!"

Rourke's eyes went wide as he continued to shoot the leaping Necks. "Goddamn, they're fast!" Now that the things were running, their jumps reached new heights. The leaps would easily clear an entire house.

He fired a short burst that caught a Neck mid-flight. One of its arms flew off. The other three went limp as the remaining rounds slammed into the center of the bot's white torso. The robot crashed to the floor and slid to a stop. Then it moved no more.

Vaughn's hand slammed into his chest plate. "Keep firing, or they're going to overrun us!"

Rourke tore his eyes from the dead Neck and looked up in time to see another volley of robots flying through the air. Beneath them, several others were racing up the criss-crossing stairway that led up to the landing occupied by the humans.

The decking lurched beneath his boots as a Neck slammed down right in front of Rourke. In a blur, two of the robot's arms drew back lightning-fast, but before the machine could land the twinned blow that surely would've killed Rourke, the lower half of the Neck's body and a section of railing behind it vanished, sent to Hell by a flash of light from BOb's BFG.

Its severed head and shoulders along with part of an arm toppled to the floor and rocked back and forth. BOb leaned over the remnants of the Neck and shouted into its dead face, his voice a near-perfect imitation of Arnold Schwarzenegger. "Consider that a divorce!"

Vaughn grabbed Rourke's utility belt and yanked him away from the railing, nearly pulling him off his feet. "Fall back! They're overrunning us."

"No!" Rourke shouted as he shrugged out of the man's grasp. He raised his gun and aimed at the next wave of bots. "We can do this! Just keep—"

"Look!" Vaughn shouted, cutting him off and thrusting a hand over Rourke's shoulder to point at the far side of the facility. "There's more coming!"

"Oh, shit! ... That's at least a hundred of them!"

Vaughn fired a burst into another group of robots as they arced toward them. The shots robbed the now-dead bodies of just enough inertia to cause them to fall short of the landing's metal deck.

"Doctor Geller, I'd very much appreciate it if you'd follow my orders." As the captain continued to fire, he tilted his head toward the opposite side of the facility. "There's probably a thousand or more behind those. We don't have enough bullets or grenades to kill 'em all."

Vaughn paused long enough to fire into another wave of bots. The dead machines bounced off the side of the railing. The body of one crashed through the gap left by BOb's gun and then slowly slid off the deck.

"But if we stay here, we'll be overrun long before we have a chance to fire a fraction of those rounds."

Teddy fired his weapon into the robots and then looked over. "What's the plan, El Capitan?"

"I saw a side door just before we reached ATLAS. Fall back to that. It'll be on your right, just beyond the top of the stairs."

Hennessy stopped firing long enough to look back. "Why in the hell didn't we stop there the first time?"

Vaughn shrugged and fired at another robot. "We were a bit busy at the time."

Peterson pointed up the stairs. "Well, we're about to be giraffe ass-deep in Necks. I say we go now!"

Vaughn pursed his lips and shook his head. "I'm so glad you guys all agree." He grabbed Rourke and shoved him toward the stairs. "Move it already, Doctor. If we're lucky, there'll be a working network terminal in there."

Nodding, Rourke began sprinting up the stairs. Considering its proximity to the facility, he agreed with the captain's logic. Whatever waited for them beyond that door, it likely tied to the ATLAS experiment either physically or better yet digitally.

In the short moment it took for Rourke to consider those facts, he passed behind ATLAS's massive network of pipes and conduits.

He flinched as shots rang out behind him.

Then footsteps.

Looking back, he allowed himself a breath as Bill and Teddy ran through the gap, hot on his heels, followed shortly by Mark and then Vaughn.

BOb entered the tunnel behind them. Turning, the battle operations bot fired a ray of white light at an unseen attacker.

At the same moment, Vaughn ran past the others. Then he shot past Rourke and shouted over his shoulder. "I saw the door up here, Geller."

Rourke sprinted after the captain.

Sounding as if it were firing continuously, the high-pitched squeal of BOb's weapon filled the curving tunnel.

Actually, the sound went on too long, Rourke realized. It should have already faded.

Was the thing capable of continuous fire?

He didn't think so.

Instead of dropping, the squeal grew louder.

Glancing back, Rourke did a double-take at the sight of BOb running backward just behind Major Peterson and Cosmonaut Petrovich. The robot had its weapon trained on targets to their rear, and it was firing periodically, but the sound of it was lost beneath the now cacophonous assault of the high-pitched wail. The noise he'd mistaken for the discharge of the light wave-equipped EMP cannon now took on an all-too-familiar harmonic warble.

Looking forward, he saw the captain shaking his head. "Fucking Taters! A shit-ton of them this time, coming from both ends!"

The sound seemed intent on grinding Rourke's bones to dust.

"Here it is," Vaughn shouted. He stepped up to a door in the side of the tunnel and then twisted its latch. The heavy-looking panel swung outward. "Get in!"

When Rourke hesitated, Vaughn grabbed his arm and shoved him through. Before letting him go, the man scanned the room beyond the door and then gave a quick nod. He shouted into Rourke's ear, his words just audible above the rising din. "There are too many Taters coming. We'll hold them off as long as we can, but you need to get to a terminal and initiate the overload."

Rourke chewed his lip nervously and looked past Vaughn, trying to see what was happening in the tunnel.

"Goddammit, Geller! For once, do what I say without questioning it!"

Nodding, Rourke spoke with more confidence than he felt. "I'll get it done, Captain."

Vaughn gave him a hard look and then jabbed a pointed finger into his chest plate. "Do it exactly as Angela trained you. Don't get fucking cute!"

Then the man turned and stepped back into the tunnel. The door closed behind him, and the riotous noises pouring through it suddenly halved.

CHAPTER 33

After closing the door behind the young doctor, Vaughn stepped back and glanced left and right, scanning the tunnel in both directions. He saw no Taters or Necks, meaning none had seen him deposit Rourke into the side corridor. "Thank God for small favors."

Mark's rifle barked to life. "Need a little help over here!"

Bill and Teddy opened fire. From the sound of it, they were engaging at least two Taters.

Vaughn shouted in their direction. "Hold them off. I have to help Mark."

The two men waved distractedly. Bill Peterson looked back. Sweat glistened on the man's dark face. "We'll do the best we can."

Nodding, Vaughn turned toward ATLAS and started running. The sound from that direction had an echoing quality to it. The Taters coming from the facility hadn't yet entered the tunnel.

The spaghetti tangle of pipes and conduits that led into ATLAS choked this portion of the shaft, blocking all but the passageway that ran along its inner circumference.

A Neck emerged through the gap and charged straight at Hennessy.

Vaughn fired a three-round burst into the center of its chest.

The machine's arms and legs went limp, and it collapsed to the floor.

Vaughn slid to a stop next to Mark. He looked at the battlebot. "BOb, switch to rifle. Let the bodies stack up. They'll block the Taters."

"Affirmative, Captain Asshole."

Shaking his head, Vaughn pulled the shotgun from the scabbard that ran down the side of his backpack. As he pumped a slug into the chamber, he looked at Mark. "Same to you. Single shots now."

His friend threw a questioning look his way and then shouted over the droning drives of the approaching Taters. "Shouldn't we try to lead them away?"

Vaughn glanced back toward Bill and Teddy and saw them firing multiple rounds. Then he looked at Mark and shook his head. "We have to hold this position. Gotta give Rourke time to complete the overload. If we draw them down the tunnel, a thousand more will come in behind them." He gestured toward the closed door. "They'll start searching the corridors." He shook his head. "Can't let that happen. We have to keep the Necks at bay."

Mark dispatched another robot and then glanced toward the side door. "What makes you think they aren't already searching the corridors?"

Vaughn looked at the door and furrowed his brow. "Well, fuck. Thanks for that."

Another Neck charged into the passageway.

Vaughn turned and fired a shot into its torso.

The slug blasted a massive hole through the over-eager bastard's chest. The machine fell to the floor, landing on top of one of its dead comrades.

"Goddamn! That felt good!" He looked at Mark and shrugged. "We'll just have to hope Rourke finishes his job before the Necks get too industrious."

Nodding grimly, Mark patted the empty pouches on his vest. "Getting low on munitions." The man snapped his rifle up and took down two more Necks.

Vaughn killed a third. He pumped another round into the shotgun's chamber. "Me, too." He glanced over his shoulder. "BOb, load us up with ammo and then go top up Major Peterson and Cosmonaut Petrovich."

Holding his weapon and firing single-handedly, BOb rummaged through his backpack with his free arm, bending it in an unanatomical direction. While the battlebot worked, it kept nailing enemy robots with precise single shots targeted to their heads.

As Neck after Neck dropped, the battlebot chanted the same phrase repeatedly in a harsh whisper: "Let the robots hit the floor. Let the robots hit the floor." Then BOb raised his voice. "Let the robots hit the … *Floor!*" He shouted the last part. Then screaming guitar music streamed from the bot's mouth speaker. All the while, BOb continued to extract munitions from its backpack, distributing them to Mark and Vaughn smoothly, without missing a shot.

As he accepted the offered magazines and stuffed them into his pouches, Vaughn recognized the song as a modified version of Drowning Pool's *Bodies*. He smiled inwardly. It was a hard-rockin' song that his mom would've loved.

Blaring hard rock music in the middle of a battle wasn't exactly a sound tactic, but the thing was a prototype that hadn't been released for full combat duty. However, all things considered, Vaughn thought BOb was doing a pretty damned good job, Captain Asshole and all. Besides, at this point, he couldn't give two shits about stealth. The whole goddamn robot world already knew where they were.

Screw it. He patted the bot on the shoulder. "Play it loud, BOb!"

The volume increased. Banging its head, the bot sang the refrain as it continued to pour fire into the enemy with one hand and distribute munitions with the other. "Let the robots hit the floor. Let the robots hit the floor!"

Vaughn stuffed a final magazine into his vest. "Nice!" He pointed toward the other end of the tunnel. "Now go reload the others. We'll hold this end."

As BOb ran to Bill and Ted's end of the tunnel, he pumped a fist overhead. "Let the robots hit the … *Floor!*"

Bouncing his head to the beat, Vaughn raised his rifle and poured fire into the endless stream of invading Necks.

While the battlebot had reloaded Mark and Vaughn, it had done an excellent job against the enemy robots. The bodies had indeed hit the floor. Dead Necks now sat four and five deep across the tunnel's entire breadth.

Vaughn shot another one. Its pancake-like head flew into the air, and its lifeless body collapsed, adding to the heap.

Did it mean the end for the Neck?

Were the robots actually dying?

Did they experience real death, or did their consciousness upload to a new machine?

Vaughn sure as hell hoped not. He was taking a great deal of satisfaction in the thought that each kill represented a small payback for the Hell that these bastards had put them through, literally. He was doling out justice for the billions of lives they'd taken—trillions when you considered the bastards had killed all animal life on the planet.

Vaughn glanced at the doorway. He kept hoping to hear the ramping-up power of an impending overload, but none came.

What the hell was Rourke doing back there?

A Neck emerged through a gap, crawling over its fallen comrades.

Mark placed a bullet in its head, and it fell limp.

Their tactic appeared to be working. No Taters had entered the tunnel from ATLAS. Vaughn and Mark were making the most of their limited ammunition. One shot-one kill. However, they were slowly being backed up by the continuous onslaught of new arrivals. Every time the bodies threatened to clog the tunnel entirely, another wave would yank back a few of them and begin to scramble through.

Looking over his shoulder, Vaughn saw the same was happening on the other end of their battle. The Taters were slowly pushing back Bill and Teddy.

Exploding grenades, shotgun blasts, and dozens of rifle shots shredded the smoky atmosphere.

No Necks approached from their end, but the carcasses of dead Taters were stacking up.

The high-pitched wail of BOb's modified weapon echoed loudly in the ever-shrinking space.

Vaughn frowned. "BOb! Keep using your rifle!"

The bot shook its head. "Out of ammo."

It looked over its shoulder and held up the modified EMP cannon. "And the BFG is overheating."

"Shit!" Vaughn glanced at the door to the side corridor.

Where was the overload?

BOb raised the cannon and fired at a Tater that had drawn dangerously close to Bill and Teddy.

The white ovoid vanished.

Vaughn saw several lights on the side of the modified weapon shift to red.

BOb holstered the cannon across its back. After giving Vaughn a short nod, the bot turned and leaped toward the nearest of the remaining Taters, clenched fists held high overhead. Before it could land the blow, a white light shot out from the belly of the targeted craft and BOb vanished.

In the ensuing silence, Vaughn heard a new sound.

He looked at Mark with widening eyes. "He's doing it!"

"What?"

Vaughn pointed to his own ear. "That's the sound of an overload. Rourke must've found a working terminal!"

"He's overloading the collider?"

Vaughn nodded, but the smile faded from his face. He remembered the wave of fire that had erupted from the back of the ATLAS experiment when Angela had overloaded it. The wormhole had enveloped them before the churning plasma could. He was pretty sure a successful reset would restore all of them to the timeline, but he didn't know if it would be this version of them that returned if they died.

These weren't new thoughts.

Vaughn had agonized over the issue ad nauseam since they'd set off on this mission.

He shrugged. It would be what it would be.

Looking back, he saw Taters pressing in on Bill and Teddy.

"Mark! Go shore up the other end. I'll keep my finger in the dam here."

Sweating profusely, Mark gave him a short nod. "See you on the other side, friend."

As the sound of the building power levels continued to rise, Vaughn nodded and tried for a confident grin. "It shouldn't be long, buddy."

Mark returned the wry smile. Then he gave the conduit a nervous glance. He'd heard the stories about the collider exploding at the end of their last reset.

After bumping fists, the two men parted.

Vaughn continued to pump single shots into the head of each Neck as they appeared in the opening.

Behind him, the battle raged with ear-splitting intensity.

A trio of grenade launches echoed off the walls.

The sharp cracks of multiple rifle shots pierced the air.

Another Neck poked its flat head into the gap between the top of the piled bodies and the ceiling. Vaughn did the robot the favor of placing a slug right in the center of its disc-shaped head. The Neck went limp, dying on the top of the pile.

Vaughn flipped it the bird. "How's that lead taste, Fucker?"

He blinked as the decapitated Neck and several of its equally dead comrades flew backward, yanked bodily from the heap.

A massive insectile head poked through the opening.

After an involuntary backward step, Vaughn raised his shotgun again and aimed at the mechanical monstrosity.

The slug ricocheted off the head, leaving only a faint scratch.

White carapaces shattered under the churning legs of the caterpillar bot. The large, fearsome machine began to inch through the opening.

Vaughn tried to rack another round, but the shotgun was empty.

After sliding the depleted weapon back into its scabbard, he pulled out his rifle again. He shifted his hand to its grenade launcher and fingered its trigger. The exterior of the Taters had proven soft enough to absorb most of the explosive force that hit them. However, the caterpillar's hard metals and sharp angles would direct much of the explosion outward. The deflected blast would likely damage the collider.

Vaughn shook his head. Not an option.

The guns behind him fell silent.

Taking advantage of the gap, he shouted over the collider's rising whine as he continued to back away from the multi-legged robot. "We've got company!"

No one responded.

"Guys—!" Turning, Vaughn came face-to-face with a hovering Tater.

Dropping back a step, he yanked his M4 assault rifle, swinging its muzzle around to fire on the bastard. He squeezed the trigger, loosing a short burst at the Tater.

Two of the rounds stitched holes in the left side of the machine's body.

However, before Vaughn could hit the thing center of mass, white light shot from the Tater's emitter.

CHAPTER 34

Hands held over tortured ears, Rourke stared at the computer terminal's display.

He'd done everything just as Angela had prescribed. However, the buildup seemed to be taking much longer than what he had expected, given the descriptions shared by both her and Captain Singleton.

Glancing upward, he stared into the cloud-covered sky. It hung low above the pit's opening which, itself, sat a hundred meters above Rourke's head.

He cast a furtive glance toward the doorway that had led him there. A wave of Necks was sure to sweep through it at any moment.

After Vaughn had pushed him from the collider tunnel, Rourke had passed back through another pair of security booths. He'd wandered through seemingly endless corridors, searching for a work-station in a fruitless, horror-filled trek. The smell of death permeated that portion of the facility.

Visions of stacked bodies had filled Rourke's head. He'd felt pretty silly when he'd discovered the source to be an open refrigerator full of rotted and spoiled food. It had been in a break room replete with reminders of what they'd lost during the Great Disappearance, as Vaughn called it.

Rourke had been on the verge of despair when he'd finally seen light coming through a hatch at the end of a long corridor. Every door he'd found had been unlocked, just as Vaughn had predicted. Initially, he'd worried that the illuminated hatchway portended a waiting army of the bots, but the light coming through the window set in the door glowed with an unmistakably natural hue. Somehow, daylight was streaming through it.

When he'd inspected the area beyond, Rourke couldn't see the ceiling. It appeared to be a large maintenance facility. Heavy equipment and tools lined many of its walls, and a large overhead hoist hung from a beam at its center.

Rourke had stepped through the door and seen a leaden sky above.

Presently, he peeked from under the workstation's overhead cover. He didn't think the pit had been initially designed to have an open sky as it did now. It looked like the robots had modified the structure.

Rourke supposed that originally the vertical tube had served as one of the main shafts through which the collider's builders had lowered equipment into the tunnel. However, there was no way they had left it open to the sky all this time.

It occurred to him that the top of the shaft formed a pit just like they had seen from Mont Salève when they'd looked down on the other experiments.

Dragging his eyes away from the steep walls of the vertical shaft, Rourke shook his head. At least there weren't any of the caterpillar bots here.

Not yet, anyway.

Dust mingled with water from the recent rain, leaving muddy puddles at the bottom of the shaft. Leaves had drifted down, coming to rest among the dropped hardware that dotted the floor. Fortunately, the cover that had probably been designed to protect the computer terminal from overhead hazards had also protected it from both falling rain and hardware. The workstation's computer remained undamaged and still functioned.

He hadn't received any network errors, and Angela's access code still worked as advertised.

Using her instructions, Rourke had quickly identified the spatial and chronological coordinates for the formation of the first micro black hole. Targeting that MBH, he'd programmed the overload Angela specified and added the interference pattern, engaging her two-tiered approach to resetting the timeline.

Then Rourke had hit the enter key, and the sequence had started.

The power had been steadily ramping up ever since.

He just hoped the scientists at CERN would find the message he'd inserted into the interference pattern. It had better cue them not to repeat the experiment. Rourke had wanted to add more to the message, but Angela wasn't sure of the bandwidth they'd be able to pump into the interference pattern. It might be so narrow as to only permit an SOS sent via Morse code, or it might be wide enough to allow the passage of a video. However, with an army of robots seeking him out at this very moment, Rourke hadn't had time to experiment or dig deeper into the code. He could only go with their basic plan: injecting an interference pattern embedded with an SOS in, you guessed it, Morse code.

Now, hands covering ears, he was just relegated to waiting—a wait that seemed to be taking forever.

Suddenly, something crashed behind him.

Rourke spun around, raising his rifle and pointing it towards the now open door.

A Neck glared back at him from the opening.

Reflexively, Rourke yanked the trigger. A three-round burst stitched across the doorway. Only the middle bullet found its target. It caught the robot in a glancing blow to its shoulder.

The Neck looked at its wound and then turned on Rourke. Raising all four arms menacingly, it charged him.

Stepping backward, Rourke loosed another three-round shot. This time all of the bullets struck the robot center of mass.

The Neck crumpled to the ground, dead.

A shadow inched across the floor beside him.

His shoulders slumped. "Oh, geez..."

Rourke spun toward the movement but didn't see anything.

Leaning out from underneath the overhang, he glanced upward and caught a horrifying glimpse of at least four of the mechanical caterpillars climbing down the pit's walls. The sound of their descent was drowned out by the ever-increasing scream of the building overload.

At the same time, he heard something rising above the screaming collider. The noise sounded as if it were coming from the light fixture above his head. It blared down from above the workstation's ceiling.

Looking up, rooted in place, Rourke stared at the lamp.

He heard the clatter of another Neck arriving behind him, but before he could turn to fire on the new arrival, the light fixture flared blindingly bright.

Rourke winced and threw a hand up to protect his eyes, but then the light extinguished, plunging him into sudden darkness. Somehow, the riotous noise disappeared with it.

Disoriented, Rourke stood motionlessly. Flexing his jaw and blinking, he struggled in vain to hear or see something, anything.

With the sudden disappearance of both light and sound, he felt as if he'd plunged into a sensory deprivation tank.

Was this the timeline reset?

Had it worked?

Was he teleporting back to the past?

CHAPTER 35

R ourke stood motionlessly.
Wait.

How was he standing?

Angela and Vaughn had said they'd felt like they were falling when the reset had sent them back.

He must still be standing in the pit.

Finally allowing himself a breath, Rourke pulled in a lungful of air. It burst from him in hacking coughs.

"Oh geez ...! What ...? What the hell is that?"

Somehow, a suffocating, putrid odor had filled the suddenly dark pit.

Had the storm blown over? Was it robbing the overhead light?

Rourke nodded. That must be it. The wind must've blown in the smell of rot from a nearby structure.

He coughed and spat as the odor threatened to overwhelm him.

The floor lurched beneath his feet, nearly sending him sprawling headfirst.

Rourke turned left and right, struggling to spot a visual cue. Blinking, he realized there was still some light in the work area.

As the last of the flare's afterimage faded, he looked up at the lamp.

It wasn't there.

Hell, the ceiling was gone, too.

Now he could see straight up into the suddenly darkened sky.

Could the storm clouds block out that much light?

Still looking up, he realized he could no longer see the sides of the shaft.

A droning buzz rose to fill the void left in the wake of the suddenly silenced collider.

Still looking up, Rourke thought he could just make out the edges of the shaft. However, they seemed fluid, moving like dark black clouds surrounding the small patch of sky visible overhead.

He took a backward step.

The ground gave beneath his feet.

Somehow, the rank odor worsened. The fetor wafting up from beneath him became nearly thick enough to see.

Rourke breathed through his mouth in a futile attempt to save his sinus cavities from the assault.

The potent stench took root in his very taste buds.

He choked and spluttered.

A shredding noise came from his left. He looked over and saw Captain Singleton walking up to him. The lower half of the man's face lay hidden beneath a strip of cloth, only his eyes visible. A world of sorrow hung in them.

As Vaughn walked up, he finished tearing the left sleeve from his uniform.

The man tied the strip of cloth over Rourke's mouth and nose.

While it wasn't perfect, the material filtered out enough of the foul odor to permit him an unmolested breath.

Three other silhouettes emerged from the gloom. Studying their faces, Rourke saw that it was Bill, Teddy, and Mark, each with their own makeshift mask covering their mouth and nose. BOb stepped up behind them.

Rourke shifted his footing on the unstable surface. Looking down, he saw his boots had sunk to the ankle in an unidentifiable black and dark red mass. Then something crackled under its sole.

Dark smoke wafted between Rourke and the men. Following it visually into the black sky, he blinked in sudden recognition. The onyx obscuration that he'd mistaken for the walls of the shaft was swirling above him.

Rourke stared at a churning swarm of flies so thick they blotted out the sky.

He suddenly understood it all.

Tearing his eyes from the image, Rourke looked at Captain Singleton. "Is this...?" Fearing the answer—knowing the answer, he left the question unfinished.

Vaughn stared back at him and nodded slowly. He waved a hand through the buzzing swarm, clearing them from his face. "Welcome to Hell."

PART IV

"Hell is empty, and all the devils are here!"

—William Shakespeare, The Tempest

CHAPTER 36

Vaughn stood over the retching doctor. The sky continued to darken. It had been close to dusk in Geneva, so it was the same here. The rapidly setting sun afforded little light.

Rourke finally found the bottom of his previous meal and fell quiet.

Vaughn spoke through his mask, the cloth muffling his words. "I heard the power rising! We should all be home now. What the hell happened?!"

The young man stood upright and, after wiping a sleeve across his mouth, slid the makeshift mask back into place. He held out his hands. "I don't know. I started the overload, but it was taking too long."

Vaughn took Rourke by the elbow and walked after BOb. The bot was retracing their steps using its built-in inertial nav.

Scanning the ground, Vaughn waved flies from his face. To his left and right, Mark, Bill, and Teddy paralleled their course as they, too, searched the surface.

Walking between him and Mark, Rourke fanned the air. "What are we looking for?"

"The starting point. We're trying to find the place we were before we went looking for you. Never mind that, though. Just answer the goddamn question. How did you end up here? What happened?"

Rourke tripped and nearly went sprawling. A bone cracked beneath his boots. He gasped and then bit back a gag. "I'm—" He dry-heaved. "I'm not sure how I got here. I found a working terminal and started the overload, but, like I said, it was taking longer than what you and Angela described. Probably had something to do with the new setting. Anyway, they found me. I was able to kill one of the Necks, but a bunch of the caterpillar bots came after me. Then the lights flared, and I ended up here. A Tater must have hit me through the ceiling."

"Shit!" Vaughn shook his head. "The Necks stopped the overload. That's why we're all still here."

"Son of a bitch!" Peterson said, emotions twisting his words. "That's it, then. We … We failed."

Teddy looked from the man to Vaughn. His forehead drew into a point above his makeshift mask. "We're trapped here?"

The robot stopped and turned around.

Halting, Vaughn glanced at Teddy. Then he looked at all of them. "I don't know anything except that we have people out there some-where. We need to find them. Once we're all together, we'll figure out what to do next."

Peterson threw his hands into the air. "What is there to do?!" He jabbed a finger toward the ground. "There's nothing that a few billion people haven't already tried. We're screwed!"

"No, Bill." Vaughn locked eyes with the man. "One thing all of this has taught me is that we're only screwed if we give up. Hang in there." Pausing, he looked from man to man. "Don't quit on me, guys. Don't quit on your families."

Mark nodded somberly. "We're with you, Vaughn."

Bill and Teddy exchanged looks and then nodded as well.

In the day's wan light, the portion of Rourke's face visible above the mask looked ash-white. The young doctor stared back at him for a moment. Then his head dipped.

After returning the gesture, Vaughn pointed at the ground in front of him. "Is this it, BOb?"

"I believe so, Captain Assho—"

Vaughn's hand shot up. "Not now!" He turned ninety degrees and pointed ahead. "It should be that way."

Rourke looked at him. "What should be?"

"A dead Tater." Pausing, Vaughn pointed to Rourke. "Hold this position. You'll be our anchor. Otherwise, we'll get disoriented and never find anyone." He waved away the flies. "Once we find one of the dead Taters, BOb can extrapolate the curve of the tunnel. Then we should be able to find our people."

The young doctor nodded pensively. "Got—" The man retched. "Got it."

Vaughn pointed to Mark, Bill, and Teddy. "Spread out but not so far you lose sight of the man next to you."

Major Peterson looked at him askance. "What makes you think the Tater would've hung around?" He pointed at the battle operations bot. "Once BOb beamed it here, the thing probably flew away."

"I don't think they're autonomous. Once the Tater lost contact with its home base, it probably shut down." Vaughn shrugged. "Besides, where's it going to beam us? We're already in Hell."

Bill looked ready to say more, but Mark waved him off. "Let's give it a try."

Vaughn nodded his thanks. "Agreed." He pointed ahead. "Let's see what we see."

As he walked across the uneven surface, Vaughn's thoughts returned to his arrival. He'd found the other three men and BOb almost immediately after the Tater had beamed him to Hell.

After fashioning their masks, they had waited in anticipation for the timeline to reset. Vaughn had expected the ground to drop out from beneath him at any moment. However, several minutes later and still firmly in Hell, they'd set out in search of Rourke.

While they looked for the man, they had discussed how they might find the rest of the crew. From their initial dispositions, it appeared that the beams fired by the Taters dropped them into this world in roughly the same position as they'd been back in their home dimension, unlike the global light wave which had deposited the entirety of Earth's animal biosphere in one location. Fortunately, it had deposited them on top of the mountain of the dead instead of beneath it.

Vaughn was so deep in thought he almost tripped over the Tater. Looking up, he waved for the rest of the team. "Over here!" He turned and extended a hand toward Rourke. "You! Stay!"

Couldn't have the young man moving. If Vaughn was right, they should be able to draw a line from Rourke's position to that of the fallen Tater and then extrapolate the curve of the collider tunnel. Then they could start searching for the rest of the group. It wasn't much, but it was all he had to go on. Angela was still out there somewhere.

They stood over the fallen Tater. A sliver of the tunnel's concrete wall along with some miscellaneous hardware lay strewn around the machine.

Bill Peterson looked at him and nodded. "Looks like you're right. Thing looks dead as a doornail."

Vaughn nodded soberly as he walked around to its far side. He did a double-take. "It's one of the ones you guys hit with a grenade. This whole end is blown out."

Teddy stepped over and then nodded. "Must be the Tater they beamed out."

"Huh? Who?"

Peterson leaned in and studied it. "Yep. That's the last one I hit. They were starting to stack up. For a moment it blocked the next Tater from getting at us, but then the bastard beamed the thing out of its way. Next thing I know, I'm here."

Vaughn stood and looked around. "Where are the ones BOb beamed out?"

Teddy shrugged.

Peterson gave Vaughn a meaningful look. "Maybe it flew away."

Vaughn continued to scan the hill to the limit of his vision. "I doubt it." He shrugged. "Doesn't matter. At least we know we're on the right path." Looking over his shoulder, he waved the robot over. "Come here, BOb." The bot stepped to his side. Vaughn pointed at

Rourke and then drew an imaginary line with his finger across the bloodied earth to their position. Then he turned and extended the line toward the horizon. "Cross-referencing Doctor Geller's position and ours, I want you to plot the curve of the tunnel using an arc that follows a seventeen-mile circumference. Can you do that?"

The robot looked from Rourke to the direction Vaughn had pointed. Finally, it nodded. "I believe so, Captain."

"Good."

Looking back, Vaughn could just make out the silhouette of Rourke in the distance. Batting away the flies, he cupped his hands around his mouth. "Come on up!"

Rourke took a couple of steps and then stumbled to a stop. The man bent over and vomited.

Apparently, the good doctor hadn't yet found the bottom of that meal.

After a final heave, Rourke stood and slid his mask back into place. A moment later, he stumbled to a stop next to the dead Tater.

Vaughn placed a hand on the young man's shoulder. "Hang in there. As soon as we find everyone else, we'll get the hell off this ..." He faltered, unable to finish the statement.

What the hell were they going to do?

What *could* they do?

Honestly, he didn't know. But he sure as hell wasn't going to leave Angela or anyone else out there by themselves. They might be destined to die here, but no one was going to die alone.

Not no, but hell no. Not while he had anything to say about it.

His gaze had fallen to the gore beneath their boots. Vaughn dragged his eyes back to Rourke. "We'll figure it out from there."

The doctor gave a single nod.

Vaughn addressed the whole team. "If this works, we should be able to follow the line all the way back to Monique and Chance and Angela and Rachel beyond them."

They nodded absently. Each man looked distracted, lost in thought.

"Stop it, guys. Don't think about it. Just keep going. That's all we can do right now."

No one responded.

Vaughn sighed and gestured ahead. "Lead the way, BOb. Everyone else, spread out, but be careful. Don't lose sight of the man next to you, or you might get lost."

Mark waved a hand through the swarming bugs. "Can't see more than a few dozen feet thanks to these damned flies."

As BOb began to walk, they fanned out beside him. Periodically, Vaughn heard bones cracking under boots followed closely by groans and strung-together curse words.

The sticky blood of the dead started to soak through his pant legs. Vaughn shook his head. They had to get the hell off this mountain. He'd thought Hell was terrible before, but this was orders of magnitude worse. The immensity of it pressed at his sanity. It was all he could do to keep a brave face, to keep pushing the men. But he would be damned if he'd ever leave any of his people up here—not even Chance, and especially not Angela.

A horrified female voice rose above the buzzing din. "Who … Who is that?!"

Bill yelled into the darkness, his voice cracking. "Mo-Monique?"

"Oh my God! William?"

Vaughn turned and walked toward the voices. A moment later, he found the man and woman hugging each other.

Chance Bingham stared back at Vaughn from the far side of the two. A haunted look now filled his previously pompous and self-assured visage. "I'm so sorry, mate." He slowly shook his head. "I-I had no idea. I don't know how the two of you survived so many trips through …" He surveyed the scene with haunted eyes. "Through this."

"I …" Vaughn swallowed. "We just—"

Distant gunfire cut off his words.

Vaughn turned toward the sound. "Angela!"

Before he knew it, he was running across the mass of blood and gore. Bones crunched underfoot.

Flies bounced off his face.

He coughed and spat.

"Angela?!"

Another shot rang out, followed by a sharp yelp.

That wasn't human.

Had it been a dog?

Then he heard a deep growl followed by multiple sharp yelps.

Vaughn spotted something large writhing on the ground ahead. Several smaller shapes yanked and tugged at it.

Eyes flying wide, Vaughn turned and charged. "No, no, no, no!" He ran straight at the churning mass. "Get the hell off her!"

Charging into the writhing pile, Vaughn kicked the nearest animal. The thing tumbled away from the pinned victim, squealing as it rolled across the turbid ground.

Looking down, Vaughn realized that the dark silhouette at the bottom of the pile wasn't human at all. The mortally wounded beast appeared to be the scrawny, withered remnant of a bear.

Its attackers dissolved into the night. Looking after them, Vaughn couldn't tell what they were. Gore-covered, matted fur hung from emaciated bodies. The animals could've been hyenas, pigs, wolves, or coyotes. He couldn't be certain.

Another shot rang out to his front right.

He cupped hands around his mouth. "Angela! Rachel!"

"Vaughn?" Major Lee shouted back. "What the hell are you doing here?"

He struggled forward, head on a swivel, watching for additional wild animals. "We got beamed—"

"That was a rhetorical question, Captain. Get your ass over here! We need help."

Vaughn released a pent-up breath and whispered a thank you. She had said *we*. Angela must still be alive.

Vaughn swatted at the flies that were threatening to choke him. Storming forward, he heard a rustling sound ahead. "Angela? Are you okay?"

"Yes, but be careful. There's some crazy shit over here, and we're almost out of ammo."

Then Vaughn saw them.

A pack of large, horse-sized animals surrounded Angela and Rachel. On one side, a massive buck swayed unsteadily. Chunks of tattered and torn, rotted flesh swung from its expansive rack. Next to the beast, another bear was swatting at a pair of moose. None of them seemed to be attacking one another. It was more like they were fighting to see who was going to get the fresh meat represented by the two women.

Vaughn raised his rifle and aimed at the animal he perceived to be the most dangerous threat. He shot the bear square in the head. In his adrenaline-fueled rage, he pulled the shot, hitting the bear near the top of its cranium. The round must have ricocheted off the animal's thick skull because the emaciated bear suddenly turned insane eyes toward Vaughn.

It charged without hesitation.

Vaughn raised his rifle and fired into the chest of the onrushing bear. At the same time, two additional shots rang out, one from each side of him.

The huge beast stumbled to a crashing halt in front of his blood-soaked boots.

"Vaughn!"

He raised a hand. "I'm okay. We got it."

The mechanical click of a dry-fired weapon snapped through the omnipresent buzzing of the flies.

"Vaughn!" Angela repeated, her voice raising an octave. "We're not okay at all."

The firing pin clicked into an empty chamber again.

Looking up, he saw the two women standing back to back. The insane buck was bearing down on Angela. While the pair of moose, no longer hampered by the bear, seemed intent on having Major Lee for dinner.

Rachel glanced his way. "I'm so happy to hear you're okay, Captain." Still pointing her empty gun at the slowly advancing animals, she added, "How about you do us a solid and take care of Bambi and the Bullwinkle twins before the big-assed son of a bitches make the two of us their next meal?"

Multiple gunshots split the pungent air as Vaughn and the rest of the men fired into the surreal pack. All three animals dropped to the ground, their hooves kicking and spraying fetid gore as the last vestige of life streamed from each.

Lowering his weapon, Vaughn ran to Angela and wrapped her in his arms. "I thought I lost you."

He felt her look past him. Then her shoulders slumped. "You're all here." She said it matter-of-factly, her voice steady and cold. It wasn't a question.

Vaughn pulled back. He nodded. "We started the overload but got beamed out before it could finish. The Necks must have canceled it."

Angela looked past him and addressed Rourke. "You started the override?"

For a moment, Vaughn felt hurt that she had automatically assumed it had been Rourke, but considering his paltry computer skills, he didn't blame her.

Rourke nodded. "Found a connected computer terminal. I was able to initiate the override using your new settings. I even managed to put in the code you specified."

Looking around, Angela shrugged. "Then what happened? Why are we still here?"

"The build-up was taking a lot longer than what you described. Guess it had something to do with the new settings. Anyway, just before I got beamed out, I heard a Neck come in behind me. It must have stopped the overload before it could blow."

Angela waved the flies from her face. "How long ago was that?"

Rourke shook his head. "I don't know. Fifteen or twenty minutes, I'd guess."

"Then we're all lost."

Opening his mouth, Vaughn started to protest but then reconsidered.

Angela was right.

They were fucked.

There was no coming back from this.

The hair on his neck stood out as a growl cut through the darkness behind him. An instant later, dozens of additional snarls and squeals joined in.

Everyone turned and scanned the horizon. The sun had finished setting. Vaughn couldn't see anything in the gloom. Between the constant black cloud of flies and the lowlight afforded by the moon-less night, he was all but blind.

Reaching for the light attached to his gun, Vaughn called out, "Turn on your flashlights. Whatever it is, they know we're here. We might as well be able to see them, too."

Choked with the billowing mass of uncountable black flies, the beam that streamed from the Maglite attached to his rifle looked like a laser formed from swirling, dark energy.

In every direction Vaughn looked, he saw paired points of reflected light. Dozens of glowing, white eyes stared back from the black night.

He shook his head. "Really?!"

They had already been low on ammunition. Now they faced an army of predators.

Peterson flipped on his flashlight. "You gotta be shitting me!"

Bingham shrugged. "We're all going to die anyway. May as well get it over with, mate."

Vaughn gave the man a sideways glance. "Being dismembered by a pack of animals with a hankering for live flesh doesn't top my list of ways to go."

Raising his rifle, Vaughn fired at one of the nearest beasts. It fell, but another stepped into its place.

Several other shots rang out. However, each time one animal dropped, the night birthed two more.

The group of nine humans slowly backed into an ever-tightening circle as the animals continued to approach. Every time one broke from the pack and tried to dart in toward them, a shot took it out.

One of them ran right at Vaughn. He raised his weapon and fired, but the hammer fell on an empty chamber.

Then a rifle barked on his right. He looked over to see Mark lowering his M4.

A dark shape arced through the air, leaping over the tightening circle of wild beasts and landing just in front of Vaughn.

He aimed his empty weapon at the new arrival and then shouted, "Hold your fire! It's BOb."

Several of the animals pounced on the robot. However, the bot shook them off like so many rags. BOb threw punches that crushed heads. The bot snatched up one animal. The apparent hog released a horrified squeal as BOb threw it bodily into the pack.

The animals backed away from the machine.

Seeing Vaughn, BOb tilted his dark head. "What are your orders, Captain?" The bot extracted the modified EMP cannon and held it up. "Would you like me to beam the animals away?"

Doing a double-take, Vaughn looked at the weapon. "I thought it overheated."

BOb aimed the cannon at the still encircling mass of beasts. "It had, but it's back online. Would you like me to beam them out?"

Vaughn started to nod but then hesitated. "Wait. Won't it just send them here? We'll be right back where we started."

"No, Captain. I adjusted the coordinates. I can beam them several miles away."

"What? How can you do that?"

The pack of animals inched closer. Vaughn could see their exposed teeth and eyes even without the aid of a flashlight.

Rourke stepped up next to him. "BOb, did you access the latitude and longitude coordinates in the table?"

The robot nodded. "Yes, Doctor Geller. The coordinates here perfectly matched those of our location at CERN. One of the values was a variable. I believe it represents—"

Vaughn waved the robot silent. He pointed at a group of nearby animals. "Yeah, take out..." He hesitated, looking at the shredded remnants of the bodies beneath their boots. Then he looked at the modified cannon and canted his head. "I wonder. Could we …?"

Teddy nudged him. "Earth to El Capitan. I think now would be a good time."

Slowly nodding, Vaughn looked at BOb. "Can you hit yourself with the light while still holding the cannon?"

Bingham looked incredulous. "Have you gone nutters?!"

"Shut up, Chance," Angela said. "I think he's onto something." She pointed at the robot. "Go ahead, BOb. Answer the question."

"Yes, my arm is long enough to aim the device at myself while still holding it."

"Good. We won't lose the cannon." Vaughn saw confused faces staring back at him. He held up a hand. "Anything you're holding when the light hits gets beamed out with you."

After a quick scan of his mental map of the place, he turned back to the robot. "Can you set the destination coordinates approximately five miles to the northwest of our current position?"

After the slightest hesitation, the robot nodded. "Done."

"Okay. I want you to beam us and yourself to that destination."

As he spoke, the animals continued to tighten the noose. Fortunately, none of them seemed ready to jump after seeing what happened to the few who tried it so far. However, Vaughn didn't think that would last much longer.

Bingham bristled. "Are you trying to get us killed?!"

Vaughn pointed at the Brit. "Start with him."

Without hesitating, BOb swept the EMP cannon toward the man.

Chance's hands flew up, and his eyes went wide. "Wait—!"

White light shot from the end of the device, and the man vanished.

The surrounding pack of wild animals flinched backward but then quickly recovered and resumed their stalking.

Vaughn saw concerned looks on the faces of the others. He gestured toward the animals and then the cannon. "Pick your poison."

Everyone acquiesced.

Angela stepped in front of the robot. "Do it, BOb."

The bot nodded and then leveled the gun. The light flared, and

Angela vanished. BOb proceeded through the team, beaming out the remaining humans in groups of two and three.

At the sight of their rapidly diminishing source of live feed, the animals suddenly became more aggressive. Snarling and squealing, they surged closer.

Vaughn and Rourke stepped in front of the bot. Looking at the approaching animals, the young doctor held up his hands. "Nothing to see here: so skinny I can Hula Hoop a Cheerio."

Vaughn waved the bot over urgently. "Beam out yourself and the two of us at the same time, all three at once."

BOb nodded and held the large cannon at the end of its long arm.

"Do it!" Rourke urged.

The snarling pack lunged en masse.

White light shot out from the emitter.

CHAPTER 37

The buzz of a trillion flies vanished, and the light faded.

Blinking, Vaughn stared across a dusty expanse of desert plane.

Urgent voices rose from behind him.

He turned.

An arcing fist shot out from the darkness.

Ducking under it, Vaughn stepped into Bingham's swing and thrust a hard punch into the man's gut. Air burst from Chance's mouth as he doubled over.

Vaughn stood over him. "You're welcome, jackass."

After several coughing hacks, the man found his voice. "We're all dead anyway, you fucking wanker."

"A lot of people are dead. Unfortunately for us, you're not one of them."

Vaughn turned from the man and instantly felt guilty. He'd earned his Captain Asshole moniker, but he wasn't about to apologize to Wing Commander Arsehole.

Looking up, he studied the faces of his comrades. They stared back at him with mixed levels of amusement and disgust. Dark gore covered much of their lower halves. Rachel grinned crookedly and gave him a thumbs-up. Then the humor fell from her face as she went back to digging under a fingernail with her Ka-Bar.

Mark walked over and placed a hand on his shoulder. "Quick thinking. Good job."

Vaughn pursed his lips and tilted his head toward the still coughing Brit. "He's got a point, you know. We're still screwed."

"You bought us more time."

Twisting his face, he looked up at his friend. "Considering what lies ahead of us, you might not appreciate that so much in the day to come."

Mark shrugged. "I'll take my chances. At least some animal isn't chewing my taint at the moment."

"Thanks," Vaughn said, stretching out the word. "Could've done without that particular image."

Their shared chuckle faded fast.

As the new reality set in, everyone began to spread out. Vaughn saw defeat hanging in the faces of all but one.

The only person that didn't look lost was Angela.

She stared across the desert, but she wasn't focused on anything.

Vaughn knew that look.

He walked over to her. "What are you working on?"

She blinked and then looked past him and pointed at Rourke. "Do you still have your tablet computer?"

The young man looked up from the ground and regarded her with a confused face. "Yeah ... Why?"

Angela waved him over. "Connect it to the robot."

Nodding, Rourke extracted the device from a pouch on his side. He stepped over to the bot. "BOb, I need to access your port."

"Certainly, Doctor Geller."

"What are you doing, Command-Oh?"

Moving to stand next to Rourke, Angela looked at Teddy. "I want to have another look at the data the Necks programmed into the emitter."

Rourke connected the harness from his tablet to the port on the side of the robot.

Angela placed a hand on his shoulder. "Bring up that table again."

"Already on it."

Vaughn joined them. "What are we looking at?"

Staring at the tablet, Angela said, "BOb was able to change our destination coordinates. I remembered that there was a lot more data than latitude and longitude in the table." She pointed as a set of numbers popped up on the device's screen. "Like these."

Raising his eyebrows, Vaughn leaned in. "What do you think they are?"

"At the time, I wasn't sure, but now I think they might be astronomical coordinates."

"Astronomical, Command-Oh? Like for planets?"

"Yeah but not planets outside of Earth, but for ones outside our dimension. If I'm right, they're dimensional coordinates."

Rourke nodded excitedly. "There are two sets of them. I think one is the origin and the other the destination."

Angela grinned. "Exactly!"

Looking at her, Vaughn repressed a smile. He didn't want to get his hopes up, nor those of anyone else.

Bill Peterson stepped up. "Origin? Are you saying you can pull the coordinates for our dimension out of that database?"

Chewing on her lip, Angela nodded tentatively. "Maybe." She turned back to Rourke and then gestured at a portion of the screen. Can you reverse these two tables?"

"I can sure try."

The man began to tap commands into the tablet.

Vaughn once again wondered how the hell US standard hardware and software had found its way into the device. He looked at Monique. "Is there any way that MIL-Standard One-Eighty-Eight hardware and software was being used at CERN?"

In the corner of his eye, he saw Angela shake her head. "I can tell you that it was all based on international standards. All of it, including my gravity wave experiment on the space station, was built using the same standard."

Mark pointed at the light wave emitter. "Then how did US tech get in this thing?"

Leaning in, Monique looked at Angela. "You said the President sent a plane full of special forces operatives at them. When they beamed the people out of it, the plane crashed. Maybe the Necks recovered some of the equipment from the wreckage and reverse-engineered it."

"Got it!" Rourke said, nearly shouting the words.

Angela held out a hand. "Let me see."

The young man handed her the tablet. Angela scrolled through the data. Then she held it up for the robot to look at. "Is this where you adjusted the destination coordinates?"

BOb nodded. "Affirmative, Commander Brown."

"Good." She pointed to a cell on the top right of the screen. "I want you to beam us to these coordinates, starting with me."

Stepping back, the robot raised the modified cannon.

Eyes flying wide, Vaughn held up his hands. "Belay that order."

Angela turned to him confusedly.

He held his palms out. "Are you crazy?! What if you're wrong? You could end up somewhere else altogether, like the middle of the ocean or in outer space."

Remaining frustratingly indifferent to his words, Angela merely shrugged. She looked around and then back at him. "Is staying here any better? Are we any less likely to die?"

Vaughn's jaw worked, but he had no counter.

Monique stepped up and saved him. "Should we not test it first?"

Blinking, Vaughn nodded. "What she said."

Angela appeared to consider her words for a moment. Then she gestured at the robot. "BOb, can you beam out both of us simultaneously, like you did last time?"

The robot dipped its head. "Yes, Commander Brown."

Angela turned to Vaughn, a satisfied look on her face.

He shrugged. "How does that change anything? Then we're all stuck here." He shook his head. "Screw it. Maybe Chance has the right idea. Let's just end it right here."

Angela grinned wryly. "Not the time for Captain Asshole to make a showing. What I was *trying* to say is that, if we survive the trip and end up anywhere close to where we anticipate, I will have BOb beam us back here."

Monique pursed her lips and nodded. "That should suffice. If you can make a round trip, then BOb will be able to beam all of us back home."

Vaughn stared back at her, trying his utmost to come up with a better plan and failing miserably. Then he raised his eyebrows. "I'll go. There's no sense in you taking a chance."

Smile softening, Angela said, "That's sweet of you, but what will you do if you need to adjust coordinates?"

"I know how to program coordinates."

"Astronomical coordinates?"

His mouth closed with a click.

Not waiting for his reply, Angela continued. "Either way, we'll return or we won't. Nothing ventured, nothing gained."

It was Vaughn's turn to chew on his lip. Finally, he nodded—a lump forming in his throat.

Bill Peterson looked around. "What do you say we get this going? The longer we wait, the more likely some animal or the entire pack catches a whiff and finds us here. The sooner we get out of here, the better."

Monique pointed at the modified cannon. "Where are those coordinates going to take you? Did you shift them away from ATLAS?"

Angela nodded appreciably. "Good point." She looked at BOb. "Change the coordinates to the center of the field where we left the tiltrotor."

Again, the robot paused for a beat and then nodded. "Adjustment complete."

Mark looked at her, fresh concern on his face. "You could end up inside the mountain."

Vaughn's eyes widened and his already tight throat constricted further.

Angela shook her head. "The light has never left us even ankle-deep in the surface. It always deposits us on top of the ground." She gestured at the tablet. "There are some digits here adjacent to a symbol that I don't recognize. It must be a variable that identifies the elevation or top of the dimension's solid surface. Otherwise, the light wave would've deposited Vaughn and me inside the mountain of dead, not on top of it. Same for the rest of us this time."

Chance Bingham emerged from the periphery. He tossed Vaughn a contrite glance and then looked at Angela. "You know, you're betting your life on that?"

Angela shrugged. "Anyone got a better idea?"

No one did—not even Vaughn.

All but he began to slowly back away from BOb and Angela.

Teddy pulled a Roscosmos hat from his backpack and pushed it down over his wild tangles of curly, red hair. He held out a thumb. "Hurry back to us, Command-Oh."

Vaughn hugged her tightly. Then he backed away and finally found his voice. "Yeah, Command-Oh, hur—" Voice cracking, he coughed. "Hurry back to us."

She held up a finger and gave a hopeful smile. "I'll be right back."

With his long arm held high, BOb positioned the muzzle just as he'd done with Vaughn and Rourke. The bot pointed the weapon at himself at an angle such that the light beam would sweep across itself and Angela.

The robot looked down at her. "Are you ready, Commander Brown?"

Angela glanced over at Vaughn and winked. Her next words made him realize that she hadn't led quite the sheltered life he'd thought.

Smiling nervously, Angela nodded. "Beam me up, Scotty."

CHAPTER 38

Vaughn paced back and forth. Now that the blood had dried, his stiff pant legs scraped together noisily.

A full moon had risen shortly after Angela and BOb had vanished. It had climbed a good way above the eastern mountains since.

Scanning the land illuminated by its pale light, Vaughn searched for any sign of them. Even using the zoom capability of his night-vision goggles, he'd seen no evidence of Angela since she and the robot left.

"Wh-Where are they?!" he stuttered, failing to hide his apprehension. Apprehension, hell. He was on the verge of full-blown panic. Every second seemed to stretch into a minute—every minute an hour. The anticipation and expectation that any moment now he'd turn and find her standing right behind him were drawing out the night painfully. "Where are they?" he said again, this time in barely a whisper.

Rourke shifted on his feet. "I'm sure it's just the quantum variability."

Vaughn spun on him. "What the hell does that even mean?"

The young man looked from him to Monique and then back. "It means that, at the atomic level and below, nothing is set in stone."

"Were not operating at anything close to that level."

Rourke nodded. "You're right, but for that device to work as it does, it must manipulate matter at the plank level."

Vaughn's eyebrows stitched together.

Monique spoke up. "It is the smallest scale we have. Suffice it to say it is firmly in the realm of quantum variability. At that level, particles pop in and out of existence. Time does not even exist as we perceive it."

"Yeah, of course. You're talking about Ant-Man space."

Rourke nodded, but Monique stared her confusion back at him.

Vaughn rolled his eyes. "You know, the realm where Ant-Man got lost for a long time, like between-movies long?" He held out his hands. "But what does that have to do with them not being back yet?"

Monique continued to stare at him. Finally, she shook her head. "The churn of particles popping in and out of existence in *Ant-Man space* introduces variables for which no calculation can completely compensate."

Teddy, who appeared just as miserable as Vaughn felt, looked at Monique, concern twisting his face. "What would this variability do to Angela?"

Monique released a frustrated growl and looked at Rourke.

The young man started to speak, but Vaughn held up a hand. "English, please."

Rourke appeared to consider his words for a moment. Then he continued. "Quantum variability—"

Vaughn gave the man a hard look.

He held up his hands in surrender. "*Ant-Man-churn* can screw up the calculations, cause them to end up in a slightly different position than what was targeted."

Eyes widening, Vaughn stared at the man. He felt the color drain from his face. He looked around, searching the horizon. "You picked a hell of a time to mention this. She could be back on that mountain of decaying bodies, trying to fight off Hell's guard dogs."

"No," Monique said. "I do not think the error would be that large."

Vaughn turned toward her. "Thanks, Data. I am so happy to hear you do not think so."

She stared back at him from beneath scrunched eyebrows. "My name is not Data."

"Are you sure it *isn't?*" Vaughn said, emphasizing the last word. "You sure as hell sound like him, what with your seeming inability to use a goddamn contraction."

"Vaughn, that's enough!"

Turning, he saw Mark looking back at him disapprovingly.

After a moment, Vaughn's chin dropped to his chest. He released a long sigh. "Sorry, Lieutenant Gheist, you didn't deserve that."

The woman glared at him, her mouth pressed into a thin line. Finally, she dipped her head.

Struggling mightily, Vaughn managed to keep his tone level as he continued. "Why do you think the error wouldn't be that big?"

"When you were beamed here by the Taters, did you ever end up somewhere other than on the mountain of the dead?"

As understanding dawned on him, Vaughn began to nod slowly. "You're right. We always returned to it. Wasn't the same exact spot every time, but close enough."

A new realization struck Vaughn. "Wait. If it's quantum variability, then how did we all end up right here, together?"

Both Monique and Rourke stared back at him, struck dumb by his question. After a moment, the young doctor shook his head. "Shit. I don't know."

Vaughn would have taken pride in his ability to stump the two scientists, but unfortunately, it just meant they were no closer to figuring out the mystery.

He released a long growl and laced his fingers through his hair as if trying to pull it out. Turning from them, he looked across the dusty plane. "It may not be that, but it doesn't mean you're wrong. They could be here already, just not close enough to see us in the dark."

He cupped his hands around his mouth. "Angela!"

"What the hell are you doing?!" Bill Peterson said in a harsh whisper. "You trying to get us eaten?" He stormed over and grabbed

Vaughn by the shoulder and spun him around. He pointed toward the distant mountain of the dead. "May as well walk out there and shout 'dinner is served!'" Looking over Vaughn's shoulder, the man paused. His eyes went round. "Oh, shit …!"

Behind Bill, Mark craned his neck. "Something's coming."

Major Peterson released him. "Now you've done it."

Vaughn turned and immediately spotted the movement.

A faint voice drifted across the dark plane. "Vaughn?"

"Oh, thank God. Angela! Hang on. I'm coming." He sprinted past Bill and ran toward the movement. A few steps later, the twinned silhouettes of Angela and BOb resolved from the desert gloom.

Vaughn crossed the gap and scooped up Angela. "I was so worried." He kissed her dusty forehead and then lowered her to the ground. "What happened?"

"What happened is that it works!" Angela leaned back and smiled up at him. "We're not stuck here. More importantly, we're not beaten."

The knot in Vaughn's gut eased a bit, but it seemed too good to be true. "Where have you been? Why have you been gone so long?"

Turning, Angela waved for him to follow as she continued walking toward their makeshift camp. "Come on. I'll tell everyone at once."

CHAPTER 39

Vaughn glanced at BOb. The robot continued watching for wild animals. The bot had assured them that it would be able to beam threats elsewhere should they approach.

BOb's giant backpack looked full to bursting point. Angela had returned with hers stuffed full of munitions as well.

Vaughn turned from the image and looked at Angela.

He felt the knot in his gut relax another notch.

She wasn't lost to him.

Angela had returned.

The hug she'd given him upon her arrival had awoken something within Vaughn, reminding him what they were fighting for.

He smiled inwardly as Angela shared the story of her and BOb's trek.

The light wave emitter had beamed the two of them to a field about a mile from the tiltrotor, leaving them with a lengthy hike to get back to the aircraft.

Hearing Monique and Rourke's theory about quantum variability causing the error, Angela rocked her head equivocally. "That would account for the irregular shape of the mountain of the dead. If everyone had been beamed to precisely the same point, it would've been cone-shaped."

Teddy shook his head and pointed to Vaughn. "I think El Capitan is right. That can't be it. When he had BOb beam us off Mont de Los Muertos, we ended up in one place." He gestured at the group. "If it were Ant-Man-churn, all of us would end up in different locations, no?"

"Ant-Man?"

Vaughn held up a hand. "Long story."

Rourke glanced at him and then looked at Angela. "He means quantum variability."

Smiling, she scoffed. "I get it." Then Angela shrugged. "I think it's more likely that the interface between our EMP cannon and their bastardized One-Eighty-Eight hardware is introducing calibration errors."

Vaughn nodded as a realization struck. "That's why we never saw any of the Taters that BOb hit with the light. We only found the dead one that another Tater beamed out."

"What do you mean, El Capitan?"

"I was starting to think Bill might be right, that those Taters had flown away, but they might have simply ended up elsewhere."

Angela waved dismissively. "None of that matters now. It works well enough, and from what happened when BOb beamed us here, it looks like you stay in close proximity to each other if you do the shots in short order." She gave them all a significant look. "We still have a chance to reset the timeline."

Bill glanced into the dusty night sky and wrinkled his nose. "I'll take anything over this place."

Monique faced the man. "William, have we decided there are worse things than monster caterpillar bots?"

He cast a nervous glance at the outline of Teddy's Mont de Los Muertos. The man shivered visibly and then nodded. "Yes ... yes, we have."

Mark looked at Angela. "What did you do when you got to the tiltrotor?"

"When we reached the edge of the field, we held back for a bit, making sure there were no robots around. Then I sent BOb in to check it out. He didn't find anything, and nothing had been disturbed, so we dug through the crates in the cargo bay and loaded up." She patted the backpack that sat next to her. "We brought as much ammo as we could carry." She paused and stared across the land. Her eyes lost focus. "It's a good thing we did. Ended up having to leave some of it behind." She shook her head, and her eyes cleared. "I'll go into that in a minute."

"That's okay, Command-Oh," Teddy interrupted. He gestured toward the group. "We can all stock up on ammo when we go back."

Angela shook her head. "I don't think that's a good idea."

Bill scoffed. "Since when is too much ammo a bad thing?"

"It's not that. It's the uncertainty thing. The device dropped us only a few feet from the Balcony."

"What balcony?" Monique asked.

A chill ran down Vaughn's spine as understanding washed over him. "The cliff?"

Angela looked at him, soberly. "Yeah, we emerged just a couple of meters from the drop-off. A few feet farther left, and we would have ended up somewhere on that cliff ... or over it. Even if I somehow managed to hang on and not to fall, I would've been stuck. It's not like I had ropes or climbing gear. BOb might have been able to scale it, but I would've been stranded."

That sobering image silenced everyone for a moment.

"Anyway," Angela continued, "after we finished loading up, I had BOb beam us back here. Initially, I had planned to shift the coordinates so that we didn't end up right on top of you, but once I saw the variability, I realized right here," she pointed at the ground, "was the best place to aim. It was the one spot we were least likely to hit." She shrugged. "Of course, we ended up a pretty good way north of here, a couple of miles according to BOb's estimation. He offered to beam us the last bit back to here."

"Why the hell didn't you?" Bill asked.

"Same problem. We could have ended up just as far off, maybe even more. Besides ..." Angela paused and gave Vaughn a meaningful look. "I saw something I recognized ... from before."

Staring back at her, he tilted his head. "What?"

"That tall rock, the one that marked the location of the alien ship."

A stream of mental images suddenly flowed through Vaughn's mind. A broken alien vessel. An equally shattered exoskeleton of a large, lobster-like creature. He and Angela had spent countless nights there, often shivering and on the verge of death. He recalled splitting headaches, something he was already beginning to re-experience now.

He released his breath in a long, hissing sigh. "Yeah, I remember it alright. Don't care if I never see the place again."

Standing, Angela walked up to the robot. "Turn around and take a knee, BOb."

The bot complied.

Standing on her tiptoes, she tugged at the top of BOb's backpack and then released a frustrated growl. "Crap! You're still too tall. Bend over."

Vaughn had noticed earlier that they had indeed filled the robot's backpack. The thing was bulging as well as Angela's.

They walked over to see what she was doing.

The robot lowered its other knee and then, leaning forward, came to rest on all fours. BOb looked over his shoulder and eyed them warily, giving the group the fisheye. "Can I at least get a kiss first?"

Angela rolled her eyes as she unzipped the large backpack. She peeled back the top and then stood back and pointed. "That boulder also marked the location of these."

Seeing the look on Vaughn's face, she held up a hand. "They're safe. BOb has both a neutron detector and a gamma-ray detector. He says there's nothing coming from them."

"Nothing above what one would expect, Commander Brown," the robot corrected, still on all fours. "The nuclear warheads are emitting normal levels of radiation for their type. I do not detect any leakage."

Standing upright, several of the members started to back away. However, Monique held her ground. She looked at Angela. "I take it this is a pair of the nuclear warheads that the Necks beamed out before they could hit Geneva?"

"Yes." Angela pointed at the robot. "He identified these two as having come from a naval missile. Trident, I believe. Previously, you'd mentioned that you started off in the Navy as a Nuclear Surface Warfare Officer, so I had him load up these two."

Lieutenant Gheist peered down at the devices and then nodded appreciably. "BOb is correct. These are MIRV warheads." Seeing their confused looks, she added, "It is an acronym that stands for multiple independently targetable reentry vehicle. Each Trident can carry twelve MIRVs, although treaties limit them to four or five." Still seeing concerned looks, she held up a hand. "They are safe enough if there are no leaks."

BOb gave them the fisheye again. "If leakage concerns you, I highly recommend you avoid diet pills, as some have been shown to cause anal leakage."

Angela cast an arched brow at Monique.

The naval lieutenant shrugged. "That is not my fault. I did not program BOb's responses." She placed a hand on the tip of one of the devices. "Anal leakage notwithstanding, I think the missiles are safe enough. I will have to make sure they're disarmed. From what you have told us, I imagine they were configured for ground penetration. So it should require a large impact followed by a certain amount of time, albeit very short, before the nuclear device would activate."

Bill, who had been looking a little green under the gills, scoffed. "Activate? Is that a euphemism for blow the hell up?"

Monique nodded. "Yes, William, it is."

After holding up a hand, Angela gestured at the robot. "Turns out BOb has the appropriate protocols and," she paused and gave the group an inscrutable glance, then added, "One-Eighty-Eight hardware. He was able to ascertain that the missiles had reverted to safe mode before shutting down."

For a moment, Vaughn wondered how the missiles could still have power after so many months, but then he remembered that, in this timeline, little more than a week had passed since the President had dispatched these warheads on their awful mission.

Bingham had initially held back from the discussion. However, he'd started creeping closer at the mention of nuclear devices. Now the man looked like a Doberman eyeing a prime rib, ears rotated to front.

Vaughn extended a hand toward the man in a hold-on gesture. "No, Chance, were still not going to nuke them." Then he looked at the rest of the group. "Not unless we have to. If we don't succeed this time, we can at least deny the bastards our world."

CHAPTER 40

"Here you go, Doctor Geller," Monique said, handing the young man the now disconnected tablet. "That will do."

The naval lieutenant had connected the device to the nuclear warheads using the same One-Eighty-Eight-compliant interface as they had with the light wave emitter.

Vaughn understood why the nukes had the US MIL-Standard interface but was still at a loss as to why the Necks had incorporated the tech into the Taters. None of the theories advanced by the other team members fit. Monique's theory about it having come from the crashed quick-reaction force aircraft didn't hold water. The thing hadn't been anywhere close to this area when it crossed the light wave, and as far as Vaughn knew, the Necks had not yet gone that far afield. He doubted they would've already come across the wreckage in this timeline.

He also didn't think the hardware had come from anything in the Geneva area. Angela had been adamant that they weren't using the mil-standard interface in CERN.

Monique stepped back from the boulder she was using as a makeshift workbench. Holding out her hands, she gave them a meaningful look. "The nuclear devices are now armed ... again. However, they are no longer on impact-initiated timers."

Bingham's face soured. "What kind of ops-sec are you Yanks running? How on earth could you arm a nuke that easily in the field?"

"I assure you, our nuclear operations security is the best in the world." Nodding, Monique pointed to the devices. "If these had not been previously armed, I would not have been able to bypass their built-in security measures, even with my access codes. They would have self-destructed."

Vaughn did a double-take. "Now is a fine time to tell us that."

Monique merely shrugged.

Teddy adjusted his hat as he craned his neck for a better look. "How do you arm nuclear device now?"

She pointed at the small keypad that she had exposed along the back of one of the warheads. "Type in the desired number of minutes and then press the enter key three times. Then you must repeat the process. That will prevent accidental detonation."

Bill Peterson bent over to inspect her work and then gave Monique a sideward glance. "So you're saying that we need to enter the number of minutes a second time and then press the enter key three times ... again?"

"Yes, William."

Teddy chuckled. "Da, no butt-dialing the nuclear device."

Mark looked at Vaughn and then back at Monique. "What happens if we punch in zero minutes?"

Lieutenant Gheist stared back at him somberly. "The device detonates the third time you press the Enter key."

"Instantly?"

Monique nodded. "If it is the second time around, yes. Instantly."

The group stared at the nuke for a long moment.

A distant wail descended from the dark desert air. It was a lonely, sad thing, full of agony and despair.

Staring at the device, Vaughn asked, "What's the yield on this thing? Is it an H-bomb?"

Monique chuckled. "No, this is not a thermonuclear device. There is no way they could have carried anything that powerful, even with BOb's strength. This is one of the new submarine-deployed tactical nukes, a W76-2 warhead. Its yield is only six kilotons, about half of what we dropped on Hiroshima. I am not even sure it would have done much damage to the collider." Frowning, she looked down at the nuke. "I suppose it is just further evidence that the President was throwing everything he had at the problem."

Vaughn nodded and then looked at the robot. The machine was still vigilantly scanning the horizon around their perimeter. "BOb, can you beam all of us out at one time, including yourself?"

"Negative, Captain Asshole."

Vaughn felt his face flush as someone guffawed behind him. Then a loud snort issued. He looked back to see Angela covering her mouth. Several of the others were also laughing.

Pointing at the robot, he looked at Rachel. "Thanks for this."

Major Lee lifted one shoulder. "I told you, you shouldn't have said that within my earshot."

Vaughn pursed his lips and turned back to the robot. "BOb, address me as Captain Singleton from now on." Remembering Monique's suggestion that the robot seemed to react positively to politeness, he added, "Please."

The bot's head dipped. "Roger, Captain Asshole."

"That's not …!" He shook his head in surrender. "Shit!"

Pursing his lips, Vaughn turned his ire on Monique. "Really? You and your friends at DARPA couldn't do any better than this?"

The woman made a face. Holding out her hands, she shrugged. "Beta software."

Vaughn blew air through his nose and turned back to the robot. "Can you beam five out at once and then the other four plus yourself?"

"Yes, Captain Singleton."

"Thank you. Now, was that so difficult?"

"Not at all, Captain Asshole."

Vaughn closed his eyes for a moment and then turned back to the team members. Several of them were dabbing tears. "We're going to break back into our two groups. We'll use the same teams as we did back in the city." He pointed at Rachel. "Major Pain, I mean, Lee, I'd like you to take Wing Commander Bingham, Lieutenant Gheist, Lieutenant Colonel Hennessy, and Doctor Geller with you." He gestured at the others, pointing as he called out their names. "I'll take Angela, Bill, and Teddy and, God help me, BOb."

Smiles dissolved as they exchanged nervous glances, but after a few moments, everyone looked back at him and nodded.

They had already reloaded all of the weapons. Mark and the robot had retrieved the munitions Angela had left in the nuke field. It had been more than enough to rearm and resupply everyone.

"Where are we going?" Major Lee asked.

"I've been giving that some thought." Vaughn paused and looked at Rourke. "Can I borrow your tablet?"

The young man gave him a quick nod and handed over the device.

Vaughn opened the map app and zoomed in on a portion of the city. "When we were checking out the airport, I noticed that its west half was empty. I didn't see any buildings or robots there. That's a couple of miles of wide-open territory that's not too far from ATLAS." He slid his finger to a point in the middle of the open space. "We'll designate this as our target. The emitter's margin of error falls within the clear area. Even if we're off by a mile, we'll still be far enough away from the buildings and the bots."

Bingham held up both hands. "Wait, wait, wait! Why not just beam ourselves to the far side of Mont Salève? We can regroup, rearm, and come at this another day."

Rachel shook her head. "We've already depleted their forces significantly. If we fall back now, we'll never have a better chance."

"Exactly," Vaughn said. "And now they know that some humans survived." He held up a hand. "I know they think they beamed us out, but to them, we're nothing but cockroaches, and when you see one cockroach you know there's a hundred more in the walls."

Angela leaned in, raising her eyebrows. "And don't forget, they know what we tried to do to the collider. We have to act now, before they can formulate a defense against that kind of attack."

Bingham stared back at them for a moment. Finally, he dipped his head.

"What if the teams are too far apart?" Mark asked. "What's the plan if we can't find each other?"

Vaughn nodded slowly. He'd been working through the problem since they'd discovered the emitter's margin for error. "We'll have to proceed separately. It'll double our chances of success."

Bill Peterson's eyebrows peaked. "I thought you said it would double our chances of detection, too."

Rachel waved her hand dismissively. "There's nothing we can do about that now. It's not like we're going to hang around here instead." She looked at Vaughn. "What is our plan of attack?"

"It's still night. We'll beam out in a prone position. The field will have drainage easements. Work your way into the nearest one and then follow it as best you can to the airport perimeter. That'll limit our exposure and mask our thermal profile."

Rachel stared at the map for a long moment. Finally, she patted her rifle. "If they see us, we just start shooting. It'll become a running battle, but that's okay. We've proven we can take 'em out." She pulled her gaze from the tablet and looked at Vaughn. "How are we getting into ATLAS? The Necks closed off all of our ingress points."

"Not all of them. Angela and I discussed that a minute ago." He pointed to her. "Tell them your idea."

She nodded. "I think we might still be able to find one of the emergency exit shafts."

"Really?" Mark said. "I thought you didn't know where they were."

"I don't, not exactly, anyway." She pointed her chin at the tablet. "Can I see that for a moment?"

Vaughn handed it to her.

Angela zoomed in on the area between ATLAS and the airfield. She activated the drawing tool and then circled two points. "This is the ATLAS experiment on the west end and the LHCb or Beauty to the east." Then she dragged her finger from ATLAS toward the airfield, leaving a green arc on the screen. "The tunnel should follow this line between them. There will be a small fireproof building at the top of each emergency exit shaft, so they should still be standing if the Necks haven't bulldozed them."

Mark studied the line she'd drawn. "How big are they?"

She rocked her head equivocally. "They're small, cinder block buildings. About the size of a two-car garage, maybe?"

"Lovely," Bingham said acidly. "So the plan is to wander through a dark city filled with killer robots that may or may not be able to see us, all while looking for a building we've never seen. And then, if that hare-brained plan succeeds, we'll descend into a tunnel that has already proven full of enemy combatants."

Vaughn nodded. "Pretty much sums it up."

"Lovely!" Bingham repeated.

Vaughn looked at the robot. "BOb, from now on, please refer to Wing Commander Bingham as Commander Jackass."

The robot looked at him and nodded. "Roger, Captain Asshole."

Rachel gave the man a hard look. "You're welcome to stay here, Chauncey-Baby."

Unfortunately, Chance declined.

Addressing the rest of the group, Vaughn said, "So that's the plan." He regarded Bingham askance. "Unless anyone has a better idea."

Commander Jackass glared back at him but, for once, kept his trap shut.

Vaughn pointed at the map. "BOb, add that curved line to your navigation system."

After a slight pause, the battle operations bot nodded. "Complete."

Looking at Angela, Vaughn held out his hand. "Are you done with that?"

She nodded and handed it to him. Vaughn relayed it to Rourke. "Take this with you. Team Two will rely on Angela's mental map and the one inside BOb."

After a moment, Vaughn gave a short nod. "Let's divide into our groups and get ready to beam the hell out of … Hell."

CHAPTER 41

"Sure that's not too much for you?"

Breathing heavily, Mark slid his thumbs under the backpack's shoulder straps and shifted them. With its nuclear cargo, the bag was now quite heavy. "I can handle it."

Vaughn patted him on the shoulder. "Knew you could, Chewie." He paused for breath as the lack of oxygen wrought its effect on him as well. Then the smile faded from his face. "Be careful, friend. Take care of these guys."

"Hey, that's on Major Lee. You put her in charge." Seeing Vaughn's reaction, Mark held up his hands. "Just screwing with you, buddy." He drew a deep breath. "I'd be lying if I said I wasn't a bit nervous, but it will be good to get some oxygen in these lungs." He wrinkled his nose. "And some fresh-ish air, too."

"Hear! Hear!" Bingham said and then coughed. "What do you say we get a move on?"

Vaughn gave the man a nod. It was good to see Chance getting on board with the idea. Turning from the wing commander, he stepped over to Rachel. "You ready?"

"Yeah," she gestured at Angela, "but I'd almost feel better if one of you was with us. You're the ones with all the experience here."

"Not really. You may not have been there for the whole battle, but you and your team already have more combat experience against the enemy than Angela and I ever had during our travels."

She cocked a skeptical eyebrow and then turned to address her team. "If everyone is ready, let's get in position."

Having donned their combat gear and placed their night-vision goggles atop their heads, the five of them lay down next to one another.

To make sure they all fit within the fan of light, they positioned Rachel, the shortest of the team, closest to the robot. The two tallest members, Monique and Mark, occupied the other end. Rourke and Bingham lay prone in the middle.

Vaughn thought it probably didn't matter, but he wouldn't want anyone's appendages or extremities left here in the desert ... Unless it was Bingham, of course. That would be just fine with him.

BOb stepped into position and looked at Vaughn.

After receiving a nod from Rachel, he turned back to the robot. "Give them a three count and then beam them out."

Raising the gun into firing position, BOb aimed over their heads and began to count down in a voice that sounded like Captain Picard. "Three. Two. One ... Engage." The white light shot in a wide fan over their heads. However, instead of continuing toward the horizon, it simply terminated like a flattened lightsaber blade, its far end only reaching a couple of feet past Mark.

To minimize the degradation of their night vision, the team was facing away from the light. Vaughn narrowed his eyes in a belated effort to preserve his own.

The members of Team One twitched in unison as the light shot over their heads. However, before the movement could complete, the beam had swept over them and then vanished, leaving nothing but a ten-foot-wide crater where the light had scooped out a section of the dusty desert floor as well.

Cursing himself, Vaughn tried to blink the dazzle from his eyes. After a moment, he recovered.

BOb was looking at the side of the BFG. He appeared to be studying its display.

"Are you ready to beam the rest of us out, BOb?"

After staring at the small display for another moment, the robot looked up. "The device shut down."

CHAPTER 42

"Son of a bitch!" Eyes widening, Vaughn looked back at the crater where the group had been lying. "Did they all make it?"

He walked over to the pit and scanned the ground. Fortunately, no bodyparts sat within the depression, not even Bingham's.

"I believe so, Captain. The error occurred when I released the trigger."

Looking at Angela, Vaughn swallowed. His throat clicked in his ears. She stared back at him wordlessly, her face looking ghostly white in the moon's pale light.

Bill and Teddy exchanged nervous glances as well and then looked at him.

Major Peterson looked at the empty crater and then at the modified cannon. "Is it bricked?"

"I am sorry, Major Peterson. I do not understand the question."

Craning her neck, Angela tried to read the display. "He's asking if the device is completely offline. Is it dead?"

"Oh, no. It is simply rebooting. My software's built-in test detected an error with the device."

Vaughn saw new concern register on Angela's face. "Did the error occur during the beaming?"

"I cannot say for certain, ma'am." The robot tilted its head. "Only that the BIT-fail logged shortly after I released the trigger."

"How shortly after?"

"Approximately three hundred and thirteen milliseconds after trigger release."

"Whew," Vaughn said. "He had me worried—"

Angela cut him off. "That's less than a third of a second."

Vaughn's eyes went wide. "Oh, shit."

"What do we do, Command-Oh?"

After staring at the modified EMP cannon for a moment, Angela slowly shook her head. Then she looked at the robot. "Has this happened before?"

"Yes, Commander Brown. However, this is the first time that a built-in test failed close to the activation of the device."

"How many BIT fails have there been?" Vaughn asked.

He could feel his pulse quickening.

Were they stuck here?

Had the others made it back to Geneva, and if so, had they even ended up in the right Geneva?

When a Tater had partially beamed him and Angela from the top floor of that building in the machine city, they'd ended up back in a different dimension. Fortunately, in that case, it had dropped them into their home dimension.

"There have been thirty-one failures since integration of the device."

Angela's mouth formed a thin line. Then she pointed at the modified weapon. "Is there any kind of pattern? Are the failures happening on a specific schedule?"

"No, Commander Brown. I can detect no pattern or timeline for the failures, although they have begun to happen more often. The time interval between them has shortened slightly."

"What is the nature of the failures?"

"They are related to a communication error nested within the One-Eighty-Eight databus."

"What's that mean?" Bill Peterson asked.

Angela's eyes lost focus as she stared off into the distance for a moment. Then she tilted her head. "I think it ties to the fact that this device isn't strictly native to this architecture."

Vaughn saw an idea form on Angela's face. She looked at BOb. "What's been the minimum and maximum times between failures?"

The robot hesitated for a barely perceptible moment and then looked as if it was ready to answer, but Angela held up a hand. "Rounded to the nearest minute and second, please."

BOb dipped his head. "The longest time between failures was approximately one hour thirty-two minutes and ten seconds."

"That's not bad," Teddy said, relief evident on his face.

"The shortest time between failures was approximately four minutes, thirty-one seconds."

Bill Peterson shook his head. "Well, that sucks."

"Da, comrade. Seriously sketchy."

Vaughn could feel time slipping away. "Angela, remember how we ended up back in Geneva that last time?"

"Yeah, I was just thinking about that."

"Maybe a failure or partial beaming returns us to Geneva anyway."

She looked dubious. "Maybe, but I think we just got lucky on that one. If the light fails while it's beaming us out this time, we could end up somewhere else completely."

Teddy's eyebrows rose. "Like, not in the city?"

"No ..." Angela looked at the man. "More like, not in our universe."

Bill's mouth went round. "Oh, shit."

"Agreed," Vaughn said as he stared at the depression left in the wake of the departed team. After a moment, he looked at BOb. "Let me know when the next failure occurs."

"Wilco, Captain."

Bill looked at Vaughn. "What's the plan?"

"After the BIT failure, it'll reboot. We'll beam out as soon as it completes."

Angela nodded. "Good idea. That'll minimize the chance we get glitched into another dimension."

The next several minutes were the longest of Vaughn's life. Finally,

BOb perked up. "I just detected another BIT failure. The device is rebooting."

Having been in the middle of pacing a groove into the desert floor, Vaughn broke from the slot and ran over to the predesignated position. He lay down, and the rest of Team Two gathered around him. Being shortest, Angela and Teddy lay prone at the front, with Vaughn and Bill in the back. BOb folded himself in half next to Angela.

Vaughn activated his night-vision goggles. "Make sure your NVGs are on."

BOb stared at the datapad on the side of the device. Vaughn thought it an affectation as the robot clearly could access the data directly without having to look at it on a small screen. Then the robot nodded. "Reboot complete."

As the bot held the device at the end of its long arm, Vaughn said, "Hold onto it tightly, BOb. We wouldn't want that to get left behind."

"Roger, Captain Asshole."

Vaughn pursed his lips and shook his head. "Energize, jackass."

CHAPTER 43

The light flickered over Vaughn and just as quickly disappeared. Then the ground shifted beneath him. Fortunately, he remembered to close his eyes this time, so it didn't take long for them to adjust.

He made a quick scan of their surroundings and then lay flat on the mounded dust that had come with them. "We're back," he whispered. "Looks like we finally caught a break. We're in a low spot, so we don't have to move right away." He jabbed a finger ahead. "And the western perimeter is a couple hundred meters that way."

He looked at Angela. She and the two men nodded silently.

A hazy moon stared down from their south. Clouds of unknown intensity hung overhead. Looking up into the dark sky, Vaughn couldn't determine whether it was just another squall line or if the main body of the storm had finally arrived.

Beyond Angela and the boys, BOb was scanning left and right. Then his head rotated a full three hundred sixty degrees. The anatomically incorrect movement still gave Vaughn the willies.

"Any sign of the other team?"

"Negative, Captain."

Vaughn shook his head and whispered under his breath, "Shit.

Shit. Shit." Still peering through his night-vision goggles, he scanned the horizon alongside the robot.

Where had they gone? He tried to think what he would've done in Rachel's position. He supposed he would've given them less than fifteen minutes before he moved on. It'd easily been more than that.

He looked to Angela, Bill, and Teddy. "I think they've already gone."

Angela raised her eyebrows. "Either that or..." She left the last part unsaid.

After a moment, Vaughn sighed. "This doesn't change anything for us. We'll proceed as planned." He looked at the robot and gestured west. "BOb, do you see any movement or heat signatures in those buildings?"

The battle operations bot stared in the indicated direction for a long moment and then shook its head. "Negative, Captain Singleton." The robot turned one hundred eighty degrees and gestured toward the far end of the airport. "I am detecting movement near the terminal," BOb shifted the gesture ninety degrees to the right, "and more of it farther south, into the city. However, as we observed previously," the robot turned the last ninety degrees and pointed west again, "this area still appears to be clear of enemy combatants."

Having followed the movements of the robot, Vaughn zoomed in with his NVGs and scanned the buildings, looking for any indication that their comrades had entered them. "You're certain there are no heat signatures?"

"I am sorry, Captain. I do not see any evidence of Team One."

Angela extended a hand and pointed at a structure protruding above the debris. "There's a building standing over there. Let's get up inside one, and maybe we'll see them from higher up."

After a moment, Vaughn gave a slow nod. "Good idea. Might spot one of your cinder block buildings from there as well."

Looking past Angela, he nodded to the other two men. "You guys ready?"

"Da, El Capitan."

Bill held up a thumb. "R-Ready as I'll ever be." The major's hand shook unsteadily.

Vaughn nodded. He knew how the man felt.

"BOb, cover our six." Pausing, he swallowed hard and then pointed to their right front. "There's a drainage easement over there. Everyone stay low and follow me."

CHAPTER 44

Breathing heavily, Angela low-crawled up to the building's edge and then drew up to a seated position next to Vaughn. She ran her hand along its brick exterior. Leaning toward him, she kept her voice low and asked, "Think it'll hold us?"

He wiped sweaty grime from his forehead and then nodded. "Looks stable enough," he said, also keeping his voice down. He pointed back down the path they'd come up. "When we rounded the bend, I saw that its roof and second-floor walls are gone. Fortunately, it looks like most of it spilled into the street. What's left looks sturdy." He patted the bricks firmly.

The wall creaked.

Vaughn did a double-take. Seeing Angela staring at him, he nodded confidently. "It's just settling." He held up a hand. "Don't be giving me the eyebrow-o-skepticism."

"Oh, now you're a building expert? Tell me, Captain Construction, what kind of electricity did they use here, one-ten or two-twenty?"

Vaughn shrugged. "Two-twenty, two-twenty-one, whatever it takes."

Angela shook her head. "Thanks, Mr. Mom."

"Wow, Michael Keaton, nice. Figured that one would go right over your head."

Rolling her eyes, she peeked around the corner of the building and gazed west along its northern perimeter. After a quick scan, she leaned back against the wall. "There's a clear area across the street."

"Yeah, saw that. Should give us a pretty good line of sight west, toward ATLAS."

The scent of death wafted up from her pant legs. Angela wrinkled her nose. "Smells like the rinse didn't do as good a job as I'd hoped."

"No shit." Vaughn inspected the lower half of his camouflage pants. "At least it's a little better. I don't see any more bones or fur stuck to it."

"Yeah, thank goodness for the run-off."

They'd found a stream of rainwater running through the bottom of one of the drainage easements. All four of them plus the robot had used it to rinse off the worst of Hell's deposits.

Lightning flashed across the sky directly overhead.

Vaughn looked up and frowned. "Wonderful."

In the stuttering illumination, Angela saw Bill, Teddy, and BOb inching up to them.

Thunder shattered the night, shaking the very earth. She took a measure of comfort in the fact that the building didn't topple.

Using the cover of the still rolling reverberations, the two men and the robot scrambled the last few feet to the back wall and then moved to sit on either side of them.

Angela hitched a thumb toward an opening a few meters to their right. "Let's head up before the rain hits. Otherwise, we may not be able to see much from up there."

Vaughn nodded and then gestured left and right. "Bill, Teddy, move to the corners and keep an eye out for company. BOb, I need your infrared vision. You're with us."

The two men gave a single nod and then, in the renewed silence, crept toward their assigned positions.

Rising to a crouch, Angela followed Vaughn to the back door. BOb came up behind her, holding the BFG at the ready.

Vaughn pressed his back to the wall and then leaned in and peered through the opening. "All clear." Moving to the far side of the door, he extended an arm. "Go ahead. I'll cover your back. Just be careful not to knock anything over."

Pursing her lips, she moved past him. "Don't worry. I'll try not to make any of the classic B-movie mistakes."

A few steps in, she found a debris-cluttered stairwell. She worked her way up the treads, choosing her path cautiously.

Vaughn and the robot followed her.

A moment later, she emerged under a tumultuous sky. Vaughn had been correct. The entire roof, along with all the walls of the second floor, was gone. It looked as if they'd been wiped entirely off the building.

Lightning flared overhead followed almost instantly by bone-shaking thunder.

Reaching the top floor, she lay prone on damp carpet and started to low-crawl toward the western edge of the structure.

Vaughn and the robot crept alongside, paralleling her path over the squelching rug.

Low clouds churned above them.

As another thunderclap rolled across the city, Angela shook her head. "That damned storm front has been threatening all day. Guess it decided it was time to get off the pot."

Vaughn glanced up. "Won't be long now. Those clouds are hauling ass."

The moon still ruled the southeastern sky, but it was losing ground quickly. Glowing under its light, the ragged edge of the front raced northeast as the body of the storm slid inexorably closer to the lunar disc.

Lightning strobed within the tumult.

"Careful," Vaughn whispered. "We're almost to the edge."

Angela shifted her gaze forward as she crept the last two feet. Reaching the sharp precipice, she stared at the land immediately west of the building.

The moon's tenuous effulgence drew muted shadows across the scene.

A vision of heart-wrenching loss wormed its way into her eyes.

The building that served as their vantage point stood in silent vigil, watching over the night-veiled town square that had once been a beautiful park. From its floor, stunted, burned trees reached skyward like the yearning, skeletal fingers of a dying earth. A debris-choked fountain sat in its southeastern corner. The flotsam of the broken lunar disc rode unsteadily atop its rippling black water.

Another white-hot bolt silently bridged the heavens, drawing Angela's gaze west.

Thunder cracked the night again as the report of the lightning's brief presence finally reached their observation point.

A bifurcated city lay beyond the ruined park.

The coming storm cast a deep shadow that blanketed everything to Angela's right, leaving only a hint of what lay beneath. Rapid-fire lightning pulsed within the clouds. With each flash of electricity, sharp angles jutted up from the shadowed depths of shattered apartment blocks only to vanish between strokes, as if the ruined structures had manifest from the light itself.

Shifting her gaze to the south, Angela studied the portion of the city not yet covered by the storm's shadow. It shone eerily beneath the lunar light. Mont Salève backdropped all of it. The moon's recycled sunlight haunted its cliffs, painting the range in an ectoplasmic glow.

Pulling her gaze from the scene, she lowered her night-vision goggles into place and activated them. Geneva's remnants blossomed back into existence. The light intensification capabilities of the tubes revealed the entire city, painting it in shades of green, gray, and black.

The construction site above ATLAS sat at the farthest reaches of her enhanced vision. Angela ignored the area for the moment. Instead, she glassed the broken cityscape between, desperately seeking any sign of movement.

After a fruitless search, she shook her head. "I don't see Team One."

"Shit," Vaughn said through a growl. "Neither do I."

Angela raised her goggles and looked at the battlebot. The dark gray machine was all but invisible. Its silhouette cut a black hole across the remnants of the next building over. "Do you see Team One, BOb?"

"No, Commander Brown. I see no signs of life."

Vaughn flipped up his NVGs. "No heat signatures?"

The dark silhouette of the robot's head shook side-to-side. "Only those that match the profile of enemy combatants."

Vaughn nodded slowly as he continued to look across the city. Finally, he said, "Godspeed, Mark. Good luck, my friend." He paused and then looked at her. "We'll just have to go on without them."

Angela nodded. "Who knows? They could be working their way in right now. The timeline could reset at any moment."

Vaughn scoffed. "Yeah, wouldn't that be nice?" Falling silent, he continued to stare into the night. Brief spats of lightning illuminated his face. Finally, he sighed. "Well, shit. We're still here. Guess it's up to us."

"Guess so."

Flipping her NVGs back into position, Angela scanned the line that she believed the collider followed, this time searching for the cube-shaped buildings that sat atop the emergency exit shafts. She didn't see any nearby. Shifting her gaze farther west, she adjusted the optics of the goggles and zoomed in on the construction site above the ATLAS experiment.

Freeing a hand, Angela pointed at the giant, stadium-sized vat. "They've just about completed the cauldron."

"Yeah, I can see the foundry machinery beneath it. Looks like they're still working on that stuff."

Angela shifted the aim of her goggles and saw the indicated equipment. It lay in various states of assembly. Every surface within the massive machinery appeared to be moving. She swallowed hard. "A lot of activity there. Looks like someone kicked over a damned ant bed."

Her scan faltered as a recognizable structure panned into view to the right of the construction site: a brown, dome-shaped building. She knew that, up close, it would look more like a partially embedded brown marble formed from horizontal slats. "I ... I see something!"

"What? One of the emergency escape shafts?"

"No. It's ... It's CERN's Globe of Science and Innovation, their exposition center."

"Where?!"

Extending an arm, she pointed. "There, in the shadow of all the construction. It's just to the right of the cauldron. That's why I didn't see it before. The city builder was blocking it from view when we were on the cliff."

Beside her, Vaughn fumbled with his NVGs. "What am I looking for? What's it look like?"

"It's that dome-shaped structure. Looks like a big sphere with its bottom third embedded in the ground."

"Yeah! ... Yeah, I see it!"

As she stared at it, Angela shook her head. "I can't believe it's still standing. It should've burned up with everything else. The thing is like a hundred feet tall and half a football field wide, and its entire exterior is made from thick, horizontal, wood planks."

Vaughn adjusted the magnification and zoomed in. "That's made of wood?"

"Yeah, there's a gap between each board, like the slats on Venetian blinds. They enable the globe to act as a natural carbon sink." She shook her head. "No idea how it survived the fires."

"Would there be a HiLumi-networked computer terminal in there?"

Angela nodded excitedly. "The Research Area exhibit displays live collisions. It's like a mini-control room. It uses the HiLumi network feed to display real-time data. It's tied directly into ATLAS. Gets both its power and its data from the main experiment."

Vaughn zoomed in further. His shoulders slumped. "Ah, shit." Rolling onto his side, he flipped up his goggles and looked at Angela. "A lot of good that does us." He hitched a thumb toward CERN. "The place is crawling with caterpillar bots."

Still staring at the scene, Angela adjusted the magnification of her goggles to max. The ground around the structure looked like it was moving. "Shit!" she said, drawing out the word. "It sure the hell is."

Vaughn chuckled. "I doubt we'll ever convince Bill to head into that."

Angela smiled wryly and dropped her voice an octave. "Nope! Nope! Nope! I ain't fucking with no army of ten-foot-long caterpillar monsters."

"That's not exactly what he said."

"Close enough." Angela raised her eyebrows. "Besides, I'm kinda with him on that sentiment."

Rolling back onto his stomach, Vaughn flipped his night-vision goggles back into position and continued his scan. "I still don't see any of your cinder block cubes."

"Me neither. There's a lot of debris blocking our view, though." Shifting her gaze right, Angela studied the area that lay between them and the city builder. Then she raised an arm and traced an imaginary arc toward ATLAS. "On the bright side, I don't see anything moving along the path we need to search. What about you, BOb? Do you see anything moving along the line we plotted?"

"Negative, Commander Brown. The only movement I detect along that path is immediately around and within the enemy construction site."

Angela gestured ahead, indicating an east-west thoroughfare. "That main road roughly follows the line of the collider. If we're lucky, we'll spot a cube along it somewhere."

"That's what I was thinking, but I don't know." He raised an arm and pointed to the left of the street. "I see a shit-ton of scavenger bots moving around in that neighborhood."

Angela looked in the indicated direction and then nodded. "The one that skirts the south side of the road?"

"Yeah, that one."

"We don't have to go that far south." Angela patted Vaughn's shoulder and gestured at the leveled cityscape that skirted the right side of the street. "We can hang a couple of blocks north and run parallel to it." She traced a finger left and right, gesturing at the narrow north-south streets that intersected the main road. "These are so choked with debris we shouldn't have any problem staying out of sight. The bots working in the southern neighborhood won't even be able to see us."

Full darkness descended over them as the moon finally lost its battle with the advancing storm front.

They both flinched as a bolt of lightning hammered into the ground some distance to their right. A few moments later, thunder shook the earth once more.

Fat droplets of rain began to pelt them, first in ones and twos and then quickly crescendoing into a torrential downpour.

Vaughn rolled onto his side and looked at her. "Wonderful."

Blinking against the spray, Angela shrugged. "The rain should make it harder for them to see us."

A long breath hissed through his teeth. "Yeah, it'll make it harder for us to see them, too."

CHAPTER 45

Having circumnavigated around to the decimated park's west side, Vaughn led the group behind the remnants of another building and ducked into cover.

They still hadn't seen any bots, but he knew that didn't mean a lot at the moment. He pulled the rest of the group close and whispered, "The primary objective, for now, is not to be seen. The Necks don't know we're back. If we encounter anything, get behind cover, let BOb take care of it, especially if it's a solitary scavenger bot. He can beam it to Hell in relative silence."

Teddy scoffed and then matched Vaughn's whisper. "You did hear that thing in the tunnel, right?"

"Yeah, I did, but that was in small confines. It won't be as loud here, and it sure as hell won't be as distinctive as an explosion or gunfire. If one of us opens up, the entire goddamn alien army will know we're here."

Eyebrows raising with sudden realization, Vaughn paused and looked at the robot. "BOb, have you changed the destination coordinates to Hell?"

"No, Captain, I have not," BOb said in a barely audible whisper. "Would you like me to do so now?"

"Uh, yeah. Let's do that."

Shaking his head, Vaughn looked into the rain. "Should have thought of that sooner." He felt his face flush as he looked at Angela. "If BOb had beamed out an enemy bot, the damn thing would've just ended up back at the airport, free to alert its robotic alien overlords."

She shrugged. "Better late than never."

Vaughn rocked his head equivocally and then peered around the corner. He scanned the intersection to their south. Zooming in with his night-vision goggles, he glassed the main thoroughfare. Nothing was moving, and there wasn't a cube-shaped building in sight.

He ducked back behind the corner.

Teddy gave him a crooked grin. "See any ten-foot-long monster caterpillar bots, El Capitan?"

Bill's eyes narrowed, and he gave the man a hard look. "Shut. The hell. Up! That shit is not funny."

Vaughn winced and raised a hand. "Jesus Christ! Keep it down." He flipped up his NVGs and shook his head at Teddy. "Focus, guys. This is not the time to be whistling past the graveyard."

Bill and the cosmonaut exchanged looks and then nodded.

"Outstanding. I want you to cover the three of us while we advance, and then we'll cover you. We'll work our way block-to-block that way. Just like last time: move then cover, move then cover." Pausing, he leaned out and signaled their direction. "Stay low. We'll stop at every intersection, see if we can spot one of Angela's buildings. Any questions?"

None came.

Lowering his goggles, Vaughn glanced around the corner one more time and then, pointing a bladed hand, mouthed, "Let's go."

Sometime later, they crossed another of the many intersections that spanned the gap between the airport and the ATLAS experiment.

As planned, they had held back a block, sometimes two, from the main road to stay out of sight.

Vaughn chewed his lip as he peered out from behind cover. Scanning the visible portion of the major thoroughfare they'd been tracking, he saw yet another intersection with nothing approximating

377

Angela's buildings. The things were starting to take on the feel of vaporware: something promised but never delivered.

The five of them were getting damned close to CERN, and they still hadn't found a way into the collider. Additionally, they had seen no sign of the other team's passage, not so much as an out of place scuff mark or disturbed dust.

That and the fact that he and his team were still firmly rooted within this timeline made him wonder all the more about what had happened to the other team.

All along, Vaughn had held out hope that he'd suddenly find himself falling through the ether of another reset, one initiated by the other team.

That hope was waning rapidly.

Where were they?

Had he lost Mark, his one true friend, again?

Was it his own fault? Had he rushed them into action?

Vaughn shook the thoughts from his head.

Angela looked at him and whispered, "Everything okay?"

He sighed and then nodded.

Glancing around the corner, he eyed the next block.

As they'd drawn closer to ATLAS, the noise generated by the alien construction site had reached them. The racket had risen in volume with each block they'd advanced.

The din now sounded like a nearing freight train clawing its way down a track riddled with failing foundations.

Looking around, Vaughn saw the other members of the team scanning the surrounding cityscape. "See anything?"

They looked at him, but before anyone could answer, they all flinched as a metallic clang rang out.

The five of them turned as one toward the source of the clatter.

The twisted frame of a metal table sat crumpled in the street ten feet from where they crouched in hiding. It hadn't been there a moment before. As they watched, a dark object flew out of the structure that stood across the street from them. The item hit the pavement, loosing another loud, metallic keen. It bounced loudly and then rolled twice before finally coming to rest.

Looking at the green rendering generated by the NVGs, Vaughn thought the thing had been a metal television stand or an entertainment center. He imagined it had once been a modern assembly, probably from Ikea.

The sound of metallic feet scraping across a concrete floor confirmed Vaughn's suspicions: a scavenger bot was working inside the building.

Gesturing silently, he pointed northeast, signaling for the group to fall back. They'd move a few blocks farther away from the main road and then head west again.

Everyone nodded their understanding.

Vaughn gestured at BOb and pointed for him to lead the way.

The battle operations bot looked left and right and then darted across the street. The team followed close on its heels.

After they'd advanced one block to the north, they turned ninety degrees, intending to head west. However, Vaughn ran straight into BOb's nuke-filled backpack.

The battlebot had lurched to a stop in the middle of the intersection.

As Vaughn bounced backward, BOb raised the modified cannon, aiming it at an obviously startled scavenger bot. The thing stood next to a pile of metallic refuse.

Before the machine could raise an arm or sound an alarm, blue-white light flared from the emitter.

The scavenger bot vanished along with several pieces of metal and a divot of charred pavement.

The howling screech of the weapon's discharge echoed loudly off the crumbled walls that surrounded them.

Vaughn stood transfixed for a moment, unsure of what to do. If they ran farther north, they might stumble into occupied territory.

Had the two bots simply been outliers?

He didn't know, but one fact screamed inside his head: they'd been seen!

Looking back, he whispered harshly, "We need to get the hell away from this spot!"

Matching his volume, Angela said, "Yeah, but where? Where do we go from here?"

The others stared at him apprehensively.

Vaughn shook his head. "Retreat isn't an option. There's nothing back there for us." He looked around, frantically searching for an exit path. "We've already checked everything to the east and south, and going farther north just takes us farther from the collider."

Lightning strobed the night and the rain redoubled as its thunder shook the ground, momentarily eclipsing the cacophony coming from the construction site.

Vaughn growled in frustration. "Fuck it." He jabbed a finger, pointing west. "Go now! We'll regroup and reevaluate after a few blocks."

As everyone broke into a run, he whispered urgently, "Keep your head on a swivel. Watch for one of the cube-shaped buildings."

They had gone less than a block when an all-too-familiar noise rose above the sound of falling rain and the cacophony coming from the construction site.

The screaming wail of an onrushing Tater suddenly filled the night.

Vaughn shook his head. "Fuck!"

Then he saw it through his night-vision goggles. Glowing light green in the phosphorescent display, the onrushing ovoid rocketed straight at them from the direction of the ATLAS experiment. Water sprayed off its body as the thing raced over the broken walls of the city's burned-out buildings.

BOb and the rest of the group slid to a stop. Darting sideways, they threw themselves against a half-crumpled wall.

The Tater came to a hover about a hundred feet away, stopping ten feet above the roadbed, outside the range of the modified EMP cannon.

Vaughn tapped BOb's shoulder. "Hit the bastard as soon as it's in range."

The robot shook his head. "Unable, Captain."

"Why the hell not?!"

"The device is rebooting. It experienced a BIT failure a moment ago."

Bill growled and slammed the back of his helmet against the wall. "You gotta be shitting me!"

Looking around, Vaughn desperately sought a way out of their situation, but the Tater appeared to be staring right at them, its long axis pointing directly at their position.

The damned thing had them pinned.

Vaughn shook his head. "Fuck it. They already know we're here."

Switching to full auto, he pushed off the wall and stepped out.

He squeezed the trigger.

The rifle danced in his hands, spraying dozens of 5.56mm rounds at the Tater.

None of the bullets found their target. Strobing, blue-white light zapped each one mid-flight.

The rest of the team leaped out and launched a fusillade at the alien machine. Fire, bullets, and grenades belched from their weapons, dousing the surrounding structures in flickering yellow light.

The Tater darted left and then right, dodging some of their shots and zapping away the rest.

As the thing moved, Vaughn blinked in sudden recognition. Nothing had hit it yet, but two bullet holes already marred the left side of the machine.

It was the same Tater that had beamed him to Hell.

The ovoid jinked left and then instantly back to the right. Between movements, it rapidly advanced on their position.

Vaughn and his team members managed to keep its light beam emitter at bay, overloading it with incoming fire, but still, none found their mark.

BOb had been firing both bullets and grenades. Suddenly, the battlebot stowed its rifle and drew the BFG.

Before Vaughn could ask whether the thing had finished its reboot, a wedge of white light shot out from the weapon.

Then the light vanished, taking the Tater with it.

Blinking, Vaughn stared at the spot and then looked up urgently. "We need to put some distance between ourselves and our last known position." He jabbed a finger toward the west. "Go! Go! Go!"

Needing no further prodding, the group sprinted in the indicated direction.

Rain pelted them.

Lightning strobed the sky.

Thunder shook Vaughn's chests and rocked the ground beneath his feet.

A few blocks later, he waved them to a stop. They took cover beneath the leeward side of a partially toppled structure. It blocked the team from view from all but one direction and sheltered them from the wind and the rain.

Breathing heavily, they exchanged frightened glances.

Finally, Vaughn found his voice. "Anyone see an entry point?"

They all shook their heads.

Still panting, Bill Peterson tilted his NVGs back and wiped water from his face. "Can't see a damned thing through all this rain."

The others nodded their agreement.

Thunder split the air again. As it rumbled across the city and faded, the rain began to taper.

Vaughn tilted his head, listening for the expected arrival of more Taters.

Something struck him as odd. "Do you hear that?"

He watched the others, including BOb, crane their necks out as they listened intently. After a moment, they each shook their heads.

"What is it?" Angela asked.

Vaughn shrugged. "I don't know. Something sounds ... different."

Teddy's eyes flew wide. "It's too quiet!"

That was it. That's what was wrong. Not only did he not hear the shriek of approaching Taters, but the rest of the background noise had also faded.

Angela looked at him, comprehension dawning on her face. "The noise from the Necks' construction site ... It's gone. I ... I don't hear it anymore."

The rain subsided further. Then it ceased completely. The only thing left in its wake was their heavy breathing and intermittent drips of water dribbling from broken masonry.

All other sound had ceased.

Vaughn flipped his night-vision goggles back into place. Around him, the others did the same. Craning their necks, they stepped out from underneath their overhead cover and peered around.

The five of them, four humans and one battle operations bot, edged into the middle of the road.

Turning slowly, Vaughn searched the surrounding rubble. It appeared the Necks had removed all metal from this section of the city. A brick chimney lay across a portion of the road. Although he could see where part of it had been plowed out of the way to permit vehicle traffic, probably the trucks the Necks had used to transport metal through the area.

Vaughn scrunched up his face. "You guys seeing *any* movement?"

Bill shook his head. "Nothing."

"Nada, El Capitan," Teddy whispered.

Angela looked at him and gave a single shake of her head.

BOb's dark gray head shifted side-to-side. "Negative, Captain Singleton. I detect no movement within the range of my passive sensors."

Vaughn scanned the dark sky. "I thought they'd be sending a whole other wave of Taters after us."

The tubes of Bill's goggles bobbed. "Me, too. What do you make of it?"

Continuing to scan the ruined cityscape, Vaughn raised his eyebrows. "I ... I don't know."

"Maybe that was ..." Teddy paused and then continued. "Maybe that was their last Tater."

Vaughn blinked. "Holy shit! You might be right. That last one had a couple of bullet holes in it." He gestured at Bill and Teddy. "I think it's the one that sent us to Hell. I managed to hit it with two rounds before it got me."

Angela placed a hand on his arm. "I'll bet it's the same one that beamed Rourke out, too. It probably sped over there to take him out right after it finished off you guys."

"You may be right." Vaughn paused and then nodded. "We still need to get into CERN, and we sure as hell aren't going to accomplish that standing here."

He scanned their surroundings for a moment and then shook his head. "I can't see the thoroughfare we've been following."

"Me neither, El Capitan."

"BOb, still no movement?"

"Negative, Captain Asshole."

Gnashing his teeth, Vaughn pointed south. "Okay, COC-RING, how about you lead us to the main drag? We still need to find an ingress point."

The robot did a double-take, but for once, the machine started in the indicated direction without further comment.

They'd traversed less than a block when BOb suddenly stopped in front of a narrow alleyway. Spinning toward it, the bot raised its weapon, aiming the light wave emitter into the dark crevice.

Vaughn looked into the brick-lined fissure. His night-vision goggles revealed the outline of a scavenger bot staring back at him. He almost ordered BOb to fire on the thing, but the enemy machine sat outside the emitter's range.

The two robots stared at each other for a moment. Then BOb raised an arm as if waving to the thing. His hand cut a slow, wide arc as he spoke with a British accent. "These aren't the droids you're looking for."

As if startled into motion by BOb's voice, the scavenger bot began to back away. Then it spun around and disappeared into the night.

Teddy looked at BOb and chuckled. "Nice work, Obi-BOb! I can't believe that worked."

Vaughn shook his head. "It didn't. Something has changed. The robots always attack or at least sound an alarm." He searched the sky again. "I don't like this. The Necks obviously know exactly where we are, but they're not sending anything after us."

Bill's eyebrows rose. "I'd say that's a win."

"I'm not so sure about that." Vaughn paused and then pointed south again. "Keep going, BOb. We need to see what the hell's going on."

The others exchanged concerned glances, but they fell in behind Vaughn and the battlebot as they continued toward the main road.

Another block later, they stopped under a partially collapsed awning. It sat at the corner where the narrow lane they'd been following intersected the main thoroughfare.

Leaning out, the robot peered up and down the street, gazing east and west.

"Any movement, BOb?"

"Negative, Captain."

Angela tapped Vaughn's arm and pointed at the roadbed. "Look at those grooves. They've already scavenged all the streetcar rails." She shifted the gesture to indicate overhead. "All the power lines are gone as well."

Bill nodded. "Maybe that's why we don't see anyone working the area. They've already scavenged all of the steel."

"I don't know." Vaughn shook his head. "I still don't hear any construction. Should be pretty close to it by now."

"You are correct, Captain Asshole." BOb leaned out and pointed west. "I can see it now."

"What?" Vaughn blinked. "I thought you don't see any movement."

"I do not."

"That doesn't make any sense," Angela said. "That place is crawling with those caterpillar bots."

"Not anymore, Commander Brown."

After exchanging confused glances, the team slowly stepped out from behind their cover and walked out into the middle of the street. Then they all stopped as they stood staring at the monstrous assembly.

It was like standing at the base of an enormous football stadium.

Vaughn had to crane his neck to see its top.

Viewed through his NVGs, the thinning clouds gliding across the upper reaches of the cauldron looked like wispy cotton balls caressing a wide, green balloon.

The clouds broke, and the moon emerged.

Vaughn flipped up his night-vision goggles, wanting to see the thing with his own eyes. Nothing moved on or beneath the massive machinery. At its base, huge tracks, like those on a tank or bulldozer, protruded from the machine like the crooked teeth of a steel giant.

Earlier, the entire assembly had been teeming with moving caterpillar bots. Now it looked like an abandoned project.

Bill Peterson moved to stand next to him. "Where the hell did everything go?"

"I don't know."

Angela patted his arm insistently.

Vaughn dragged his gaze from the insane assembly and looked at her.

She pointed down the road, indicating an area to the bottom right of the partially constructed city builder. "Look at the exhibition center!"

Vaughn lowered his night-vision goggles back into place and then zoomed into the area. "Holy shit ... It's clear. I don't see a single robot around any of it, even using max magnification."

Angela nodded excitedly. "There's something else. Look at its base."

Complying, Vaughn aimed his NVGs at the bottom of the structure and then blinked in surprise. "I ... I can't believe it."

"What are you seeing?" Bill asked.

"The entrance ... It's glowing. Only a little, but there's some light coming from somewhere inside the building."

"What does it mean, El Capitan?"

"It means, Teddy, that we don't need to find a way into the collider. There's not a goddamn thing between us and a HiLumi-networked computer terminal." Flipping up his goggles, he turned to look at the cosmonaut. "And it has power."

CHAPTER 46

V aughn grabbed the right handle and pulled.

The door eased open.

Turning, he whispered urgently. "Hurry! Get in here before something sees us."

Angela emerged from cover and darted through the entrance followed closely by Bill and Teddy.

Waving over the robot, Vaughn nodded toward the open field they'd crossed. "See any movement?"

"Negative, Captain. All sectors still clear."

Vaughn regarded the field and city beyond warily. He didn't like this one damned bit. Something was wrong.

He scoffed and shook his head. Since when *wasn't* something wrong?

Finally, he nodded and waved the robot in.

After following BOb through the opening, Vaughn pointed to a spot on the ground a few feet inside the door. "Stand guard here. Come get us immediately if you hear or see anything. Understood?"

"Understood."

Vaughn started to step away but then did a double-take.

The robot held up a hand. "Sorry. Understood, Captain Asshole."

Shaking his head, Vaughn swore under his breath. If they survived this and managed to reset the timeline, he was going to have a serious man-to-geek discussion with BOb's programmers.

Turning, he ran after the rest of the team members.

He saw the source of the light they'd seen from the street. Pale illumination haloed a pair of doors set into the back wall of the entry foyer.

As Vaughn approached Bill and Teddy, he looked at Angela and nodded toward the source of the light. "Is that the Research Area exhibit?"

"No." She gestured at the doors. "It's through there, down a corridor."

After glancing toward BOb, Vaughn pointed to either side of the double doors. "Cover me."

Bill moved to the left side while Angela and Teddy stepped over to the right.

Vaughn crouched in front of the left panel. As he'd done with the main entrance, he eased open the right door. The crack widened, and light began to flow through the opening. Leaning in just far enough to see with one eye, he scanned the hallway beyond.

"I don't see any movement," he whispered. "The light is coming from the far end."

Pulling back from the opening, he looked at Angela. "I'll take point. Where are we going?"

"I'm not sure how far down the hallway it is. There should be a large set of double glass doors on the right."

He pointed at Bill and Teddy. "You guys stay right behind us, watch our six. I've got BOb keeping an eye on the entrance."

"Got it, El Capitan," Teddy said. Some of his reddish-blond mane had come loose. The long, wiry hair protruded from the back of his helmet. It bobbed comically when the man nodded.

Bill Peterson simply held up a thumb.

Vaughn looked at Angela. "Stay right behind me."

She pressed her lips into a thin line and gave a short nod.

He pulled the right door fully open and then eased into the

hallway beyond.

Vaughn made sure the others had entered behind him and then started down the long passageway. After proceeding a good distance down its length, he spotted a pair of glass doors on the right side. The light was coming through them. Looking over his shoulder, he pointed ahead. "Are those the doors?"

Angela nodded.

Vaughn gave her a hold gesture and then eased up to the glass. Hugging the right wall, he leaned left and peered in with just one eye.

A room similar to NASA's Mission Control sat on the other side of the glass panels. This had to be the Research Area exhibit. Two rows of workstations occupied its center. It all looked very modern. Large TV screens adorned the back wall, covering its entire surface. Only one of them was working at the moment. A static image of arcane plumbing and electrical machinery filled its display.

After trying the doors and finding them unlocked, Vaughn looked back at the other three team members. "This is it." He waved them forward. "Looks clear, but keep your head on a swivel."

After passing through the opening, Angela made a beeline straight for a specific workspace. Vaughn saw a sign above it that read 'ATLAS Experiment'.

After posting Bill and Teddy on either side of the glass doors, Vaughn jogged over and joined her.

His pulse began to pound in his ears.

Swallowing, Vaughn shook his head. He had to temper his excitement. They still didn't know if the Necks had isolated the collider from this section of CERN.

Angela had already pulled out a chair and taken a seat.

He glanced back toward the glass doors as doubt crept into his thoughts. He couldn't help but feel like something was wrong. The place was a ghost town. That would be fine if they were anywhere else, but here, in the middle of alien Grand Fucking Central, it felt damned wrong.

He looked back to see Angela pressing buttons on the keyboard with apparent frustration.

Nothing happened on the monitor.

It was still black, dead.

Her shoulders slumped, and a short laugh escaped her.

She reached up and pressed the monitor's power button.

The screen sprang to life.

Angela gave him an embarrassed grin. "Guess it works better when the pesky O-N - O-F-F button is in the right position."

A generic sign-in box hovered in the center of the display.

Angela entered her credentials, and a new screen popped up, full of application icons.

Vaughn released his held breath. "Oh, thank you."

Angela shook her head. "We're not all the way in yet. I've only logged into this building's server. It gives me access to everything in this control room."

"What about the HiLumi Intranet?"

Angela continued clicking through items. "Working on it."

She descended a layer deeper into the menu and was rewarded with a new sign-on page that featured the HiLumi icon.

Vaughn clenched his fists nervously as he watched.

Angela entered her credentials and then looked back at him, her finger hovering over the return key. "This should get me in."

"Hit it already."

Lowering her finger, Angela pressed the key.

The screen turned black, leaving only the spinning collider logo at its center.

As Vaughn watched in breathless anticipation, he realized the room wasn't as quiet as he'd initially thought. There was an underlying rumble, so deep it was almost imperceptible, the vibration more felt than heard. The building seemed to be thrumming. He wondered idly if it might be a failing pump. Without the constant maintenance usually provided by its human crew, much of the machinery might be on the verge of failure. He pictured an air-conditioning compressor or a water pump somewhere in the structure vibrating itself to pieces.

The computer monitor flickered, and a new window popped up. A HiLumi logo adorned the page's top-left corner.

Smiling victoriously, Angela pumped both fists into the air. "Yes! Yes! Yes! I'm in!"

Vaughn's pulse began to hammer in his ear as hope threatened to breach his barricades.

A smile crept across his face.

Could this finally be it?

Did they finally have a leg up on the life-stealing bastards?

The smile faltered.

He looked around the room.

Something had his teeth on edge.

Between the quiet outside and the thrumming of this building, Vaughn felt like he was missing something.

He glanced back toward Bill and Teddy. The two men were high-fiving.

"Stay sharp, guys. Keep an eye out for the robots."

Turning to look back at Vaughn, they both nodded soberly.

Teddy screwed up his face. "Where did robots go?"

Vaughn shook his head. "I don't know. That's what's got my short hairs standing on end." He paused and glanced at the image on the single functioning display. Looking back at the cosmonaut, he added, "There's another thing, too. I keep wondering why the Necks were all standing around the wormhole like that."

Teddy's eyes lost their focus, and his ginger complexion turned a shade whiter. He slowly shook his head. "That was some seriously sketchy shit, El Capitan. ATLAS was rotten with Necks. We nearly got worked by that place."

"Seriously sketchy," Vaughn agreed, nodding absently. "I don't understand why they were standing around it. At first, I thought they were a welcoming party, but the bastards looked surprised to see us."

Typing furiously into her keyboard, Angela shook her head. "None of that matters now. I'm almost ready to start the overload."

Vaughn looked at the floor. The tremors were intensifying. Whatever that component was, it was going to fail soon. He could feel the vibrations through the soles of his boots now.

Dragging his gaze from the floor, he frowned. "I still don't like this.

Something is wrong. Where did all the caterpillar bots go?"

Teddy's brow furrowed. "Maybe … they're all … sleeping?"

Angela shook her head. "Robots don't need sleep."

"Sorry, I meant recharging, Command-Oh."

Bill Peterson nodded. "Maybe that's why they've all disappeared. Good riddance, if you ask me."

"Uh." Vaughn scrunched up his face. "I don't know. The whole time Angela and I were stuck in that loop, I never saw a resting or recharging robot."

Angela looked up from her terminal. "Are you guys feeling that?"

"Yeah," Vaughn said with a shrug. "Sounds like a pump going bad in the basement. Probably has an imbalanced shaft that's getting ready to fail." Looking past her, he pointed at the large screens that adorned the back wall. "Can you bring up the inside of ATLAS on one of these? I want to take a look inside."

Nodding quickly, Angela bent back over her workstation. She cycled through menu items.

A moment later, the monitors began to spring to life. A large cylinder sat at the center of one of the images. Vaughn recognized it as the CMS experiment. Then he saw the hardware for ALICE, the experiment they'd passed through en route to ATLAS.

He searched through each of the images but saw no movement. "None of these look like ATLAS."

"Hold your horses. I'm working on it."

Vaughn looked at the floor again. That shaft was going to let go soon. The vibration was starting to get pretty intense.

"Got it!" Angela said. "What? … What on earth are they doing?"

Before Vaughn could look up, Teddy moaned. "This is bogus, El Capitan. The bastards are still in there."

Dragging his eyes from the skittering dust on the floor, Vaughn looked up at the screen. It was ATLAS alright. He imagined the live feed had initially been set up to feature the large, cylindrical body of the experiment. However, the mercurial sphere of the wormhole now served as the video's focal point.

Necks stood atop every horizontal surface within the camera's field of view. None of them were moving. They all seemed transfixed.

Then one of them leaped high into the air, startling a shout from Bill. "Geezus Christ!"

The robot flew in a high, arcing trajectory. Then it slammed down onto the top of the sphere, not stopping until it was knee-deep in the now churning mercurial orb.

As Vaughn watched in shocked silence, the Neck slowly subsided into the wormhole. Just as the last part of the robot passed out of sight, a brilliant flash of white light washed out the image. When the video recovered, it revealed another Neck flying through the air. Then it, too, disappeared into the wormhole.

Vaughn's jaw worked silently for a moment. Then he finally found his voice. "Where...? Where are they going?"

Behind them, Teddy spoke up. "Da, Command-Oh, why are they leaving?"

"Ha!" Bill shouted triumphantly. "I'll tell you why, because we kicked their asses, that's why. The bastards are running for the hills."

Angela was slowly shaking her head. "I ... I don't think so." She turned and looked at Vaughn, her face ash-white. When she spoke, her voice sounded reed-thin. "They're falling back so they can do it again." She bent over the keyboard, and her fingers became a blur of activity.

"Do what again, Command-Oh?"

"Yeah, Angela. What are you talking about?" Bill asked.

Vaughn felt his guts begin to churn.

This is what he had been missing.

It all fit with Angela's theory about the Necks not being able to send the light wave through when they were on this side of the wormhole.

A white flash announced the passage of another Neck.

Vaughn looked at Bill and Teddy. "It means they're going to send the light through again."

Still typing, Angela nodded. "Exactly. It's only a temporary retreat. They'll be back as soon as they finish wiping the planet."

The two men stared at her wordlessly. In the ensuing silence, the failing machinery in the basement neared the finish of its unscheduled self-destruction. Then Vaughn's eyes flew wide as the vibrations traveling through the floor rapidly crescendoed into bone-jarring waves.

"What the hell?!"

The tiles between himself and the two men heaved upward. An instant later, the chewing and gnashing maw of a massive, mechanical monstrosity burst through the floor.

Vaughn stepped back. "Caterpillar bot!"

Teddy stumbled backward and slammed into the wall.

Bill Peterson's eyes went round. "Oh, hell no!"

Realizing that he and Angela were about to be cut off from the exit, Vaughn turned around, intending to grab her, but she was already up and backpedaling.

Beyond the computer terminal she'd been working, two more of the insectile machines were clawing their way through the floor. Concrete and tiles spilled outward from them. Desks and terminals tipped over.

Vaughn grabbed Angela's arm and turned her to face him. "Did you start the overload?!"

Eyes wide with panic, she shook her head. "I was almost done! Just a few more keystrokes to go."

They turned back toward the terminal.

Angela reached out for the keyboard.

Then dust shot into the air, and the entire workstation dropped into a new hole and fell from sight.

"Shit!" Still holding her arm, Vaughn pulled Angela toward the exit. "Come on. We gotta go!"

The floor bucked beneath their churning boots.

Vaughn cursed with each unsteady footfall. "Shit! ... Shit! ... Shi—!"

Air burst from him as he and Angela slammed into each other painfully as another pair of caterpillar bots burst through the foundation to either side of the double doors.

The safety glass shattered and fell to the heaving floor.

Angela tugged desperately at his sleeve. "Vaughn! We need to run!"

"Ya think?!"

CHAPTER 47

Bill and Teddy crashed through the double doors at the end of the hallway.

The floor lurched behind them.

Angela screamed and launched herself over the rising tiles.

Running alongside her, Vaughn also jumped. An open, metallic mouth emerged beneath him and snapped at his boots. He pulled his knees to his chest, throwing off his balance and causing him to land awkwardly and tumble.

Rolling to his feet, he jumped up and followed Angela through the double doors.

BOb still stood guard at the front. He looked back with evident surprise. "What is happening, Captain Asshole?"

Vaughn ran across the large room. "We've got company!"

BOb turned and kicked open the exterior doors with extreme prejudice. Knocked from their hinges, both of the heavy steel panels flew out and disappeared into the night. Then the battlebot stepped aside and raised both its weapons, aiming behind the running humans.

The floor heaved beneath Angela and Vaughn, launching both of them into the air. They stumbled forward but somehow managed to stay on their feet.

Glancing back, Vaughn saw another caterpillar bot climbing up through the floor.

BOb slewed the BFG and beamed away the massive machine.

Following Bill, Teddy, and Angela through the exit, Vaughn waved for BOb to follow. "Cover our retreat. If anything gets too close, beam it out. Otherwise, hold your fire."

The robot gave a quick nod and then followed Vaughn out of the building.

As they sprinted across the lawn, the sound of wrenching concrete and cracking timbers filled the previously quiet night.

After they had run about a hundred meters across the overgrown field, everyone stopped and looked back.

Nothing had followed them out of the exposition center.

Transfixed, they watched as the massive, spherical structure collapsed inward. Then the entire building fell from sight, launching a cloud of dust into the night.

After a moment, Bill Peterson looked at Vaughn. "I told you I wasn't fucking with these things." He shook his head. "Nope! Nope! Nope! Not doing it." The man turned and started to run toward the south.

Blinking against the dust, Vaughn ran after the major. Angela and Teddy exchanged nervous glances and then followed.

Bill was heading toward a long strip of cleared, completely flat land. The smooth expanse extended south to the limit of Vaughn's vision. It was the strip they'd seen from Mont Salève, the one that appeared to follow the subway line.

"Where the hell are you going, Bill?"

"Away from here."

"Hang on! We need to—"

Vaughn saw movement beyond the major. "Bill! Wait!"

"Nope!"

The man kept running.

Vaughn flipped down his NVGs and zoomed in on the movement.

His eyes went wide.

Peterson slid to a stop and started backpedaling. "Ah, man! Come on! Really?"

Beyond the major, a swarm of caterpillars was climbing from a hole in the ground.

Vaughn realized they were coming from one of the shafts they'd seen from the Balcony of Geneva.

Bill shook his head as he stared at the swarm. "That's a whole fuckload of *Nope!*" He turned to sprint back to the group, but then Bill froze again. "Ah, shit!"

Angela and Teddy looked behind Vaughn and flinched.

Vaughn's blood ran cold.

Turning, he saw another swarm of caterpillar bots streaming from the hole left where the exposition center had stood a minute earlier. They emerged from the spreading dust cloud and quickly fanned out to encircle his team.

Vaughn looked around, frantically searching for a way out. Their options were diminishing quickly. The caterpillar bots were trying to flank them.

He pointed east, back in the direction from which they had come. "Fall back!"

Pulled from their paralysis, Bill, Teddy, and Angela ran for their lives, heading back down the thoroughfare.

Vaughn turned and looked at BOb. The bot was aiming the BFG at the swarm, but none of the caterpillars had closed to within its range. The machines were holding back. It looked like they were intentionally staying outside its reach.

Waving, Vaughn shouted, "BOb! Come on!"

The robot disengaged and started running behind Vaughn.

The shrieking squeal of thousands of mechanical actuators echoed from every surface within the broken city, seeming to come from all directions simultaneously.

Looking past his running comrades, Vaughn narrowed his eyes as he studied the street ahead through his NVGs. The road appeared to be moving. Then the moon slid out from behind a cloud, bathing the scene in its pale light. "Ah, you have got to be shitting me!"

Vaughn slid to a stop.

Ahead, Bill seized, nearly falling as he bounced to a stuttering halt. His shoulders slumped. "Ah, come on! Shit!"

Teddy and Angela pulled up next to them and silently stared down the street.

An ocean of gnashing black maws filled the thoroughfare. It looked as if the night had taken on a life of its own, becoming animated and hungry.

The five members of Team Two drew together.

Vaughn pointed north. "Go left!"

Teddy held out an arm. "No good, El Capitan."

Turning, Vaughn watched caterpillar bots stream from every nook and cranny of the shattered apartment block that lined the left side of the street.

"Shit!" Vaughn growled as he stared at the alien horde. He hitched a thumb over his shoulder. "South!"

They turned and started running toward the field that lined the right side of the road.

The bots that had swarmed from the shafts south of CERN were circling in from their right. The gap of empty earth between them and the army of caterpillar bots that choked the street to the team's east closed before the five of them could even reach the far curb.

The team slid to a skipping stop.

Teddy released a string of Russian curse words.

Shocked into silence and backing up, Bill aimed his rifle at the encircling mass of machinery. He fingered the trigger of the M4's integral grenade launcher. Beneath arched brows, the man's mouth hung open in an unrealized scream.

Clutching Vaughn's arm, Angela swallowed hard and looked up at him. "What do we do now?"

Vaughn could only shake his head as he, too, aimed his grenade launcher at the caterpillars.

BOb swept the BFG left and right threateningly.

Huddled together, weapons pointing outward, the five of them stood at the center of an ever-tightening circle of mechanical monstrosities.

Then the bots stopped drawing in.

The encircling mass rotated about them clockwise. They held back thirty or forty feet, well outside the range of the BFG's light wave emitter. The caterpillars looked like a swarm of giant ants as they crawled over each other, hungrily stalking their prey, but reluctant to taste its defenses.

"Wh-What …?" Major Peterson stammered. "What are they doing? Why aren't they attacking?"

Teddy pumped a fist at the bots. "They fear the BOb!"

Angela shook her head. Pointing her weapon at the churning mass, she said, "They're just holding us at bay until the Necks finish their withdrawal."

One of the bots ventured in.

Bill backed into Vaughn. "I think that one disagrees." He fired a grenade into the caterpillar's gnashing mouth. The front third of the machine disintegrated.

Teddy slapped the man's shoulder. "Great shot, Bill!"

The major looked at the side of his M4. Curling the corners of his mouth down, he nodded appreciably. "Damn!"

A grin spread across Vaughn's face. The machines were vulnerable to their grenades. Then he looked across the circling horde of enemy bots, and the smile dissolved.

He shook his head. "Dammit! We have to fall back."

Angela's head snapped toward Vaughn. "Why? You saw what Bill's grenade did to the thing."

Vaughn dipped his head toward the encircling bots. "We don't have anything close to enough grenades to get through that. Not a chance. We have to retreat."

Teddy looked at him as if he'd lost his mind. The cosmonaut pointed at the circling machines. "How on earth are we going to do that, El Capitan? We're surrounded."

Vaughn pointed at the battlebot. "BOb! Beam us to Mont Salève!"

Angela's eyes went wide. She held her hand out toward the robot. "We can't! If we leave, there will be nothing to stop the Necks from sending out the light again."

Bill pointed at Vaughn. "I'm with him. If we stay here, we'll be human giblets."

A caterpillar broke from the formation and darted toward Vaughn. He fired a grenade and hit the thing center-of-mass, blowing it in half.

The enemy robots were becoming more aggressive.

"We don't have time to discuss it." Vaughn looked at the battlebot. "Beam us out now, BOb!"

"Wilco, Captain."

The robot turned and held the BFG at the end of its long arm, aiming back at itself such that it would sweep across all of them.

Angela began to protest, but Vaughn wrapped his arms around her and pulled her into a huddle with the other two men. He looked at the robot and nodded. "Do it."

BOb squeezed the trigger.

Nothing happened.

Then a series of red lights illuminated on the side of the BFG.

"BOb!" Bill Peterson said shakily. "You need to beam us the hell out of here right goddamn now!"

"Unable, Major."

"What?! Why the hell not?"

The battlebot peeled away from the group. "The device is offline." BOb stowed the BFG across his backpack and pulled out a second M4. "Switching to guns."

Vaughn stared at the machine as it aimed both of its grenade launchers at the circling caterpillars. "I-I thought it reboots after a BIT failure!"

BOb dispatched an enemy robot. As the echoing thunder of the explosion dissipated, the battlebot shook its head. "Negative. This was not a built-in-test failure. The device shut down. I cannot bring it back online at the moment."

Vaughn shook his head. "Shit, shit, shit ... *Shit!*" They were trapped.

Pulling out of his grasp, Angela leveled her weapon on an approaching caterpillar. "We needed a better plan anyway."

Eyes widening, Bill looked back at her. "You're kidding, right?"

A bot scrambled toward the major. "Fuck!" Bill turned and blasted the thing.

Vaughn pointed at BOb. "Let me know the *instant* it comes back online!"

"Will do, Captain Asshole."

A caterpillar on Vaughn's side of the formation split off and made a beeline for him. He fired a grenade that caught the thing right in its open mouth. The head of the bot vanished behind a rapidly expanding cloud of shrapnel.

Another grenade launcher barked behind him, followed closely by a piercing detonation. Looking over his shoulder, he saw one of the insectile machines collapse into a heap of broken and shattered parts.

Angela pumped her fist. "What can Brown do for you?! Ha! That's what, bitch!"

Vaughn reached back and slapped her on the arm. "Great shot!"

As she loaded another grenade, she shouted over her shoulder. "That felt damned good, but it won't last. This is going to take more than a visit to Home Depot. We have to find another way, Vaughn."

He knew she was right on the first part. There were significantly more robots than grenades—or even bullets, for that matter—and the latter of the two was useless against the machines. The slug he'd fired at the caterpillar in the tunnel had barely scratched the thing.

Moving with incredible speed, BOb darted in and out of the group, shoring up a side of the formation when it looked ready to collapse. Maneuvering with inhuman dexterity, the battle operations bot earned its name, firing both grenade launchers over and over.

Between shots of his own, Vaughn watched as the bot blasted two caterpillars. In a smooth movement, BOb flipped over both rifles, grabbed the grenade breaches and ejected the spent shells. Then he tossed the weapons into the air. As the two assault rifles pinwheeled overhead, the bot's arms blurred with speed, extracting two more grenades from the bandolier draped across its chest. Then it slid the rounds into the still open breaches mid-flip. Finally, it snatched the rifles out of the air.

Snapping the breaches shut, BOb fired the grenades into the next targets and then repeated the entire process, pouring a steady stream of explosive rounds into the encroaching caterpillars.

Each iteration took less than a second. Vaughn thought the speed-blurred actions would've been indiscernible if not for the time-dilating effect of combat.

Despite the bot's incredible kill-count and those racked up by the rest of the team, the caterpillars continued to draw closer.

Vaughn didn't think the machines would settle for holding them at bay much longer.

He needed a way out right now, or else …

Turning, he stared at the nuke bouncing on BOb's back.

He shook his head.

Not yet.

Vaughn's eyes widened as he remembered something from his last trip through Geneva.

He began to scan the ground. "Anyone see a manhole cover! They lead to the subway tunnels."

"Manhole cover?" Bill said incredulously as he fired another grenade, taking out a caterpillar that was crowding his side of the formation. "You wanna go underground? Are you crazy?! That's where all these bastards came fr—!"

Bill shrieked as two caterpillars darted toward him. He and Teddy quickly dispatched the pair.

"N-Never mind," Peterson stuttered. "U-Underground is good."

"Great idea!" Angela shouted after firing another grenade. "But you can't call them that. They're utility holes."

Scanning the surrounding roadbed, Bill scoffed loudly. "Really, Commander? Now you wanna be PC?"

Teddy blasted another caterpillar and started searching the ground. "Manhole - shmanhole. Whatever! I'll take anything."

Raising eyebrows, Vaughn nodded.

"Uh … Problem, El Capitan. How we find shmanhole?" Teddy

paused to fire another grenade and then released a frustrated growl. "There's too much ash. I can't even see pavement!"

"Shit!" Vaughn shouted as he cycled between scanning the ground beneath his feet and watching for incoming caterpillars. He swept the soles of his boots left and right, trying to clear space in the muddy ash as he desperately sought the circular outline of one of the access covers. "I'm having the same problem. Just do what I'm doing."

Angela nodded. "Vaughn's right. We have to get down there. Once the Necks are back through the wormhole, they'll fire the light wave again. Then we are finished, especially if the BFG doesn't come back online."

BOb got involved in the exercise between grenade shots, dragging his dark gray foot across the ground.

Looking like a five-person formation of back-to-back River-dancers, they began to rotate slowly, each one of them manically sweeping the soles of their boots through the ash and dust as if tap dancing to the beat of an Irish ballad.

They tried to shift the search to another portion of the pavement, but the caterpillars tightened the noose.

Vaughn swore under his breath. They hadn't found a goddamn manhole … utility hole … whatever the fuck. Soon the enemy robots would be too close to engage with grenades.

He eyed the backpack slung across BOb's back again. The heavy nuclear device jumped and lurched with each of the bot's sporadic movements.

Gnashing his teeth, Vaughn looked away from the nuke and focused his ire on the next contender. The head of the offending caterpillar vanished under another shower of smoke and fractured metal.

The ring tightened another notch as the mechanical monsters inched closer.

Behind the circling horde, Vaughn could see a steady stream of additional caterpillar bots still emerging from the ground.

Regarding the backpack askance, Vaughn contemplated their rapidly diminishing options.

His choices were quickly distilling down to one.

"BOb! BFG status?"

"Still offline, Captain Asshole."

Angela looked at Vaughn and gave a single nod. "Do what you have to."

Bill nodded. "Fuck it. Do it."

Behind him, Teddy's head bobbed somberly. "Da, El Capitan. Nuke the bastards."

Vaughn dispatched another caterpillar. This one had gotten almost within the minimum range of his grenade launcher. If the bot had been any closer, the round would not have spun enough times to arm its tiny warhead before striking its target. The thing would've just bounced off ineffectually.

Vaughn continued to grind his teeth. "Shit! Shit! Shit!"

Aiming at another of the caterpillars, he gestured to the battle operations bot. "BOb, take the nuke out of your backpack and set it behind you."

The bot tossed its rifles into the air. Reaching back with both hands, BOb snatched the nuke from his backpack. He bent backward and placed the device on the pavement so fast it launched a spray of ash. Then the bot stood and plucked the pinwheeling assault rifles from the air and launched a fresh salvo at two caterpillars.

Vaughn dropped to a knee next to the bomb. "Cover my sector!"

Everyone shifted position.

Looking up, he received a nod from each of the team members.

Grenade explosions shook the ground beneath him.

Vaughn extended a trembling finger toward the keypad. He tried to press the zero key but inadvertently hit the asterisk. He blinked and yanked his finger away.

Apparently, that wasn't the detonate now button.

Extending the trembling finger again, he finally pressed the correct key. Bracing his hand on the chassis of the device, he hit the enter key three times.

Then he depressed the zero key again.

He pressed the enter key.

Once.

Twice.

Vaughn swallowed.

Grenades exploded.

Then Angela was next to Vaughn, wrapping her arms around him. She placed her hand on top of his.

Steadied by her presence, he extended his finger. The tip of it caressed the enter key.

He felt Angela's lips press against his ear. "I love you, Captain."

Her hand tightened on his. "Now press the damned—"

"Wait!" Bill shouted.

Vaughn flinched. The movement almost caused his finger to press the key.

He yanked back his hand. "Wh-wh-why?!" He looked up at the major. "What—?"

Brilliant orange fire vanquished the night as a rapidly spreading line of explosions burned through the enemy formation, launching metallic chunks of twisted caterpillar bodies into the air.

Watching the pieces arc across the sky as if in slow motion, he blinked, unable to comprehend what was happening.

Bill and Teddy pointed into the sky, gesturing wildly at something behind Vaughn.

Then the growl of churning propellers rose above the fading explosions.

He turned and stared into the sky.

Narrowing his eyes, he spotted the distant silhouette of the onrushing tiltrotor aircraft.

Still small but closing quickly, the V-22 continued to dive straight at him.

Vaughn flinched as yellow fire strobed from the airplane's belly cannon.

His eyes flew wide.

The white-hot stream of explosive rounds was going to drop right on their heads.

"Get down!"

PART V

"Every normal man must be tempted at times to spit upon his hands, hoist the black flag, and begin slitting throats."

—H.L. Menkin, Prejudices: First Series

CHAPTER 48

R ourke watched the bullets he'd fired trace arcing lines across the screen of his gun camera control display. They raced toward the target, sweeping from left to right well ahead of the diving airplane.

"Everyone keep an eye out for those damned Taters," Colonel Hennessy yelled from the cockpit. "If one of those things sees us before we see it, you might find yourself riding in the back of a pilot-less airplane."

As the man spoke, Rourke watched the rounds arc over the heads of Team Two.

He and the rest of Team One should have been down there with them. They would have, had they not somehow ended up on Mont Salève.

When they had first emerged back into reality, they'd found themselves standing in a small clearing, grass beneath their feet and trees surrounding them.

They'd had no idea where they were, and the jump seemed to have flummoxed Major Lee's GPS. It couldn't find itself, so it was of no use.

Then they had stumbled upon the Balcony of Geneva and realized that the emitter had deposited them close to the same spot specified for Angela's practice jump.

They didn't know whether it had been a glitch in the device or a mistake made by the robot ...

Or a mistake made by Rourke.

He'd felt more than one accusatory glare cast his way.

Presently, white-hot fire erupted across the gun camera's infrared display. Explosions danced through the far side of the scrambling formation of caterpillars.

"Still too high, Rourky!" Rachel shouted over the intercom. "I know you're trying to be careful, but we gotta push them away from our people, not toward them!"

Rourke shook his head. "Dammit."

The last thing he wanted to do was accidentally drop even one explosive-tipped round next to his friends—the damned things had a kill radius of five meters—but, she was right, that volley had only pushed the caterpillars closer to the other team, and the first one had been even worse.

Grimacing, Rourke reluctantly shifted the stabilized aiming reticle closer to Team Two. He had to fire over their heads, aiming at the inner circumference of the ring's far side. He feared a round would fall short and drop in right on their heads, but if he hit the near side of the ring, the explosions would launch shrapnel and heavy chunks of metal machinery into his comrades.

In the infrared display, the humans stood out as four white-hot points at the center of the undulating ring of moving mechanical appendages. BOb darted back and forth between the team members, barely visible as a ghostly gray shadow that all but merged with the background.

Scarcely thirty meters separated them from the closest portion of the circling robots. On his display, the five of them sat just outside the thin, white, oblong ring that denoted the Fire Control Computer's calculated blast-damage radius.

It was close.

Too damned close.

But Rourke knew it could've been much worse. If not for Major Lee's quick reactions and her rapid combat start-up of the aircraft, they never would have made it there in time.

"Dry-fuck 'em, Rourky!" Rachel yelled over the intercom. "No 10W-40 for these bastards."

Pressing his lips paper-thin, he fired the gun and walked the crosshairs clockwise as another fifty-round burst barked from its muzzle.

"Give 'em what for, mate!" Bingham said as he scrambled from the left portal to the right, scanning each window for approaching Taters.

Holding his breath, Rourke watched the bullets arc through the magnified, infrared image. The hot rounds shone like tiny light bulbs. They sailed through the display like a rapidly fired line of glowing baseballs, flying up from the bottom. As they neared the top of the image, they reached the zenith of their arc and, slowly curving downward, dropped into the target.

Explosions stitched a left-to-right line through the inner ring of the caterpillars. Blossoming like white flowers across the gun camera's thermal image, heat plumes momentarily washed out portions of the display. The blasts hammered the machines, burning through those closest to the far side of Team Two and launching white-hot chunks of metal into the surrounding enemy formation.

Rourke pumped his fist. "Yes!"

Rachel leaned out from her pilot's seat. "Hell, yeah! Get some!" Looking back, she shook a thumb up and down. "Great shooting, Rourky! Now slew it around to aim backward. We're about to overfly the battle."

Returning to her flight controls, she continued over the intercom system. "You're up next, Monique! Cover our six. Rourky already hit the front side. Now both of you can hit the back half."

Lieutenant Gheist looked at Rourke and winked. She adjusted her mic boom and turned the tailgunner pedestal to face fully aft. "You just fly the airplane, Major Lee. I understand what needs doing."

Reaching the bottom of the attack dive, Rachel pulled back on the controls of the V-22. "Hold on tight, Chauncey-Baby!"

Rourke's face sagged, and momentarily, his arms felt as if they weighed a hundred pounds each. In his peripheral vision, he saw Bingham's knees buckle and almost drop him to the floor.

The aircraft heaved upward and then raced back into the sky.

As he slewed the gun to face aft, Rourke stared through the open ramp.

Inertia and propellers thrust the tiltrotor higher. The rectangular patch of Geneva visible through the opening quickly shrank, revealing the full breadth of the churning swarm of attacking robots in the blink of an eye.

Even unaided, Rourke could see the now jagged, ring-shaped outline of caterpillars appeared wider. They continued to circle the five members of Team Two, but his third volley had pushed back the enemy robots.

Monique's tail-mounted automatic grenade cannon pedestal swiveled the last few degrees as she adjusted her aim. The outline of her head and closely shorn hair glowed faintly, haloed by the light streaming from the gun camera display.

Pulsing fire belched from her cannon. A steady stream of grenades coursed from its muzzle.

Explosive rounds hammered into the enemy formation.

The flashes strobed the night, illuminating the interior of the aircraft and cutting long, frenetic shadows across its cluttered ceiling. Each flicker froze time, forming a series of snapshots forever emblazoned upon Rourke's psyche like a mental photo album of the apocalypse.

The belly cannon finished slewing aftward, finally pointing back at the circling robots.

Rourke placed the crosshairs on the left side of the formation and pressed the fire button.

Guttering yellow light flared within the belly cannon's hellhole.

He again walked the targeting reticle clockwise, slowly sweeping it around Team Two.

Even though the aircraft's speed was quickly carrying it away from the scene, the optics of the scope made it appear as if the tiltrotor was barely moving.

Again, white-hot explosions blossomed around the ringing formation of caterpillars. The widening flares quickly moved in a clockwise pattern, following the path of his aiming reticle.

Then a second group of more powerful detonations began to dance through the enemy machines, moving in the opposite direction, as had Rourke's.

Monique had picked up on what he was laying down. She'd swept fire across the enemy machines in the same manner as had Rourke but in the opposite direction.

Between the two of them, they obliterated the inner ring of bots.

"Good shooting!" Colonel Hennessy called from the copilot seat. "Everyone keep an eye out for Taters. We're going to swing it around and bring us back in, see if y'all cleared out enough space for us to land."

Peering through the left portal, Chance Bingham craned his neck. Then he darted to the other side of the aircraft and looked out that window again. He toggled his mic. "Still don't see the buggers."

Rourke glanced forward and saw Rachel and Mark scanning the sky. They shook their heads. "Haven't seen any up here either," Colonel Hennessy announced over the intercom.

Rachel banked the aircraft hard left and then looked over her shoulder. "That doesn't mean they're not out here. Keep your head on a swivel, people."

Nodding, Rourke thought back on what they'd witnessed from the Balcony. They had been scanning the city, looking for Team Two, but at first, they'd detected no movement.

None—not even the robots that they'd previously seen from the location.

Then a dust cloud had risen from behind the city builder construction site.

They'd zoomed in using their night-vision goggles and seen Team Two running out from behind the massive structure.

All hell had broken loose after that.

Caterpillar bots had swarmed from a shaft in front of the team just as hundreds of the horse-sized machines came pouring out of the dust behind them.

Major Lee had ordered them to the aircraft. By then, her GPS had started working again. She'd thrown the thing to Mark—who was weighed down by a nuclear-armed backpack—and then sprinted ahead.

By the time they reached the clearing, Rachel already had the tiltrotor blades spinning.

After strapping the nuke into a crate, Colonel Hennessy had joined her in the cockpit. Monique had strapped herself into the tailgunner pedestal. She'd helped program the autocannon for BOb and was the most familiar with its operation. Rourke had taken his assigned position controlling the belly cannon, and Wing Commander Bingham had agreed to act as their roving eyes, scanning each quadrant around the aircraft for Taters.

Presently, Rourke's face sagged as the nose of the aircraft pitched up.

Major Lee's voice broke over the intercom. "Transitioning to helicopter mode. Bingham! Be ready to fire out the left side. Help cover that quadrant."

Grabbing a grenade launcher, Bingham moved to the indicated position. "I'm on it." He jettisoned the window and aimed his weapon through the opening.

Suddenly, the man's entire body spasmed. "Bloody hell! Watch out!" He pushed himself back from the window.

A tremendous crash rang out as something slammed into the left side of the airframe. A portion of the fuselage in front of Bingham caved in, and the V-22 lurched sideways.

Hennessy's voice exploded over the intercom. "What the hell was that?!"

Hanging from his harness and swinging like a pendulum, Bingham waved his arms wildly as he tried to get his feet back under him. "It looked like a bloody boulder."

The aircraft had been slowing, but now Rourke felt it begin to accelerate again. Looking aft, he saw something flash by, passing just behind the V-22.

If Major Lee had not reacted so quickly, the object would've struck the aircraft.

"Something else just missed us!" Monique called out. "It passed directly behind the aircraft."

Rachel looked back, eyes widening. "Was it a Tater?"

Monique shook her head. "I do not think so. It looked like a rock to me as well."

"Anyone see where they're coming from?" Colonel Hennessy shouted from the front.

No one had.

Panning the gun left and right, Rourke searched the battlefield. He saw a sole caterpillar bot in the center of a long street to the aircraft's front left. The thing was holding a large boulder high over its head. The forward third of the robot heaved into the air. Then it and the rock slammed down, causing the rear half of the caterpillar to heave up. It folded over the robot's back like a scorpion's tail, but it didn't stop there. The movement accelerated as the thing rolled up like an inverted doodlebug, its appendages protruding outward instead of in. Rolling like a wheel, the robot rapidly accelerated. Soon, it was speeding across the ground, racing toward the left side of the V-22.

Then the caterpillar seized and flung the boulder into the air.

Blinking, Rourke stared at it for a moment before he suddenly realized what was happening. Breaking his paralysis, he shouted, "Incoming!"

Rachel yanked the plane sideways.

Chance Bingham flew off his feet. "Oh, for fuck's sake!" The man swung through a wide arc as the major snapped the aircraft level again.

She looked back. "What happened?"

Staring at his display, Rourke watched the boulder pass behind the aircraft and arc downward. Then he turned wide eyes to Rachel. "The caterpillars are hurling rocks at us."

"Well ... shoot 'em!"

"The rocks?"

"No. The caterpillars."

He blinked. "Y-Yes, ma'am."

She shifted her gaze to Bingham's swinging body. "Chauncey-baby, quit screwing around. I need you watching for Taters."

"Oh, bloody hell."

Returning his attention to the display, Rourke spotted another caterpillar-turned-doodlebug rolling down a sidestreet. A short burst of fire later, the spinning monstrosity dissolved beneath a blossoming onslaught of white-hot explosions.

Cursing and swinging his arms, Bingham finally got his feet back underneath him. He scrambled to each of the port windows and shook his head. "Still no Taters."

Major Lee spoke over the intercom as she maneuvered the airplane. "Maybe you guys killed all of them."

As Rachel started another diving run, Rourke quickly dispatched three more rock-wielding robots.

The formation was beginning to tighten around Team Two again.

Shifting his aim, he fired another fifty-round burst into the circling ring of bots. As he did, two more of the caterpillars began to roll toward the aircraft. He managed to blow up one of them before it could launch its cargo, but the other sent a large chunk of broken masonry flying into the sky.

"Incoming!"

Rachel banked the aircraft sharply.

Bingham's feet shot out from under him. "Blimey! Come on!"

Continuing to focus his fire, Rourke shouted over the intercom. "I don't have enough rounds. I can either keep them away from our people, or I can stop them from throwing the rocks, but I can't do both."

Monique shook her head. "I cannot help from back here. The weapon will not slew past ninety degrees left or right."

Bingham regained his feet and held up a finger. "If our Asian-American princess can keep the aircraft level for just a moment, I might be able to do something about your problem."

Walking unsteadily, the wing commander moved over to a crate strapped to the center of the cargo flooring. He started opening the large box with one hand while extracting a device from his pant pocket with the other.

"Major Lee, can you bring us to a high hover, well above the range of those damned boulders?"

"Uh, I guess so, what's your plan, Chauncey-Baby?"

Ignoring the question, Bingham stared into the open crate and punched commands into the face of his smartphone.

Suddenly lights began to twinkle inside the box.

The wing commander looked at Rourke and Monique. "Don't worry about the rock-chucking bots for now. Just focus on clearing a landing zone around our people."

CHAPTER 49

Vaughn stared into the sky, watching the now hovering tiltrotor aircraft as it climbed straight up. It quickly passed out of the range of the rocks.

When the V-22 had first shown up, its initial shots had slammed into the far side of the enemy formation, driving some of the robots closer to his team. However, the belly cannon operator, likely Rourke, had adjusted fire and, on the third attempt, hit the caterpillars closest to Vaughn and the rest of Team Two, driving the machines back.

The tiltrotor aircraft had screamed overhead and began to climb. It quickly faded into the night.

Standing up from the nuke, Vaughn had held his arms out. "Where you going?!"

Then a line of white-hot rounds had streamed from the tail of the V-22 and flown over his head. He had started to duck, but before the signal could reach his legs, the grenades had slammed into the ground behind him.

The near flank of the robotic horde had dissolved beneath an expanding cloud of flailing metallic limbs and disembodied heads, the direction of the blasts carrying all of it away from the team.

Vaughn had shouted, "Oh, thank you!" Then he'd bent over the nuke, and, keeping his finger well clear of the enter key, disarmed the device. Afterward, they had returned it to BOb's backpack.

Now staring up at the hovering tiltrotor and watching another line of explosive rounds stream from its belly cannon, Vaughn saw a boulder rise into the air.

Teddy pointed at it. "Check it out, El Capitan." He chuckled. "Stupid caterpillars still throw rocks. Aircraft too high now."

Vaughn shrugged as he watched the hunk of broken concrete lose energy and fall earthward well before it reached the aircraft. "Everyone keep an eye out. Eventually, they're going to figure out that they can't hit the thing. Then they might start chucking 'em at us."

The smile dissolved from Teddy's face, and the man turned and scanned the horizon.

Once again, Vaughn wished they'd been able to use radios. He had worried about what the Necks might do with the radio signal, especially to BOb. However, his primary concern lay with the digital underpinnings of modern military transceivers. The Necks could possibly track or sense a modern radio, even if it were off, just as hackers had often done with mobile phones.

Firing almost straight down, both of the tiltrotor's weapons began to pound the entire ring of caterpillars.

Dozens of robots disintegrated under the twinned assault.

The aircraft began a slow rotation.

No longer having to split its efforts between the stone-chucking robots and those encircling Team Two, the belly cannon was able to focus all its attention on the ring of caterpillar bots. Combined with the firepower coming from the tailgunner's automatic grenade launcher, the attack radically reversed the flow of the battle.

Explosions leaped into the air all around the team. Like a stadium wave made from expanding clouds of yellow fire, dual lines of explosions raced through the enemy formation.

The fusillade of incoming grenades and exploding belly cannon rounds finally forced the caterpillar bots to retreat. The circle of clear ground around the team expanded. Soon, more than a football field's worth of open land sat between the team and the nearest still functional caterpillar. The force of the blasts had even swept much of the metallic detritus from the field.

Then Vaughn realized it wasn't just the blasts. He saw one of the horse-sized robots carrying away the fractured body of a destroyed caterpillar. He wondered idly if it was to scavenge the metal, or if the machine saw it as a fallen brother.

As he watched the two cannons continue to pour fire into the enemy formation, Vaughn saw a problem with their tactic. There were more bots than the tiltrotor had rounds. They had already cleared more than enough room to permit a landing, but as soon as the V-22 touched the ground, the caterpillar bots would just rush in and pounce on the aircraft. The belly cannon wouldn't be of much use after the landing, and the grenade launcher on the ramp could only cover about a hundred and eighty degrees around the back of the aircraft. There'd be little to stop the robots from starting a full-on attack.

Vaughn saw something falling from the back of the V-22.

The tiltrotor continued to rotate about its vertical axis slowly. As it did, a stream of small dots flowed from its tail, falling like black rain in a wide perimeter around Vaughn and his team. If not for the night-vision goggles, he wouldn't have seen them.

Looking down, he saw the small objects now littered the ground in an arc between him and the circling caterpillar bots. However, they'd left a wide, clear area at the center. It was more than big enough to permit the aircraft's landing.

The belly cannon and tail gun continued to pour fire into the enemy formation. However, two of the large, segmented robots broke from the group and started to sprint toward Vaughn.

He took an involuntary backward step. "Oh, shit! Watch out! Incoming!"

It appeared no one in the aircraft had seen the movement. They hadn't adjusted fire.

Vaughn raised his grenade launcher. Beside him, BOb did the

same. However, before either of them could finish the movement, both robots exploded.

No fire had come down from the aircraft. The machines had simply detonated.

Then Vaughn understood. Those small black cubes had to be magnetically activated explosives. Team One had covered the land between his team and the retreating robots with the SLAM mines they'd loaded into the aircraft. The metallic debris that littered the field wasn't big enough to trigger them. If programmed correctly, the Selectable Lightweight Attack Munitions would only detonate when something with the mass of an armored vehicle, or caterpillar bot in this case, crossed its magnetic sensor.

Looking up, he saw the V-22 had started to descend. As the aircraft dropped lower in the sky, a couple of caterpillar bots began to roll across the ground. However, each time, a line of explosive-tipped rounds or grenades would slam down into them. The robots disintegrated before they could build sufficient inertia to throw their stones.

He wondered why the robots hadn't used the same technique to attack him and the rest of his team remotely. Then he remembered what Angela had said about the caterpillars simply just holding them at bay until the Necks could escape.

Vaughn had a pretty good idea of what would come out of that wormhole once the last Neck passed from this world.

Bill, Teddy, and BOb were preoccupied with keeping the cater-pillar bots at bay and hadn't noticed the descending aircraft. Angela was standing next to him, staring up at it transfixed.

He reached out and grabbed her arm and started pulling her back from the center of the clearing. Then he yelled to the two men and the robot. "They're coming in. Back up! Give 'em room to land."

Vaughn turned to BOb and raised hopeful eyebrows. Shouting over the noise of the descending tiltrotor, he asked, "Is the BFG working yet?"

The robot looked back at him and shook its head.

Staring up into the tail of the still descending V-22, they all squinted as Monique fired the autocannon, sending yellow flames over their heads.

Rescue was imminent, and he didn't know whether to laugh or cry.

Where the hell could they go?

CHAPTER 50

One of the caterpillar bots appeared to be staring straight at Vaughn. It began to slither its way inward from the north side of the ring. He felt his pulse quickening as he watched it successfully negotiate its way around several of the black dots. Then it garnered magnetic attention and blew up. Fortunately, the surrounding mines weren't sensitive to nearby explosions. Monique had told them that they had been hardened to prevent cascading detonations. Otherwise, if one of them detonated, they could all light off.

As the V-22 dropped below twenty feet, its belly turret fell silent. However, the tail gun continued to roar overhead as the slowly rotating aircraft descended the last few meters. Monique was doing a damned good job of wiping out the robots. Each time a new one curled into a wheel and started to roll in their direction, the end of the automatic grenade launcher would slew toward it and quickly dispatch the thing.

Vaughn and Angela alongside Bill and Teddy crouched as the rotor wash threatened to topple them. Only BOb remained fully upright. The robot turned and fired a grenade at a caterpillar that was inching closer to the minefield.

Rachel and Mark turned the V-22 so that the tail was just over his team.

Beneath the exhausts of the aircraft's massive jet turbines, steam rose from the street's wet ash. Then, cooked into flaky cakes, the long-dead embers began to fly away in large chunks. They rapidly devolved into a cloud of dust that drifted over the minefield.

As the aircraft descended the last few feet, Vaughn squinted against the flying debris and peered under the ramp, looking toward the front of the tiltrotor. He saw a caterpillar beyond the main body of the formation curl into a wheel and start rolling toward the aircraft's unguarded front side.

Eyes widening, he looked up at Monique. He pointed forward, gesticulating wildly. "Incoming!"

Apparently, someone inside had seen the same thing. The tiltrotor stopped its descent and then rapidly spun about its vertical axis. Monique wrenched the automatic grenade launcher ninety degrees left, pointing it over the side of the ramp. She loosed a short burst at the accelerating robot. The rounds quickly found their target, obliterating the articulated, multifaceted body of the machine, but not before it could launch the rock. The chunk of masonry flew in a shallow arc straight at the hovering V-22.

Grabbing Angela, Vaughn pulled her sideways. "Everyone down!"

As the two of them dropped to the pavement, the rotor wash turned into a hurricane, blowing them across the ground. At the same time, the aircraft rocketed up into the sky.

The tumbling hunk of broken bricks and concrete narrowly missed slamming into the cockpit. Instead, it passed just beneath the aircraft.

Vaughn slid to a stop and rolled onto his back. He watched the rock sail toward them. It looked like it was going to strike BOb. The machine raised its arms as if it were going to deflect the boulder. However, it glanced back at the team members and saw that the rock would easily clear them. At the last instant, the robot stepped aside, opting for self-preservation.

Just as quickly as it had ascended, the tiltrotor dropped back down, this time landing in a low spot right next to Vaughn and his team.

He helped Angela up and pulled her toward the aircraft. Beside him, Bill and Teddy jumped to their feet and ran up the open ramp.

Angela pulled up short, refusing to enter.

Vaughn grabbed her hand and urged her forward. "What are you doing?! Get in!"

She shook her head and yelled something, but he couldn't hear her over the raucous roar of the tiltrotor's engines and rotor blades.

Bingham leaned out and shouted in their faces. "Get in the bloody aircraft!"

Angela looked across the field and continued shaking her head.

Rourke ran to the back of the aircraft and tossed a pair of headsets to them.

As soon as Vaughn slid one over his ears, Rachel's voice barked from its speakers. "What's going on back there? Why in the hell aren't they getting on?!"

Angela shook her head. "We can't leave. We have to get below ground!"

"Negative, Commander Brown!" Rachel shouted over the intercom. "We have to fall back, regroup. We'll figure out a different way to come at the problem. Now, hurry up, and get your ass in here before another one of these damned robots chunks a rock at us."

"We don't have time for that. The Necks are retreating through the wormhole."

Chance Bingham smiled. "Good riddance! Let the buggers go."

"No, you don't understand. Once they're finished retreating, they're going to send the light through again."

This was taking too long. Vaughn pointed to BOb. "Go around front, and guard that side of the aircraft."

The battle operations bot nodded. It turned to head out but looked back. Leaning in close, the bot spoke over the roar of the V-22. "FYI, Captain Asshole, the BFG has rebooted. I estimate it has one discharge left. After that, I fear the circuitry will be irrevocably compromised."

Vaughn started to wave the bot on but then held up a finger. "Save it! Use grenades only for now."

BOb dipped his head and then disappeared around the side of the V-22. At the same moment, Monique loosed another burst of grenade shots. In his peripheral vision, Vaughn saw a rolling caterpillar disintegrate.

As he looked across the battlefield, an idea struck him.

Vaughn turned and stared into the cabin. "Let's take the Osprey over the nearest shaft." He pointed at Doctor Geller. "Rourke said there was a workstation at its bottom. We can fast-rope down." Vaughn looked at Angela. "We'll cover you while you start the reset. Between the guns on this thing and all of us, we should be able to keep the caterpillars at bay."

Angela's face started to light up, but before she could reply, Rourke's voice crackled over the intercom. "I'm sorry, Captain. That's not gonna work. I saw the bots welding steel plates over the shafts … all three of them."

Detonations rang out from BOb's side of the enemy formation.

"Oh, bloody hell!" Bingham blurted out, sounding as if he'd had a realization of his own. "The chap is right. I saw the welding arcs. And from the way those caterpillars were struggling with the panels, it must be some damned heavy steel plating, too."

"Get down!" Monique yelled. The muzzle of her grenade launcher swung straight at Vaughn and Angela. The two of them ducked. Then fire erupted over their heads as the autocannon launched a volley at the ringing formation of robots. Vaughn looked over in time to see the rounds punch into another rolling caterpillar, disassembling the thing before it could launch its cargo. "Get some!" Monique yelled. "Take that, you son of a bitch!"

Vaughn did a double-take and then nodded appreciably.

"Angela," Mark called from the cockpit. "We're out of options. We have to retreat. If the light comes again and we end up in Hell, we'll just have BOb beam us back."

She shook her head vigorously. "The emitter has been glitching, and now it's completely offline."

Vaughn held up a hand. "BOb said it's back up now, but he thinks it only has one more shot left before the whole thing goes Tango Uniform."

"Doesn't matter. BOb and the BFG won't be there. The light the Necks shoot through the wormhole only beams out life. It doesn't send everything to Hell, just living beings."

"Oh, shit," Bill said.

Teddy's pale face stared out at them from inside the cargo bay. "You're right, Command-Oh."

Twinned explosions came from the front. "BOb just took out two more caterpillars," Mark announced.

Monique swung the cannon left and destroyed one coming in from the right. Releasing the trigger, she looked at Vaughn and shook her head. "Whatever we are going to do, it needs to be soon!"

Frustration building, Vaughn looked around, desperately seeking a solution?

What *could* they do?

The Necks had systematically cut off every point of ingress.

Turning, he looked east. "Has anyone seen one of the emergency exit buildings?"

No one had.

Either Angela was wrong about their location, or the Necks had already leveled them.

"Shit!"

Bingham grinned sardonically. "You could always try talking one of the caterpillars into digging a hole through the pavement?"

Vaughn turned widening eyes toward the man. "Bingham, you're a fucking genius!"

"Wh-What?"

Remembering how the V-22's twinned jet blast and massive rotors had swept the ash from the street, Vaughn scanned the ground around the aircraft but saw nothing. He dropped to a knee and looked beneath the Osprey.

A smile spread across his face. "I'll be a son of a ..."

Directly under the center of the aircraft sat a circular outline that could be only one thing.

As Vaughn stood, Mark leaned out and looked back from the flight deck. "What, what, what?"

Grinning, he stepped onto the ramp and hustled inside. "I think I found a way out!"

Vaughn spotted the tool he needed on a pallet behind Bingham. He pointed. "Hand me that crowbar, the one you've been using to open crates."

Confusion twisted the man's face.

"Now!" Vaughn shouted.

Startled into motion, Bingham grabbed the tool and handed it to Vaughn. "What are you going to do, spear one of the robots? They're not mechanical vampires. You can't drive a metal stake through their hearts, Captain. That's not going to work."

"Just make sure my headset cable doesn't get tangled up." Turning from the man, he looked at Rourke and pointed at the belly turret. "Retract the gun. I need to go through the hellhole."

"Why?"

"Goddamn civilians! Just do it!"

Rourke flinched but then toggled a command. The gun flipped to vertical and then slid up and out of the square hole in the belly of the aircraft.

As the mechanism moved, Vaughn pointed through the opening and addressed the entire crew. "The rotor wash exposed a manhole cover under the belly. You landed in a low spot, so the robots won't see me go down there." He pointed at Monique. "But let's keep 'em busy. Cover me. I'm going under."

Monique nodded. "My pleasure."

As she turned and opened fire, Vaughn dropped through the hatch and lay flat on the ground. Looking around, he saw that the low spot was indeed obscuring him from view. The depression in the road was sufficient that he couldn't see any of the surrounding robots, which meant that they couldn't see him either.

He started to low-crawl toward the outline of the ring. "Bingham, make sure Monique doesn't run out of ammo. This is going to take a minute."

The man grumbled something about not being a crew chief, but it sounded like he was doing as asked.

"Teddy!" Vaughn called out. "I need you to make sure that BOb isn't low on ammo either."

"On it, El Capitan."

Mark's voice came over the intercom. "What's the plan?"

"Hang on. I'm almost there." Vaughn reached the circular outline and smiled. "Yes! Something finally broke our way. It's a manhole cover alright. Even has the same design as the one Angela and I used last time we entered the subway tunnel." He glanced at the bandage that still adorned his wrist from when the scavenger bot had dragged him down the streets. It seemed like a lifetime ago, but it had been barely more than a week.

Shaking his head, he jabbed the end of the crowbar into the hole on one side of the ring and began to lever it. Through a grunt, he said, "Everyone, get ready. I'm opening it now. We'll pop smoke and head down. By the time the caterpillars know we're gone, we'll be halfway to ATLAS."

Another round of automatic grenade fire belched from the back of the airplane. Then Vaughn heard a shot come from the front as BOb blasted a caterpillar.

The far end of the lid finally levered upward. "Got it!" Vaughn shouted, his voice straining as he shoved the plate out of its frame and slid it across the pavement. He narrowly avoided crushing his fingers as it dropped to the ground. He pulled his flashlight from his battle rattle and aimed it into the hole. Metal rungs disappeared into the subterranean depths. "Yes! Looks just like the last one. Goes straight down."

"That won't work," Angela said.

Vaughn looked across the ground, his forehead puckering. "Why the hell not? It did last time!"

"These caterpillar bots won't simply let us go, Vaughn. Remember, they can dig. Once they figure out we're not in the aircraft, they'll come after us."

Vaughn blinked and then hammered the side of his fist into the pavement. "Shit!" Clenching his jaw, he shook his head. "We'll just have to stay ahead of them."

"No, Captain," Rachel said from the flight deck. "*We* won't have to stay ahead of them. *You* will."

"What are you talking about?"

"I'm going to take the Osprey back up. Once all of you are below ground, I'll take off and make them think we're still in the fight."

"No! We don't need to separate. The battlebot can fly just about anything, including the tiltrotor. Let BOb do it. It's in his programming. We can all go down."

"That won't work either, mate," Bingham said. "The robot is the only one that can fire the BFG. The thing may only have one more shot left, but that might be the shot you need. No, Major Lee is right. Some of us need to stay on the aircraft. We'll have to keep firing on them, or they'll come after you."

The autocannon roared as Monique fired another volley into the robotic horde.

"There's one other thing, Singleton," Rachel said over the intercom, her voice uncharacteristically dour. "You need to get as deep as you can as fast as you can. If I see that light start to come out of the ground, I'll detonate the nuke."

Vaughn's eyes flew wide. "What?! Why?"

"It will take a while for the light wave to reach you underground, but if it beams us out, it'll leave a few thousand caterpillar bots up here with nothing to do but look for stragglers. The collider tunnel will get crowded in a hurry."

Everyone fell silent.

Rachel continued. "No. I'm not going to let that happen. The light is fast, but not so much that we won't have time to fire the nuke. We'll fly around, make them think we're looking for another way in, keep them engaged until the end. When the light comes, I'll fry 'em up nice and crispy-like. It's a low-yield tactical nuke, and there's two hundred feet of earth between you and the explosion. You'll be safe enough, especially considering the steel plates they welded over the shafts."

Vaughn tried to swallow but couldn't against the lump that had formed in his throat. She was right. This was it. This was their all-or-nothing final dash.

Mistaking his silence as disagreement, Monique said, "If you succeed and Angela resets the timeline, it will not matter if we die here now. All of us will return to our previous lives, back where we were just before the Necks first opened the portal."

Gnashing his teeth, Vaughn nodded his agreement. "Okay, you're right. Team Two, let's get ready to head down. Mark and Chance, I want the two of you down here, too. You weren't firing weapons. The bots won't know you're not on board."

"Negative, Captain Singleton," Bingham said. "The others will be too busy doing their jobs. I'll be firing the biggest weapon of them all. Been itching to 'pop a nuke' as you Yanks like to say. I can't very well bail out now."

Before Vaughn could argue, Mark chimed in. "Same answer here, buddy. I need to stay on board. If something happens to Rachel, this thing won't fly for long. We have to sell this. If we fail, if the bots realize that some of us have gone underground, they'll come after you, and there'll be no stopping them this time. If you're below ground, I don't think they'll settle for keeping you cornered."

Still grinding his teeth together, Vaughn released the intercom trigger and slammed his fist into the pavement. "Shit! Shit! *Shit!*" Mark was no longer his only buddy up there. They were all good people, people he now counted as friends—even that asshole Bingham—but knowing that his oldest friend was about to sacrifice himself for the good of the mission threatened to end Vaughn.

It was almost more than he could take.

But he had to take it. Half-measures weren't going to get this done. He and the rest of Team Two would just have to make sure that their sacrifice wasn't in vain.

"Okay—" Vaughn's voice cracked. He released the mic key. After a short growl, he toggled the switch again. "Copy. We'll ... We'll make sure your ... departure ... is short-lived, have you back home in time for dinner." He sighed and then added, "Bill and Teddy, retrieve BOb and get your asses down here. You, too, Angela. And I swear to Christ, if one more person argues with me, I'll have all your asses court-martialed."

He saw Teddy's boots hit the ground behind the ramp and then run around to the front of the aircraft. Then the pair of them quickly returned to the ramp and disappeared inside. At the same time, Angela slid down through the belly hatch and soon joined him on the ground next to the open utility access. Muddy tears streaked her cheeks. A moment later, Bill, Teddy, and BOb dropped through the hellhole and lay next to Angela. The eyes of the two men glistened as well.

Vaughn pointed to the robot and shouted over the rotor noise. "You head down first, BOb. Don't stop until you reach the bottom of the shaft. Wait for us there." He started to turn away but then gave the bot a meaningful look. "But make sure you're the *only* thing waiting for us. Visually verify the adjoining tunnel is clear before we reach you."

The robot dipped its head. If BOb had responded, Vaughn couldn't hear it. That was just as well. He could do without being called Captain Asshole for the moment.

The battlebot eased down through the opening. With the second nuke still strapped to its back, the machine barely fit through the ring, but a moment later, both BOb and the nuclear-armed backpack disappeared down the black hole.

The autocannon mounted to the tail barked to life again. Looking toward the sound, Vaughn shouted over his shoulder, "Alright, the rest of you get your asses down there."

He could've saved his breath. When he looked back, Angela was already halfway through the opening. She rapidly descended out of sight. Bill and Teddy zipped through after her.

As Vaughn swung his legs over and started to descend, he looked at the belly of the aircraft and toggled his headset. "Everyone's down the hole, and I'm going now. Godspeed, Team One. We'll see you on the other side."

He started to yank off the headset, but then Mark's now unsteady voice crackled in his ear. "We're all counting on you, Singleton. Don't … Don't fuck up."

"Oh, shit. Th-Thanks …" Vaughn swallowed and then took an unsteady breath. "Thanks for that, Chewie. I almost jinxed everything."

"Yeah, you did. Now, get the hell out of here. We got work to do."

Vaughn gave a short nod and pulled off the headset.

Bingham leaned down through the hellhole and took it from him. Then the man pointed. "Get your arse down there ASAP, Singleton. I'll not wait until I'm back in Hell to detonate this thing. If I see that light coming, I'm pulling the bloody trigger."

CHAPTER 51

Vaughn looked down as he descended the last few rungs of the long ladder. Even using the night-vision goggles, he could barely see the four other members of the team beneath him. The two small holes in the utility access cover didn't provide much light for the tubes to amplify.

Team One had taken off in the V-22 shortly after he had slid the steel plate back into place. Even now, he could hear the distant sound of sporadic cannon fire. They were doing an excellent job of keeping the bots occupied.

Vaughn felt solid ground beneath his boots. He could also feel the other four members of the team standing around him. "What are you waiting for? Head down the tunnel!"

Bill, Teddy, and Angela exchanged confused looks in the murky darkness. Then their night-vision goggles swung back and forth as they glanced left and right. Teddy stared back at him. "Okay, El Capitan. Which way?"

"Geez!" Vaughn looked at the other pilot. "Come on, Bill. Am I the only one with a sense of direction?"

The man merely shrugged. "You're the one that's been down here before. I have no idea where this leads, and I can't see shit with these goggles. There's not enough light."

Vaughn nodded. He flipped up his NVGs and motioned for the others to do the same. Then he activated his flashlight, shielding it so that its illumination wouldn't reach the small holes in the lid above them. After directing its beam down the tunnel, he looked back at the robot. "BOb, cover our six. I'll take point. The rest of you, try to keep up."

Not waiting for them, he headed toward the end of the shaft that ran toward ATLAS.

His flashlight's beam glinted back at him from multiple points along the tunnel's damp walls. He doubted this was the passageway that he and Angela had traversed before, but he hoped it followed the same routing structure as had the last one.

He ran as fast as the range of the light cast by his flashlight permitted. The multitudinous clattering footfalls behind Vaughn made it sound as if an entire army were chasing after him. Unfortunately, he couldn't run full-tilt lest he outrun his vision and fall down another vertical shaft.

Just as Vaughn had the thought, a dark pit emerged ahead, swallowing the beam of his flashlight like the event horizon of a black hole.

He shouted over his shoulder. "Careful! there's a drop ahead."

By the time the others caught up with him, Vaughn had already started down the shaft. He descended twenty feet through the darkness before he felt firm ground beneath his boots once again. Above him, he could hear the breaths and steps of the rest of the team as they descended. This time, he didn't wait for them to join him, he just continued, heading farther down the tunnel.

Over the next few minutes, they negotiated one more vertical descent before running into a closed steel hatch.

Inspecting it with his flashlight, Vaughn tilted his head. "This is new." It looked like the type you would see on a ship. He tried to spin the wheel, grunting with the exertion. "Dammit!"

Angela peered over his shoulder in the narrow passageway. "What's wrong?"

"It won't budge!"

"Try it the other way."

He started to argue but reconsidered. Maybe this wasn't a righty-tighty-lefty-loosy configuration.

Vaughn heaved against the wheel, trying to turn it in the other direction. "Ah! It still won't move."

He stepped back and shouted over his shoulder. "BOb! Get your ass up here. Open this door."

"Yes, Captain Asshole."

The robot squeezed past him in the tunnel's narrow confines. Vaughn moved back, giving the obstinate shit room to work.

The machine grabbed the wheel and began to wrench on it. The handle moved half an inch, but then it seized.

Expecting the blast wave to pulverize them at any moment, Vaughn peered back over his shoulder nervously.

This was taking too much time. They'd already been underground for more than ten minutes.

It wouldn't be long before the last Neck passed through the wormhole.

Then the light would come, and the nuke would follow.

Vaughn and his team had descended a fair distance, but he had no illusion that the manhole cover alone would protect them from the overpressurization that was sure to come. The heat and radiation might not reach this depth, but the shockwave would likely pulverize their bodies.

Everything would be lost.

The electronic muscles of the robot strained audibly against the latching mechanism of the door.

Vaughn tried to reach around the bot, but the tunnel was too narrow.

"BOb! You need to hurry!"

"I am hurrying, Captain Asshole. I believe the door has been locked from the other side. I'm detecting the sound of a chain moving when I turn the handle."

Vaughn swore under his breath. He knew ATLAS likely lay just beyond this door. Of course, they would keep the sewer-access hatch locked, but if he and his team couldn't find a way past the thing, it was all going to end very soon.

He eyed the nuke warily. They were much closer to the wormhole now. If they detonated the bomb here, it would almost certainly collapse the near part of the tunnel, including ATLAS. They'd at least be able to deny the bastards this world.

As Vaughn stared at BOb's backpack, the BFG strapped alongside it drew his attention. Seeing its long length, he reached up and tried to pull the bot away from the door. "Get back. I have an idea!"

CHAPTER 52

R ourke searched the ground, slewing the belly turret's gun camera with an unsteady hand. Seeing another sharp-edged rectangle, he keyed his mic. "Th-This shaft is covered, too."

In his peripheral vision, he saw Rachel nod as she guided the aircraft across the city. "Good, that makes all of them. The caterpillars even plated off the new hole behind their construction site."

"What about the emergency escape shafts that Angela told us about?" Mark Hennessy asked.

Monique looked forward from her position on the tail ramp. "I just saw the remnants of one." She pointed to their back left. "There is a steel plate surrounded by some rubble. Looks to be about the size and position Angela described."

Returning her attention to the autocannon's monitor, the naval lieutenant shook her head. "Oh, you naughty bastards." Adjusting her aim, she squeezed the trigger, releasing a short burst of grenades. "I will give them one thing: these caterpillars are tenacious."

Rachel leaned out and looked back. "They still following us?"

Straddling the nuke atop a crate in the center of the cargo area, Bingham released a snort. "Yes, my Asian-American princess. They swallowed our ruse hook, line, and nuclear device." He looked outside. "They're quite anxious, kicking up one hell of a dust cloud in their wake, too." He laughed and then patted the missile. "Come and get it, you little shits."

Rourke couldn't believe the light-hearted way the rest of the team members were going about this. He was shaking in his boots, literally, and his hands were so unsteady, he could barely keep the gun camera under control. "Y-You people are cr-crazy," he blurted. "This is ridiculous! We're about to die, and you're cracking jokes!"

Bingham looked over at him and winked. "We've all got to die someday, boy-oh, but it's not every day you get to do it with a good chance of coming back."

Rourke glared at the man. "I guess you finally get to have your nuke and eat it, too."

Chance's smile broadened. "Now you're getting the hang of it, chap." He pointed at the belly cannon. "How about you give that thing a little exercise. Want the bastards to know we're still in the game, right?"

Rourke blinked and then looked back at the display. "Oh shit." Slewing the camera to point aft again, he quickly found the horde of chasing caterpillar bots. The things were racing over structures, mowing down what little bit was left and launching a cloud of dust behind themselves.

He aimed at the lead element and fired the weapon. It barked to life, lighting up the inside frame of the hellhole with rapid yellow pulses. The concussive discharge of each shot shook his innards, making his guts feel as if they were trembling every bit as much as were his hands.

The front flank of the advancing caterpillars dissolved under the fusillade of explosive bullets. Vaughn had told him the 30mm rounds had the same hitting power as those fired by the Apache attack helicopter. Rourke didn't know about that, but he thought they did an excellent job against the metal bodies of the caterpillar bots.

Monique looked forward and held up a thumb. "Good shooting,

Doctor Geller. Chance's delivery may leave something to be desired. However, the wing commander is correct. At least we have the consolation of knowing we may come back. If we do not, then … we have lost, and there was nothing left here for us anyway."

Rourke tightened the corner of his mouth. "What if it's not us that comes back? What if …? What if we don't remember any of this?"

This time, no one issued a sharp retort. The looks on their faces told Rourke he'd struck a nerve. A wave of guilt washed over him. They'd been having the same thought, but he'd been the only one stupid enough to give it voice. "Ah, shit … I'm sorry."

Rachel gave him a wan smile. "You remember what I told you about ifs?"

For a moment, Rourke stared back blankly. Then a grin inched across his face. "Yeah. *If* my aunt had balls, she'd be my uncle."

"Exactly. Let's leave the what-ifs behind." She pointed at the belly cannon's controller. "Put your energy into getting a little payback while you still can."

He looked at Rachel a moment and then gave her a short nod before returning his attention to the weapon's display.

The bastards were still chasing after the slowly advancing aircraft, following it as if the thing were the Pied Piper. Focusing his anger, Rourke gnashed his teeth and pressed the fire button. "Die, you pieces of shit!"

"Good job, Rourky," Rachel called from the front. "Keep engaging them. I'm going to climb higher. Need to put some room between us and the ground. Don't want to create a crater that might cave in the collider tunnel."

Looking up, Rourke swallowed. They were actually going to do it. These might be the last moments of his life.

In spite of their big talk, Monique and Bingham exchanged nervous glances.

The whine of the tiltrotor's engines ramped up, and the aircraft started to climb.

Major Lee looked back. "Not yet, Chauncey-Baby. We'll wait till we see the light. Need to give Team Two all the time we can."

"Are you sure about that, Major?" Bingham asked, turning raised eyebrows toward Rachel. "Judging by the number of mechanical eyes staring at us right now, I'm pretty sure they have a good fix on our exact location. The first light that comes through may be the one that takes us out. We might blink and suddenly find we're flying through Hell."

"I don't care. It's just a chance we'll have to take, Chance." Rachel paused and winked at Rourke. "See what I did there?" She returned her attention to Bingham. "I won't have you wiping out both teams. If you detonate that thing too early, you'll risk the entire mission."

The wing commander pointed through the open rear ramp. "If we get beamed to Hell, all those bastards will be free to seek out the other team. Our delay might doom humanity." The man's eyes lost focus, and his voice dropped. "My family will stay buried at the bottom of that damned mountain."

Momentarily forgetting his own worries, Rourke watched the man struggle with his emotions. Head lowered, Chance stared through the floor of the cargo bay.

Finally, Bingham sighed and keyed his microphone again. "Don't worry, Major. I'll not get trigger-happy. Just … Just let me know when you see the bloody light. I'll do the rest."

Rachel's eyes softened. "I know you will, Chance."

They spent the next several minutes circling Geneva as if searching for a way back into the collider complex, while not getting too close to the construction site.

Both Rourke and Monique continued to pour fire into the pursuing caterpillar bots. The machine army was starting to cut a circular path of destruction around the already pulverized city. Their passage raised dust high into the atmosphere. However, the strong north wind was sweeping the cloud toward Mont Salève on the south side of the city.

As they flew over the airport, Rachel turned the V-22 east, affording Rourke a view of the Necks' cauldron through the back of the airplane. It looked like they were only about a half-mile from it. The sky had started to glow faintly with the coming sunrise. While it was still relatively dark outside, Rourke found he could make out some of the structures without the need for night-vision goggles.

Between the alien construction site and the remainder of the burned-out city lay a few rectangular plots of scorched farmland. The east-west highway they'd initially planned to follow from the airport cut a gray line across the monochromatic scene.

With mounting dread, Rourke eyed the alien edifice that now squatted over CERN, wondering when the Necks would complete their evacuation and reinitiate their purge.

How many more of them could there be?

Surely the light would come soon.

Hope inched its way into his thoughts.

What if Angela had been wrong?

What if the robots were giving up on this world?

Maybe they—

Flinching, Rourke and his two fellow teammates in the back of the aircraft winced and raised arms reflexively.

As if heralded by thought alone, a brilliant beam of blue-white light shot through the base of the stadium-sized cauldron and burned into the sky, incinerating Rourke's short-lived pipe dream.

Dust swirled through the vertically oriented laser beam-like column of fluorescing energy.

"It's here," Bingham said flatly, lowering the arm he'd raised. Bending over the device, he looked toward the cockpit. "I have the weapon ready to fire. Need only press the enter key one more time."

Eyes wide, Rourke looked forward and saw both Rachel and Mark staring back. The two pilots exchanged a glance. Then Rachel looked at Rourke and winked. "It'll all be okay, Rourky." Addressing the rest of the team, she added, "It's been an honor to serve with all of—"

Her eyes went round with shock as she stared past them. "Oh God! Fire it! Fire it now, Chance!"

Snapping his head left, Rourke looked outside.

The light beam no longer looked like a laser. It had ballooned into a rapidly expanding cone, a narrow wedge with its point of origin buried two-hundred feet underground. The wall of ethereal light raced toward the back of the airplane with incredible speed.

Rourke's brain sent a signal to his arm, ordering it to raise as a shield.

The electrical impulse never reached its destination.

CHAPTER 53

Vaughn watched the barrel of his ruined M4 rifle bend as BOb wrenched its stock. Wedged into the spokes of the wheel, the weapon made an excellent lever. He had considered having the bot beam them into ATLAS with the BFG's final discharge, but it would have simply deposited them on the surface above the facility. He didn't see emerging into a nuclear blast front as being an improvement in their situation. However, seeing the length of the BFG had reminded him of the benefits of leverage.

A loud snap echoed through the narrow tunnel.

Vaughn's eyes went wide. "Did the barrel break?"

A severe squeal cut across his words.

Finally, the handle began to turn.

A moment later, the robot wrenched open the door, revealing a wider, metal-lined passageway beyond. A broken length of chain sat on its floor.

Vaughn urged the others through. "Go! Go! Go!"

Guns raised, Bill and Teddy darted through the opening followed closely by Angela.

Passing through the hatch, Vaughn pulled BOb in behind him. "Latch it! Hurry!"

Deciding the robot was moving too slow, he lunged forward and pulled the large metal panel.

The massive door slammed home with enough force to cause the ground to shake.

The trembling continued as BOb spun the wheel.

Then the hatch lurched in its frame.

Dust shot out from its entire periphery, and the ground heaved.

At the same moment, a pressure wave drove agonizing daggers of pain into Vaughn's ears.

Hands thrown over ears, they all stumbled back from the hatch.

Staring at the door, Vaughn understood.

That had been the nuke.

He exchanged glances with Angela, Bill, and Teddy.

Mark was gone. The man who'd been his friend through most of his adult life had been vaporized in the blink of an eye.

Rachel, too. The woman who'd survived so many special operations combat deployments and was one of the best pilots he'd ever worked with.

Gone.

Rourke ... Monique.

Gone.

Even the loss of Bingham dug a pit in his soul.

More than half the remaining human population ...

Gone.

These were people who'd followed him into battle, and now there was nothing left of them but a cloud of disassociated atoms.

After a seeming eternity, the quaking faded and then ceased.

Vaughn shook his head. Turning from the blast door that had saved their lives, he looked at the remaining members of humanity. "We ... We need to get moving. Otherwise, their sacrifice will be for nothing."

Angela stared at him, steely resolve in her eyes. "We'll bring them back." She looked at Vaughn significantly and momentarily tilted her head to the side. "All of them, the whole damned world."

He swallowed hard and then gave a sharp nod. "You're right."

Bill and Teddy looked as shocked as Vaughn felt. The cosmonaut looked up warily. "Light wave coming, yes?"

Angela shook her head. "The light will have to travel quite a way across the surface before the beam coming from the wormhole gets low enough to reach us this far underground, but we do need to hurry."

"She's right." Vaughn gestured toward ATLAS and patted BOb's shoulder. "Nothing will be following us, so you take point. Kill anything that moves." After a moment, he winced and added, "Just try not to break the collider."

For once, the robot didn't quip or crack a joke. It merely nodded and headed deeper into the facility. Then BOb hoisted one of his grenade launchers overhead and turned it sideways.

Face twisted, Angela looked at Vaughn. "What's he doing now?"

As if in answer, the robot whispered menacingly into the darkness. "Say hello to my little friend."

Staring at the silhouette of the raised weapon, Vaughn gnashed his teeth and cursed under his breath. "After I get done kicking the ass of whoever programmed this damn thing, I'm going to have a serious talk with them about comedic timing."

Pausing, Vaughn tilted his head. Something didn't look right. At first, he couldn't put a finger on it, but then he saw the issue. It was the silhouette.

"Everyone turn off your lights."

After returning a few confused looks, they all complied.

Looking toward the robot, Vaughn raised an arm and pointed. "There's light ahead."

"Good grief!" Bill said. "You're right."

After exchanging looks, the four of them chased after the robot.

The light grew in intensity as they ventured down the hallway.

Soon, they reached a partially closed doorway.

Vaughn grabbed the robot's shoulder. "BOb, I want you to, *silently*, open that door and clear the room beyond."

The bot looked back as if to speak.

Narrowing his eyes, Vaughn held up a finger. "Uh-uh! Not a damned word."

After a momentary pause, BOb turned and eased open the door.

The three humans winced as bright light poured into the hallway.

The robot leaned through the opening. It glanced left and right. Then its mechanical muscles silently ushered the machine forward. It eased through the doorway and quickly passed out of sight.

Teddy looked after the bot and then glanced at Vaughn. "I am happy he is on our side."

Vaughn raised an eyebrow. "I guess."

He flinched as BOb's gray head popped back into the opening. Then the bot whispered, "The room is clear, Captain Asshole."

Vaughn sighed. "Shit." Shaking his head, he signaled for Bill and Teddy to proceed to the door that adorned the room's far wall, gesturing for them to position themselves to its left and right. Then he and Angela crossed the open space and took up station behind them.

Cleaning supplies lined racks of shelves. A mop bucket sat in the middle of the small room's floor. Murky water still filled its interior, but the mop was missing. Vaughn wondered if it might be at the bottom of Mont de Los Muertos, still clutched in the janitor's decaying hands.

He shook the vision from his mind and turned his attention back to the new door.

Bill and Teddy were peering through its window.

"See anything?" Angela asked.

"Da, Command-Oh. Lots of pipes."

Bill nodded. "Looks like we're close to ATLAS."

Vaughn leaned out and saw the same thing. He tapped the major's shoulder and whispered, "Do you see any movement?"

Both men shook their heads.

Bill looked back at him. "Looks like a ghost town in there."

Vaughn nodded. "Glad to hear the Necks haven't left a greeting party for us." He glanced at Angela. "Do you know where we are? Can you find your way to a network terminal from here?"

"Yeah. We're pretty close to the control room, actually."

"Good." Vaughn paused and looked around. Spotting something that should work for his purpose, he pointed. "BOb. Over here."

"What are you doing, El Capitan?"

"You two stand guard for a moment." Stepping over to the small door, he opened it and found that, as he'd suspected, it was a coat closet. He shoved aside the few hanging garments that occupied the space and pointed at the floor. "Set the nuke here."

Using its anatomically odd ability to bend its arms in multiple directions, the robot reached around itself and extracted the cone-shaped nuclear device from its large backpack. Then it gently deposited the thing onto the floor of the small closet.

Angela looked at him. "What are you doing?"

Vaughn took a knee next to the device and looked up. "How much time do you need?"

She blanched. "Why? What are you doing?"

"Setting a failsafe. This is why we brought this. If we don't make it, if they beam us out, we can at least deny the bastards this world."

Angela nodded, cold resolve in her eyes.

The look concerned Vaughn. He didn't know if it was good or bad.

She skewed her mouth as she calculated. Then she held up two fingers. "Twenty minutes should be enough. Even with the longer build-up that Rourke told us about, the actual reset shouldn't take more than ten minutes, max. It'll take us a couple of minutes to get there plus a few more for me to program the reset and insert the Morse code message."

"The SOS that you're going to put in the interference pattern?"

"Yes, so a total of twenty minutes should do it."

After looking at her for a long moment, Vaughn gave a short nod and then bent over the device. He punched in twenty-five minutes and pressed the enter key three times. Then he repeated the process, hesitating after the second press of the enter key. He looked up at Angela and pointed at her watch. "That thing still working?"

She nodded her understanding. "Yes. Hang on. Let me bring up the timer." Angela pressed a button on the side of the watch and then looked at him.

Vaughn scrunched up his face. "I sure as hell hope Monique got this right. If I press the enter key and this thing blows up immediately, I'm going to be really pissed."

Angela nodded. "Only one way to find out."

Returning the gesture, Vaughn said, "Start the timer on one."

She dipped her head.

"Three …"

Still standing by the door, Bill and Teddy watched with wide eyes.

"Two …"

Vaughn swallowed.

"One!"

He pressed the button.

Then he flinched as a single, loud chime rang out from the device. At the same time, Angela's watch beeped.

As a long breath hissed through his lips, he watched the display trip 24:59.

24:58

24:57

Vaughn looked up at Angela. "Time's-a-wasting. Better get moving."

CHAPTER 54

S tanding in a long hallway, Angela pointed at a door. "This is it. This is the control room."

Vaughn knew she was correct. He recognized the door's position and the reinforced glass frame within it. Last time the two of them had been here, a Neck had pulverized that window to the point of failure. That had been just before Angela had reset the timeline and returned them to their starting points.

Peering through the window, he couldn't see the wormhole or the light wave. A large set of cabinets blocked the sphere from observation.

It had taken less than five minutes to reach the control room this time. They'd started off slow, clearing each new corridor, but Bill had been right: the place was a ghost town.

Vaughn had heard the light wave's eerie wail the moment they left the janitorial supply closet. It had steadily grown louder since.

He tilted his head toward the door and looked at Angela. "Hear it?"

She nodded wordlessly.

"Hear what, El Capitan?"

"The light wave. Sounds just like it did back on Mon Calamari."

"Oh ... Da, the Fish-Head world."

Bill nodded. "The world full of Admiral Ackbars?"

"It used to be," Angela said plaintively. "They're gone now. We couldn't stop the Necks from wiping their planet."

Vaughn looked at her. "We did our best. It wasn't our fault."

Eyes darkening, Angela turned and gazed into the control room. A look of immense sadness clouded her features. "And here we are, about to do *our best* all over again."

Vaughn pointed to her watch. "If we don't hurry, we won't be *doing* anything."

After glancing at her wrist, she continued to stare through the window. "Twenty minutes. I'll get it done." She shook her head again. "But what about them? We're leaving all those worlds we passed through unchanged. The only thing this reset accomplishes is denying the Necks our world. All those other peoples ... they'll still be lost."

Bill and Teddy watched the two of them with mixed levels of confusion.

Extending an arm past Angela, Vaughn reached for the door handle.

She batted away his hand. "I've got this, Captain!" She stared at Vaughn. The cold, hard looked returned to her eyes. Turning away, she opened the door.

The squealing wail rose precipitously.

After a slight hesitation, Angela stepped into the control room.

Vaughn exchanged glances with the two men and then pointed at BOb. "Guard the door. If anything comes this way, kill it."

"Wilco, Captain Asshole."

He blew air through his nose and then followed the other three into the control room.

Stepping around the cabinet, he stopped and stared at the mercurial sphere that hung beyond the glass wall. Angela, Bill, and Teddy were already doing the same.

A wide cone now shone out of the top of the wormhole, an inversion of what they'd seen on Mon Calamari. However, instead of shining down through the planet, this one sent up a spreading fan of energy that cut through the ceiling of the control room.

Vaughn knew that, some distance away, it was emerging as a ring of blue-white light. At this very moment, the aurora-like curtain of fluorescing energy was racing across the planet's surface with CERN at its epicenter.

As he watched the top of the widening cone creep across the ceiling, slowly lowering over their heads, Vaughn pointed to Angela's computer console. "I'll settle for banishing them from our world for now."

Staring up at the descending wave of light with wide eyes, Teddy gestured sideways, pointing at Vaughn. "Da. What he said."

CHAPTER 55

"Bob, any movement out there?" Bill said, looking back nervously. "Negative, Major Peterson."

"None of them caterpillar bots, right?"

"No, sir."

Vaughn pursed his lips. "Major? Sir?"

Continuing to scan the corridor, the robot nodded. "Affirmative, Captain Asshole."

Ignoring the exchange, Bill pointed through the control room window. "You sure they can't see us in here, sense us through that wormhole?"

Shaking his head and trying to sound more certain that he felt, Vaughn said, "No. The other side is mirrored, designed to shield against radiation. Besides, I think they believe we're dead."

Teddy pointed at the light still streaming overhead. The curtain of white energy was now only a few feet above their heads. "Then why are they still firing that light?"

Angela continued to work on the computer, her fingers dancing across its keyboard. Without looking up, she said, "They don't know we were the only ones. The Necks see us as an infestation. Like Captain Asshole said: if you see one cockroach, there's probably a

453

hundred more hiding in the walls." She pulled her hand away from the terminal long enough to point up at the light. "This is planetary bug killer."

Dropping her hand back to the keyboard, Angela released a growl. "Shit! They've cut off my access!"

Looking at her screen, Vaughn blanched. "What!?"

"Oh, shit, Command-Oh! Password not working?"

As Teddy asked the question, another log-in fail message flashed across the terminal's screen.

Shaking her head, Angela pounded her fist into the desk's off-white surface. "The bastards locked me out."

A wave of nausea swept over Vaughn. He looked from the screen to her reddening face. "Please tell me there's another way, a backdoor or something."

Angela started to shake her head, but then she paused and sat bolt upright. "Wait. Maybe …" She reached tentatively for the keyboard. "I wonder if …?"

"What? What?" Vaughn barked.

Angela didn't answer. Her fingers started dancing across the keys again. Several screens later, she reached a new log-in window. She peered over the top of the display, her eyes losing focus. Then she nodded again and punched in a series of characters.

Finally, a new window opened. Angela pumped both fists overhead. "Yes! Yes, yes, yes!"

Vaughn shifted his gaze from the screen to her triumphant face. "You're in?"

"Pfft, yeah." Angela started typing commands into the keyboard. Apparently setting aside her earlier sadness, she gave him a lopsided grin. "Stupid robots can't stop me."

"Holy shit!" Shaking his hands, Vaughn released a pent-up breath. "You scared the shit outta me."

Bill scoffed. "Ya think?"

"I got this, guys. Just had to use my old sys-admin log-in."

"Why didn't you tell us you had another log-in, Command-Oh?"

She cast an embarrassed grin at the cosmonaut. "Didn't think it would work. IT was supposed to delete that one when I left for NASA."

"You didn't think it …?" The words fell from Vaughn's lips. He shook his head. "That … That was just dumb luck?"

She held her palms out and gave him a toothy grin. "Hey, even a blind squirrel is right twice a day."

Bill did a double-take. "I'm pretty sure that's not how the saying goes."

She waved a dismissive hand and then continued typing. "Whatever. Bottom line: we're in. It's about time something broke our way."

Looking up at the slowly descending fan of blue-white light, Vaughn sighed. He dragged his gaze from the encroaching curtain of energy and stared at the computer screen. Lines of code streamed across its surface. It was all Greek to him. From the instructions Angela had given each of them, Vaughn understood the basics of what she was doing, but the data currently crossing the screen was inscrutable.

He tapped her on the shoulder. "What are you doing now?"

"I'm accessing the alien code." The data on the screen paused. Angela pointed at a set of numbers. "Here it is!"

"What?"

Angela looked at him and smiled. "These are the space-time coordinates for the first set of collisions."

Returning her attention to the computer, she quickly copied the data and then opened a new program. A moment later, she finished, pressing the enter key with a flourish. Then she looked up. "The reset is ready to go."

Vaughn looked at her from beneath raised eyebrows. "That was faster than last time." He stepped forward for a closer look. His foot brushed against something under the desk.

Angela shrugged. "Practice makes perfect."

Vaughn bent over and blindly probed the area beneath the workstation.

"Like I told you back in the wheat field, I'm coming at the problem from multiple directions. This reset will take us back to the formation of that first micro black hole, but if the interference pattern works, it'll disrupt the flow of protons and stop it from ever forming in the first place."

She paused and looked at Vaughn. "What do you have there?"

He stood and placed the item on the desk next to the computer terminal. "It's a camcorder. Someone must've dropped it here just before the light took them."

Angela nodded absentmindedly and then continued talking as she worked on the computer. "I'm encoding the SOS into the pattern now, but even if they don't see the message, the reset should give me enough time to call Doctor Garfield before he reinitiates the collisions." She looked up. "We'll stop the Necks from ever finding us. They won't know we exist."

"What's on the video, El Capitan?"

"Let's not worry about that right now. How about we just activate the reset?"

Angela shook her head. "No, Teddy is right. There's something else I need to add, but first I want to see what's on that video."

Snatching the camcorder from the countertop, Vaughn activated it. The screen flared to life and promptly displayed a low-battery message.

Jabbing a finger at the device, Angela said, "Push play."

He pressed the button, and the face of a self-important older gentleman suddenly filled the screen.

Angela's eyes widened. "That's him. That's Doctor Garfield, the director of the HiLumi upgrade. He was going to oversee the first proton-proton collisions that day."

The little speaker in the side of the camcorder came to life. They all leaned closer, listening intently.

"Today, vee shall plumb the deepest reaches of the quantum realm," the man said with a thick German accent. "The collider's High-Luminosity upgrade vill shine the light of discovery upon hidden dimensions und singularities."

Vaughn looked at Angela and frowned. "He was right about that, but the light was shining the other way. The only thing it illuminated was us."

Angela shushed him. "Quiet! Fast forward. I need to see what happens."

Vaughn growled his impatience. "We need to get this thing moving." He tapped her watch. "Time is ticking."

"Then hurry."

Vaughn narrowed his eyes. Angela was working on a new idea, but as usual, she was reluctant to share it. This tendency of hers had really pissed him off when she'd done it before, and it wasn't helping to improve his mood at the moment.

"Fine!" Grinding his teeth, Vaughn jabbed the fast-forward button. They watched as the camera panned left and right quickly. It aimed at two other people: a woman in a dress suit and a man in a lab coat. Then the point of view lurched, and suddenly it was pointing at the ATLAS detector. Moving at an accelerated pace, the large, cylindrical device crumpled and then collapsed.

As Vaughn knew it would, the detector apparatus shrank down until it was a sphere hanging suspended in mid-air, just like the one that currently levitated beyond the control room's observation window.

Then it flashed, and something emerged from its top.

Vaughn pressed the pause button.

The four of them stared silently at the motionless Neck that now jutted from the top of the mercurial sphere. It had frozen in the act of reaching out with one of its arms. Its extended finger sat inches away from the protruding digit of the facility's mechanical manipulator. The image looked similar to Michelangelo's painting on the ceiling of the Sistine Chapel, the one where God bestows life to Adam through the touch of a finger.

"Dude," Teddy said reverently. "It's like The Creation of Adam."

The grinding wail of the light wave's overhead passage rose a notch. They all looked up. The energetic curtain had accelerated.

"Shit!" Vaughn reached to push play again but missed the button in his haste.

"Push it!" Angela ordered.

"I'm trying!"

Bill looked from the two of them up to the light and then back at Angela. "Why did it speed up?"

"Less resistance, I guess. There's no animal life for it to beam out, so it's going faster."

She looked at Vaughn. "Start the video already. I need to see how it ends."

He growled with frustration and then finally managed to finger the play button.

Coming back to life, the Neck suddenly spasmed and looked down. It pointed at something off-camera. Then the video zoomed out, and Vaughn saw two people had entered the chamber, stepping in from the left side of the ATLAS facility.

The Neck leaned over and, extending both of its free arms, pointed a pair of accusing fingers at the new arrivals.

Vaughn thought he could hear the thing's siren-like scream, but with the wail presently coming from the energy curtain, he couldn't be sure.

A moment later, the Neck dropped out of sight.

Then a beam of light shot from the sphere, and the two humans vanished.

Bill Peterson jerked as if jolted by electricity. "Son of a bitch!"

The camera's point of view fell to the floor and came to rest aimed at two pairs of shuffling shoes.

A moment later, white light washed out the video.

When the image returned, the shoes and the people who'd been in them had vanished.

Vaughn and his three teammates stared in silence.

The screen went black, and a small, red, dead-battery icon popped up.

Angela thrust out a hand. "Give me the SD card!"

Searching the exterior of the camcorder, Vaughn quickly found the small memory chip and ejected it. Then he handed it to Angela. "What are you going to do?"

She grabbed the card and jammed it into a reader on the side of the computer terminal.

"Initially, I had planned to use Morse code because I wasn't sure how much bandwidth there'd be, but now that I have full access, I can see there's plenty. I can send this video."

Teddy nodded approvingly. "Strong work, Command-Oh!"

Bill knitted his eyebrows. "How can you do that?"

Angela's fingers blurred as they sprinted across the keyboard. Not looking away from the screen, she said, "I'm uploading the file now. The video will form the interference pattern."

She hit the enter key a final time and then sat back. "Done!"

Vaughn heard a loud clunk followed by the familiar sound of ramping electrical energy.

Angela glanced at her watch and then looked back at the three of them. "Eleven minutes to go." She smiled at Vaughn. "Good thing you added that extra five. Now we just have to hope that someone on the other end recognizes the pattern as being video."

Casting a nervous glance toward the janitorial supply closet, Vaughn asked, "Should we add more time?"

After consulting her display, Angela shook her head. "The overload will peak four or five minutes before that."

Vaughn nodded. "Okay, but we're cutting it close."

Angela looked through the window, eyeing the wormhole warily. "It's still possible that the Necks somehow discover we're here. If so, they'd beam us to Hell just like they did on Mon Calamity."

"Mon Calamari," Vaughn corrected.

"Whatever. We'd survive being beamed out, but not if I leave them enough time to also find the bomb and send it after us, you know, just to keep us company."

The noise of the building overload had doubled, and Vaughn could already feel the floor starting to vibrate.

Bill nodded but cast a nervous glance at the overhead energy curtain. "Alright, Angela, but you let us know if you change your mind."

The four of them fell quiet as they looked up and gazed into the still lowering fan of white light.

Vaughn gestured at it. "Judging by its speed, I think we might have ten minutes before we'll be lying on the floor trying to stay out of its reach."

Bill raised an eyebrow. "I sure as hell hope we're gone before that. Otherwise, things are gonna get real hot."

Angela pursed her lips and nodded.

Teddy made a sour look. "If it speeds up again, we might get another trip through Hell before the reset can send us home."

Vaughn fought back a shiver as visions of circling, ravenous animals rose unbidden in his mind.

Shaking his head, he banished the mental image and glanced at the observation window. He nodded toward the sphere. "Now that Angela has started the overload, everything should be in the bag. Once it finishes, the timeline will reset, regardless of where we are, here or in Hell." He looked at Angela. "Right?"

"One can always hope."

"Thanks," Vaughn scoffed. "You're a beacon of optimism."

Bill looked from her to the computer screen. "Are you sure this is going to work?"

Angela puckered her forehead. "I'm not sure of anything. We know that the wormhole touches every point along its path in both time and space. I'm hoping there's enough of a quantum disturbance between the creation of the two micro black holes to allow us to link with the first one. That way we'll travel back to that point when the overload reaches its peak, but like I said, I'm also trying to send a message that prevents both of them from being created. If any of the approaches work, it'll collapse the wormhole and send us back to the beginning."

Bill sighed. "That's a lot of ifs."

Angela shrugged. "Several minutes passed between the formations of the two singularities. If we fail to stop the first one, I should have time to stop them from creating the second."

Teddy's face scrunched up. "How did you find the coordinates for the first MBH, Command-Oh? How do you know they're correct?"

"Hang on. I'll show you." Angela started typing again.

As she worked, Vaughn eyed the wormhole. Ripples were starting to flow across its surface, but Rourke had been right. The build-up was taking significantly longer than had their first one.

"The Necks are running the software over our computers, so the data within it has to conform to our syntax and program language." Pausing, Angela entered a final command and then pointed at a specific set of numbers. "Here. These represent both the location and time of the first event, the creation of the initial micro black hole." Angela hesitated, and her finger drifted to another location on the display. "Wait." She tilted her head. "Could that be...?"

Her eyes flew wide. "Oh my goodness!"

Vaughn pried his gaze from the now clearly quaking mercurial sphere and looked at Angela. "Wh-What?"

Ignoring him, she looked at Bill and Teddy. "Go get the nuke!"

They stared back. Teddy's bushy eyebrows knitted. "O-Okay, Command-Oh. Should we ... take BOb?"

Angela shook her head impatiently. "No, no, no." She jabbed a finger toward the exit. "Just go get it."

Looking every bit as confused as Vaughn felt, the two men stared back at her, still anchored in place.

"Now!"

Bill and Teddy flinched. Shocked into action by the sharpness of Angela's command, they quickly exited the room.

"And hurry! We don't have much time!" She looked toward the door. "BOb! Get your carbon-fiber ass in here!"

CHAPTER 56

Angela pointed at the screen. "BOb, can you load these coordinates into the BFG?"

Bending at the waist, the robot studied the display for a moment and then nodded. "Upload complete."

Vaughn looked from the robot to her face. "Uh … what are you doing, Angela?"

She held up a finger. "Hang on. We only have a couple of minutes before the overload goes critical."

The back door flew open.

Both of them flinched and turned to face it.

Vaughn raised his rifle.

Teddy peered around the opening. "Don't shoot, cowboy. It's just your friendly Rusky and his trusty sidekick." He stepped into the room, leading a cart that had the nuclear warhead riding its top. Bill entered behind him, pushing the back of the rolling shelf.

Vaughn lowered his gun.

The eyes of both men went wide as they looked past them and stared through the control room's observation window.

"Holy shit," Bill said. "It's getting bigger."

Angela nodded and waved them over impatiently. "Yeah, yeah. The wormhole is starting to respond to the power we're pumping into the collider. Get over here before it blows!"

Teddy shook his head and gestured at the nuke. "We're okay, Command-Oh. There's still five minutes left on it."

"No!" Angela pointed at the large window. She raised her voice above the increasing volume of the building energies. "I'm talking about the collider. It's gonna blow soon, but I need to do something first!"

Her eyes lost focus.

Vaughn could see that she was struggling with something. "Dammit, Angela! What are you working on?"

She ignored him. Instead, Angela turned and stared at the quaking sphere. "Why do the Necks come through the wormhole?"

Vaughn blinked at the non sequitur. "What?"

"When they got the coordinates for our dimension, why didn't they simply program a Tater to beam themselves here instead of Hell? Why only come through the wormhole?"

Bill Peterson shrugged. "I think it's for the same reason they left here before sending the light through: they must fear it."

Vaughn nodded. "Maybe it damages their circuitry."

Angela looked at Vaughn as if she'd forgotten he was still there. Then she slowly nodded as well. "It must rob them of their sentience."

Shrugging, Vaughn said, "Okay, but what the hell does that have to do with the here and now, Angela?"

The combined wail of the energy wave coupled with the coming overload threatened to shake his teeth from his jaw.

Vaughn's eyes flared. "You need to quit with your twenty questions already. This habit of yours got really old last time. What's up with the coordinates? What are you doing with the nuke? Spit it out, woman!"

Angela smiled at him and pointed at the computer screen. "I'm going to have BOb beam the nuke to those coordinates."

"To Hell?! What good does that do?"

"No. Those are the coordinates for the other end of the wormhole. It's where the Necks are coming from." She gave Vaughn a meaningful look. "It's where they are now."

A grin spread across Vaughn's face.

Bill guffawed. "Holy shit!

A laugh burst from Teddy. "Ha! Sweet!" He grabbed a Sharpie and bent over the nuclear warhead. A moment later, he stood and smiled broadly as he extended an arm and gestured to his handiwork.

The silver cone now sported a grinning visage above which was written:

From Russia With Love,
Mr. Nukey

CHAPTER 57

Standing next to Vaughn, Angela pointed at the modified BFG and looked up into BOb's emotionless gray face. "Please tell me you still have one shot left in that thing."

The bot dipped its head. "Yes, Commander Brown. I'm receiving multiple glitches per minute, and the circuitry is on the verge of burnout. However, the wiring harness still has sufficient continuity to convey one more discharge, and the time between BIT failures is long enough to permit the weapon's activation."

During the battlebot's verbose answer, Vaughn flexed his jaw against the pain rising in his ears. "Dammit, BOb! *Yes* would've been fine."

"Sorry, Captain Asshole."

Wide-eyed, Bill turned from the spasming wormhole and stared at Angela. "What are you waiting for? Beam the thing to the bastards already."

Watching the sphere, Angela shook her head and yelled over the cacophony. "Just a couple more minutes. If we do it too soon, they'll just beam it back."

A glint drew Vaughn's eye to the partially opened drawer where Teddy had found the Sharpie. A pair of small discs shone from its bottom. They looked like inch-wide CDs. Looking at Angela, he pointed. "What are these things?"

Angela glanced over and then did a double-take. Her eyes went wide, and she began to run a finger across the front of the computer. It stopped on a small opening that had 'Arch Mission Foundation' stenciled above it. An identical unit sat just beneath it.

Sitting bolt upright, she thrust out a hand. "Give 'em to me!"

He plucked the coin-sized discs from the drawer and handed them to her. "What are they?"

She plugged one into each of the two apparent drives. "They're Arch discs, like the ones Elon Musk sent up with Starman."

Vaughn nodded. "I remember that. They were in the Tesla Roadster he launched on the Falcon Heavy back in 2018. Those discs can hold a shit-ton of data."

Typing quickly, Angela nodded. "Yeah, and they're supposed to last forever."

"What are you doing with them?"

She punched in a final command, and twinned progress bars started to slide across the screen. "I'm copying the Necks' program and all the coordinates onto them."

Vaughn blinked. "You. Are. A. Fucking. Genius!" He palmed Angela's face with both hands and kissed her. "Have I mentioned how much I love you?"

Bill pulled his gaze from the slowly swelling sphere. "Are you sure that's a good idea?"

Angela shrugged. "It's insurance."

"Against what, Command-Oh?"

"I don't know, Teddy, but I'd rather have it and not need it than—"

Silvery spikes began to rupture from the exterior of the wormhole. They rose and fell in rapid waves that raced across its curved surface.

Vaughn shouted, "It's time, Angela!"

Staring at the progress bars, she nodded briskly.

BOb raised the weapon and aimed it at the nuke. Then the robot looked at Vaughn.

The floor lurched beneath their feet, nearly knocking all five of them down. The nuclear device rocked on its cart and almost toppled.

Across the ATLAS facility, curtains of lightning danced across the spiderweb-like network of conduits.

Tremendous thunder cracked the air.

Vaughn pointed at the nuke and shouted, "Beam it out now, BOb!"

In his peripheral vision, he saw Angela stand up and eject the two discs. Then she jammed them into a pant pocket.

Flames exploded from the facility's far side, launching a racing wall of churning fire straight at the control window.

Bill and Teddy took a backward step, but Angela and Vaughn stood transfixed, watching BOb.

The bot squeezed the trigger.

White light shot out from the business end of the BFG.

The nuke and most of the cart vanished just as the orange fire began to claw at the observation window's glass face.

Then the insanely undulating surface of the wormhole pushed through everything, wrapping Vaughn and the rest of his team in its weightless black void.

CHAPTER 58

"Today, vee shall plumb the deepest reaches of the quantum realm. The collider's High-Luminosity upgrade vill shine the light of discovery upon hidden dimensions und singularities."

Hans had said those words for the benefit of both the reporter and her cameraman just a few short minutes ago.

He frowned.

Now he looked like the world's biggest jackass.

As the director of CERN's High-Luminosity upgrade, he'd expected to stand the world of theoretical physics on its head, but instead, he was standing here with a thumb up his ass and a multibillion-dollar collider upgrade that didn't work.

The first attempt to generate collisions at the collider's new and significantly increased power levels had resulted in a resounding thud.

He'd been certain this was going to be his Nobel Prize.

Now he'd be the laughing stock of academia.

Hans placed a hand over his heart, fingering the place where the metal would've hung.

A slap on his back snapped him from his silent mourning.

Blinking, he spun to face the interloper. "Vhat?!"

Sampson flinched and took a backward step. He coughed. "Sorry to disturb you, Doctor." The man paused, and his face brightened. "I think I found the problem."

The scowl melted from Hans's face. He hoisted hopeful eyebrows. "Vhat, vhat? Vhat have you found?"

"It was an interference pattern, electronic noise, I think. It started the instant we applied full power, but it's gone now."

Hans stepped around the man and bent over the console. "Are you certain, Sampson?"

The man nodded. "We just applied full power for a short burst, not long enough to create any of the highest energy collisions, but there was no sign of the noise."

"Do you have a record of the anomaly? Ve vill vant to research that further later."

"Yes, Doctor Garfield. We captured all the data. I have Stillman analyzing it now."

"Sehr gut!" Hans clapped his hands together. Smiling broadly, he added, "Let us resume the experiment."

CHAPTER 59

The black void swallowed Angela.

All sense of space and time ceased to exist. She simply was.

Then light flooded back into her world, and an all-too-familiar sensation of falling gripped her.

Bill's voice burst from the speakers in her helmet. "Oh, geez! ... What's happening?!"

Squinting against the bright light, Angela shook her head. "Oh, no ... No, no, no. The reset happened, but we're still floating in our spacesuits!" She stopped fumbling for the helmet's visor lever. "Wait ... The light isn't that bright."

Blinking furiously, she finally managed to bring her surroundings into focus just as Bill's gauntleted hand struck her visor. The disoriented man was flailing his arms.

Angela reached out and grabbed his wrist. "Bill! It's okay. We're back, but we're still in the airlock."

"Wh-What?" He stopped pinwheeling his arms. Blinking, he looked around and then locked onto her eyes. "How? ... When?"

"The reset worked! It pushed us farther back in time. We haven't started our spacewalk!" She looked around, and a smile crept across her face. "We haven't even gotten to the outer half of the airlock yet."

Eyes widening, she looked toward the hatch that led to the heart of the space station. "Where are you, Teddy?"

No good. The helmet muffled her words.

Releasing Bill's wrist, Angela wrenched off her gloves and flung them aside. She clawed at her spacesuit's neck ring with scrambling fingers. Unlatching the acrylic dome, she yanked it from her suit and tossed it aside. "Teddy!"

CHAPTER 60

Hans watched the building energy levels. It appeared Sampson was correct. There'd been no further sign of the interference that had collapsed the first run.

He looked at the reporter and gave her his best smile. "Soon, vee vill reach HiLumi's maximum center-of-mass energy level."

"Oh? How high is that?"

"Vee are not quite sure yet, but it could be as high as twenty-five TeV if vee are lucky. After that, vee vill begin proton-proton collisions."

Subvocalizing, he added, "Und I vill finally earn my Nobel Prize."

The reporter's face twisted. "TeV?"

"Tera electronvolts, Miss Preston. It's a unit of energy used in particle physics. One TeV is roughly equivalent to—"

"Doctor Garfield, I think we found something."

Blinking, Hans turned away from the reporter. "Vhat did you find, Sampson?"

"Stillman was able to isolate the noise. He says it looks like a … a video."

"That is ridiculous." Shaking his head, Hans walked over to the technician's workstation. "Video? How could video enter our system?"

The man shook his head. "I'm not sure, Doctor Garfield, but here it is. I have it queued up now."

Hans pointed at the man's screen. "Let us see it, then."

The man nodded. A few mouse clicks later, a distorted video popped up on the display.

Hans blinked and stood upright. "Vhat is the meaning of this?! Is this some kind of practical joke?"

In spite of the grainy quality of the video, it was apparent that the person standing at its center was Hans. He could see his lips moving on the screen.

Looking around, he saw Stillman and Sampson shaking their heads.

Narrowing his eyes, Hans pointed to the technician. "Turn up the volume."

A moment later, Hans's voice came from the computer's small speaker. "...shine the light of discovery onto hidden dimensions und singularities."

Standing upright, Hans turned and glared at the reporter. "It's your recording!" The cameraman beside her was still filming. Hans pointed at him. "Your camcorder is interfering with our collider." He pointed toward the exit. "You must remove it at once. Leave!"

In the corner of his eye, Hans saw Stillman shaking his head. "No, Doctor Garfield. I don't think that's what it is."

Hans glanced at the collider's displayed energy level. It was nearing the threshold. He turned his ire on the technician. "Vhat are you talking about?! Of course it is the camera. Vhat else can it be, idiot?"

The man's face reddened. Extending an arm, he pointed at the screen, indicating a series of numbers at its bottom right corner. "There are more minutes of video in this file then there have been since you said those words, Doctor Garfield." The man tilted his head and then leaned in for a closer look. Then he shook his head. "And this file is more than a week old."

Hans looked from the man to the camera and back to the screen. Finally, he shook his head in disgust. "All of these *connected devices*!

Someone must've hacked the man's camcorder. It is as simple as that."

"Do you want me to stop the experiment?" Sampson asked.

Hans gave a sharp shake of his head. "No, no. Vee vill not let those bastards vin."

"But sir," Stillman interjected. "If you think we've been hacked, don't you think we should—?"

"Nein! The experiment continues." Hans eyed the power level. It was nearing the threshold. "Prepare for proton-proton collisions."

CHAPTER 61

Haloed by his now grimy mane of reddish-blond hair, Teddy's dirt-streaked, sweaty face floated into the opening at the station's side of the airlock. Still in his combat fatigues and battle rattle, the man looked like a misplaced, ginger G.I. Joe having a bad hair day. "Command-Oh! It worked!" Then the smile plastered across his freckled face faltered. "Did we go back far enough? Have we stopped robot invasion?"

"I don't know!"

"You want to call Director McCree?"

Angela shook her head and jabbed a finger toward the heart of the ISS. "No time for that. Stick to the plan. We'll do this just as we briefed. Get the IP phone booted up. I'll be right there."

The man nodded briskly and then disappeared into the station.

She looked back at Bill as she squirmed out of her spacesuit.

The major had removed his helmet. He gave her a thumbs-up. "I'll call McCree and tell him to contact CERN, just as we briefed."

"Still got the number memorized?"

He cocked an eyebrow at Angela and waved her on. "I got this, Commander. Get the hell out of here."

Angela nodded. During their travels across the Atlantic, she had made everyone in the group memorize the telephone numbers for both CERN and Doctor Garfield's mobile.

She wiggled side-to-side, struggling to extract her upper body from the spacesuit. It took a couple of extra tugs as some of her military gear hung up on the thing. Finally, she extricated herself and then quickly exited the module. "Teddy! I better hear a goddamn ringtone by the time I get there!"

CHAPTER 62

F inally rid of the reporter and her cameraman, Hans watched the energy levels build. He was happy to see that it had surpassed twenty TeV and was still climbing. Once it peaked, he would have Sampson initiate the collisions.

Just as he had the thought, Hans heard the man talking behind him.

"Stillman, fast-forward through the video. Let's see what else is in there."

Hans rolled his eyes but didn't say anything. He just continued to watch the numbers climb.

"Doctor Garfield!" Sampson shouted out a moment later, yelling sharply enough to make Hans jump. "Y-You need to see this."

Pressing his lips together, Hans shook his head.

He turned from the display and walked heavily to the technician's workstation. "Vhat is …?" He paused mid-sentence and stared at the video.

The ATLAS detector sat at its center, what was left of it anyway. The entire structure was crumbling down like paper being wadded into a ball. Light rays shot out from it, burning through the facility at odd angles.

Seeing people moving too quickly in the foreground, Hans realized that the video was still in fast-forward. The icon at the bottom right corner indicated four times normal speed. A moment later, the ATLAS detector finished its collapse, leaving nothing but a levitating metallic sphere.

Then something emerged from its top. Hans pointed at the display. "Stop the video!"

Stillman complied, and the image froze.

Unblinking, Hans stared at the orb and the apparent robot that now protruded from its top. Then he turned to look through the window at the currently intact and functional ATLAS experiment. A quick check of the power display showed that the collider had peaked at twenty-three TeV.

They were ready to begin collisions.

The power level had fallen a little short of the hoped-for twenty-five TeV, but it was sufficient to garner a Noble Prize, nonetheless.

Narrowing his eyes, he looked back at the video. Could hackers really do something this elaborate?

He thought maybe they could.

Hans flinched as the mobile phone inside the pocket of his lab coat began to ring.

Still staring at the frozen image, he extracted the device and accepted the call. Distractedly, he said, "This is Doctor—"

"Hans!" shouted a familiar-sounding female voice, cutting off his words. "Stop the experiment! Do not initiate any collisions!"

"Doctor …? Doctor Brown?"

"Yes, yes, Hans. Shut it down! Shut it down now!"

Hans eyed the energy level. Twenty-three TeV. He need only flip the switch, and he'd have his Nobel.

He turned his gaze back to the frozen video. "Vas it you, Angela? Did you send me this message? Is this some kind of practical joke?"

"It's no fucking joke, Hans. I sent you that message more than a week from today."

"A veek ago? Vhy?" Remembering his speech at the beginning of the video, he added, "That's not even possible. I just said those vords a few minutes ago."

"Not a week in the past, Hans, a week in the future, a *very bad* future. Stop the experiment, or you're going to kill us all."

Hans opened his mouth, but then it snapped shut as he recalled Stillman's words. 'The video is more than a week old.'

Doctor Hans Garfield was a rational man. The rational part of his mind told him that a message from a week in the future was impossible, but the part of him that truly understood the quantum realm knew that time didn't exist within the portion of the universe they were delving. That same part of his mind began to scream that perhaps he was about to open a door that could not be closed.

"Oh, scheisse! Stop the experiment! Kill it. Kill it now!"

Everyone turned and stared at him.

No one moved to follow his order.

Hans pushed past Sampson and bent over the workstation.

He flipped open the clear acrylic cover.

Sampson threw out his hands. "Wait! What are you doing?!"

Hans hammered the wide red button twice, activating the emergency power disconnect.

The omnipresent electrical thrumming of the collider rapidly faded and then died as mechanical actuators around the entire circumference of the ring physically cut the electrical wires, inflicting millions of dollars in damage and robbing the network of its power supply.

The overhead lights went dark, activation of the emergency lights signaling complete failure of all facility power.

Sampson stared at him with wide eyes. "What have you done?"

Breathing heavily, Hans stared at ATLAS through the control room window. "For the sake of my career, I hope I have saved the vorld."

CHAPTER 63

As she drifted toward the module, Angela heard Bill yelling inside. "You don't understand, Director!"

She allowed her inertia to carry her through the opening and into the Destiny module.

"Listen, McCree!" Bill shouted. "I need you to—!" He stopped mid-sentence as he saw her.

Angela smiled and gave him a thumbs-up.

Myriad emotions washed across the man's face, and tears began to flood his eyes. "Oh, thank you. Thank you, thank…" The man's voice cracked, and then he lost his words.

She knew thoughts of his family, now alive and well back home, would be crowding out all other thoughts.

Angela gently took the headset from Bill. She slipped it on and positioned the mic boom in front of her mouth. "Director McCree?"

"Angela! What the hell is going on up there?"

"I'll explain it all to you in a minute, sir, but first there's someone I need you to call."

"Is this more of that CERN thing? I couldn't make heads or tails of what Bill was saying." Randy paused, his voice suddenly becoming unsure. "But the damnedest thing is that, somehow, some of it seemed … familiar."

"I can't tell you how glad I am to hear that, Director. I promise, I'll tell you more soon, but first, we need to make that phone call, and no, it's not to Geneva. Teddy is on the IP phone with them now, filling in the scientists there on the rest of the details. The call that I need you to make will be to a location a bit closer than Europe."

CHAPTER 64

S tanding in the locker room and partially clad in his spacesuit, Vaughn growled in frustration at his mobile phone. "It's still busy!"

Mark shook his head. "Mine, too!"

Vaughn looked at Mark and smiled in spite of their dire situation. "I can't tell you how good it is to see you back alive, my friend."

"I can't tell you how good it is to be *seen* alive ... again. I just hope we get to stay that way. If we can't get a hold of someone soon, we're going to have to get back inside the vacuum chamber."

Vaughn blew out a breath. "God forbid."

Releasing a frustrated growl of his own, Mark hammered the end-call button. An instant later, his phone began to ring.

The two men exchanged glances.

The phone rang again.

Vaughn pointed. "Are you going to answer that?"

Mark stared at the device for a moment and then handed it to Vaughn. "I think it's for you. It's Houston."

Clutching the mobile in a suddenly shaky hand, Vaughn pressed the answer-call button and then held the phone to his ear.

"H-Hello?"

"This is Angela, Vaughn!"

He smiled. The line was crackling as if it were coming through a relay, but by the tone in Angela's words and the smile in her voice, Vaughn knew all was right with the world.

"Angela-Vaughn, huh? That's an unusual name. What are the odds?"

EPILOGUE

Angela stared around the conference room. A wan smile twisted the corners of her mouth.

Walking from her, Vaughn stepped over to Mark and wrapped his friend in a bear hug. "Good to see you, buddy."

"You, too, Vaughn."

After slapping each other on the back, the men parted, and Vaughn looked up at Mark. "Well, Chewie. How have they been treating you?"

The tall man massaged the back of his neck. "I've had worse." He winced. "Although I can't remember when."

Releasing a soft chuckle, Vaughn nodded.

Angela shifted her attention to another part of the expansive room. Bill and Teddy, the ever-inseparable pair, were reuniting, hugging each other and having a conversation similar to Mark and Vaughn's. As with the other men, the two of them looked significantly better than they had last time she'd seen them.

Teddy laughed at something Bill said. The cosmonaut shook his head, causing his puffed-out ball of tied-back, strawberry-blond ringlets to bounce back and forth comically.

Looking at the man's now much cleaner hair, Angela ran fingers through hers. The military had supplied a barber to cut and tame her near-dreadlocks. For the first time in ages, it felt soft, light, and a bit shorter. Its trimmed auburn tips slipped through her fingers.

She studied the back of her hand. The various cuts, nicks, and bruises had all but healed, leaving light, untanned marks in their wake. She hoped none would leave permanent scars.

As she brushed the hair from her face, it fell listlessly across the side of her right cheek. When the military finally released her, she was going to make a beeline straight to the nearest stylist.

Blowing the lock from her eyes, she scoffed. "First-world problems."

The smile fell from her lips.

If only minor concerns were all she had to worry about.

She sighed and then flinched as a voice spoke just a few inches from her ear.

"Looks like I'll be able to get back to the telescope soon."

Before she could stop herself, Angela spun toward the person and grabbed his shirt.

Rourke stared at her with wide eyes. He held up his hands. "S-Sorry."

"No, no." Releasing the man, Angela straightened the lapels of his blazer. "It's not you. It's me."

A crooked smile banished the shocked look. "If only I had a nickel."

Chuckling, Angela punched the man in the shoulder. "Yeah, I'm sure." She threw her arms around Rourke and hugged him fiercely. "It's so good to see you, Doctor!"

He hugged her back. It's good to see you, too, *Doctor*," he said, emphasizing her title through a chuckle. "I wanted to say hello earlier, but I saw you chatting with Monique and Rachel. Then Vaughn arrived, so ... you know."

Angela smiled. Not the wan one she'd had earlier but a full, wide grin. "I'm just happy all of you Team Two folks made it to the other side." She hugged him again and then kissed his cheek. "You were so brave, Rourke. Thank you for all you did. I don't think the world will ever know how much it owes you."

He blushed and then shrugged. "We all did it together."

Angela stared past him for a moment and then nodded. "I just wish we had more to convince the government of how desperate our situation is."

Seeing the man's confused look, she said, "Never mind about that for now."

Hair had fallen across her right eye again. She blew it out of her face. "What was that about a telescope?"

He blinked at her sudden course reversal. "Oh, that. I was just saying I'm looking forward to getting back to work on the James Webb Space Telescope."

"Oh, yeah. Guess it's back in one piece now?"

He smiled. "Yep. Safe and sound inside the vacuum chamber. My interrogators were really confused when I asked about its destruction."

Angela winced. She pointed at Bill and Teddy. "We've only been going through the grilling for the five days since we landed the Soyuz. They've been going at you guys for a week now."

He shrugged. "It hasn't been too bad. I just wish they'd answer some of my questions. They're not saying much."

"I know. Everything's a big damned secret with them."

Chance Bingham stepped up, his usual scowl firmly in place. The man positively reeked of righteous indignation. "When in bloody hell will we get to see our families?"

Angela nodded. "I hear you."

And she'd heard him the first ten times, too, although she knew the man was right to be upset, all of them were. They had saved the world, but all they were getting was questions and non-verbalized accusations.

She looked around the spacious conference room. "I just wish they'd tell us something. I mean, I've been able to track the news and contact a few people via email, but I'm sure all of that has been filtered or screened or whatever."

Bingham's frown deepened. "Yes, yes, I've been able to email my family, and I've maintained the instructed cover story: that we're in a surprise, short-duration, simulated space mission as part of our training." He gestured angrily at the conference room's distant wall. "It might only have been a few days to these twits, but dammit, it's been more than two weeks for me."

The same door through which Vaughn had entered suddenly opened, and Randall McCree walked into the room with the battle operations bot in tow.

Angela broke from her conversation and sprinted over to the two of them. "Randy!" She threw her arms around the director and hugged him tightly.

BOb watched the exchange with mechanical curiosity.

Releasing the man, she smiled up at McCree. "Thank you for all your help. We couldn't have done it without you."

The director smiled sheepishly. "I just wish I had clearer memories of whatever it is I did."

Angela nodded. "Maybe it'll come to you in time."

"Maybe. Doctor Andrew, the ass-can I supposedly sent into the chamber with the rest of you doesn't remember much either."

Vaughn walked up to him and extended a hand. "Vaughn Singleton. Pleasure to finally meet you, Director."

Randy gave Vaughn an inscrutable look but then shook the proffered hand. "Same here, Captain."

Looking back, Angela saw that the other eight members of the team had gathered around the new arrivals. Over the next several minutes, they asked the man myriad questions, but it turned out he was just as in the dark as were the rest of them.

"How are you doing, BOb?" Monique asked, smiling at the robot.

The bot looked at Lieutenant Gheist. "The week has been long." BOb drooped his shoulders and melodramatically wiped the back of a hand across his carbon-fiber forehead. "It's a dog-eat-dog world, and apparently, I'm wearing bacon-wrapped underwear."

Angela placed a hand over her mouth and stifled a laugh. Not for the first time, she wondered if BOb's programmers may have unknowingly imparted the bot with sentience or something close to it.

"Hola, BOb," Teddy said with a wide grin. "Dude! Where's your BFG?"

Monique held up a hand. "I will take this one." Turning, she addressed the group. "During my debriefings, I was permitted to contact a colleague at DARPA. I instructed her to secure any new equipment that they might find in BOb's possession, including any weapons," pausing, she gave them a meaningful look, "and the modified BFG." She nodded. "Yes, it came back with him, although it now seems completely inert. They have not been able to get anything from it. My friend said its circuits were completely fried." She frowned and added, "As were BOb's memories."

Angela peaked her brows. "All his memories?"

Shaking her head, Monique said, "Only the ones associated with his time with us."

"What about his stored archives?" Rourke asked. "Weren't there video logs?"

Monique rubbed BOb's shoulder. "All gone."

"Wait. What?" Vaughn paused and looked at the robot. "You don't remember anything prior to a week ago?"

"Of course I do, Captain Singleton. I have complete memories of my time working in DARPA. I even recall working with Lieutenant Gheist … before she left me for NASA." The robot tilted its head. "However, my internal clock tells me there is a gap of several days' worth of data."

"My associate ran a full set of diagnostics on our mechanical friend," Monique added. "Aside from the wiped memory sectors, he seems completely intact."

Bingham leaned in and inspected the bot. "How does the wanker know our names, then?"

She winked at Angela. "I had my friend upload them."

Vaughn cocked an eyebrow. "Did they work on his humor?"

BOb looked at him quizzically. "Why would they do that, Captain Asshole?"

The director guffawed, which caused the room to burst out in laughter.

Even Bingham's omnipresent scowl faded as he, too, chortled.

Seeing the look on Randy's face followed by the reactions of the others, caused Angela's initial chuckle to dissolve into one of her patented snort storms, which, in turn, led to another burst of laughter from the gathering.

After a few moments, the hysterics began to diminish.

Angela wiped tears from her eyes and saw a few others doing the same, including Vaughn.

He collected himself and cast a mock scowl at Monique. "Thanks for nothing."

An uncharacteristic smirk spread across the naval lieutenant's face. "They asked if anyone preferred a nickname, and I remembered how much you loved that one."

Vaughn pointed at BOb. "Don't make me change your name back to COC-RING."

"How did you know my original—?"

Monique waved a hand. "Never mind Captain Asshole, BOb."

The exchange elicited a short round of giggles.

Having drifted across the expansive room, the group started to sit in the chairs that ringed the large circular table that served as the chamber's focal point.

As they had moved, Angela had seen Vaughn look toward the door more than once. Even now, he was stealing glances in its general direction.

She narrowed her eyes. *What are you up to, mister?*

Turning from the door, Vaughn saw her staring at him. She gave him a pointed look. "Why are we here?"

The corners of his mouth twisted downward, and he shook his head. "No idea."

Even as he said it, Vaughn glanced at the door and then back at her. He might have fooled everyone else, but she knew him well enough to know when he had something up his sleeve. She'd seen Vaughn acting like this back in Tripoli when he was about to reveal the *Angela's Dream*.

Deciding to let it go, for now, Angela took a seat between Vaughn and Monique.

Rourke leaned forward in his chair and looked around the table. Then his eyes locked onto Angela's. "Maybe that's why the Necks won't go through the white light."

"What do you mean, Rourky?"

Turning to look at Rachel, Rourke responded, "The Necks appear to only travel between dimensions using wormholes. Maybe the light wave damages their memories like the reset wiped BOb's."

"We talked about the same thing," Angela said. "I think it might rob them of their sentience."

Monique nodded slowly. "Basically, we are the sum of our memories. They shape us, form us. We interact with the world based on what the memories of past actions have taught us."

"Exactly!" Rourke pointed to BOb. "If passing through the light robbed our bot of its memories, maybe it does the same thing to the Necks."

Vaughn grinned. "So it turns them into vegetables."

Chance smiled menacingly. "I fancy the idea of rendering their entire race into drooling dolts. They certainly didn't hesitate to do worse to us."

Angela shook her head. "I don't know. The light didn't affect BOb's memory. He didn't lose any when they beamed him to Hell … or any of the other times he beamed himself to and from the place."

"It's all a moot point now," Mark Hennessy interrupted. He held out his hands. "Vaughn told me you guys nuked the bastards. That should set 'em back a bit."

Teddy nodded excitedly. "Da! Mister Nukey should have blasted them back to Commodore-Sixty-Four age, yes?"

Angela shook her head. "No. I think the reset of the timeline undid the nuke."

Vaughn regarded her through knitted brows. "Undid it? Why? It was set to blow." He raised an arm and pointed at his scarred wrist. "We returned with our cuts and bruises. Our perceived timeline has continuity. If anything, the nuke should have ..." His eyes lost focus and then went round. "Oh shit."

Angela had already worked her way through this thought experiment. She watched as Vaughn did the same.

He looked at McCree, mounting horror evident in his face. "Did ...? Did we nuke a submarine?!"

The director looked at him, the non sequitur rendering the man mute for a moment. Finally, he shook his head. "I'm pretty sure I would have heard about something like that."

Vaughn began to nod slowly. "I imagine you'd have heard if a pair of nukes went missing, too."

"Yes ... We have contingencies to add orbital assets to the search effort should one, or two, nuclear devices go missing, but ... why ...?" Then realization dawned on the man's face. The same look suddenly registered across the visages of several other attendees.

Nodding, Angela held out a hand. "The reset returned the nukes to their starting point, just like it did to us, but fortunately, the memory dump must have wiped its timer. Regardless, we can't assume the Necks are no longer a threat." She looked around the room and gave each team member a meaningful look. "It gets worse. We also can't assume they no longer know of our dimension."

Shouts of 'What?!' rang out.

Frowning, she tilted her head. "We may have lost our multiversal anonymity." Seeing the confusion deepen on several faces, she added, "The Necks might know we're here now."

"What?!" Bingham boomed, Angela's proclamation finally drawing the man off his single-minded track. "How? We reset the timeline to a point before your mates at CERN could create a black hole. The bloody Necks had nothing to detect. They shouldn't even know we exist!"

"*You* know they exist."

The man opened his mouth to protest, but then it snapped shut.

"Son of a ..." Bill started, but then he, too, fell silent.

Angela dipped her head. "We kept our memories through the reset, so it's possible some of the Necks did as well."

"Oh, no, Command-Oh."

"I know, Teddy. It sucks." Angela paused and looked at the rest of the team members. "But that's what we're left with." She nodded to Vaughn. "Looks like we'll get to test your theory."

"My theory?"

"Yeah, back when we were trapped in the time loop, you said the Necks were right to fear us, that humanity wouldn't sit by idly if we knew a race of land-hungry robots were sitting on our multiversal doorstep."

"I still think that, but how the hell can we do anything about it now? My scenario was *if* we had the same ability to cross into other universes. We don't have the hardware or the tech, and what we did have got fried."

Angela extracted the Arch disc she'd managed to keep on her person.

Vaughn's eyes went wide. "You still have them."

Nodding, she held it up. "This one, anyway." She turned and addressed the entire group. "Turns out, physical memory isn't wiped by time resets. This one still has all the data I downloaded. It's still intact."

Confusion clouded the faces of Team One.

"I managed to pluck the Necks' program and their coordinates from CERN's network before the reset." She wagged the disc. "It's all still here."

"How do you know?" Monique asked.

"My interrogator, I mean debriefer, verified that the one I surrendered still had viable data." She held up a hand. "Don't worry. Based on my insistence, she used an air-gapped computer." Seeing confusion on a few of the faces, she added, "A computer not connected to a network. Didn't want any alien viruses getting in."

They nodded their understanding.

Vaughn pointed at the small optical disc. "What good does that do us? I thought it was just the alien software and their coordinates. Without the hardware, it's as useless as a football bat."

Angela smiled and raised an eyebrow. "I saw something else when I was loading the files."

Bill blinked. "And you're just now telling us?"

"As you may recall, we were a bit pressed for time at that moment."

Monique leaned in. "What did you see?"

"They appeared to be circuitry designs."

Rourke's face lit up. "Designs for what?"

Shrugging, Angela said, "Looked like a light wave emitter to me."

Shocked into silence, everyone stared at her mutely.

Then their heads turned as a knock rang out from the room's single entrance.

Vaughn's face lit up. Jumping to his feet, he ran over and cracked open the door. After peeking out, he nodded and then turned to face the room's occupants.

The man was practically bursting with excitement. It was the same look he'd given her when he'd pulled off her blindfold in Tripoli.

He shared a conspiratorial grin with McCree, and Angela realized that whatever this was, the two men had conspired to make it happen. That explained the mysterious look Randy had given Vaughn.

"Ladies and gentlemen." Vaughn paused theatrically and then flung open the door. "I believe I've found someone you'd all like to see."

A group of faces looked out from the opening.

The head of a small, dark-skinned girl peered through a gap. "Daddy!"

Bill bolted from his seat and ran across the room. He scooped up his daughter and hugged her tightly. Then he wrapped up his wife in the bear hug.

Angela watched the scene repeat across the room. Someone even walked in holding a pair of cats, raising a cheer from Monique.

As she watched it all develop, Angela wished her mom was still around. She'd have loved to share this with her.

It was good that the rest of them were getting this opportunity. They should enjoy the moment. Soon, it would be time for humanity to go on the offensive in this multiversal war.

Angela pictured the Neck who had tried to drag her through the wormhole during the first timeline reset. Narrowing her eyes, she swore an oath under her breath. "Whatever it takes, I'm coming for you."

Someone tapped her shoulder.

Angela turned to see Vaughn standing next to her.

An elderly waif of a woman was clutching his arm. A tattoo featuring a winged electric guitar protruded from one of her shirt-sleeves. She was positively beaming.

Vaughn smiled at Angela and winked. Then he looked down into the woman's face. "Mom, I have someone very special I'd like you to meet."

AFTERWORD

Well, what do you think? Enjoyed the ride?

Thought I would take a moment to pop in and chat with you about where we are and how we got here ... and, more importantly, where we go from this point.

A lot of people ask how I got the idea for *Solitude*. It started while I was on an apocalyptic-focused reader form. We were discussing what you would do if you woke up to discover that you were the last person on Earth. Assuming one could get past the emotional aspect, what kind of crazy shit would you get into, given the entire world at your disposal. Of course, this assumes that all of humanity's toys are still lying around just waiting to be played with.

My answer to this question led directly to the creation of *Solitude*.

As long as I can remember, I've wanted to be an astronaut. Even made it part of the way, having flown jets high up in the atmosphere. However, if the world had ended and I had nothing left to lose, why not cross into the final frontier. I'll bet there's something parked at the not-so-secret airbase in Area Fifty-One that could get me all the way there, and being a rated pilot in both helicopters and jets, I'd also bet I could fly it.

Why not? What the hell.

Cool, I had the beginnings of a story, but I needed a reason to go to space—other than just for the hell of it. So I stranded a beautiful woman up there.

What more motivation could a red-blooded hetero man want, right?

So I had the last man and the last woman along with a plausible motivation to go to space, but I needed a reason for them to be *the last*.

Enter the Necks.

You know what happened after that, but what happens next?

Those no-neck-havin' mother effers got to go, that's what.

There just ain't enough room in the multiverse for us both.

This brings me to the next Dimension Space trilogy. Magnitude, the fourth book in the series, is coming soon (cover preview on the next page). It'll kick off the second DS trilogy, *Multiverse War*, with the scale of a space marine war epic while retaining the characters you've (hopefully) come to love and adding a few more.

What do you think? What plot twists would you like to see? What crazy shit would you get into if you were the last person on the planet? Give me a shout by using the social media or email links in the About the Author page at the end of this book. I'd love to hear from you.

Finally, I need to ask a favor. I'd truly appreciate a review of *Amplitude*. In this day of e-marketing, you have the power to make or break a book. Please post a review for *Amplitude* to its page on your favorite book retailer's website.

Now for the bonus question. Did you catch all three Expeditionary Force Easter eggs? I'm a huge fan of Craig Alanson and his books. I'm also fortunate enough to count him as a friend. Thanks to our shared audiobook narrator, R.C. Bray, we also share many fans. Those Easter eggs were for you. I hope they elicited a laugh or three.

Thank you so much for reading *Amplitude* and for being my copilot on this adventure. Don't forget to follow me on your favorite site by clicking the appropriate links on the About the Author page.

Fly safe!

Dean M. Cole
Seabrook, TX

Magnitude: Dimension Space Book Four

Enter your email address at deanmcole.com/notify to get an alert when Magnitude comes out.

It's war!

We've pushed the Necks from our world, but we can't hope they won't find another way to eradicate Earth's life. When Angela sends a probe to the coordinates she tried to nuke, it reveals a massive threat. If we are to survive, we must unite. With our very existence on the line, humanity will take the battle to the enemy. If you enjoyed *Multitude*, you'll love the epic scale and plot twists in this all out war for survival.

Sector 64: Sneak Peek

The *Sector 64* Timeline
1947 - *First Contact* a *Sector 64* Prequel Novella
Today - *Ambush - Book One of the Sector 64 Duology*
Tomorrow - *Retribution - Book Two of the Sector 64 Duology*

Seventy years after the events of *First Contact*, most of humanity is completely unaware of the coming changes. We live and die believing we are alone. In 2017, Air Force fighter pilots Jake Giard and Sandra Fitzpatrick discover the decades-old secret project to integrate Earth into a galactic government, but then the plot renders our world a disposable pawn. An interstellar war spills onto our shores, plunging the planet into an otherworldly post-apocalyptic hell. Can Jake and Sandy save humanity from extinction? If you like action-packed, page-turning novels, then you'll love the electrifying action in this apocalyptic thriller.

SECTOR 64: AMBUSH SNEAK PEEK

Captain Sandra Fitzpatrick's steady rhythmic breathing, a technique born through years of cardio training, belied the horror gripping her soul. The teddy bear, oh God, the teddy bear. An image she couldn't shake, the vision would haunt her for the rest of her days.

Earlier, while jogging toward the distant terminal building, Sandy came across a still idling airport transfer bus. Hoping to use it to expedite the crossing, she peered into its closed glass doors. In spite of the eastern glow of the coming sunrise, she couldn't discern details through its dirty windows. However, the bus looked empty.

Jamming her fingers into the rubber gap between the panels, Sandy tried to pry the split glass doors apart. After a fruitless, half-minute struggle, she finally noticed a backlit, recessed emergency-release button left of the door. Activating it, Sandy heard a short blast of compressed air. She jumped as the doors popped two inches out of their opening and then parted, each sliding in opposite directions.

"Hello?"

No reply rose above the bus's droning diesel engine.

She took a tentative step into the opening. "Is anybody in here?"

Standing half in the doorway, Sandy screamed as two strong hands, squeezing from both sides, grasped her shoulders. Another blast of compressed air burped from under the bus, and the door trying to close on her retracted.

"Shit!" Sandy kicked the right panel of the retreating glass door and shook her head. Keep it together, Captain Fitzpatrick. She stepped all the way into the bus, and its doors slid closed. Air-conditioner blower noise replaced the engine's. Getting over her skittishness, she stepped into the driver's compartment. In the dawn's wan light, the seat looked empty. Groping in the darkness, Sandy worked her way closer. A few awkward seconds later, she finally dropped into it.

Something was wrong with the seat. It felt like someone had left a towel or cloth on it. Running her fingers across the material's loose, rippled surface, Sandy froze, remembering what she saw while peering down into the empty F-18's cockpit. An uncomfortable hard object dug into her right thigh. Wide-eyed in the dark, she leaned left and pulled it out from under her leg. Breathlessly holding the object up, she studied its angular silhouette against the deep turquoise hue of the early morning sky. A round ball on one end and a long rod on the other, it felt metallic. With her opposite hand, she blindly searched the instrument panel for a light switch. A huge windshield wiper arm sparked to life, its dry, rubber blade chattering against the dirty glass. Another switch later, the bus's cabin lit up like an exam room. Sandy blinked and squinted as the sudden blast of light burned her dark adapted eyes.

Finally able to see, she squinted at the device in her hand. Struggling not to scream, Sandy dropped the artificial hip. Jumping to her feet, she looked down to see a bus driver's uniform strewn across the compartment. While the driver's shirt was on the floor, the pants, belt still buckled, lay in the seat. She saw several shiny objects littering the interior of the pants. Bending, she looked closer. In a sudden epiphany, she recognized the parts as titanium screws.

What the hell could do that? She looked from the strewn articles, to the screws, and finally to the artificial hip where it had landed next to her right foot. Why isn't there any blood?

Backing away in shocked dismay, Sandy stumbled. Regaining her footing in the bus's central corridor, she looked aft and froze. Visible in the cabin's stark, white light, emptied articles of clothing littered the entire bus.

A glint of light drew her attention to one of the front left seats. A teddy bear's half-open, glass-bead eyes peered from under a vacated toddler's outfit. On the narrow bench, a little girl's tiny white and yellow dress sat between piled clothes of an apparent mother and father. Worn in anticipation of an early morning departure to some exciting destination, the tiny girl's yellow ribbons and pink bows now lay strewn about her emptied clothes.

Sandy had a mental image of the parents casting horrified glances at the monstrosity hovering overhead while they tried to calm their frightened little girl. But in Sandy's vision, she and Jake were the anxious couple. The child between them was the little girl with golden locks that she'd often imagined would grace their future. Unconsciously, her hand drifted to the point where the baby bump would soon show.

As a tear threatened to breach the levee of her lower eyelid, Sandy extended a trembling hand toward the stuffed animal. After a short hesitation, she caressed its furry belly.

The teddy bear's lifeless, doll-like eyes snapped wide open. "Are you my mommy?"

Find out why this happened and what happens next!
Get the Sector 64 Series Today!

ABOUT THE AUTHOR

Amazon Top 20 and Audible Top 10 Author Dean M. Cole, a retired combat helicopter pilot and airline pilot, has penned multiple award-winning apocalyptic tales. Solitude, book one of Dimension Space, won the 2018 ABR Listeners Choice Award for Best Science Fiction. Previously, IndieReader named Dean's first full-length novel, Sector 64: Ambush, to their Best of 2014 list. His sixth book, Amplitude, the third Dimension Space novel, is now available.

Follow Dean on BookBub!
bookbub.com/authors/dean-m-cole

For More Information:
www.deanmcole.com
dean@deanmcole.com

facebook.com/authordeanmcole
twitter.com/deanmcole
instagram.com/deanmcole

CPSIA information can be obtained
at www.ICGtesting.com
Printed in the USA
LVHW010714180520
655783LV00001B/16